D1713272

HOUSE OF BABEL

University of Nebraska Press: Lincoln & London

P.C.JERSILD

House of Babel

Babels Hus Translated by Joan Tate

Afterword by Leif Sjöberg:

A Conversation with P.C.Jersild

CONTENTS

HOUSE OF BABEL

SUMMARY

About ninety thousand people die in Sweden every year. Most of them die of heart and circulatory diseases: strokes, coronaries, or other conditions caused by the arteries ceasing to function. Either the blood vessels become blocked with fats, tissues, and calcium so that the blood flow is obstructed or cannot pass through at all to vital organs, or the arteries become as brittle as paper and split under the pressure of the blood, resulting in life-threatening hemorrhages.

We don't know very much about the reasons for this. You can study the process of disease through a microscope; you can observe the way red blood corpuscles pile on top of each other and grow into fatal embolisms. But you cannot draw the conclusion from these direct observations that this phenomenon is caused by well-being. Some people maintain that diet is to blame, others heredity. The medical profession moralistically recommends various limitations of diet and alcohol, and also increased physical exercise. The evidence is frail. No one even knows whether this is a question of disease or normal aging.

Number two on the list of causes of death are the malignant neoplasms, usually called cancer. The principle of cancer is that one or perhaps several cells start growing simultaneously unchecked, or decentralized, if you like. The tumor cell seldom allows itself to be influenced by goals other than its own uninhibited growth. In cases of malignancy, the tumor pushes aside the organs of the body and smothers them. It can also send out satellites, or metastases, to different parts of the body to occupy and exploit them. In the end the whole body dies because one single cell put individualism before solidarity and cooperation.

Billions and billions are spent on solving the cancer riddle. This is something of a paradox, as the cause of cancer is already known. WHO, the World Health Organization, has recently established that up to ninety percent of malignant diseases are probably due to environmental factors: smoke and dust, radioactivity, gasoline engine fumes, solvents, artificial chemical products, plastics, pesticides, cigarettes, and a thousand other things that are all part of the good life. And yet tens of thousands of research workers spend days and probably nights as well with test tubes and electron microscopes tracing the hidden life of the cell and the mechanisms that at a molecular level transform it into a cancer cell. What will happen if they succeed? If a Nobel prize winner comes forward and says that cancer is due to the fact that X combines with Y and under the influence of Z becomes cancer? The effect would be marginal, so long as we don't clean up our environment, which, as every child knows, is a political issue.

The third great cause of death is "injuries caused by accidents, violence and poisoning," which include accidents to children, traffic accidents, industrial accidents, suicide, etc. Enormous interest is taken in accidents, the interest in reverse proportion to the size of the problem. Great interest is at present being taken in the smallest group, industrial accidents. Increasing attention is being paid to the slightly larger group, accidents to children. The numbers of victims of traffic accidents have stabilized and there seems to be an unspoken agreement that an acceptable level is over a thousand deaths a year. Almost no interest is taken in the largest group of all, suicides, which is nearly twice the size of the traffic accident group.

One can object that the causal chain is sometimes complicated, that a great many factors are involved in a fatal accident, and that it is perfectly understandable that society is on the defensive. Maybe. But sometimes it is in fact not particularly complicated. If a sufficient number of motor vehicles are driven at high and poorly controlled speeds on a narrow, slippery asphalt strip in opposite directions, on what is called a collision course, in that case you can with the help of computers, more or less exactly anticipate the number of accidents on any given stretch. You can raise the figures the computers produce by adding fog and snow. You can lower them slightly by dropping into the stream of traffic a certain number of clearly visible police vehicles.

This shows that evidence of cause and effect of diseases and injuries is not especially important. Anyone maintaining that once the cause of a certain disease is known, it will disappear, is quite simply wrong.

It would be a gross slander to maintain that the civilized world does not spend much of its resources to prevent disease and death. That other budgetary items, defense, for instance, are double or triple those for health, should not confuse the issue. The aim of defense is to prevent deaths in armies and the civilian population. Defense has this aim in common with the health services. The fact that defense under certain circumstances claims more deaths than lives saved is true, but this cannot be taken as a pretext for placing an equals-sign between defense and health services.

In Sweden, health services have long been one of the largest budget items. Health service expenditures have also steadily increased, like an avalanche according to some people, though an avalanche usually moves downward and not upward. Neither has the cost of health services hitherto been subject to normal economic conditions. Despite great efforts in political quarters, diseases and their financial consequences have persistently followed their own curve, a continuously rising one, in spite of the depressed state of the economy. This has had the advantage that the drug industry, unlike other industries, does not have to cut down and dismiss staff during bad economic conditions. Some people even maintain that the situation is reversed, that bad times with resulting unemployment stimulate the consumption of tranquilizers, stimulants, antidepressive drugs, sleeping tablets, and medication for complaints of the digestive tract.

Have the billions and billions spent on health services had any noticeable effect? Have disease and death demonstrably decreased in

Sweden as a result of medical services? The answer is as painful as it is vague. In certain individual cases, for a number of special risk groups, they have. But for the population as a whole there is no absolute and unambiguous proven connection between increased expenditure on health services and improved states of health or longevity. But that is perhaps because we do not know how to measure medical efficiency.

So no one knows just how good Sweden's health services are. But if from that it is believed possible to discontinue or generally contract the health services, this is erroneous thinking, starting out from the presumption that modern society rests on rational foundations. It does not. But when we have no way of testing the effectiveness of defense measures, or of seriously finding out what the school system does to children, why should we then make even greater demands on health services? Health is a very sensitive chapter in a society that right into the twentieth century has been largely based on faith, axioms, and magic. From that perspective, health services must be looked on with kindly eyes. The contribution of medical magic is greater than the share of logic, open accounting, and scientific honesty. We have the health services we deserve. The fact that we cannot afford them is another matter.

There are several large hospitals in Stockholm: the Karolinska Institute, Danderyd Hospital, Sabbatsberg Hospital, St. Erik's and St. George's hospitals, and the Serafimer Hospital, all serving the northern sections of the city. In the south of Greater Stockholm, where medical and social problems are on the whole greater and consequently health service needs also greater, there are about half as many: South Hospital, Huddinge Hospital, and the most recent of all, the ultramodern Enskede Hospital.

When Enskede Hospital, the most modern in Stockholm, was opened by their Majesties in the spring of 1979, the building was not just a hospital in itself. It was equally a gigantic monument in scrap iron and stone of the 1960s health service policies. During the sixties, industrial principles were applied to health services, striving for large rational units with high efficiency; a kind of silo for health and knowledge, or medical cathedrals to lull people into faith and security. Health services came to behave like an occupying power in a foreign country, a power that entrenched itself in fortresses and built on heights, where the doctors and nurses dared not go out at night.

Now anyone who has been involved at all in health service planning knows that it is not the population that needs large hospitals. They need local health services instead, more district nurses, better homecare, more health centers, and many smaller long-term units. This does not mean that the large hospitals are not useful. On the contrary. But it means the health services in general, or as a system, function badly. Giant hospitals lack foundations, resting as they do on clay or quicksand, and are liable to list in any direction.

Years before even the first spadeful was dug for Enskede Hospital, most responsible people agreed that it was wrong to build large hospitals. But important decisions, once taken, are not gone back on just like that. To change health service policies is like trying to stop an ocean liner, impossible until it is already beyond the horizon.

Some of the newest hospitals do resemble ocean liners, or rather car ferries, tall compact metal constructions with drop gates to the car decks and garages. But most hospitals in Stockholm are not new and reflect in their architecture the atmosphere of the times during which they were designed. The Karolinska Institute comes from the years just before the war and resembles buildings for a regiment, a number of various-sized buildings dispersed among glades and rocks with no apparent connection. Children have their building, heart patients theirs, and the mentally ill one of their own with bars over the windows. It is as if the architect had wanted to keep the various sections strictly apart, in categories, so the inhabitants of the barracks should not be able to make their way to the officers' mess or the administration building. Why? For fear that the patients might one day all join together in a communal uprising?

South Hospital on its impregnable cliff forms a long, compact, high fortress wall against Stockholm's southern problem area on the other side of the moat of the Hammarby road. Huddinge Hospital from the air resembles a shipyard with a row of dry docks, as if it had been imagined that the metal-roofed apartment buildings in Västra Flemingsberg one by one would be taken in, inhabitants and all, for an overhaul and hull scraping.

The newest hospital, Enskede, is a somewhat confusing construction to the eye. It consists of some not too tall, metallic blue six-sided pavilions joined together by long connecting corridors. Some of the wings protrude blindly from these pavilions without going anywhere special. To an architect, the image is at once obviously that of the terminal building of a large modern airport.

An airport works like a chain of logical functions, with the passengers arriving, checking in, going through passport control, buying duty-free alcohol, taking an export beer in the bar, relieving themselves, then standing at the gate to choose a seat on the plane, preferably near the emergency exit.

Is there a similar chain of logical functions in a hospital? Probably. A hospital is constructed like a sorting office, the person arriving first having to produce a ticket to say he or she is ill. What is meant by being *ill*? What is disease? What does a disease look like? This is where definitions part company. But after what is sometimes a rather lengthy process at the check-in desk, someone in the hospital, usually a doctor, decides whether the illness exists or not. The person who is not ill is consequently well and has to go back home.

Next, attempts are made to investigate the kind of illness. After this has been done comes the treatment. An ill person always has to be treated, and naturally the hospital expects the patient to react to the treatment in return, which means become well again, or at least improve. To sum up, a patient must be *ill*, and after treatment must become more or less *well*. All people and events falling outside these medical demands are regarded by the health services as deviants. A person who cannot prove that he or she is ill should not be in the hospital. A patient who, despite every effort, simply gets worse and worse should not be there, either. A person who dies is showing a vote of no confidence. This rather categorical view from the health services side is necessary, as the whole system would fall to pieces if the following declaration of faith were not adhered to: the ill become well only because of medical intervention.

Unfortunately, there is no large hospital that reflects as clearly as an airport does its function in its actual architecture. A hospital can resemble anything: a farm building, an eighteenth-century palace, a barracks, or a nuclear power station. So Enskede Hospital looks like an airport. But that does not mean it has a natural entrance and obvious exit. Approaching the hospital from the air or from the ground, there is no way of judging the use of its various sections. It is tempting to think, for instance, that the little building with a pointed roof at the side is the morgue, and that the brown-glassed penthouse on the roof is the department for brine baths and heat therapy. In fact it is the other way around. So it is very difficult to find your way around the hospital. The corridors have no windows, which makes it impossible to orient oneself with the help of the landscape outside. Instead, different parts of the hospital have code names and the corridors have street names: Heart Street, Lung Street, Liver Street, etc. The walls are also of different colors. So to fetch results from the x-ray lab, a person is directed to Building David Red, Radium Street, Level IV, Door 1688.

Another important factor in a large hospital is the numerous languages spoken there. Swedish, Finnish, and Yugoslavian are spoken in the kitchens. The cleaning staff speak mostly Turkish, and English is often spoken in Rabbit, Rat, and Guinea Pig Streets, in Research House. There is also another kind of confusion of languages that has nothing to do with nationality. In the administration building, modern bureaucratic language is spoken, spattered with budgeting terms such as input and output, and in the surgery rooms short metallic orders are given: clamp! suture! blood! In the laboratories, they speak in chemical formulas, a staccato language with capital letters. In the pharmacy they talk prescriptions, in the computer department in figures, in the psychiatric clinic in behavioral terms, and in the literature archives in Latin. The various individuals and staff categories hardly speak at all among themselves.

All these languages have to be placed against the language of patients, and most patients find it hard to express themselves precisely or scientifically exactly. In the emergency room, for instance, a person is simply hurt, confused, exhausted, panic-stricken, poisoned, unconscious, helpless, quite often drunk, or fluttering around the walls like a sparrow in a culvert. It is impossible to give a comprehensive and at the same time living picture of a large hospital. I have made use of the established right of the novelist to be subjective. This account should therefore be compared with other pictures of Swedish health services.

THE AUTHOR

FIRST TREATMENT

1 In 1979, Enskede Hospital served an area taking in roughly the whole of the northwest part of southern Greater Stockholm, a mixed development of a few high-rise buildings and a large residential area of substantial villas and smaller houses all built in the late 1920s. There was also considerable industry: harbor installations, transport terminals and warehouses, as well as some fairly luxurious houses recently built on a stony ridge by Lake Mälare. But the three-story apartment buildings erected just after the Second World War dominated the whole. They had no elevators and had been badly built with substandard materials. Most of them had also been poorly maintained, the stucco now flaking off, windows ill-fitting, doors warped, and tiles blackening. The whole area looked as if it had been overwhelmed by a tremendous flood, the water rising to roof level, then slowly subsiding, leaving behind all kinds of flotsam: old Christmas trees, wheelless cars, broken play equipment, mud and sand. The few open spaces were nothing but yellowing sea grass. Families with children had lived there thirty years before, but now only the elderly were left, old-age pensioners and an unusually high percentage of people on sickness pensions.

The hospital itself stood where Stockholm's largest garden allotment area once had. The tiny wooden cabins had been demolished in the early sixties and the allotments leveled by bulldozers to prepare the ground for the building of the hospital. But the plans had been altered several times and almost twenty years had gone by before the hospital had eventually been built.

The hospital was built on a rectangular field as large as a municipal airport. The field was criss-crossed in several places by freeways, the hospital at one end and Årsta warehouses at the other, with about twenty or so allotments that had for some unfathomable reason been left roughly in the middle. Maybe funds for land purchases had run out, or the bulldozer contractors had gone bankrupt. This area was quite cut off from the world outside. Although part lay underneath one of the freeways, no road ran down to it. Whoever rented or looked after the cabins had to go there on foot or cycle along a path bordered by a ditch choked with waist-high stinging nettles. The authorities had lost all interest in the remnants of the allotment area because it was no longer in the way, and to level it all would have cost far too much, since there were no roads leading to it. The fire department had given the same reason when they had declined the offer of the cabins for fire-fighting exercises. Even vandals had shown no interest, since it was far too much trouble to get down there from the freeway.

The cabins on the allotments were of the smallest kind, unsuitable for staying overnight. They had been built for shelter in bad weather and as tool sheds. But though they were between only four and six square meters, they were designed as replicas of larger houses. They looked like playhouses, with windows, peaked roofs, verandas, and vestibules, a great deal of elaborate carpentry decorating the gables, window frames, and door frames. Some of the more recently built cabins, on the other hand, looked more like pigeon cotes or outdoor privies. All the cabins and their carpet-sized allotments were immaculately kept.

An old man was sitting on a stool on one of the allotments, stripping black currants. He had short legs, an athletic upper body, and was wearing a gray suit, the jacket hanging loosely across his shoulders and the baggy trousers reaching up to his chest, held up by wide suspenders. He had black laced boots on his feet and a long-peaked, scarlet baseball cap with an insignia in front on his head. His name was Primus Svensson; he was an ex-typographer, and had been a pensioner for exactly nine years. Every day throughout the year, weather permitting, he cycled out to his allotment.

When Primus Svensson looked up from his stained fingers and the stainless steel bowl clamped between his knees, he could see Enskede Hospital in the background to his right. It was the end of August, the sun low, so in the evening light the concrete looked blue. The sun was shining directly onto the hospital windows, reflecting a warm, yellowish light, making the façade look as if it were covered with thousands of Swedish flags.

He put on his glasses and tried to see the time in the slanting light. Guessing it to be about twenty past six, he took off his glasses, put them back in the hard, black case with its spring lid, pushed the case into his inside pocket and went on stripping black currants, faster now. He was in a hurry. He did not want to cycle home at dusk, when it would be impossible to see the potholes and deep ruts in the path.

Suddenly something happened inside his chest. There was a whirring at the back of his eyes. He took a deep breath but was forced to stop halfway, because it felt like a sudden raw swallow of icy water. The explosive feeling in his chest spread and moved up towards his jaw. He didn't dare breathe. He felt as if someone had leapt on him from behind without warning and was holding him around his chest in a wrestler's grip. A few seconds later, he found he could breathe again, but the pain was still there, dull and heavy in the middle of his chest. His arms were tingling, too. "Must be my stomach," thought Primus Svensson. "Gases pushing their way upward." He hadn't had a bowel movement for three days.

He felt dizzy and sick, his cap tight around his forehead, but he clenched his teeth and went on stripping the black currants. "It'll pass." But instead the pain got worse, and he found he could not move, did not even dare to blink. Slowly he let the air out of his lungs and the pain slackened. He wondered how he would get home. The black currants would have to wait. It would be best if he went home, took a large dose of salts, and put himself to bed. He got up slowly, constantly watchful of the pain, as if it were a tray of brimming glasses he had to balance. He managed to get across to his bicycle and empty the contents of the bowl into the basket on the rack.

He was thinking about his new red baseball cap. For several years he had cycled about in a brown hat clamped down over his ears. He had bought the baseball cap in a toyshop. It didn't blow off, and he could also be seen better in the traffic. He leaned against the bicycle, looking up at the façade of the hospital. He wondered if they could see him, whether he should take his cap off and wave it? But they probably couldn't see him. If they wanted to, they'd need binoculars. Why should they have lookouts on the roof, keeping track of who was sick and who was well? No doubt they had enough to cope with over there.

His body rigid, he managed to get the stool and bowl back into the cabin. He found it troublesome locking the patent lock and the other special lock, as his arms kept wanting to do nothing but hang down his sides. But he managed. He walked back to the bicycle, leaning slightly forward, his hand pressed against his heart. He put his head down over the handlebars and got his right leg over the saddle. Everything went black before his eyes and his vision shrank to pinpoints as he straightened up. He stood astride the bicycle for a moment, feeling his pulse, which was leaping and jerking rapidly and irregularly.

Primus Svensson took a few short, stumbling steps, getting the bicycle going while still astride the frame and holding onto the handlebars with white hands as he heaved himself up onto the saddle. Just as the bicycle began to fall, he got his foot on the pedal as it swung downward and gained speed. He was feeling a little better now, but at the same time could feel a horrible acid burning like a lighted fuse rising in his throat.

2 Hannes Gordon was a research assistant at the Institute of Education at Stockholm University. There was a Cuban look about him, with his untidy black hair, bushy beard, brown eyes, and surplus army clothing. But at this particular moment, he was wearing a white coat and was sitting behind a counter in Enskede Hospital's Emergency Room, filling in forms. Everyone who came into Emergency had to pass Gordon and answer a few simple questions: name, sex, date of birth, occupation, reason for visit, and finally what efforts had been made to seek help before elsewhere, from the district nurse, for instance, or the social services, or the doctor on call.

Hannes Gordon had sat filling in forms for seven nights now. He reckoned he could already see the pattern. Most of the people who came to Emergency really had no business there at all. When the bus arrived, between twenty and thirty people would come pouring in, apparently not particularly ill, but whose only aim was to get an extension of their sick leave. Reckoned in numbers of visits, the load on Emergency during the six months since opening was already more than two hundred percent greater than had been anticipated or prepared for. Waiting times became impossible. Drunken and sober people had to sit more or less in each other's laps in the waiting room and small children with ear aches screamed like a captive castrati choir. The staff had quailed and first the police, then later special paid guards, were detailed to keep order. The problems of Emergency came up continually at every hospital meeting, at health authority meetings on representation at work, and in submissions to the regional council. But nothing was done about it.

How had this happened? Why were the hospital's expectations of emergency patients so at odds with the patients' expectations of the hospital? Answers to that question were now being sought with the help of a statistical survey. No one really knew just who went to Emergency, or why, or with what expectations. Even age groups of patients were not known. At first, there had been well-planned computer routines for this kind of assignment. But the Head of Surgery directly responsible for Emergency considered that computerization would intrude on people's privacy too much. So he had sabotaged registration, with the result that Emergency, which resembled either a military casualty station shortly after a battle, or a major bank closed for cleaning, had become a no-man's-land. Everyone accused everyone else and the temperature rose with every drunken brawl.

According to medical tradition, an emergency room is equipped and organized to receive emergency cases, victims of traffic accidents, unconscious people, people with severe heart afflictions, epileptics, acute abdominal cases and other cases of a pressing and dramatic nature. The technical equipment was superb, the most up-to-date, and the very best in the country, even if the Head of Surgery did consider it inadequate. The staff were well trained in first aid, staunching hemorrhages, administering heart massage, intubation and artificial respiration. Up to two thousand medical preparations were available in the freezers and medicine cabinets. But this heavy medical arsenal was brought into use all too seldom. Instead, people poured in with minor injuries, chronic arthritis, drug problems, screaming but perfectly healthy infants, expired sick leave, or purely social problems. But no one had planned anything for them, and they did not correspond to the anticipated behavior of "ER patients." It was like dirt in the machinery. The new laws on alcohol had made things even worse. Drunks who had previously been thrown into jail now had to go to the hospital for treatment instead.

The department was unnaturally quiet this evening. Admissions in Emergency were always extremely erratic. Half the day could go by with only a few patients trickling in, and then came a great flood. Hannes Gordon did not like doing nothing. The clock ticked on and he became more and more bad-tempered. When he was bad-tempered, he felt a great desire to tip the whole chessboard over. It was all a matter of class. The investigation he was taking part in was utterly unnecessary. If the working classes themselves had decision-making power in the health services, then the health services would also look after the interests of the working classes. Now it was the medical industry complex, MEDCO, that decided. The capitalists were only interested in treatment involving apparatus. No; health services should go out into the community instead, go out into industry and workplaces, and together with employees expose the dangers in their work environment. They should go out and clean up the residential areas. They should carry out a restrictive alcohol policy, eliminate prostitution, and throw all the drug dealers out of the country.

Was it that simple? He felt ambivalent, one moment a preaching revolutionary at the barricades of the health services, the next moment shrinking into a frightened bookworm when faced with the complexity of reality, not daring to say boo without any proper factual basis with double-checked and graded statistical tables.

He looked at the wall clock again, at the hand jerking on from minute to minute around the face. The next feeder bus would be arriving in a quarter of an hour. Would it be full or empty? He would have a cup of coffee before the bus came. But he no longer felt welcome in the coffee room. At first it had been fine, and for two days he had sat in the coffee room with a friendly smile on his face, saying nothing until he was spoken to. But then he had thought it was about time he made it clear what he stood for, that—well, all of them sitting there squabbling and complaining in the coffee room would go on in that way if they didn't become more aware and able to see the health services in a political context, as a class matter.

But you couldn't talk to the staff at this place. Not to Mona, a seven months pregnant nurse who sat knitting all the time, her head down, her forearms propped against her stomach. Nor to Anders, an orderly studying at night school. Nor to the medical students, that snobbish gang from the Karolinska Institute who had not the slightest clue about reality. They just sat around pompously, yawning their heads off in their white coats with collars turned up, or carrying on involved discussions about tactics for their next exam. Nor to the doctors, those white-coated ostriches with their heads stuck down the patients' throats, blind and deaf to their surroundings.

But he had occasionally been able to exchange a few sensible words with the custodians. Several of them realized what it was all about, when he spoke in confidence to them separately, that is. They kept quiet in a group, apparently scared, and afraid of losing their jobs.

There was a coffee machine for the patients at the far end of the empty waiting room. Hannes Gordon fished out some coins from his large, old-fashioned purse and got up. But at that moment, a woman stepped in through the great reinforced glass doors that automatically glided apart. For a few seconds, she stood just inside the door, rummaging in her shopping bag as she hectically scanned the multitude of notices inside the entrance door, rather as people look at information boards in six-story department stores. Then she came over to him.

"Hello," said Hannes. "What are you looking for?"

The woman looked slightly disconcerted, then fished a stenciled paper from her bag and held it out, not for him to read, but as if she were showing her ticket or identity card.

"I'm supposed to take a technical course here," she said.

"Where?"

"The CTO have a course for work protection representatives within the health service. Blue House, Clamp Street, Level Two, door five hundred and sixty-six. How do I get there?"

"You've come the wrong way. You'll have to go around. This is the Emergency Room. You'll have to go right around to the main entrance."

"And then?"

"You'll have to ask. There's an information desk there. Good luck to you!"

The woman crumpled up her piece of paper and went back through the sliding doors. "CTO?" thought Hannes. "What does that mean? Technical? Central Technical Organization? That'd be it. Though what the hell did it matter what it meant? CTO could never be any influence, anyhow. Fundamentally."

The moment the woman disappeared, two policemen came in with a man between them. The man was hanging onto the policemen, the toes of his shoes dragging along the stone floor. He was wearing a bright red peaked cap. A fisherman? A drunk the policeman had knocked down? Hannes intercepted the thought; it was out of date. In his circles, only a few years ago every policeman had been a "pig," a brutal, semi-military fascist who took every opportunity to use his baton. But then quite suddenly attitudes to the police had changed course by a hundred and eighty degrees and in sections of the Left the police were no longer synonymous with "pigs." Almost overnight, "pig" had become "comrade." The police were useful, the police kept druggies and extreme lefties in their place. All that dilly-dallying with criminals had been a mistake, liberalistic sob-stuff in mock-radical disguise. But it had not been quite as simple as that. Hannes Gordon still showed a faulty primary reaction; at first glance, a policeman was something hostile.

"Get a stretcher!" shouted one of the policemen.

Hannes rose rather hesitantly. He was not there to get involved in health care, or so it said in the agreement between researchers and the hospital; register but don't get involved. An idiotic agreement. A bourgeois way of looking at science. Of course he should get involved! He rushed across and pulled out a gurney from the stretcher station, where all gurneys were dispensed on an automatic conveyor. With the help of the policemen, he lifted the man up onto the gurney. He tried to catch someone's eye behind the glass wall from where the hospital staff surveyed what was happening. No one there? Yes, he saw a plastic mug and a raised arm waving. They had been noticed. An orderly and a medical student came out of the coffee room and began pulling the gurney toward the examination room.

"Come over to the desk for a moment, would you?" said Hannes in friendly tones to the policemen.

They looked at him doubtfully, almost with disgust. The worst thing about the police was that they were so slow on the uptake. They hadn't had time to change their attitude and still reacted negatively when confronted with bearded youth in shabby or secondhand clothing. The police themselves didn't seem to have yet grasped they were no longer "pigs" but "comrades." Hannes went behind the counter, licked his ballpoint and smoothed down a form.

"Do you know what his name is?"

"Is this Registration?" said one of the policemen.

"Not exactly. We're doing a special investigation this week into everyone coming into Emergency. To check the scene, so to speak."

"Oh, kiss my ass," said the policeman, taking out a creased wallet with a thick rubber band around it. He pulled out an insurance certificate and read: "The patient is called zerothreezerothreeonefour-dashzerothreefivesix Primus Svensson. We picked him up when he fell off his bike."

"What's he come for?" Hannes Gordon had been just about to say, but without looking up, he wrote instead: *Unconscious? Does not appear to have been in contact with any other kind of health service before admission.*

3 Primus Svensson was awakened by the pain in his nose. When he tried to bring his right hand up to his nose, he found that the hand was tied down. He could now also hear ticking and humming noises all around him. "I don't want to see," he thought. "I don't want to be awake. Let me sink."

He woke up again and opened his eyes. A young man in a yellow coat and a pointed white paper cap was sitting beside his bed. He seemed to come straight out of a historical print, something to do with the Spanish Inquisition.

"My name's Klas," said the young man, winking meaningfully.

Primus tried to say "thank you," but his voice had gone, the air rasping in his dry sore throat. Instead he tried to turn his head towards the young man. That hurt his nose.

"Are you awake?" said Klas.

Primus tried to wink back. Of course he was! His nose was smarting, his left elbow throbbing, his throat aching and he hurt all over inside his ribcage. He also felt as if someone were sitting on his chest.

"Nurse's coming soon," said Klas. "She'll give you an injection."

"Why—?" Primus tried to say, but he found it impossible to get a sound out of his throat. It felt like a flute full of sand.

"My name's Klas and I work as an aide here," said Klas, nodding cheerfully so that his cap wobbled.

Primus looked up at the ceiling. It was pale gray. Diagonally in front of his face was a lamp of the kind dentists usually have. It was switched off. A television camera was hanging at the foot of his bed, a small, narrow gray one of the kind he had seen before in the subway. He looked down at his feet. They were bare and sticking out from under the sheet. He had no blanket. There was an empty bed on the other side of the room, a similar lamp and television camera above it. It was like looking at yourself in the mirror, but there was something missing from the mirror image: himself.

He glanced to the right, where there was a frame on wheels holding two tall cylinders. A welding unit? No, oxygen, of course. "I'm in the hospital and I'm being given oxygen," he said to himself. The pain in his nose came from a thin plastic tube that ran from one oxygen cylinder up into his nose. Beyond the tubes was a square metal box on wheels, as big as a dishwasher, with the kind of pleated tubes found in industrial vacuum cleaners. That must be a respirator.

To the left of his bed, where Klas was sitting, was a tall framework of shiny stainless steel, two plastic bags hanging from it, with up-turned bottles, a colorless liquid in one and a raspberry-colored liquid in the other. Thin tubes ran from the bottles into a gray container, and from the container a tube ran to a plastic knob on the inside of his left elbow. An alien feeling crept over him. He was no longer sure where his own body ended and where the machines began.

The pain in his nose had now developed into an almost unbearable desire to sneeze. He closed his eyes and tried to jerk his hands up to his face, but both hands were fastened to the bed with bandages. The sneeze started pumping up in his nose, a great red rubber balloon that grew and grew, as large as a football bladder now. "I must—I must—" With all his strength, he jerked his right arm to get it free.

"Nurse'll come and give you a shot soon," said Klas.

The sneeze faded away into a half-hearted yawn. He looked down at his bare chest. There were great white strips of tape across it, from which ran red, blue and yellow threads down to the right. He couldn't see where they went.

"You've had a myocardial infarction," said Klas, leaning forward and gently pinching the lobe of his ear.

"Myocardial infarction? Coronary thrombosis? Heart attack?" he thought. It had nothing to do with him. It wasn't his heart any longer. The hospital had taken over responsibility for it. It seemed to him that he was sitting by the bed on a stool like Klas's, looking at a stranger lying there entangled in tubes and wires on the shiny bed. That was the person *who was a myocardial infarction*. Primus Svensson had nothing to do with it.

Someone else wearing a yellow coat and a white pointed cap came into his field of vision.

"I'm Nurse Ingrid," she said, taking a hypodermic syringe out of a bowl, shaking out an air bubble, testing it up into the air, then thrusting the plastic needle into the fold of his elbow and injecting—not Primus, but the plastic knob that was taped into the crook of his arm. Slowly, she emptied the hypodermic. Then she freed his right hand from the bandage and said with her mouth to his ear: "I'm untying it. But please don't poke anything."

He lifted his hand and looked at it. The fingertips were still purplish and he had soil and green stuff under his nails. There was a fresh scratch on the back of his hand. He remembered fainting . . . and then falling off his bike.

Nurse Ingrid was talking to Klas.

"Did you go and tell them in Surgery that the hospital paid for our color tv? Now they want their black and white set exchanged for a color one. They've used their petty cash and added money of their own to it. Then someone goes and opens his big mouth and says we got ours through the hospital. It wasn't you, was it? They think it's unfair that they have to pay for theirs themselves. When we got ours, we were told that under no circumstances was it to be a precedent. Do you see?"

Primus did not listen to Klas's reply, as he was fully occupied trying to localize his own body. He put his hand back under the sheet and felt his stomach. It felt loose and sloppy. Just below his navel, he felt his upturned penis taped to his stomach, a tube coming out of it. He cautiously felt the tube. It was lukewarm.

Nurse Ingrid hurried out, and Klas said:

"You're in the Intensive Care Unit. In Room Two."

Primus nodded. He'd better remember that. Intensive Care. Room Two. This was his new home and he would have to remember the address, in case he should get lost getting up in the night for a pee. Silly! There was no possible chance of even getting out of bed. He looked down at his body again and remembered a picture he'd seen in a book, a book called *Gulliver's Travels*. In the picture, Gulliver was lying fastened to the ground by hundreds of thin threads, ladders leaning against his body in several places, and hectic Lilliputians swarming all over him.

"Have you any next of kin?" said Klas. "Would you like us to phone someone?"

Primus shook his head roughly. No, he certainly did not want them to phone Bernt. He had heard nothing from Bernt for over three months now. Bernt had his own life. He would be annoyed if they bothered him. He would drop his son a line when he was a bit better.

"Is there anyone to see to your apartment?" said Klas.

"I haven't got any houseplants . . . that need watering," he croaked.

What was his apartment to do with them? Didn't they think he'd been prepared? Didn't they realize he'd always known one day things would go wrong, and he would break a leg, or be run over, or have a heart attack? He didn't want any stranger snooping around his apartment. Everything was in order. Bernt would not be put to any extra trouble.

"No dog? Or cat?"

"No."

"So you're on your own, are you?"

Primus nodded. It hurt him to speak. They seemed to be pushing a chimney brush up and down his throat. What had they been doing to him while he was unconscious? He gathered his wits and thought about the apartment again. There was milk, yoghurt, butter and cheese in the refrigerator. They could stay there. The bread in the bin would probably go moldy. But the hard bread in the oven would keep all right. The mail and newspapers—the mail would be on the door-mat. Mail? He seldom got any real mail, but mostly advertisements, occasionally a money order or a bill. The newspaper usually got stuck in the letter slot. How many newspapers were stuck there now? How many days had he been here? He tried to lift his left wrist to look at his watch. But of course he couldn't; besides, they would have put his watch away somewhere.

"Stop the newspaper . . ."

"All right," said Klas, jotting something down on a pad. "We'll get that done as soon as we know which ward you're going to."

Ward? Wasn't this a ward? He was to be moved, it appeared. Hell, no, he wanted to go back home. As soon as they uncoupled him, he would be off home. He tried to raise his torso to tell Klas how he wanted things. But he couldn't even raise his head. His body and limbs were as heavy as if he were lying in the bath. Suddenly he felt the pressure down there. He held it back. It wasn't convenient. It was coming—

"Are you in pain?" said Klas. "The injection'll take soon. Relax. Try to sleep."

It was urgent now, he had to, now, at once, before the whole thing became a disaster. He turned to Klas and tried to reach him with his free right hand.

"Howdy, old man!" said Klas, jokingly shaking the tips of his fingers as one would a child's.

"I—I—"

"Lie back. Try to sleep. The injection's working, you'll see. You'll soon be floating on rosy pink clouds."

"Want to go."

Klas laughed and placed Primus' hand back onto the sheet. Primus didn't understand and suddenly felt sleepy, his body becoming warm, his skin tingling, and he sank and sank, warm waves lapping up over his chest.

"You don't need to," Klas explained. "It's the thermometer you feel. We've got an electronic thermometer in your rectum all the time. It tells us your temperature continuously."

4 The students' common room was on the second floor of White House, the high rise blocks of Årsta visible through the tinted glass of the windows. The room was furnished with seven circular pine tables, six chairs around each table. Only one of the tables was occupied. Two students were sitting with their white coats open and a worn pack of cards lying on the table.

"Shall we draw for it?" said one of them. *Carl Bertelskjöld, Student* was on the badge on his lapel.

"Draw? Let's do two-handed poker instead," said the other, with *Lars Borg* on his badge.

"Poker's damned hopeless with two," said Bertelskjöld.

"What about Old Maid then?"

"We might as well draw for it in that case."

"Why draw? Why not just toss?"

"Or matches? One long and one short."

"No. I lost on that last time. Not matches. I might just as well go and write up the case sheet straightaway."

"Excellent!" said Bertelskjöld. "Done!"

"I was only joking," said Borg. "That'd be damned unfair, wouldn't it?"

"But if you do this one, then you've done nine and I've done nine. Then it'll automatically be my turn next time. Automatically."

"Oh, yeah! We've just changed wards. Then you start all over again. You can't count all your old ones. If I do this one, then I've got one point. But you've got none. The way you work it out, it's one-all."

A third student came into the room, a girl of about twenty-three.

The most striking thing about her was that she looked so healthy: big without being overweight, fair hair, and red cheeks. She would have looked much too perfect if she hadn't had a wide gap between her front teeth; *Martina Bosson, Student* was on her badge.

"There's a new patient in," she said. "Which of you is doing the admission?"

"He is!" they replied simultaneously.

"For God's sake, decide which."

"And how many admissions have you managed to scrape together, Martina?"

"Eleven."

"You can't count those from your previous ward."

"Two, then."

"Not many, then."

"Oh, to hell with her!" said Bertelskjöld, holding out the deck. "Let's draw for it."

"No," said Borg. "I've changed my mind. Where's the dice shaker?"

"For Christ's sake, I'm not going to start on poker!"

"Could you two gentlemen kindly make up your minds?" said Martina.

"How many admissions has Bosco done?" said Bertelskjöld.

"He's off sick."

Juan Bosco, another medical student, was often off sick. He was a refugee from Chile. When he had started studying medicine in Stockholm, most people had been sympathetic. Naturally someone who had been hunted by the Chilean junta's secret police should be helped. But now, three years later, their sympathy had faded. It was hard on his friends having him in their group. He often found it hard to understand the lectures because of language difficulties. Yet he had managed to scrape through tests and exams by the skin of his teeth; no lecturer had had the heart or the courage to fail him. Juan Bosco was often off sick. When he was present, he sometimes burst into a veritable paroxysm of fury, accusing his friends of the most studied baseness. Sometimes he appeared to be utterly paranoid. In his first term

at the Karolinska Institute, the whole class had taken it upon themselves to look after Bosco. Now they hardly mentioned him.

"To hell with Bosco. He can't have done more than three or four at
the very most anyway," said Borg.

"Here," said Bertelskjöld to Martina. "Take these two matches,
break one behind your back and then hold them out."

"No."

"Why not?"

"I'd rather do it myself."

"The admission?" said Bertelskjöld.

"Splendid!" said Borg. "Delighted to oblige. Great! You knew it was
an old boy, didn't you? A male patient. Don't forget the rectal exam."

She went out. Why did she never learn, never learn that you change
nothing by taking on other people's work! What had just happened
would happen again. They would go on tricking her into work on the
surgery rotation, on the OB Gyn rotation, on the psych rotation, on
every damned rotation. How did they think they would ever learn
anything if they kept getting out of departmental work? What kind of
doctors would those two make? She was wrong to let them get away
with it. Hadn't they jointly agreed to help each other become good
doctors, in the days when they had started and had had a discussion
group on the subject? She was already betraying that promise, but she
couldn't stand this bickering and drawing lots for who should look
after the patients. She would rather do the job herself.

She went over to Ward 96. In the middle of the ward was a large
glassed-in cube with corridors on all four sides. The rooms were on
the other side of the corridors. In the central core was the office, the
examination room, the students' common room; the coffee room and
the domestic offices. Number 96 was an internal medicine ward. She
went over to the secretary and was given a bundle of papers. The
patient's name was Primus Svensson. He had been in Intensive Care
for a few days after a myocardial infarction. The crisis was over now
and he had been moved into an ordinary ward.

Primus Svensson was in a room for two. Normally, she would have taken him into the examination room, but as his infarct had been relatively recent, he was not allowed to be moved. Before she went into his room, she fetched a folding screen to place between the beds. This stopped his fellow patient from staring, but it wouldn't stop him listening. According to their instructions, interviews should always be held in private, but in reality they were held wherever it happened to be possible.

She pushed open the heavy door with her behind and backed into the room, dragging the screen with her. She turned her head in embarrassment and saw two elderly men staring rigidly at her in surprise.

"Good morning," she said, walking between the beds and unfolding the screen with an apologetic nod to the other patient. Then she fetched a chair and placed it close to Primus Svensson's bed. Before she sat down, she shook his hand and told him her name. She was used to people not catching it, so she held out her badge at the same time, but she was not sure if he could read it, as he was not wearing glasses.

It all seemed foolish and wrong, coming in like this, blurting out your name and then barging straight on with the most intimate questions. But it had been even worse at first, when she had sat there with the interview form on her lap, ploughing through heading after heading in the order they were in on the sheet: past medical history, family history, review of systems and so on. Nowadays, she had the courage to ask more or less freely and only now and again checked with the crib she had in her pocket.

"How are you now?" she said, feeling her way.

"Quite well, thank you."

How should she address him? They used first names straight off to all younger patients, but it was difficult with older patients. Should she say Mr. Svensson? Or just Svensson? Or Primus? Or avoid the issue? She squinted down at the paper on which it said: ex-typographer. Could she use his first name just because he was a worker? A crazy way of reasoning, but all the same, she said:

"Primus, would you mind telling me a little about what happened when you were taken ill?"

"Isn't it in the case sheet?" said Primus Svensson.

"Yes, but rather briefly, I'm afraid. You fell off your bicycle, didn't you?"

He told her that he had suddenly felt ill, and that he must have passed out and fallen off his bike. He didn't know how he had got to the hospital.

"When did you first feel there was something wrong in your chest?"

"About six or eight years ago. It nipped sometimes, a sort of stabbing feeling. I had to watch it."

"Did you do anything about it? Go to a doctor, I mean?"

"Yes, once. To Doctor Ryden, if you know him. He said I had high blood pressure and gave me a prescription."

"Do you still take anything to keep your blood pressure down?"

"No. I finished off the bottle. About two hundred, they were. Then I suppose it got better."

"Shouldn't you have gone back for a checkup then? To Doctor Ryden?"

"I don't remember that. I was to take them pills morning and night. Huge things they were, difficult to swallow."

"And the pains in your chest, did they just disappear?"

"Well, I don't know about that. I got used to it. Took things a bit quieter, like. Didn't bike up hills and that sort of thing. No, it didn't bother me that much."

She tried to get him to describe exactly what it felt like when the pains had begun the day he had been brought in. What time they had started, whether they had come on suddenly, whether he had been upset beforehand, whether he'd exerted himself or eaten a heavy meal, whether he had been cold, or whether anything unusual had happened. She also wanted to know what kind of pain it had been, whether it had been just there in his chest or whether it had spread out in any direction, along his left arm, for instance, or up toward his throat. Was the pain *exactly* the same all the time, or had it varied?

She went on to *Past Medical History. Previous illnesses.* There was nothing much there. He had been healthy as a child. In 1918, he had had a touch of Spanish 'flu. In the forties and fifties, he had gone to the staff medical officer several times for stomach trouble and been given various medicines. He had also been off sick with his back. The years just before he had retired he had found it difficult to see and had even thought the air in the compositors' room had got heavier and heavier to breathe. She went on to *Social History* and was told that he had been divorced from his wife for thirty years and he had a son called Bernt. The son had had his fiftieth birthday the previous year. Primus had no real contact with his son, a telephone call about twice a year, a brief visit at Christmas. The son was very busy and was nearly always away, traveling.

Then she came to the more intricate questions. She began with the easiest, smoking.

"I smoke a good cigar sometimes, on occasions, party occasions, you know."

"A drink or two, as well? On those party occasions?"

He looked up at the ceiling for a few seconds.

"Do you mean do I drink, Miss?"

"Not exactly drink. Perhaps you're a teetotaler?"

"Should have been. When you see the misery drink brings. No, but to be honest, I do take a drink sometimes."

"What did that mean?" Martina wondered. "Was it a confession? Or did he mean he hardly drank at all?"

"How many centiliters?" she said, feeling idiotic.

"I never drink during the week. Not even light ale. I've heard there's alcohol in full-cream yoghurt. So I get the skimmed kind."

She jotted down "Alc. insignif." Then they came to the next section: drugs including sleeping pills and tranquilizers.

"What about sleep; do you sleep well?"

"I worked shifts when I was younger. That was O.K. I could sleep anywhere as long as there was something to lean against. But it's not so good these days. I get to sleep all right. But in the summer I wake up between three and four."

"And do what?"

"Do what? Lie there thinking, I suppose. Wait for the paper to come."

"Don't you ever take sleeping pills?"

"My wife used to. But I never touched them. You get to depend on them."

Now they had come to the most awkward questions of all, the ones you were supposed to squeeze in between other things so that it seemed natural. But she'd not done that. She was tired. They had had four hours of lectures, the professor's round, and she'd already done one case history on a Finnish woman, with the help of an interpreter.

"Have you ever been to sea?" she said, feeling her way again.

"National service?"

"Yes, or been in the Navy?"

"Yes, I was at Oscar Fredriksborg. And was in the Coastal Artillery."

She couldn't ask the shameful question that way, then. She was tired, so asked straight out: "Have you ever had venereal disease?"

He picked up his spectacle case, opened it, closed it, then put it into the drawer in the locker. Then he looked straight at her.

"I've not had either gonorrhea or syphilis."

She breathed out. Now the case history was practically done and she could dictate it. No, hell! She'd almost forgotten the form. Every infarct patient was to be interviewed according to a special stress form. It was part of a research project the head of the unit was doing. He was going to write a dissertation on it. She hadn't the energy to ask any more questions, so she decided to do the form after the physical examination.

She went into the examination room and fetched the little cart with the examination tray on it.

When she returned, he had fallen asleep. But she had to wake him and start on the laborious exploration from head to foot. She checked his pupils and made an attempt to see into the base of his eyes, but it was difficult. She put the ophthalmoscope a few centimeters from his eye and leaned close to peer through the minute hole of the black disc. She held her breath, all the time afraid their cheeks or noses would touch. She couldn't adjust the focus properly and saw nothing but a glimpse of something yellow and red. She gave up. At this stage, before she'd done the ophthalmology rotation, they couldn't expect her to be able to do eye examinations.

She moved on to his mouth and throat, then to the lymph glands in his neck and armpits, then to listening to his heart and lungs. The lung examination wasn't complete, because she was not allowed to raise him up. She went on to his heart and tried to listen to the rhythm. It was irregular. He had a slow fibrillation, but she could see that already on the EKG strip. She heard a murmur, a systolic blowing sound. The really tricky murmurs or extra sounds were the diastolic ones, the ones that come about when the heart valves open to receive fresh blood. She listened for a long time. Hitherto she had never heard diastolic extra sounds except on a phonograph record.

The rest went quickly. She took his blood pressure and felt his abdomen and inguinals. Nothing abnormal, a slight "grittiness" in the loins perhaps. She tested his reflexes and did a Babinski. Nothing special, but for some reason, she could never remember whether the big toe should point upward or downward with a Babinski.

Then she did something she was deeply ashamed of. She skipped the palpation of the rectum and prostate. Perhaps it wasn't the end of the world, but although she hadn't carried out the examination, she wrote: "Prostate normal size, normal consistency. Rectum norm." It was a falsification. She wondered how many of her friends occasionally cheated in the same way, writing down examinations they had never made. She was much too tired. To examine his backside, she would have to overcome her embarrassment and she simply couldn't now. In addition, to be fair, Primus Svensson wasn't even her patient, but the men's.

She washed her hands and set about the stress form. She didn't really understand the point of some of the questions. The form was a direct translation from an American original.

SOCIAL READJUSTMENT SCORE

Events ≦ 1 year	Possible points	Patients points
Death of a spouse	100	o
Divorce	73	o
Separation from mother	65	o
Detention in jail	63	o
Death of member of family (not children)	63	o
Personal injury or illness	53	o N.B! ?
Marriage	50	o
Being fired from work	47	o
Illness of member of family	44	o
Pregnancy	40	o
Sexual difficulties	39	o
Arrival of new member of family	39	o
Financial problems	38	o
Death of close friend	37	o
Change in line of work	35	o
Changed responsibility at work	29	o
Son or daughter leaving home	29	o
Trouble with son/daughter-in-law	29	o
Promotion	28	o
Husband/Wife started/stopped work	26	o
Troubles with the boss	23	o
Change in working hours	20	o
Change in residence	20	o
Change in recreational habits	19	o
Joined/left a society or union	19	o
Change in friends	18	o
Change in sleeping habits	16	o
Change in eating habits	15	o
Vacation in last month	13	o
Christmas/New Year in last month	12	o
Minor violation of the law	11	o
		o

Score: - 150 points, no clear risk
         - 199 points, some risk
         - 299 points, moderate risk
         - 300 points, high risk

Martina Bosson put the form into a red plastic file marked *For punching*. Primus Svensson had not managed to scrape up a single point, only a question mark under the heading *Personal injury or illness*. And yet he had suffered a myocardial infarction as clear as day.

5 The atmosphere at the hospital switchboard was often charged. This was one of the most stressful areas of work. So much aggression came in and so little was allowed out, the surplus remaining at the switchboard and increasing the tension.

From outside it was possible to reach the various telephones inside the hospital in two ways, either via the switchboard or by dialing direct. If no one replied after dialing direct, then after a couple of minutes the call was automatically put through to the switchboard, which had to go on searching.

There were two more communication systems alongside the telephone network, the intercom and the wireless radio. All duty and emergency staff carried small radio receivers in their top pockets. When the switchboard wanted to reach them, the receiver would bleep. Whoever it concerned then had to go to the nearest telephone and contact the switchboard.

The switchboard area at Enskede Hospital was light and modern, but the air was dry, as in most places with indirect ventilation. The dry air gave rise to static electricity, and although the actual equipment was easily worked and ergonomically designed, the problems for those who worked there were considerable. At certain times of the day the switchboard almost jammed with all the incoming calls from people making appointments, asking for results of tests or other information. The staff at the switchboard were like living fuses; if the tension grew too great, they blew.

Hospital staff rarely sit still in their rooms. Doctors had special telephoning times, often far too short, or the person concerned could not be found or perhaps an operation had taken longer than expected.

Or else holidays, comp time in lieu of them, or some other irregularity came in between. Usually, the switchboard had not been informed.

Inpatients were not allowed to use the hospital telephones. There were public telephones for them. Ambulatory patients could phone from special telephone booths or glass hoods; bed patients had telephone carts that could be moved between wards.

Primus had asked to have a telephone brought. The telephone was constantly in use, and the staff put up a notice on the door stating TELEPHONE HERE, so that they knew where it was.

He had really meant to write to Bernt, which would be easier than talking. Whenever they spoke to each other, the conversation always ended coldly or in open discord. Bernt was his mother's son. Ellen had been dead for twelve years now, but that made no difference. Bernt went on behaving like a defense lawyer for a person who no longer existed. If Bernt had been small when Primus and Ellen had separated, this would be understandable. But that wasn't so. Bernt had been over twenty and doing his military service when it happened. Ellen and Primus had been on the point of separating for seven or eight years by then, but the boy had made them hold off. They had wanted him to have flown from the nest first. But it had made no difference. Perhaps it would have been easier if Bernt had had brothers and sisters.

Primus didn't have Bernt's current address, only a telephone number he'd been given about six months before. Could he rely on Bernt? "If I'm going to die now," thought Primus. "I must make sure everything's in order. The announcement mustn't go in until after the funeral." No guests were to be invited—who was there to invite, anyhow? He was to be cremated. The urn was to be placed in Sandborg churchyard in the same grave as Ellen's. He had agreed on that with Ellen when she had been on her deathbed. They had done this with Bernt in mind. Bernt shouldn't have to care for two graves in different places. But they had decided without consulting Bernt. Several years later, when Primus had told Bernt, he had said: "How do I know Mom agreed to that? You might have made it all up."

What else was there to tell them? Bernt was his sole heir, so there shouldn't be any trouble. Might there be difficulties getting out his funeral money? Primus had put seven thousand kronor in a special bankbook labeled *For my funeral*. At first it had been only five thousand, but he had recently increased the sum. If he survived this coronary and inflation went on, it would be just as well to raise it to ten thousand.

Primus had two more bankbooks, one for current expenses, which now stood at—. He put on his glasses and checked on a scrap of paper in his wallet; one thousand, nine hundred and thirty-four kronor, sixteen öre, plus interest for the year. In the third bankbook, he had exactly twenty three thousand. That was the money Bernt was to have. Not much for a lifetime's savings. He had recently sold his premium bonds, as it was too worrying trying to keep track of the drawings. He couldn't think why they didn't bring in some automatic computerized system and simply pay out the money to whoever bought the winning lottery ticket.

He had hardly any possessions of value. His furniture was mostly junk. No one would pay anything for the old books he had bought at secondhand bookshops or at auctions, so they could be sold in lots. Bernt could get a few hundred for the chest of drawers of domestic rococo if he were patient enough. But patience was just what Bernt lacked. He wasn't stupid but he gave up too easily. He had got that from Ellen.

Could he get anything for the apartment? Hardly, as it was rented in the usual way and would no doubt go back onto the housing list. But there were quite a few ways around that, weren't there? Picking up his pen and tearing a page out of his notebook, he wrote: Talk with Bernt about *funeral money, funeral, burial (take that last), bankbooks, chest of drawers, apartment, allotment.*

The allotment was on city ground. It was not really worth anything, a tiny shack with an old couch and a few tools in it, a rain gauge, a sundial, a few raspberry canes and black currant bushes, and some flowers. He had heard from an allotment neighbor that young people had begun to be interested in having allotments. A lot of them wanted to be closer to the soil. Farms sold well enough, but not everyone could form an extended family and go and live in the country. So allotments had become popular. One or two younger families had appeared out in Enskede and it was said that they paid well to take over. But the market swung so quickly, especially when it was anything to do with young people. And things were no longer going well for the Farmer's Party.

He had been waiting for more than three hours for a telephone now. Should he ring for the nurse? He picked up the call button hanging by his bed and weighed it in his hand. They might be cross, of course. You had to stay in the staff's good graces. But at the same time, they had often said: "If there's anything special, then ring the bell." Even the Professor had said that. The day before, not at the ordinary round time, the Professor had suddenly appeared with a jittery nurse and two black men in white coats. Primus hadn't met the Professor before. But he had come in, shaken hands and introduced himself, looked at his temperature chart and said: "Things are going fine here!" In the doorway on his way out, the Professor had turned around and added: "Don't hesitate to ring if you want anything."

There was no one to ask. His fellow patient who had diabetes had grown worse last Friday, so they had moved him and no one else had come yet. It was a trifle lonely, but nice at the same time, because it wasn't all that easy to share a room with a total stranger, who might also be seriously ill.

Primus pressed the button. He felt himself starting to sweat and his pulse racing. That was hardly a good thing. Damned silly being so nervous! Like a schoolboy. Being in the hospital was very much like going to school or doing your national service. They were friendlier, of course, but you felt uncertain at the same time. You had to watch it. You had to try to be exemplary. For a moment he wondered whether they stuck gold stars on the case sheets of patients they liked best; of course they didn't, but that was what it felt like.

A nurse he had never seen before came into the room, a file pressed to her bosom. She did not introduce herself.

"Yes?" she said. "You rang?"

"It was the telephone cart. I asked for it this morning."

The nurse took a pad out of her pocket and read: "You're not on the list. You're Primus Svensson, aren't you? B2."

"Yes."

"I'll speak to the orderlies."

She was out of the room before he had time to say that it wasn't that important and he could write a letter instead. It was not the end of the world that he hadn't got Bernt's address. He could write to the firm instead. Bernt was employed by a very well-known firm. Luna Pharmaceuticals in Södertälje. The letter ought to get there without a street address.

6 Nurse Sirkka went out of Primus Svensson's room and pushed the door shut with her heel. Where *was* the telephone? She couldn't see the TELEPHONE HERE notice anywhere. Where were the girls? All of a sudden they could simply vanish without trace. Either they were out on the wards or else they were all huddled together having a smoke. Where? The coffee room was empty except for a student asleep with his head on an open textbook. The dirty utility room? One of the male orderlies was sitting in there talking on the patients' telephone. When she opened the door, he turned away, and giggling, he put his hand over his mouth.

"You must go downstairs to phone," said Sirkka. "Or borrow my phone if it's something urgent."

He took no notice of her, but turned his bent back to her. He had put seven one-krona coins in a neat row along the top of the telephone cart, so it was clearly going to be a long call. Sirkka gave up and went into the office, unlocked the medicine cabinet and took two Alka-Seltzers dissolved in a plastic mug of water. Her headache had started at the back of her neck and was now a tight band around her forehead. She felt like crying. She would never cope with this. She was moved around from one ward to another, without a chance of getting to know any one ward properly. It was hopeless being put in charge of fifteen to twenty new people every day. Here on number 96 they had an old *cadre* of nurses who did as they pleased. They did a good job, but decided when and how for themselves.

She sat down and looked at the medication schedule; she would soon have to make rounds. It was all so damned unfair. At staff-meetings, they all said: "Nurses must go out in the ward more and not sit in the office, in their little cabins." And when she made an effort to clear off the paperwork and then went out into the ward to deal with all the rest, they ignored her completely, acting as if she were invisible, or else treated her like a child.

She could feel her eyes growing hot and her nose thick. She really mustn't start crying. Once you started, you simply couldn't stop.

She had talked to Berit, who was in charge of the whole ward, but Berit couldn't really be bothered to listen. She had no disciplinary problems. There seemed to be an unspoken agreement between Berit and the staff nurses. They obeyed Berit as long as Berit didn't interfere with certain things. If anyone came late or left too early, Berit pretended not to notice as long as the work was done. But when Sirkka tried the same thing, everything went wrong. Suddenly she would find herself standing there alone with the food cart, with no help at all. The others were so confoundedly unfair.

It had all got worse with all this crazy talk about democracy. For democracy to function, a certain order was necessary, certain agreements and regulations. It was the organization that didn't function. And then if she complained at meetings, the others said she was too rigid. One evening she had started crying as she sat there having something to eat with the doctor on call. He had brought it on. She had told him what hell it all was, and then the bastard had talked to the Unit Supervisor. And the Unit Supervisor had had the nurses union representative in to discuss the "Sirkka case." After that everything was ruined. Now the staff nurses wouldn't obey her, so neither would the "girls," the orderlies, either. But there was such a turnover of girls that after a month she had a completely new gang of them.

That was good, because then she could start again with a clean slate. If it hadn't been for those damned staff nurses in the way, that is.

They had had departmental meetings and talked and talked. At first it had been fine. Fresh matters kept coming up and some people had said what they really thought. But then it all turned out to be hot air. People pretended they were still being honest and open toward each other, and that they were deciding important things together. But it wasn't like that. A child could see there was another system, that the people with power in the ward settled in private how things should be done. The departmental meetings had become lousy theater, the work decided on by unspoken agreement.

She began counting out the different tablets into the plastic cups. It was like playing a game. There were thirty-six compartments in the tray, one for each patient in the ward. At the bottom of each compartment was a piece of paper with room, name, and prescription written on it. The pieces of paper were often changed, not just because new patients came in, but because the prescription had been changed. After some Grand Rounds, she had to sit down and rewrite practically every single paper. Or when the doctors had been to a drug conference and had decided to try something new.

Sirkka had thought about becoming a teacher instead, a teacher in the nursing school. Some of her classmates wanted to start studying medicine, but she didn't dare think in those terms. Seven or eight more years! She was twenty-three already. She would be over thirty before she qualified, and then you had to specialize. How long did that take—five years? No, teaching would be better. You could do that in two years, once you had been accepted. But at the same time, she was scared. What did teaching involve? She'd made a big blooper once already; when she'd decided to become a nurse and thought she would be able to care for people and nurse them. Instead she had become a foreman and a slave to paperwork, a kind of corporal whom no one paid attention to, and yet who still had responsibility for what they all did. She had no intention of falling into that trap again.

The male orderly who had carelessly written his name KENTA directly on his coat with a marker pen was standing in the doorway.

"The telephone's free now."

"Then take it to B2 for God's sake! Primus Svensson!"

Kenta shrugged his shoulders, rolling up his eyes and looking offended, then dragged the telephone cart off as if he were pulling along a portable x-ray machine or a cart loaded with lead.

7 It was half-past eight in the morning and the medical unit was doing x-ray rounds. About twenty doctors had collected between the narrow view boxes, on the glass panels of which hung the black and white x-ray films, some of them dark patches with white contrasting blood vessels looking like lightning in the night sky. Other photographs looked like those taken by astronauts, with kernels of light like stars against a dark background, and milky white swirls of nebulae. The Chief Radiologist was demonstrating his findings. He was a remarkably tall man and could not stand upright for long without feeling faint, so he had a specially constructed chair of his own on round casters. He swung back and forth between the cabinets in his chair, pointing and waving with a light metal stick that could be extended or collapsed like a radio antenna.

"Ward 96, Primus Svensson," said the Chief Radiologist. "Heart and lungs. We see here a slight enlargement of the left ventricle and a calcified aortic arch. Heart volume: five hundred and fifty. Nothing special about the lungs except some calcified nodes in the hilus from an old primary lesion."

"Thank you," said Gustaf Nyström, Acting Head of Ward 96 and responsible at the moment for Primus Svensson.

The x-ray rounds were calm and efficient, as usual when the Head of Medicine, Professor Erik Ask, was absent. The Chief Radiologist and Ask were not friends. The Chief Radiologist had applied for the as yet unfilled post of Professor of Diagnostic Radiology at Enskede Hospital, but Ask had intrigued to get a professor in the same subject transferred from Serafimer Hospital, which now faced almost certain closure. Another reason for the calm and efficiency was that Ask usually used the x-ray round to comment on the events of the day, to complain about the editorials in the *Dagens Nyheter* which he considered to be more like hastily scrabbled together readers' letters. But the conservative *Svenska Dagbladet* received eulogies for its journalistic reforms. No comment was ever made on the evening tabloids.

They went through more x-ray films, and two of them gave rise to brief discussion. The Chief Radiologist was in a hurry, because he was due at a meeting with the administration, to whom he had proposed a 3.2-million grant for the purchase of a computerized scanner.

The demonstration was over and the physicians all returned to their respective departments to do their morning rounds and to take morning coffee. Gustaf Nyström handed his rounds over to an intern, in order to snatch some time to do a little research before it was time for discharges. He had a research room in Rabbit Row in the Research Institute, although he did not do experiments on animals. Nearly all the others were involved in various ways in animal experiments, which was why the Research Institute had been constructed according to their needs. The equipment had been largely paid for with American dollars.

Nyström took off his coat and flung it on top of a heap of books with bits of paper protruding from them to mark interesting sections. He yawned, scratched at his crotch and fell into his chair. In front of him lay a bundle of Social Readjustment score forms of MI patients. He leafed through them—could any pattern be discerned? No, it was dangerous to look for patterns at this stage, as he might be biased; that is, allow faulty expectations to influence his judgments. The computer would have its say first.

Nyström's investigation was to attempt to distinguish psychosocial factors that might cause or give rise to myocardial infarction. That stress situations of various kinds led to infarcts was an ancient clinical observation: stress at work, trouble at home, deaths in the family and other events that threw people off balance. Many people had done research in this field before, and there were plenty of theories, but no clear evidence.

Gustaf Nyström wanted to compare three groups of men: a hundred who had had infarctions, a hundred who had been brought into the hospital for other reasons, and a hundred who lived out in the community apparently quite healthily. The idea was to interview them all with the Social Readjustment forms and complement this with various investigations primarily of a chemical nature.

Was this a sensible investigation? Unfortunately, the reply to that was no, and Gustaf Nyström was aware of the fact. As the aim was to be able to show certain definite connections, it was possible to reckon beforehand how many people would be needed in the three different groups. If too few were examined, the results would quite simply be uncertain. Nowadays there were complete epidemiological tables on how many people had to be examined for certain connections to be proved or discarded. The statisticians had worked these out and all you had to do was to look them up . . . it was as simple as a logarithm table. According to the tables, Gustaf Nyström would need 1,350 people in each group for the statistical methods to be applied with reasonable certainty.

Wouldn't it be just as well to stop at once, or make sure he got 1,350 patients in each group? Both alternatives were impractical. Examining and interviewing 4,050 people was quite out of the question, as a team of at least twelve people would be required. Abandoning the project was also impossible. Professor Ask was the guarantor and sponsor and he had originally approved the project. So it was a good project. If Gustaf Nyström now openly maintained anything to the contrary, he would have to find a job in another hospital, but as the professors stuck together firmly on certain matters, he would have great difficulty getting into any other teaching unit. For all practical purposes, his career opportunities would be closed if he opposed the project.

But if Nyström produced a poor thesis . . . would the examiner not then ensure that it was not accepted? Probably not. His examiner would also have his career to think about. Attacking all too fiercely a thesis that one of the country's leading professors of internal medicine was behind would demand courage very few examiners could afford.

An even more obvious danger threatened, namely that there would be no difference at all among Nyström's three groups. That would be a very dangerous situation. Every investigation worth its name had to show certain differences, no matter whether they were bizarre or contradicted by proven experience. Gustaf Nyström knew that this attitude was also wrong. If the theory that stress could give rise to myocardial infarction was fundamentally crazy, which would be reflected in no differences appearing among the three groups, in that case this would be a great and important scientific discovery. Research could then devote all its resources to testing other theories.

Gustaf Nyström was forty-one years old and the eldest of the doctors who had not yet presented a thesis. If he didn't produce one in the near future, he would be weeded out. Then there would be no alternative but to go into the public health field, move out into the sticks, become a company medical officer or try to get into a decent health center. Internal medicine was a fine and popular special field in which no deviators or stragglers would be tolerated.

He had not started studying medicine until he was twenty-four and so had felt out of it from the start. Before he had started at the Karolinska Institute, he had read humanities, practical and theoretical philosophy, among other subjects. That was a dangerous background, as medicine had for a long time had its own theoretical system, which was considered by the medical men themselves to be superior to all other modes of thought and laws of logic. Philosophers in the faculty were treated as statistics were treated: you could listen willingly and with amusement, you could consider discussing and asking certain questions. But when it came to the crunch, no one ever took anyone without a medical training seriously.

Lately, Gustaf Nyström had found himself in yet another dilemma.

The younger politically-interested thinkers had revived an old debate, that of the difference between describing and understanding. Nearly all medical research was based on description, charting or demonstrating connections. Very seldom did anyone ever take the trouble to understand. In theoretical science, this was done to a certain extent, trying to "understand" molecules and cells, but in this way the theoretical models became confused with reality: it was thought that the modes and reality were identical. In the field of clinical research, most people, almost without exception, were content with description. To try to "understand" was somewhat subjective. To try to find out just how people really functioned was not science. Or to be more exact, not natural science. One of the strangest features of modern medicine was just this logical clumsiness: equating science or knowledge with natural science, which naturally would function as a brake and a limitation. When a medical man talked about, for instance, the necessity of medical training being based on scientific foundations, he would mean natural science, that is, science—knowledge—in a limited and abbreviated form.

Gustaf Nyström's heart began to flutter, and he got up to walk around his desk to work off some of his aggressiveness. But it was impossible to get around the desk, as the floor was covered with cardboard boxes full of computer sheets and photocopies of medical articles. He sat down again and glared at Primus Svensson's Social Readjustment score. What the hell did Martina Bosson mean by putting a question mark against question number six, "Personal Injury or illness"? Presumably she had confused the patient's present disease, the MI, with some other disease that might have occurred during the previous years. He raised his red pen to put it right. No, he mustn't do things so sloppily. If he began messing about with the forms in his own hand, that would be deception. You could not do that. It was unethical. Cheating on a large scale, in the theoretical field, that was all right, provided it happened within an acceptable scientific framework.

He left the room and set off for Ward 96, where the students were sitting waiting for him in the coffee room. His coffee was already cold, but he drank it all the same. During recent months he had begun to detect signs of a gastric ulcer and he tolerated cold coffee better than hot.

"On Friday, you've got a written test on Diseases of the Heart and Great Vessels," he said. "Which individual characteristic or factor is most strongly correlated to myocardial infarction? Anyone?"

Carl Bertelskjöld held up his hand, although there were only six people around the table.

"Yes?"

"Sex."

"No."

"But men are a much greater infarct risk than women."

"I asked which characteristic or factor is most strongly correlated to MI."

Bertelskjöld looked offended. Nyström turned instead to the Chilean, Juan Bosco.

"Herdi . . . hereder . . ."

"If you mean hereditary factors, then that is also incorrect."

"Cholesterol," said Borg. "Triglycerides . . ."

"No. Think now. It's much simpler than you think. Martina? Hans?"

Hans Berling scratched his head with the stem of his stethoscope. Martina looked angrily dismissive.

"I think it's a silly question."

"The answer is age," said Gustaf Nyström. "It's as simple as that. The incidence of myocardial infarction increases with age. Like two almost parallel graphs. Carl is right in that when it is a question of early MI's, then there is a much higher incidence in men. But that wasn't what I asked."

"Will we get a letter grade for the test?" said Martina.

"No."

"But we'll get points?"

"Yes."

"How many times do we have to remind you lecturers that letter grades have been abolished now?"

"In your finals, yes," said Gustaf Nyström. "But this is just a minor test."

"If it's that minor, then I don't understand the point of giving points for it. It'll just mean a whole lot more work for whoever has to mark them."

"Will it be multiple choice?" said Hans Berling. "Will we be having that sort of card that's optically scanned, when you fill in the blanks with a soft pencil?"

"Yes," said Nyström. "That we check with computers. Then you get points automatically. There's nothing you can do about it. You'll have to look on it as a diagnostic test, a way for us lecturers to see what level of knowledge the class has reached in general. Not as a way of picking out individuals."

"In that case," said Martina. "Can't we do the test anonymously? You don't need all our names to know what level the whole year has reached in general."

"Now listen, I didn't think up these things. It's your own course director who decides them. The Professor. If you've any suggestions to make, then you must go to him directly."

"He's just gone to Honolulu, hasn't he?" said Martina.

"Hong Kong. He's at a conference in Hong Kong. That's right."

She looked at the others and snorted. Gustaf Nyström did not like this conversation. In actual fact, he agreed with the students, but he was forced to speak on behalf of the Professor.

"You know we've agreed that lectures and exams are to be *problem-oriented*," Martina went on.

"That's a matter of definition. What do you mean by problem-orientation?"

"Well, what do *you* mean by it?"

"That one solves certain questions. That may be of a limited kind."

"But that's just what the whole thing's about . . . to avoid questions of a limited kind. To avoid having to answer what percent and how much this and that all over the place. Don't you see that?"

"I can't say any more," said Nyström. "Your course director has interpreted the concept of problem-orientation in his own way. You'll have to make do with that for now, until you can speak to him directly."

"Which'll be *after* the test?"

"Oh, lay off now, Martina!" said Carl Bertelskjöld. "We can sneak you the answers."

"You slob!" said Martina. "Don't you see this is a matter of principle. Principles we've been fighting for for several years."

"What do you mean, we?" said Lars Borg. "I've never been consulted."

"You have! You've a vote, just like everyone else. If you're not satisfied with student politics, then you can vote for other candidates. Or run yourself. Don't go saying you've not been asked, now."

Gustaf Nyström got up. He would have to do the discharges now. Three patients were due out today, one of them, a boy of twenty, suffering from bone cancer. Nyström felt he had to gather all his strength to face the boy, to answer his questions on his treatment, about how long it would be before he would be well again. The boy would never be well again. He was going to die.

"If we go on strike?" said Martina. "What happens then? What happens if we don't turn up on Friday?"

"Don't do anything silly, now," he said.

"I just want to know what would happen?"

"I don't know. But there'd be one hell of a row, that I do know."

He took the file with Primus Svensson's Social Readjustment score and left the coffee room. He would have to try to find out about the question mark by question six on the afternoon round. He couldn't face another clash with Martina now. She was such a damned pain. Officious.

8 Bernt Svensson, Pharmaceutical Sales Representative, was on his way out of Luna Pharmaceutical's head office in Södertälje. At his side was Tony Bygren, a newly appointed rep. They were both carrying cardboard boxes out toward the pale green leased Volvo 245 in the parking lot.

"Are you driving?" said Bernt.

"It's your car, isn't it?"

"I'm feeling a bit off color. If you don't mind."

They loaded the boxes through the hatchback door of the Volvo and got in. How much longer would Bernt be able to hide the fact that he had lost his license? As long as there were two of them, the loss of his license hardly affected his work. But if they gave him a solo job? Did the driving-license bureau pass on the information to one's employer? The thought was not entirely absurd, as the Chief of Police for the whole country was on the board of Luna Pharmaceutical. In addition to that, it was the second time for Bernt. The first time they had taken his license away had been in 1961, when he hadn't been with the company for more than six months. But no one took it so seriously in those days. Several of the Sales reps had been found guilty of driving with too much alcohol in their blood. It went along with the job, so to speak. You might have to entertain people anything up to three times a week, salmon and champagne for the staff physicians, steak and red wine for the students, and schnapps and hash for the staff of a pharmacy. And you had to get home, even if it was in the middle of the night. In those days, it was almost a point in your favor to have lost your license, evidence that you were on really good terms with the customers.

Now things were different. Lately they'd tightened things up considerably. Meals had become simpler and less alcoholic. Instead, more and more money went on traveling expenses and grants for testing medicines. In other words, they were concentrating on a smaller group of interested doctors instead of splurging money any old way. Nowadays, as a consultant, a man might even have to stick to soft drinks. But whoever stuck to soft drinks had to put up with being regarded as an ex-alcoholic.

They drove up onto the freeway toward Stockholm, Tony accelerating sharply.

"We've plenty of time," said Bernt, who didn't like traveling fast.

"What's Enskede like?" said Tony. "Might it be a bitch?"

"Don't think so. Not that many come to these Friday afternoons. There aren't many long questions, either. They're all in a hurry to get back home, just like everyone else."

When Bernt had been younger, he had also worried about facing several doctors at once. They could gang up and ask awkward questions. Some chemist or pharmacologist might throw out a technical term he didn't understand. But in reality, unpleasantnesses were rare. The firm gave you a good training. They had special psychologists who trained the representatives how to get out of tight corners. The training was mostly about psychology rather than medical knowledge, a question of creating a psychological climate that kept aggressiveness down. What could be troublesome was being confronted with the really young physicians, the ones who dragged the discussion into the fields of politics and morality. But that soon passed. When they'd done about three or four years study, the red coxcomb had usually fallen off them. In the seventies, larger companies like Luna had started training some young reps in political theory, which on the medical level was concerned not so much with insight and knowledge, but with the use of a certain kind of language, with knowing a few fashionable terms and bringing them out in a natural way. When things got tricky, you had to force your opponent to define himself. And when he had done so, then you hit back with another definition plus a quote from one of the big guns, Mao or Marx or Rexed.

At the New Year, Luna had got a new director, a Professor of Medicine who had left the fold. That had made things much easier. That had made the industry cleaner in a lot of critics' eyes. Another bright idea had been to form a society to bring some of the student leaders at the Karolinska Institute into contact with Luna's own younger researchers.

"How do you think the election'll go?" said Tony.

"To hell," said Bernt, leaving Tony to interpret that whichever way he wished. Within the company, a number of people were worried that the Social Democrats would return to power, which in its turn would mean renewed demands for nationalization of the drug industry. But only middle management was worried. Bernt had been employed there so long, he knew the bosses weren't in the slightest worried. They hadn't even been frightened when the Marxists had had such an impact on the trade union congress. All talk, that had been. The socialists wouldn't nationalize any drug industry. At the most, they might contribute state capital. Like when the state had bought up Kabi a few years earlier—was there any difference? None! They all went on working exactly like anyone else. The industry was wholly protected. There was a Director-General from the Civil Service in the chairman's seat of the Association of Medical Suppliers. There were professors in cahoots with top bureaucrats from the state, the provincial councils as well as the local councils on the boards of all the firms. At this particular moment there was a vacancy on the board of Luna. Rumor had it that it had been reserved for the head of an insurance company. No more than just: in practice, it was health insurance money that provided most of the capital, wasn't it?

If the situation was bright for the drug firms, then it was rather less than bright for Bernt Svensson personally. He was one of a number of older "consultants" who had not been promoted within the firm, who had neither become an area manager, manager of an overseas branch, nor even managed to wangle himself into the personnel department. He was fifty-one now, had lost his license for a second time, and he had also twice had a couple of months off sick recently. So he was really worried that the Social Democrats might win the election. If they did, it would be used as an argument for "rationalization." The bosses would say there were bad times ahead, now we must see who earns his bread and who is dead wood. In fact, Bernt thought the drug industry was hoping for a change of government. Other industries could "rationalize" and cut down on staff when business was bad. But business was never bad in the drug industry. The Swedish people simply grew older and sicker. So to be able to "rationalize," Luna would have to prove some other threat than a financial one, the threat of nationalization.

"Here's the turn off to Huddinge," said Tony Bygren, as they passed Barby. "When I was last in Huddinge Hospital, there was someone there talking about coordinating the hospital's purchases of drugs and that clinical pharmacologists together with the other physicians should make a ranking list of their final choice of preparations. To reduce the number of synonymous ones."

"Bullshit!" said Bernt. "That never works at a big teaching hospital. How would the pharmacologists have time to do that? How many duties do they have? Two, three, three and a half. And Huddinge has become a giant transit station. The professors just sit there, longing for the Karolinska Institute. As soon as you change the head of clinical medicine, you have to start all over again with your attempts at coordination."

They drove on toward Stockholm. Bernt was not feeling well. He fished out a couple of Novalucol and swallowed them to settle his stomach. A drink would have done the trick, a bitter or a Fernet Branca, but he must not think like that. He had been on the wagon for almost two weeks. His job depended on it. His life, even. If they kicked him out now, even if with some kind of early pension, there would be nothing left to fight for. There would be nothing left to do but to drink himself to death. Or set up on his own.

"You had southern Norrland before, didn't you?" said Tony.

"No, not all of it. District Nine. Hälsingland, Dalarna and Gästrikland."

"Why did you give it up? Did you get sick of the sticks?"

"The boss thought I'd done enough traveling. And they'd reorganized everything then, and were thinking of basing it all on medical specialties instead of districts. Damned silly, actually. It means even more reps. If two boys had had to cover all the pediatric clinics in the whole of Norrland, they would have had to spin around like madmen, and at the same time, two other boys would have had to rush around the same circuit visiting the psychiatric clinics. It would have been a disaster. But then he was given the push, too, that Knut Iversen. Did you hear what the boss said afterwards? Of course things were bound to go to hell with someone who spoke Norwegian!"

"I had the chance of Jämtland and Härjedalen. In the new organization," said Tony.

"Watch out for Jämtland. They have central registrations of all prescriptions there. They're developing a bloody great bureaucracy up there. Some of the doctors are furious. You might find yourself in a fix."

They turned off at Årsta, went on up toward Enskede Hospital and drove straight into the staff multistory car park. Luna paid for three spaces there. They unloaded their boxes and took the elevator up to the medical unit lecture room. It was twenty minutes to three. Bernt usually reckoned to be in place at least a quarter of an hour early. There were certain simple and catastrophic mistakes a "consultant" could make. Arriving late, for instance. If you arrived late, you were not showing sufficient respect for your audience.

They went in and familiarized themselves with the room, tried out the overhead-projector, got out fresh chalk, which they broke into two so that it would not squeak, then laid out the contents of their boxes, a heap of nicely bound anatomical charts, a pile of ballpoint pens, an abstract color print in a numbered series, a bundle of scientific papers, a pile of order forms and three dozen phonograph records of the Moon-light Sonata on one side and information about the drug Harmonyl on the other.

They hadn't called them drug advertisements for a long time. Drug information, it was called nowadays. It was easier to work with the concept of information than with that soiled word "advertisement." But Bernt wondered how long "information" would be able to keep its luster of objectivity. Other firms, car dealers, for instance, had also started exchanging the word for information advertisement. The word "announcement" was on its ways out to the advantage of the more neutral "declaration." But language was like that. Words had a brief life and were soon burnt out. Serious firms had to keep off the rubbish and change words in good time.

At five to three, two more people appeared in the lecture room, a man and a woman in ordinary clothes.

"Are you going to be in here?" said the man, rather peevishly.

"Yes, there's a clinical conference at three, isn't there?" said Tony.

"But we were asked to be here at three," said the man. "We're speaking on a socio-medical investigation of Finnish gypsies."

"For the doctors in the medical unit?"

"For the doctors in the medical unit."

The two civilians simply sat down behind the long bench that functioned as a lecturer's desk. Bernt wondered if they were doctors. Their definite manner implied that they were. Best to lie low. He and Tony left the room.

At ten past three, people began to arrive, some younger hospital physicians and some doctors from private practices in the area around the hospital. The visitors at once began to take things from the gifts on the bench. The socio-medics stayed where they were, sullenly sitting on the same bench, but no one took any notice of them.

At twenty past three, Lock, the senior lecturer, appeared. He was Assistant Chief Physician and responsible for conferences. The socio-medics leaped on him.

"What's going on? We were invited here by your chief to give an account of our investigation. And now these advertising guys are here."

"We always start our Friday clinical conferences with ten minutes on drug information," Lock replied, unmoved.

The socio-medics looked disconcerted, but stubbornly stayed put. Bernt sensed he had Lock on his side, so he gave Tony a sign to start his little lecture. This was on Harmonyl and its tranquilizing, relaxing, and sleep-inducing effect. Harmonyl was nothing new. It had been in

Luna's arsenal for about fifteen years and was manufactured on license after a German patent. But now they had produced a new preparation, a two-level tablet that gave a more even concentration in the blood.

Everything went well, if in a somewhat Friday-afternoonish way. After thirty-five minutes, Bernt and Tony had answered the few questions and taken orders for more drugs. When they handed the floor over to the two sullen socio-medics, about half the audience got to its feet and left.

Bernt lived on the south side of Stockholm. He left Tony with the car and took a taxi home. Well, home . . . for the last six months, he had lived with a girlfriend called Kitty. Kitty was not at home when he got there, but in the middle of the kitchen floor, in a direct line leading to the refrigerator, lay a large sheet of paper. On it was written: *Your dad phoned He's in Enskede Hospital. Ward 96.*

Bernt picked up the piece of paper. Oh, so the old man was in a bad way? Well, so the time had come at last, had it?

9 Hardy had been trained at the Library School in Borås. By the time he had graduated, there was no work. During the summer he had worked as a swimming instructor, but this September, he had got a substitute job in the hospital library. It was a modern and well-organized library with two essential main aims, firstly to provide the patients and staff with good literature, and secondly to be a scientific branch of the Medical Library at the Karolinska Institute. For that purpose, there was a direct link with the central computerized literature search system, called Medline. Enskede Hospital library, however, was lacking in one minor field. Almost all its funds went into salaries, premises, shelving, photocopying and fees to Medline, so there was very little left for the purchase of books.

Hardy pushed the book cart. If he were lucky, he could travel a few hundred meters at a time if he hooked himself onto the train of food carts hauled by an electric truck. Otherwise he had to push the book cart manually. He often thought the choice of books he had to offer the patients was poor, but he had soon found that he also had other functions. In many ways, he served as a living encyclopedia on medical matters. The patients didn't dare ask the doctors and nurses directly, but they felt able to ask him. At first Hardy had been evasive and had referred the patients to the hospital staff. But then he had thought over the situation. The system was such that the patients didn't dare ask directly. It was a bad system and should be changed, but that would take many years. Meanwhile, he could be quite useful and calm down anxious patients, if he tried to answer as best he could and at the same time keep his tongue under control.

Hardy had a small library of popular medicine on his cart. *The Great Medical Book, Medical Terminology, Medical Law, Doctor Spock, What I Look Like Inside* and *Encyclopedia for Nurses*. After only two weeks he had begun to feel quite informed. The hard part was not so much patients' questions on diagnoses or the side-effects of medicines; the real difficulty was the psychological and social problems he was faced with. He was librarian, barefoot-doctor, welfare officer, and priest all rolled into one. He often tried to shuffle his patients off onto the chaplain, or the social worker or the departmental staff. But that wasn't easy. There seemed to be no cross-communications in the hospital. If the patient happened to have got onto the particular track—in this case Hardy's—then the patient had to continue along that track regardless of what questions arose. Perhaps that was right. Perhaps many of them had a greater need for personal contact than for a specialist.

Hardy went into Department 96. He had in fact been there as recently as two days ago, but there was a nurse's aide called Yvonne in 96 whom Hardy was attracted to. She was perhaps not so strikingly pretty and he knew very little about her spiritual life, but he could not forget her complexion. Yvonne was blond and the skin on her upper arms and throat was almost golden. Hardy wondered what color the rest of her body was.

He called through the door of the coffee room, in which about ten people were sitting. Yvonne was not there, nor did anyone ask him in. An older staff nurse Hardy was slightly afraid of was in the dirty utility room.

"Are you busy? Have you had a lot of new patients in?"

"Ask at the office," the staff nurse replied curtly.

Hardy did not ask at the office. He caught sight of an old woman sitting slumped in a wheelchair in the corridor, so he pulled the book cart over to her and stopped beside her.

"How are you?" he said, putting a hand on her bony shoulder.

She didn't answer, but sat there gumming the air—they must have taken her dentures away. She was clutching a handkerchief in her hands.

"Are you waiting for something?" he said, trying to catch her eye.

She didn't see him. When he leaned over her, he smelt the rank, slightly waxlike smell of old people. But he did not draw back, for he had begun to get used to it. Not everyone could smell of eau de cologne. In her lap, beneath her knotted hands, was a large brown envelope. "To x-ray. 15.30 hrs," Hardy read. What was the time now? Quarter to three. Was the old woman to sit there for almost an hour waiting to be pushed to x-ray? What if he took her with him on his book round? She could come with him as a kind of trailer cart into a few wards, and then he could deliver her to x-ray at 15.30. Everyone would be pleased and the old woman would see a few different sights and might even meet an acquaintance. But that was out of the question. There would be a fuss. Everyone stuck to his or her routine. Or someone would say he was spreading dangerous germs by dragging a 96 patient around the other wards. But she couldn't very well stay there, could she? He patted the old woman on the cheek, straightened up and turned around to go and tell them in the coffee room: "You can't just let her sit there like that!"

"*Evening Express* . . ." the old woman said faintly.

Hardy stopped and looked at her. She was looking at the book cart now, vaguely waving her trembling right hand in the air.

"Can I have an *Evening Express* . . . ?"

"Sorry," said Hardy. "This isn't the paper cart. It's the book cart."

"*Evening News*, then," said the little old woman. "Have they all gone, too?"

He squatted down beside her and started explaining that this was the book cart and that the newspaper cart wouldn't be coming until after four. But if she liked, he would ask someone in the department to buy an *Express* for her, as she would sure to be still in x-ray when the newspaper cart came around. But she wasn't listening to him and had slipped back into staring and gumming the air. He gave up and went into the nearest room, Room B.

There were two patients in Room B. Over by the window was a bed with extra side-bars containing an almost invisible and unconscious patient, looking as if he were lying in an open coffin. An elderly man was in the bed by the door. Hardy introduced himself.

"Svensson," said the man.

Hardy looked at his chart: Primus Svensson. Fabulous name! Wonder what they called him in the army? Kitchen?

"Well, here we are with a few books," said Hardy. "Perhaps you've already got something to read."

"No, I haven't much really. What kind of books have you got?"

Hardy attempted a quick judgment. Was the patient interested in books? Ex-typographer, it said on the open envelope on the nightstand. Working-class, then. But that was nothing to go by. There was an old quarry worker in 98 who was a specialist on T. S. Eliot, for instance. Hardy tried checking his nightstand . . . were there any books there? There weren't. Nothing but the daily papers and a flora. A flora. Excellent.

"You're interested in flowers, I see."

"I've got an allotment quite near here. You can see it from the other side."

"Who's looking after it now? Now you're in the hospital?"

"No one. But there's not much to see to. The birds'll get the berries. But it's tough on the asters."

"Is it far from here?"

"A kilometer maybe, as the crow flies. But it's not easy to get there, if you haven't got a bike."

Hardy had a bicycle. He was temporarily living with his mother in Hökarängen and he biked to work. It was the quickest way for anyone without a car. There were no buses from Hökarängen to Enskede Hospital.

"What about me nipping over to your allotment one day and bringing a few flowers."

"That's far too much trouble," said Primus. "I wouldn't dream of asking you."

"No trouble at all. It'd be fun. That's an offer."

"Well, thank you, then. But it won't be easy to find."

They set about drawing a map together. It took time, but Hardy was in no hurry. The longer he stayed in 96, the greater were his chances of meeting Yvonne. Why not take her with him, for that matter? How about a spin in the country, eh?

"Can you get inside the cabin? I mean if it rains or something?"

"I'll give you the key. No, darn it, it's in my apartment. No, it's not, it's in my closet."

"If you had it with you when you came in, then the nurse's probably got it."

"No, it's here," said Primus, fishing his key ring out of the nightstand drawer.

"Great!" said Hardy. "In a few days, I expect. This week with any luck."

He put the key into his pocket and got up to go and find Yvonne. He could take a bottle of wine with him, perhaps, and sit in the garden for a while before . . . before, hmm, yes, before checking up on the little cabin.

"What kind of books have you got?" said Primus.

"Bit of everything. Vilhelm Moberg, Fridegård, Widding . . . what would you like to read?"

"*Guilliver's Travels*," said Primus. "But it must have illustrations in it."

"*Gulliver's Travels*? I haven't got that on the cart. I don't even know if they've got it in the library. It'd be on the children's shelves, if they have. But I could order it for you."

He took out an order-form and wrote: *J. Swift: Guilliver's Travels, Illustrated edition.*

"There's some packets of seeds in the porch," said Primus. "Can you bring them with you, so that they don't go germinating in the damp?"

"Shall do," said Hardy, stuffing the order-form into his top pocket. " 'Bye for now."

Hardy pulled the cart over to the office and asked after Yvonne, but although she was on duty, she wasn't in the ward. She had gone to the staff doctor.

10
Yvonne Meyer was of Jewish extraction. She was blond, blue-eyed and rather short. She was wearing a little gold star of David around her neck and sitting in the staff doctor's waiting room . . . or rather, in the corridor outside the staff doctor's office, as there was no real waiting room. She was feeling uneasy. She had been there only once before, and that was for a medical examination in early June when she had applied for the job. She had no training. She had started at the Enskede Hospital straight from school.

There were two men from southern Europe sitting there, fingering brown envelopes. Turks? She didn't know. But she recognized the envelopes. They contained health records for medical examinations for prospective employees. What a lot of trouble all those forms must cause in Sweden! It was nearly four o'clock. You could see that from the staff, who had started hustling and looking agitated. The office closed at four o'clock.

Yvonne was allowed in before the Turks, although they had been there before her. There was a new staff doctor, a woman of about forty wearing thick glasses, who was speaking on the telephone when

Yvonne went in. With a silent gesture, she indicated to Yvonne that she should sit down. It was a long telephone call. The doctor was phoning in prescriptions. At last she put down the receiver with a bang and said:

"Are you allergic, or what?"

"I get cracks between my fingers," said Yvonne, holding up her hands.

The doctor leaned across her desk to reach her hands.

"Chapped," she said. "How long have you had this?"

"Since the summer, I think."

"You think? When did you start working here?"

"Fifteenth of June. I've been getting those cracks since I started here. Could it be the detergent?"

"Do you wear gloves when you're washing? You should, according to your instructions."

"Yes," lied Yvonne. Sometimes she didn't bother with the gloves; they were so horrid to pull on.

"I suppose you do washing lots of times a day? Do you use hand-cream?"

"Yes."

"If you do a lot of washing, your skin dries out if you don't use cream on them."

"But I do."

"Good. Go on doing so."

"But I get these cracks between my fingers all the same. They bleed sometimes."

The doctor leaned back and removed her glasses, looking tired and only moderately interested.

"Should I go to the work safety representative?" said Yvonne.

"No, why should you?"

"Well, it's to do with the job, isn't it? Working conditions, I mean."

"No, they're just chapped. They get that way if you have tender skin and do a lot of washing without using handcream afterwards."

"But I do."

"If you like, I'll give you a prescription for an ointment you can buy at the hospital pharmacy."

"Will that help?"

"I hope so. We'll have to try it out. Skin problems can take a lot of clearing up."

"Do you think I ought to change my job, doctor?"

"Change your job? No, that'd be going rather too far. I don't think you'd be recommended for a transfer. Not at this stage. See if your skin gets used to it. Be careful."

"And what if it doesn't get better?"

"It's too early to talk about that yet."

"Perhaps I could get a job in reception? Or in the office?"

"I'm afraid there's a long wait for transfers. People with bad backs, sleeping problems, asthma, drug allergies, arthritic necks, deafness. I don't think you can reckon on a recommendation for transfer just because of chapped hands. You have to put up with some things. That's all part of life, you see."

"I don't want to get washerwoman's hands," said Yvonne.

"I think perhaps you've got a bit of a fixation about it," said the doctor.

Fixation? What did that mean? That you'd got a fixed idea? No, she wasn't crazy. A lot of people in the ward had trouble with their hands, with cracking and chapped skin, with sore cuticles, not to mention aching wrists.

"My wrists hurt sometimes, too." said Yvonne. "When the weather's bad."

"Oh, yes," said the doctor. "Well, listen now, let's do this—try that ointment first and then—"

"And if it doesn't help?"

"Then I'll refer you to the dermatology clinic. O.K?"

11 Professor Ask was in his room and feeling extremely annoyed. A row of signed photographs hung on the wall, mostly of foreign visitors, among them two Nobel prizewinners, but a few famous Swedes, too. The most famous was Prince Bertil. Erik Ask had never actually treated the prince personally, but many years ago, Prince Bira of Thailand had visited the racing prince. Prince Bira, a famous racing driver, had been taken ill with a sudden chill. Erik Ask had happened to be at the Grand Hotel and had arranged for an x-ray at the Royal Sophia Hospital. Prince Bertil had been kind enough to thank him personally with a signed portrait.

Erik Ask was looking at the photographs in order not to have to look at the person sitting in his visitor's chair, Gustaf Nyström.

"I told them they could expect countermeasures if they sabotaged the test," said Nyström.

"Countermeasures?" said Erik Ask, feeling the collar of his white coat to see whether it were half turned up as it should be.

"That you as their course director would react."

"React?" said Ask. Yes, of course he would react. The students shouldn't imagine that this was some kind of play-school. But why hadn't Nyström reacted? Immediately! Why hadn't he come down on this nonsense like a ton of bricks? Now it had already gone too far. The students would count what had happened as a semi-victory even if the consequences would be hard in the end.

"Are you going to give them another test?"

"Another test?" thought Erik Ask. "Why should I? They'll have to take their chance." The new curriculum was so crowded, there was no time for retesting. They simply had to keep up, or go and do something else. The general level of students had already sunk disastrously in recent years. They seemed to get in nowadays on nothing but experience. Some of them were as old as forty or fifty when they started. But it wasn't experience they needed; they needed something inside their heads. Where had all the intelligent people gone to nowadays? Had they just sunk in the general wave of egalitarianism? It would be even worse now that politics had crept into medical training, with the unions beginning to interfere, especially the trade union congress. What did they know about medical training? They were even demanding a special professor in industrial medicine. Industrial medicine? Just as if there hadn't been a chair in hygiene and occupational medicine since the forties. At the same time, they were cutting down on research. Soon there would be no medical science worth speaking of any longer and the biologists and other non-physicians would have taken over. Instead of knowledge, the students would have to learn to *think* right, not know anything.

"It's a sensitive area," said Nyström. "Letter grades have been abolished and you can understand that they think giving points is a kind of grading."

Sensitive? Gustaf Nyström was the sensitive one. He hadn't really the right touch with the students and didn't dare stand up against them. He wanted to be everyone's friend. It wouldn't work in the long run. You simply had to keep to your line and make it quite clear to others what that line was. Then there wasn't so much discussion. Nyström was no up-and-coming young man. Unfortunately that had become obvious far too late. Now he would simply have to produce his thesis. Ford money was at stake and the Americans had been inquiring how things were going. There might have been trouble if he hadn't had such good connections in the USA. That's what it was all about—you had to have an international reputation or the money dried up. There was less and less of that commodity around in Sweden. The Medical Research Council had a budget of eighty million. Alms! The grants for educational development alone in the new school came to forty million! Forty million wasted to be able to think this way or that way about training! When all it came down to was such simple things as intelligence and motivation.

"I thought we'd got rid of the leftist element," said Ask. "The ones who made such a fuss a few years ago? I thought a sense of responsibility was on the increase among the students."

"There's a risk they'll bring the Curriculum Commission into this. That they'll try to make it into a discussion on principles."

Discussion on principles? In the Curriculum Commission? Where would the Curriculum Commission find the capacity to carry out a discussion on principles? The Curriculum Commission was a new invention that had come in with the new higher education reforms; before that there had been nothing but the Training Council, over which the faculty at least had had some influence. But all those good relations had gone now. Now the so-called people's movements could be found at all levels. Trade unions dictated terms for training. That was the final disaster.

"What do you want me to do?" said Nyström.

"Nothing," said Ask.

"Nothing? I think we ought to give the students some information about whether they are to take a test or not. Or whether this'll be one of those things they'll have to repeat at the end of their ordinary course."

"Information? Why should they be given information?"

"I think it would make relations with them easier. If they know what their course director's going to do about it."

"They didn't inform us that they were thinking of boycotting the test."

"Well, it was mentioned, I suppose. But not so that I took it seriously."

"Who mentioned it?"

"That doesn't really matter. I'm not really very sure myself."

So Nyström knew exactly how this fuss had brewed up and who the instigator was, but he wasn't going to tell his superior that. Nyström was actually almost as childish as the students, and just as dishonest. How could a course director possibly carry out any sensible teaching if valuable information was withheld from him? Nyström was a serpent in the bosom of medicine. Not an open and honest rebel—just a serpent. That should have been noticed at an earlier stage; he should never have got a foothold here in the unit. But a head of department can never keep track of everything or examine the seams of every subordinate. Heads of departments are very busy men. International contracts, faculty work and relations with grant authorities had to come first. And your own research project, of course. On top of that, you had to lecture, administer, and see to the medical work. There was simply no time to create intimate and personal relations with the interns necessary for both parties to know where they stood. What if he now saw to it that Nyström left the unit? There were plenty of hopefuls in line. Nyström had certified in his specialty a long time ago. The regulation that certified residents could not remain in units could be brought into use. Someone else could take over his research, or else the project could be broken up into a number of smaller investigations.

"They can't expect fair play from our side," said Ask. "When they don't play fair themselves."

"Well, then, there's nothing much more to discuss, is there?" said Nyström, putting his hands on the arms of his chair as if about to get up.

Ask said nothing, wondering whether Nyström were going to leave now, or if he were waiting for a signal from his superior. Nyström got up, nodded and left the room.

It was an insult. Even if Nyström were not wholly aware of it himself, it was clearly an insult. Doctors nowadays had little common politeness. Ask had produced a small leaflet entitled *Conduct in the Unit*, describing in it elementary rules of behavior, modes of address, suitable clothing and other useful items. He had done this quite selflessly. He did not even ask his subordinates to pay the twelve kronor the pamphlet cost—it was available on loan from his secretary.

He should have got rid of Nyström a long time ago, but there was one inhibiting factor: Nyström was the grandson of one of the great pioneers of heart diseases in the country, Professor Gustaf Nyström, now deceased. "On that score alone, he'll have to stay in my unit," thought Ask. A man had a heart, after all. The trouble was, he, Ask, had too much empathy, too much insight into what other people were thinking and feeling. It was a handicap. It made him sentimental. Sensitivity and authority didn't go together. "But you're human, after all," said Ask to himself, smiling at the photograph of Prince Bertil.

12 Primus Svensson had been moved to Room D. There were four beds in it and someone to talk to. The windows also faced west, where his allotment was. He couldn't actually see the allotment, as a freeway curve lay in between. But with the help of various landmarks, Primus could pinpoint its exact position.

There was a young engineer in the next bed for a stomach examination, an old tram worker with something wrong with his liver opposite him, and alongside the tram worker a retired policeman with an embolism in his leg. All except Primus were allowed up. They put themselves at his disposal, bringing him newspapers, shaving implements and the like. Primus had suggested that they should play cards together, but that wasn't possible. The policeman was a member of some kind of congregation and didn't play cards. He hadn't said straight out that he was against playing cards, only maintained that he couldn't and that he found all games difficult. But Primus had drawn his own conclusions from the Bible on the policeman's nightstand—and from his visitors, who had suddenly sung a hymn around his bed.

There were no fixed visiting hours. But all the same, most people came at the usual times, on Saturday and Sunday afternoons. You had to be discreet when other people had visitors. If you could, you went out to the dayroom. Primus was bedridden, so he put on his earphones and pretended to be deep in his newspaper. Today was Saturday. Lunch had been served, the dishes collected up and the medication cups emptied. On Saturdays, x-rays and labs were closed except for emergencies. The whole ward appeared to be lying fallow, waiting for visiting hours.

Primus had not yet had a visitor. Bernt had phoned the nurse and confirmed that he had received his father's message, and he had also said he would look in one day. Primus was nervous. They hadn't seen each other for almost a year, only telephoned a few times. Would they have anything to say to each other when Bernt came? Well, they had a great deal to say to each other, so much that presumably they wouldn't be able even to start. Primus reckoned that after a brief exchange of greetings, they would sit in troubled silence. Why couldn't he get through to Bernt? When Bernt had been small, before puberty, Primus had got on very well with the boy. They had made pictures with matchsticks together, and had gone to museums and to Skansen. He had often gone cycling in the summer with Bernt on the child's saddle on the bar holding onto the handlebars. They had cycled for miles from their home, once as far as to the newly started airport at Bromma, then to the seaplane station at Lindarängen, to the rifle range at Stora Skuggan, or down south to the green slopes of Värmdö or Södertörn.

It had been the best time of Primus's life. He had had work all through the Depression, so his money situation had been all right, in fact so good that in 1938 he had bought a house in Enskede Valley. While they were still living in Asö Street they had acquired the allotment. Bernt had loved the allotment. At the end of the day's work, Primus often used to cycle out there with him. Ellen never came with them, as she couldn't ride a bicycle.

Then he had done his military service. At the outbreak of war, Primus was thirty-six, and because of his age he had at first been exempt. But after 9th April, 1940, he, too, had been called up. He was in the Coastal Artillery and had been posted to Askö in the Trosa archipelago, where he had been one of the crew in charge of a listening apparatus consisting of large metal funnels held over the ears, with which he had to try to catch the sound of the engines of foreign planes. That was before the days of radar. In 1944, Primus had been posted back home and had joined the Reserves. Then he had been able to go back to printing, as the Reserves waged war only on weekends. At first during his military service, money had been very tight indeed, and at one time the family had as little as five kronor a day to manage on.

Was it during his absence that things had begun to go wrong with Bernt? It appeared so. The boy had reached puberty and began to go wild—1943, wasn't it? Primus did not remember his own puberty as anything especially troublesome. He had been a printer's apprentice then, and he could remember more about that than puberty itself. That had been during the Great War, or the First World War, as it came to be known later.

Bernt had probably had his difficulties, and unfortunately it had no doubt been his parents' fault. Because before things began to go wrong between him and Bernt, they had started going wrong between him and Ellen. He had never understood Ellen. He had liked her very much at first, but he had never understood her. She lived in a world of her own and he couldn't get through to her. She wasn't particularly interested in their intimate life, either, anyhow not after Bernt's arrival. He had thought it would get better when they moved to the house in Enskede, but it was the opposite. Ellen wasn't like the other wives out there. She made no contacts and just sat up late at home on her own.

The only person she made contact with was Bernt. Roughly when Bernt went to secondary school, a change set in. Ellen and Bernt began ganging up against him. If Primus happened to come into the kitchen, Bernt and Ellen would be sitting there laughing and talking, and they would instantly turn silent and look furtively at him. He had tried to talk to Ellen, to tell her she was taking the boy away from him, but it hadn't worked. Ellen simply evaded him, would never discuss it. But Bernt wanted to when he was a bit older. Everything Dad did was wrong. Everything Dad thought was wrong. They took the wrong newspaper. Dad listened to nothing but silly radio programs—but what was wrong with them? His clothes were all wrong. Exchanging his tobacco coupons for coffee was criminal. Doing things for the union was wrong. The matchstick pictures should be burnt at once, and so on. Once when the boy had made fun of his first name, Primus had slapped him. Then Primus had said no man could help the names he had, as he had never had any veto power in the matter.

What harm had he ever done Bernt? None! He had many a time tried to sort it out quite honestly, but the response had always been the same—nothing. Where had Bernt acquired his aggressiveness? From Ellen. It was Ellen and Primus who didn't get on, but Ellen never said that straight out. Instead she thrust Bernt in front, probably almost unconsciously. It was as if Ellen herself were the microphone and Bernt her loudspeaker.

When Ellen had reached the menopause, Primus found he couldn't go on any longer. She grew more and more introverted and started imagining there was a smell of gas everywhere. They had people from the gas company to come and look for leaks in the stove, but they never found any. But that didn't make any difference. Gradually, he had realized that she was not well. Then when she suddenly refused to take the housekeeping money, he understood. She needed the help of a doctor. But that was impossible. He had tried to talk to Ellen's mother about it, but had been more or less thrown out. In the end, divorce had been inevitable. They had got a good price for the house and Ellen had moved in with her mother, and he had got himself a small apartment in Årsta. But Bernt was twenty years old by then and was himself doing his military service.

Many years later, when Ellen was dying, they had in their own way been reconciled. He had sat with her to the last, although they were no longer married. He had got her back then, but he had never got Bernt back. Instead, Bernt had accused him of taking advantage of Ellen's illness.

Things had not gone too well for Bernt at the start of his adult life. After he left school, he worked for the post office for a while, but then did his military service, where he had met some kind of wholesale importer. Bernt went in with him. The goods varied and Primus had never been really clear over what the business was. Then the firm had gone bust. Not only that, but there had been complications over the accounts as well. Not until some years later had Primus found out that Bernt had done time for that. It had been a blow. No one in the family had ever had anything to do with the police before.

But then Bernt had pulled his socks up. He had married and got an engineering certificate in the evenings, not a very good one, true, but quite an achievement in the fifties. Bernt had started with a firm that made glass equipment for laboratories. Then he had separated from Birgitta, the marriage fortunately childless. For a few years Primus had had practically no contact with Bernt at all, but he had read on the business page that Bernt had been transferred to the sales department. For some years now, Bernt had been employed as a drugs salesman, first with Pharmacia in Uppsala, and then with Luna. Primus had gathered it was interesting work and Bernt was clearly well paid. He always had a new car every time they met.

The others in Room D already had visitors and had taken them to the dayroom or the cafeteria. It was half past three, but no sign of Bernt. But he was always late for everything. Primus was always punctual, but Bernt functioned in the opposite way and might turn up hours late for a meeting. But that was probably some kind of protest.

There was one thing he wanted to know about Bernt, and that was whether he was thinking of having a family. Bernt had no children, unless of course he had some on the side and didn't want anyone to know. But now, after his heart attack, Primus's thoughts stubbornly spun around this point. If there weren't any grandchildren now— might there be in the future? At the same time, he thought he was being ridiculous, having romantic ideas about there having to be a continuation, someone who went on living. Not just anyone, but someone of his own flesh and blood. He stopped himself. He was lying there thinking almost like a Nazi. But at the same time he couldn't deny his feelings. With all the strength he could muster, he wanted Bernt to settle down and have children.

13 Sirkka was on duty in 96 on Saturday afternoon. She had had to dash hither and thither because they had virtually no staff at all. Then there were visiting hours and she had to answer all the questions from worried relatives. In the middle of it all, Bergelin in Room A had become acutely ill and she had had to arrange for someone to come and watch him and phone to his family. The doctor on call had been up to look at him and he had ordered a whole lot of tests. But they also had a great deal to do in the lab, too, and it would be some time before anyone could get over. They wanted her to take the blood samples herself, but she really hadn't time to do that. Someone had to be in the office and she couldn't just leave the ward to look after itself. She felt safer in the office. When things were especially bad, it was like being on the bridge of a ship in a storm. Things could certainly be critical in the office, too, but not for anything on earth did she want to go out on deck.

She leafed through the shift schedule. Two orderlies were off sick, so they probably wouldn't turn up tomorrow, Sunday, either. The staff pool had produced only one substitute. On top of that, Intensive Care were putting on the pressure and wanted to send up a woman who had had a pulmonary edema. Sirkka tried to resist it. Anyone who had had one pulmonary edema could easily have another, and who would see to that? But she supposed she would have to give in later on in the evening when the cases began to pour in and threaten to overload Emergency. Emergency was not on principle allowed to be overloaded, which the ordinary departments certainly were. The last weekend she had been on duty, Ward 96 had had two patients in the corridor, one in the student's room and one in the examination room.

Where were the girls? The girls—this weekend there were more boys than girls, young boys who were students and did odd jobs as orderlies. They were generally easier to deal with. They could be lazy, dragging their jeans-clad legs along. But on the other hand they did occasionally joke and flirt, which made life a little easier. You couldn't joke with the girls. They misinterpreted everything and considered themselves unfairly treated or thought you were making fun of them.

Sirkka looked at the schedule. In five weeks time exactly, she would be back here again. But with any luck, she might be off sick. Or why not take some compensatory leave? The question was only whether she should sacrifice any of her free time to get out of duty in 96. One of the students sauntered past along the corridor. Where on earth was Kenta? He was the most hopeless of them all. Had he stolen the patients' telephone cart and was sitting in the dirty utility room phoning long distance again? She got up to go and look. At that moment her own telephone rang.

"Ward 96, Nurse Sirkka speaking," she said.

"Good afternoon, nurse. This is Dr. Wallén."

Wallén? Wallén? She had not heard the name before, but there were several hundred doctors in this hospital.

"Yes?" she said.

"Nurse, I was just wondering how one of your patients is, a Primus Svensson."

"One moment," she said, stretching out for the file. The doctor on the line sounded rather strange, panting into the receiver and rather overfamiliar in some way.

"Have you the chart there, Nurse Sirkka?" he said, when she picked up the receiver from her desk.

"Yes. Is there anything special you wish to know, Doctor?"

"I want to know if he's in prime condition. If Primus is in prime condition."

He sounded very peculiar, but doctors did make silly jokes sometimes. Very few of them knew how to mix naturally in a relaxed way with the nurses. Some of them were always trying to be funny, telling fatuous stories or discussing new medical findings. Others were authoritatively sullen and acted like they were in the military. The worst were the uncertain ones, the new substitutes who didn't dare make decisions on their own—and who didn't want to disturb the second doctor on call, so tried to heap the responsibility onto the nurses. But this doctor sounded quite crazy.

"Are you the doctor on call in the clinic?" she said, feverishly looking down the doctors' call schedule stuck on the wall. There was no Wallén there, but they were always changing the schedule, so it was never up to date.

"No, I'm phoning from outside. Mr. Svensson was my patient before he was taken into the hospital."

"I think you'd better speak to the doctor on call, in that case," said Sirkka.

"Can't you just read it out to me, nurse?"

He sounded almost as if he were drunk, or under the influence of drugs. What was going on?

"If I put you through to the exchange, they'll find the doctor on call for you."

"Just read it out to me. From the chart," said Wallén.

"I'm afraid I can't do that," she said. She could hear music in the background and then the panting started again. He said nothing for a while, just panted into her ear. In the end, she hung up. What was it all about?

She leafed through Primus' chart. He would presumably be allowed home soon. They hadn't cleared the fibrillation yet, but that wasn't all that important in 96. In other wards, the dysrhythmia would be mercilessly regularized. But Dr. Nyström used to say that a slight fibrillation was all right—you could live with it. Nyström was a good doctor. He didn't treat absolutely everything at all costs.

The phone rang again.

"Ward 96," said Sirkka.

"Um . . . my name's Bernt Svensson. I was just wondering how my father was."

It was the same voice. The same music in the background and the same puffing.

"Under the circumstances, your father is very well," she said.

"Good." There was a long silence, then the voice said: "That's good."

"Can I take a message?"

"I can't get away today. I'm . . . damned busy. Do you understand. Got it?"

"Yes," she said. "I'll tell your father. Good-by."

The same voice! What gall to phone and pretend you're a doctor! She had heard about people doing that, but she'd never come across it herself before. What a damned gall! But easy, I suppose, a method of getting past the exchange or to talk to people outside their telephone time.

She went in to Primus, but he had fallen asleep. She tore a page off her pad and wrote: *Your son is not coming. He is busy today. He sends his regards.*

Out in the corridor she was almost knocked down by a male orderly, Minos, from Greece.

"A.4., blood all over the place!" he was yelling.

Sirkka stopped for a second to gather her wits. She froze, feeling just like that time at school when the gymnastics teacher had tried to force her to dive from the diving board. There was no turning back. With controlled steps, she went across to Room A and opened the door. In bed four, a middle aged man was sitting surrounded by three fellow-patients. There was dark blood everywhere, on the sheets, on the floor, a huge patch on the wall. The man's mouth was half open and blood was running out of both corners of it.

"Phone the doctor on call!" cried Sirkka to Minos.

She went over to the patient and put her hands on his shoulders. It was disgusting. One rarely saw heavy bleeding in patients in medical wards. She found blood difficult, which was one of the reasons she had chosen internal medicine. Why was the patient bleeding? What was the diagnosis? What was his name? She didn't even know that because she kept flitting from ward to ward.

"Is there anyone here who knows anything?" she said to his fellow-patients, who had withdrawn as soon as she had arrived.

"Something to do with his liver," one of them said.

The sick man suddenly leaned over towards her and vomited again. Dark coagulated blood poured over her bare arms. She tried to steel herself and think. If the blood came from his lungs, he would cough, so it came from his mouth, his throat, his gullet or even further down. Liver? Why did someone who had something wrong with the liver bleed? Who usually had something wrong with the liver? Alcoholics!

The pale and perspiring patient drooped in her arms. She had calmed down now that she was covered with filth and there was no longer any cleanliness to lose.

"Run and ask one of the girls to come here," she said to one of the patients. "What's his name?" she said to another.

"Karlgren."

"Karlgren. How are you feeling?" she said, but he did not react.

Minos came back with Kenta in tow. Kenta rushed forward and tried to raise the patient up.

"Don't!" said Sirkka. She was quite calm now. It must be bleeding of the stomach or a varicose vein in the esophagus that had ruptured.

Kenta was running around between the beds like a bolting horse.

"Try to get him outside!" she shouted to Minos.

Minos and two patients began to chase Kenta. Suddenly he stopped in a corner, put his hands over his eyes and slowly sank to the floor with his back pressed to the wall. Minos stood astride over him to stop him getting up again.

"Try to get hold of someone else," she said. "Get them to phone for the anesthesiologist on call. He must have fluid."

She sat down on the edge of the bed, the man's head over her shoulder as if she were holding a baby. Should she lie him down? People in shock should lie with their heads low—but if he vomited again he would choke. What if she lay him face down, his head over the floor? She tried easing him around and turning him over on his side. Suddenly he came to life and threw himself backwards, grabbing her by the throat, staring wildeyed at the ceiling as if he were about to drown. She tried to twist herself free.

"Minos!"

Soon four people were trying to hold the panic-stricken patient. Sirkka managed to pull herself back and wriggle out. She sat up and massaged her throat. There was blood everywhere.

At last a doctor arrived. She presumed he was the doctor on call. He was young and looked extremely frightened.

"What's going on here?"

"Karlgren is vomiting blood," she said.

"Phone for the surgeon, then. There's nothing we can do."

"Might be an esophageal varices," said Sirkka. "He's here for his liver."

"I'll go and phone the surgeon on call," said the doctor.

"Don't leave!"

The doctor did not leave. He stood quite still as if paralyzed. Sirkka could feel panic rising. If it damn well wasn't a greenhorn on duty. But that was so common on weekends. The youngest always had to take on the most inconvenient calls.

"Phone the second doctor on call," said Sirkka, but the doctor did not move. He appeared utterly at a loss.

Sirkka turned back to the patient instead. He had calmed down and some of the color had come back into his face. Perhaps he wouldn't bleed to death after all. Hemorrhages always looked much worse than they in fact were. Quite small amounts of blood could look like a veritable bloodbath. What should she do now? The doctor on call was standing over by the door just as before, staring. Kenta was collapsed on the floor with Minos standing over him. The only calm people apart from herself were the two patients holding Karlgren. How much time had gone by? Quarter of an hour?

At that moment, the door opened and in stormed a doctor and two nurses with a crash cart. People from Intensive Care. They took over with practiced hands.

"We'll give him a blood transfusion and insert a Sengstaken tube," said the anesthesiologist. "If you would phone for blood, we'll fix the rest."

Sirkka wiped her bloodstained hands on the sheet and went out. The doctor on call had come to life. He was standing there looking up something in a little blue book about emergency medicine.

An hour later, Sirkka was standing under the shower. For the first time for a long time, she felt sure and happy. She had not lost her head. Strangely enough. She had never been involved in an acute hemorrhage on that scale before. One did not expect to in a medical ward, and yet it had happened. She felt she had acquired a new authority as well. The others in the ward, the orderlies most of all, would not be able to ignore her again. She turned her face up and laughed, filling her mouth and nose with warm water.

14 Martina Bosson and Hans Berling were going around the wards listening to bad hearts. Martina had a piece of paper on which was written:

Ward 77	E.4.	Aortic stenosis?
Ward 78	A.I.	Mitral insufficiency (can easily be heard!)
	C.I.	Septal defect
Ward 86	G.I.	Aortic stenosis plus insufficiency
Ward 89	E.2.	Op. Mitral stenosis
Ward 96	D.2.	Fibrillation with deficit.

One of the greatest difficulties on the medical course was learning to differentiate between different heart sounds. There were records and tapes of heart sounds, but that wasn't at all the same thing. Finals included tests in which you had to listen to an unknown patient. There was a long time to go before finals, but Martina had persuaded Hans Berling they might as well start now, as there would probably be a line for bad hearts nearer to finals.

They went into 77 and suddenly found themselves faced with Professor Ask on his way out. Both students backed up against the wall and said good morning to him. Ask did not return the greeting. He gazed between their heads, raised his eyebrows slightly and left the ward.

"The bastard's got a long memory," said Hans.

"He's sure to know it was me. He doesn't give a damn about the rest of you," said Martina.

"He could at least say something. He's said nothing at all, although he's given several lectures since that test."

They went on into the ward and reported to the supervisor, Nurse Staffan. Male nurses were rare in the medical wards. Male nurses preferred to work in the heroic jobs in Intensive Care or Anesthesiology.

The patient they were to listen to was having a catheterization, an examination in which they pushed a wire-thin instrument via a vein into the heart itself. The two of them trudged on to Ward 73. The office was empty, but in the students' room were two of the ward's five students listening to the hospital social worker going through social problems in the ward.

"We're going into A.1. to listen to your mitral insufficiency," said Hans.

"O.K.," said one of the students, who had slipped so far down in his chair that he had his head on the back-rest.

They went into Room A and introduced themselves. The patient with heart trouble was a Yugoslavian woman of forty-six, now clutching her clothing to her throat, and apparently less than thrilled by the visit.

"What do you want?" she said.

"We would like to listen to your heart," said Martina. "If you don't mind. We have to learn to listen to hearts, you see?"

The woman did not move, nor did she make any move to help them.

"We're sorry to come and disturb you . . ." said Hans.

"No," said the woman.

"What do you mean?" said Martina. "Do you mean you'd rather we left you in peace, or—?"

"It doesn't hurt," said Hans.

"Not him," said the woman, pointing quickly at Hans Berling, then bringing her hand back to her throat.

"Hans, perhaps you'd better go out," said Martina.

Hans Berling loped out. The woman took her hand away from her throat and allowed Martina to help loosen her clothes. Soon she was lying with her torso naked, propped up against a heap of pillows. Martina listened with her stethoscope, over the breastbone, in the space between the second and third ribs, above the top of the heart and back across the ribcage. Then she listened in the armpit and on the back. She half-closed her eyes as she listened, but not so she could concentrate; it was just a trick she had learned in the fundamentals course: if you are listening to women with naked torsos, you should close your eyes, then the woman didn't feel so embarrassed. Martina felt her own pulse quickening as her annoyance rose. Why should a woman be embarrassed about her breasts? Who could help what they looked like? Women were not only embarrassed to show themselves naked to men, but also between themselves. Oppression of women was so deep-rooted, they were even ashamed of their sex in front of their own kind.

She brushed aside her anger and started listening all over again from the beginning, the whole routine, looking at the woman this time. The woman did not look back at her, but lay there with her eyes tight shut. Martina thought she had heard what she ought to have heard, a high frequency, raw systolic extra sound loudest above the apex of the heart. But she wasn't certain. When she had finished, she helped the woman on with her clothes.

"Will there be an operation?" the woman said suddenly.

Martina knew nothing about the woman except that she had a mitral insufficiency, a dangerous valvular disorder of the heart. She was presumably in for examination and the result of the examination might be an operation. What would they do—give her artificial valves?

"I don't know," said Martina. "Ask the doctor on his round."

The woman leaned back against the pillows without another word. It was useless even saying goodbye to her, as she was lying in a defensive position again, her eyes closed and both hands pressed against her throat.

15 At night, Wards 96 and 97 were "linked," which meant that the night nurse was responsible for both wards containing altogether seventy to eighty patients.

The nurse had taken Yvonne Meyer into one of the isolation rooms, and they were looking down at a woman of about thirty in a railed bed gazing tentatively up at the ceiling. An i.v. was fastened to one of her feet.

"If she gets restless, hold her by the hand," said the nurse. "And please don't ring for me unless it is absolutely necessary. 'Bye now."

When she was alone, Yvonne took a few hesitant steps toward the bed. Did she dare sit down? She had never been alone with a dying person before. The woman in the bed had an incurable blood disease and they had been expecting the end for a long time. The doctor on call had been up and looked a short while before and he had said: "The patient is now clearly at the terminal stage."

Yvonne pulled out the chair and sat down at the foot of the bed. The patient was lying quite still, taking small, shaky breaths. What if Hardy appeared soon? The day before, Yvonne had cycled with Hardy out to Primus Svensson's allotment to fetch some things. When they had gone inside the cabin, Hardy had stubbornly insisted they should take their clothes off. When she had refused, he had taken his off and had stood stark naked in front of her. Was he crazy? He was nice and rather fun . . . but a man whipping his clothes off first like that?

"Are you there?" the patient said suddenly in a clear and shockingly strong voice.

"Yes . . ."

"Sit here."

Yvonne dragged the chair up and sat on a level with the patient's stomach. When the woman fumbled for her hand, Yvonne stretched out her arm and leaned forward so that their fingertips touched. Yvonne had to hunch up to reach. She was very frightened of being close to the dying woman's face. She was also trying to breathe with her nose down toward her chest; it seemed as if there was already the smell of corpse in the room.

After a while, her shoulder started aching from her unnatural position. Cautiously, she tried to free herself from the woman's fingers, but the woman held on tight. She would have to think about something else, about Hardy? No, about a good film—which one? No, about something important. What was important? The most important thing that had happened to her for a long time was her skin being ruined, beginning with "chapping" between her fingers, and now coming on her neck as well. The usual creases in her neck had turned red and begun to ooze. What if it was eczema!

"Hi!"

Yvonne started. Hardy was bending over her, a skateboard in his hand. There was a wide sloping corridor underneath the hospital, where the boys skateboarded. It was forbidden, of course, but late at night, there was no one to check.

"Hi, Yvonne! Can we get away for about five or ten minutes?"

She lifted her free hand and held his arm. It was marvelous someone else had come into the room, a living person.

"Sit down."

"We could go into the linen closet. Five minutes?"

"Sit down."

But Hardy did not sit down. Instead he took a closer look at the patient, then whispered into Yvonne's ear:

"But she's punching out!"

"Don't go, Hardy—"

"Ring for the nurse."

Had the time come? Yvonne tried looking at the patient's face, but it looked just the same as before.

"Sit down. We can whisper to each other."

"I didn't realize you were stuck like this. I thought you and I—are you going to sleep here afterwards?"

"What do you mean—afterwards?"

"Well, when . . . you have to go and get some sleep, don't you?"

"No."

"Don't you?"

"No . . . if you're on nights, you can't sleep."

"Oh, I see. But you must have a break some time, surely? Later on. When you're not needed. We could go to the lounge in 97, couldn't we?"

"Sit here and keep me company."

"All night?"

Hardy glanced at his watch.

"Now look, I've got to get up and go to work tomorrow, you know."

"Don't go!"

"They shouldn't make you sit here alone with someone who's so bad off. Shall I go and tell . . . ?"

Hardy was obviously on his way out. She didn't ever want to have anything more to do with him, ever. What a friend!

"Go on, go to hell then!" she hissed.

"We could go to a film sometime, couldn't we?"

She turned away. He stood stroking her hair for a moment, then padded quickly out. Anger had made Yvonne slightly braver. She moved closer to the patient and held her whole hand in hers. The woman's pale thin nostrils were fluttering, her eyes wide open and moving regularly back and forth, as if she were reading a text on the ceiling.

Yvonne glanced at the i.v. bottle. It was almost full. No one would have to come along and change it for a long time. Was there any such thing as death throes? The moment she thought about her own death, she was filled with terror. But when the time really came, perhaps by then you would have found some clarity, a different . . . ? She wanted to ask the woman what it was like to die. But you couldn't ask a dying person such a question, could you? Who else could you put such a question to?

Death throes, what was that? When did they start? How long did they go on? Her mother had told her about people who became unnaturally strong when they were about to die, people who leaped out of bed and fought. . . But that was probably only when they had pneumonia . . . or Spanish 'flu.

Yvonne nodded and without her noticing, her forehead fell down onto the pillow. She woke . . . how long had she been asleep? Had the patient—? No, the woman was still alive. She was lying there looking at the i.v. bottle at the foot of the bed. Her hand was still warm. Yvonne had to go to the bathroom, but she didn't dare let the hand go. If she did, the woman might suddenly drop dead.

At 03.20 hours that night, the woman died. It happened almost imperceptibly. She drew a couple of slightly deeper breaths and turned her eyes upwards, that was all. Yvonne felt relieved, as if she had only just escaped going, too. She sat still for a moment, holding the dead woman's hand. The thin face was very beautiful.

16 Professor Ask was lecturing on heart diseases. Among clinical subjects, internal medicine came first, and within internal medicine the greatest thing to devote yourself to was the heart. Internal medicine was the oldest section of academic medicine with its roots in the ancient world, in Antiquity, the Arab world and the urine examinations of the Middle Ages. Its practitioners had always liked occupying themselves with theoretical superstructures that had always threatened to freeze development into dogmas and axioms. The latest rapidly expanding branch of internal medicine was called immunology. But Erik Ask stood on a firm traditional ground and was a heart specialist.

Ask was also a traditionalist as a lecturer. He spoke the entire time himself, asking his students an occasional brief question, but largely keeping his audience in a state of passiveness. His students listened and took notes. Erik Ask had one weakness as a teacher: the slides he showed, always blue with white text in English, contained far too much information, figures, parameters, graphs or graph sounds, all so complicated and overloaded that few students could keep up with him.

Twenty-eight of the thirty-one members of the year's class were present, an unusually high number. Erik Ask always counted his students and if more than five were absent, he abused those who were present. But that seldom happened. He was proud of never using the lists those present had to sign to show they were present.

Martina Bosson was sitting with her group roughly in the center of the lecture room. Today it was Bertelskjöld's turn to take notes. They had a system that meant each member of the group took notes one in five times. The notes were then duplicated free of charge on the communal xerox. But Martina was taking notes, although she wasn't "on duty." Years of medical studies had meant that she could not keep awake if she didn't. Her ability simply to sit and listen had gone, and so it was a question of getting as much down as possible of what was said and what the pictures showed. The aim was that the notes should be virtually identical with the lecturer's manuscript. So the students really functioned as a kind of duplicating machine driven by manpower. The lecturer delivered the original, the students producing identical copies. If it had not all taken place at such a high level, it might have been suspected that the job-creation authorities were providing occupational therapy for twenty-eight young academics.

Martina usually felt pleased after a double lecture that produced plenty of notes, as if she had really done something worthwhile. She had produced something. That hundreds of students over the years had produced almost identical notes did not diminish the value of her work. Why should it? The procedure was not rationally determined. Instead it was an altar service, a medical mass. It was like the Benediction or the Lord's Prayer. For the parson and his confirmation-students, the Lord's Prayer was just as important whether it was being read for the very first time or the thousandth.

Professor Ask might occasionally move away from his script and illustrate his theme with a case history, apparently always an improvisation, but in fact even that had been planned beforehand. This morning he was talking about endocarditis, or inflammation of the valves and membranes of the heart. All diseases that affected the function of the valves were dangerous. Nowadays many types of endocarditis could be treated with antibiotics, but by no means all patients were cured in that way.

Professor Ask told them about a medical student, a young man of their own age, who had been afflicted with a fatal and rapidly developing inflammation of the heart, how he had gone to his teachers when the first symptoms had appeared, and how he had been placed in the clinic in which he was a student. Ask gave a detailed account of the merciless progress of the disease and the boy's reactions to it, how he had first confidently seen himself as a "case," but then how he had gradually become childishly dependent on his teachers and doctor. Finally, he had not wished to discuss his illness at all. All he had wanted was that they should sit by his bedside and hold his hand.

Martina felt sick. Ask really had no need to pile on the hypochondria, the fear of diseases students already possessed. After a lecture, they all went home and felt themselves. Isn't my pulse in fact rather irregular? Don't I feel pressure at the back of my head when I wake up—like with a brain tumor? A dull ache in the back, like with cystic kidneys? Don't I see flashes sometimes that might herald epileptic fits? With all his knowledge and modest manner—Ask used to whisper in a husky voice when being truly melodramatic—despite all his polish, the Professor was a sadist. This no longer had anything to do with teaching. It was a sort of theater of cruelty.

Martina wondered what Ask would do if he himself fell ill. Whom would he consult? Whom could he possibly trust? Perhaps the same thing would happen to Ask as had happened to a great many famous clinicians? When they fell seriously ill, they consulted someone far too late, or not at all. Many doctors behaved like people who live in thinly populated areas.

After a lecture, the assistant, one of the youngest residents, asked the students to remain behind. A schedule change had arisen. The week before All Saint's that had hitherto been blank on the schedule, had now been filled with lectures taking up to four to six hours a day. A loud wail arose from the students.

"We were going on our trip that week!"

"Hell, what's going on? We've always had that every term before. A week's trip."

The students were well-informed. Last term, the whole class, with Ask in the lead, had been to London for a week. The class before had all gone to Warsaw. This year, preparations were well underway for a trip to Finland. No promises had been made, that was true. The trip always had to appear to be a surprise and a reward. But in actual fact the financial backers, a number of large drug firms, had already been approached in August. Martina, who undertook jobs in the student union, had also seen letters from the Finnish Medical Society, Thorax.

"We know the trip isn't really part of the course. But the others have all been allowed to go. Why not us?"

The assistant was evasive and talked about the new curriculum making teaching more difficult. They were trying to integrate medical and surgical courses, as they all knew perfectly well. At this stage, the course directors could not take the responsibility of allowing the whole class to be away in Finland for a week. There had also been directives from the Higher Education Section of the Department of Education to say that every subject had to show minimum necessary proficiency earlier than before. The clinic had now found some sections had been taken rather too lightly, so more was to be demanded of them. For that they needed an extra week.

"Is it because we boycotted the test?" said Martina.

"You'll have to ask the Professor that," said the assistant. "I'm just telling you what I've been told."

17 Primus Svensson was now in his seventh week in the hospital. His M.I. was largely considered to have healed. His blood pressure was under control. His heart was working calmly and surely, but still with a small irregularity. It was time for rounds.

"Ah, yes, Primus Svensson, yes," said Dr. Nyström. "Things look good here."

Everyone standing around the bed, the nurse, the hospital social worker, the students and student nurses—they all smiled.

"Where will you go, Primus, after your discharge?"

"Home."

"How are things at home? Is there anyone there to help out?"

"I can manage on my own."

Nyström hesitated for a moment. Could he take the responsibility of a seventy-six-year-old who had just had quite a massive coronary living alone?

"Haven't you got a relative, or someone, Mr. Svensson? Someone you could stay with for a while? To recuperate?"

"No, I don't think so."

Nyström leafed through the chart and looked under "social history."

"But your son? Does he live in town?"

"Impossible," said Primus.

"Perhaps it'd be a good thing to have a little chat with the social worker?"

Nyström turned to the social worker.

"We know about long term care, don't we . . . but what about a convalescent home?"

"If he's up and can manage, that'd be quite possible."

"What do you think, Primus? About going away for a while to a place with pleasant surroundings?"

"I've got my allotment."

"Hmm," said Nyström. "I can't really recommend gardening. Not this autumn. But by the spring that should be all right. If you take things easy."

"Must I?"

"I don't know about must," said Nyström. "But it'd be a kind of continuation of your treatment. After all, a heart attack is a heart attack."

"I suppose I'll have another," said Primus. "I've read about that."

Nyström looked troubled. He knew Primus was right, but it

seemed wrong to be discussing that now, when everything was looking fairly rosy. The risk of Primus dying of the M.I. he had just gone through had been considerable.

"We'd thought of putting you on a diet, too, Primus," he went on. "To reduce the amount of fat and sugar in your food. That'd mean getting a new cook book. You can't learn to cook different food at the drop of a hat. So it'd be better if you had a brief transit period. Nurse, can we book a time with the dietician?"

Nurse Margareta was on the ward today. She moved closer to Nyström and said in a low voice:

"Have you seen the latest lab results?"

Nyström took the chart and looked. Blood and urine samples were taken once a week, the usual pattern with an M.I. What were called the transaminases had been very high at first. Now nearly everything was quite normal, except a test that showed some disorder in the thyroid glands. It was a new test that Nyström knew little about.

"Why have they taken this?" said Nyström to Nurse Margareta. "No one here asked for it."

"No, it was all part of the package."

The new chemical laboratories were so automated that it was no longer possible to arrange for individual tests, so they all had to keep to the packaged sets. So they also got results of tests that had not been requested. The trickiest thing was to decide what attitude to take to these results that had not been asked for. If the test results were normal, there was no need to do anything. But they were often not normal. A secondary test would suddenly return abnormal. What was to be done about these red lights? Had the patient another undetected disease that had not yet started producing symptoms? A cancer lying in wait somewhere? An early hormone disturbance? Deterioration of the nervous system? Should further investigations be made, or shouldn't they? If they were, then a whole new set of laboratory packages would be involved as well as more questions to unasked questions. If one more step were taken, there was the risk of a third generation of unasked-for answers, wasn't there? This phenomenon was known as the Odysseus syndrome: the patient was sent on to an auto-chemical voyage that perhaps would never produce any definite answers.

"We'll do the same tests as before," said Nyström. "No extra ones." That was the simplest way out. The same tests could quite simply be checked once again. Not infrequently the results then proved quite normal, but there was a risk that the laboratory doctors themselves went on without asking the department, and nothing whatsoever could be done about that.

"Is there something wrong?" said Primus.

"No, no, not at all. We'll do a last round of tests. You'll have to stay in a few more days. Think it over about the convalescent home."

18 The staff cafeteria was one of the largest in Stockholm. There was only one cafeteria in modern hospitals. When Gustaf Nyström had been a student, he had been in a hospital with a doctors' cafeteria, a students' cafeteria, a nurses' cafeteria, a staff-nurses' cafeteria, and another for the rest. That had all gone now, which did not stop the various staff categories from sticking together. There were thick invisible walls. No outsider, for instance, ever sat at the doctors' tables.

Nyström carried his tray of cod and almond sauce and potatoes to the salad table. While he was helping himself to salad, he looked quickly around. He didn't want to eat lunch with just anyone. Professor Erik Ask was sitting at a large round table, drinking coffee with his food. Should he take the chance? It was hard to find time to talk to Ask, who was sometimes away for weeks on end. Nyström went over to him.

"Hello. All right if I sit here?"

"Of course, of course. Sit yourself down."

He sat down and spread margarine onto his roll, his appetite gone.

"I'd like to have a few words with you about my research. If that's all right with you?"

"I've been expecting you," said Ask. "You know I don't go around sticking my nose into people's business. I wait for people to come on their own steam."

"Exactly," said Nyström, "I was just wondering about extending it a bit?"

"Within the time specified? We reckoned you'd present it in the spring, didn't we?"

"Not this coming spring. In the autumn, or next spring."

"I had a distinct idea we decided on this coming spring?"

"Well, you wanted that, but I said I didn't reckon with that."

Ask looked at his coffee dregs and swirled them around. Nyström felt everything already beginning to go wrong with the conversation.

"To be honest, we know that my material is really almost minimal, don't we? If you remember, I showed you from those calculations I'd be forced to go as far as thirteen hundred and fifty subjects in each group. Four thousand and fifty altogether."

"You can perfectly well use the material you've already got. I've never asked that it should be greater."

"No, exactly. But I'd thought of improving the investigation qualitatively. Not quantitively."

"How?"

"That epidemiological model we started using. It lacks time factors. And the time factor is beginning to become more and more important in international literature."

"I've not noticed that," said Ask. "At the cardiology congress in Chicago as recently as in June, they were all quite content with the traditional model. Jerry McGuire included. As you know, he's the biggest name in cardiovascular epidemiology. So it can't be in the medical literature you've come up against that criticism."

"No, not actually. I've started looking at what the ethnogeographers are up to."

"Ethnogeography, is that a science?"

"Yes, it is. There are about ten professors of ethnogeography in Sweden."

Ask got up and put his cup onto Gustaf Nyström's tray. Nyström also got up, although he had eaten nothing but the roll, and he took his tray across to the dishwashing conveyor. When they got out to the culvert, Ask said:

"You may be in trouble with your examiner if you drag in models that aren't approved."

"I could ask the ethnogeographers themselves to have a representative at the defense. Just to stop the discussion getting bogged down in methodology. They've used these models for fifteen or twenty years."

They took the elevator up to Ask's office. They didn't go into the office, but Ask stopped in the annex, his secretary's office. His secretary was sitting with earphones on, filling in invitation-cards to a dinner the professor and his wife were giving. Ask took Nyström by the arm and sat him on the edge of the desk, he himself remaining standing. He put his thumb against Nyström's collarbone and massaged it, a habit of his when he wanted to talk seriously to subordinates, or apparently out of pure distraction whenever he was standing close to a younger woman resident or student. He said nothing, but looked at Nyström like a troubled father.

"The ethnogeographers use a three-dimensional system of coordinates." Nyström went on. "Imagine an aquarium. If you look at it from above, you see an ordinary map of places or events that relate to each other. But if you look at it from the side, you can see that the points and their connecting lines are at different heights. It is the height that marks the time."

"I can't see that that glass box has any advantages over our model with environment, human beings, and agents."

"Yes, it has, actually. You can illustrate graphically a more complex development. If we can link some of the causes of M.I.'s to preexisting stress, then we have gained something more. Then we could use a smaller sample. We wouldn't have to struggle with thirteen hundred and fifty patients in each group. It's obvious that—"

"What's obvious?"

"I only mean that such a simple thing as trying to pinpoint the causes in a previous time-period—"

"I suppose you think we cardiologists don't know anything about epidemiology."

Nyström tried to avoid Ask's eyes, and instead looked at the secretary tapping out her invitations on small cards. The dinner was to be held at Skeppsholm. Ask's voice was crackling out of the microphone, listing names.

"I can't see what we would lose by learning from other sources of knowledge. From the ethnogeographers, for instance. Their models actually go back to military games. The Pentagon's strategists started trying to describe complex processes with this kind of model some time in the fifties, when the first computers came out."

"I'll be honest with you," said Ask. "Fairly soon after you started at my previous clinic, I realized you didn't have much theoretical talent. On the other hand, you are a good clinician. You have a certain practical understanding. That's nothing to be ashamed of. A university clinic shouldn't benefit just the bright boys. We also have to produce senior physicians for the countryside. So a thesis doesn't have to be a work of genius. But it must stick to certain scientific fundamentals. It is true that research has changed in many directions in this country. Educators and psychologists or whatever they're all called have begun to produce work, supposedly scientific work, that is no more scientific than the telephone directory. Or a Marxist rebellion. But in my clinic, the level has not yet sunk that low. If you see what I mean."

"I'm afraid I don't, really."

"You disappoint me, you really do. Your grandfather, Gustaf Nyström senior, was my teacher once. At old St. Erik's."

Ask let go his thumb-grip on Nyström's collarbone. The hollow above the bone hurt.

"I see that we're not on the same wavelength, you and I," Ask went on in his creaking, almost whispering voice, a St. George who has shouted himself hoarse at all the dragons, or who has laryngitis from the sulphurous fumes of Evil.

"I don't know whether it's really worth going on with," said Nyström.

"I haven't abandoned you," said Ask, now almost inaudible.

"Haven't you?"

"In my clinic, everyone gets the help he needs to complete a thesis."

"Wouldn't it be just as well to give it up, if we have such different views?"

"No. You will complete the work as planned. Exactly according to the old plan."

"It's difficult to do something you don't believe in."

"I wasn't thinking of you personally, my friend, I was thinking of the clinic. I've been responsible for more than fifty theses. Everyone who has defended his thesis here has sooner or later become at least a senior lecturer. Only one was unable to complete his doctorate. He threw himself in front of a train."

"And if I give up? Without committing suicide?"

"Naturally, the whole world is open to you, in that case. With the exception of internal medicine."

Professor Ask picked up one of the telephones and leaning the receiver against his shoulder, started dialing a number. The audience was at an end. Gustaf Nyström bowed rather carelessly and left. There was nothing more to discuss. Ask was not going to tolerate any defectors. So that was that. All he had to do now was to decide whether to write a thesis in which he didn't believe, or to become something else. What? A company doctor? An army doctor? A medical officer? A private practitioner? A "head of research" in a drug company?

He had been in a similar situation many years before, when a temporary assistant in Anatomy. Up to the end of the fifties, it was a fundamental scientific truth that human beings had forty-eight chromosomes. But then those solid foundations had suddenly been shaken, when two researchers had shown that human beings in fact had no more than forty-six chromosomes.

The interesting thing was that during the previous few years, anyone had been able to see that human beings had no more than forty-six chromosomes. There were excellent microscopic photographs to show this. All you had to do was to count them on such a photograph. But the dogma that human beings had forty-eight was so established that it proved impossible to shift for several years. One evening, Gustaf Nyström and two younger colleagues had counted the chromosomes on a microscopic photograph for fun. Whichever way they counted, they could not make the number more than forty-six. But in the text underneath the photograph, it said the photograph showed that human beings had forty-eight chromosomes. Nyström and his friends had sat up half the night counting, not believing their own eyes. Then they gave up and went out for some beer, preferring to forget the whole story.

19 Greten Sohlberg was a laboratory nurse. She was one of the last remaining nurses in the laboratory, for nowadays only lab technicians were trained. In the mornings, she went around the wards and took blood samples. In the afternoons, she sat in the lab, sorting the samples, doing analyses, watching over the complicated machines that had taken over most of the routine work, counting cells through a microscope and laying out glass tubes and other materials for the following day's test samples. She was fifty-four and had suffered for a long time from constant pains in her neck and shoulders.

Nowadays she had a small cart on which was everything she needed, but for more than twenty years, she had gone around carrying a heavy tray. At her previous place of employment, there had been a great many years' discussion over whether they should switch to using carts. The younger girls had preferred trays, which were quicker and meant they finished earlier. Their employer had agreed with the younger ones. It cost money to change to carts.

But at Enskede Hospital, they had had carts from the beginning, though too late for Nurse Greten, so she would have to live with her pain. But she wasn't unhappy. She had been allowed to go on working.

If the tray system had continued she would have been forced to stop working and live off disability, or ask for a transfer. And where could she be transferred to? Nearly all nursing jobs involved heavy or difficult work that put a strain on back and shoulders. With a little luck, she might have got a full time job in the laboratory itself, but she didn't want to be shut up all day long among all that apparatus, her glasses on her nose, peering at instrument panels or calculators. Or worse, being stuck in front of a little television screen that wobbled out gray combinations of figures against a blurred background.

Most of the patients were scared of Nurse Greten. She could see the fear in their eyes as she pushed her little supermarket cart around the rooms. She pricked fingertips, extracted blood from veins in the crook of arms, took blood from hands and feet, or stabbed lobes of ears if that was necessary. She was tormented by the patients being so afraid of her that grown men sometimes fainted at the sight of her in the corridor. Oddly enough, it was often much calmer in the pediatrics ward. Children got used to her. They could be as affectionate as lab animals, despite the pain. Diabetics also became stoic over the years, although they were punctured from head to foot with insulin injections and extractions for blood sugar tests.

Many patients accepted the tests with a kind of forced gaiety. They gave her nicknames, often greeting her with loud cries of "Hi, Nurse Wasp." Or "Little Hedgehog," or "Our Mosquito," or "Dracula's Sister," or "The White Vampire." If she had time, she used to try to spend a few minutes talking before she took the sample. But it was easy to slip behind with her schedule. Going around taking tests was something that could be relatively easily timed, in contrast with other hospital work. So the administration was extremely interested in Nurse Greten's pace of work. The fact that the electronic analyzers down in the laboratory represented a vastly greater capital investment was perfectly obvious, but to criticize the Health Service's latest progress demanded far greater courage than harassing an old nurse with a stopwatch.

In Ward 96, people were rushing in and out through the heavy doors, for it was time for major rounds, or Grand Rounds, as it was called when the Professor was present. Greten picked up the charts from 96 and sorted them room by room. A, B, C and so on. The first patient, in B.1. had gone to x-ray. The next, C.4., had been discharged the day before, but they had forgotten to cancel the test. She went into Room D to take a sample of Primus Svensson's blood.

When she came into the room, he was asleep with a pillow over his face. She turned the cart around to take the other rooms first, but one of the other patients quickly went across and lifted the pillow.

"Wake up, Primus! Time to give your blood for the Fatherland!"

Primus Svensson sat up in a daze and mouthed vacantly.

"It's me again," said Greten. "Here I am with my stings and antennae."

"Good morning, Nurse Cockroach," said Primus.

It was the first time anyone had called her Cockroach. Did cockroaches really sting? She parked the cart by the nightstand, sat down on the edge of the bed and took hold of the tip of his middle finger. It seemed cold and pale. She massaged and washed it for a while to get the blood into it. Swiftly and routinely, she thrust the lance into his finger, squeezed out the first drop, wiped it away, and let the next one fill out into a large ruby-red marble. Then she sucked up the blood into a pipette and emptied it into the square plexiglass tube.

Then it was time for a vein test. She looked at the crooks of both arms. He had good veins that protruded bluish-green beneath the thin old skin. Men were generally easier to stick than women, but if you were unlucky, the thick veins would roll away so that you couldn't puncture them, or else they were so delicate, especially in old people, that you stuck the point right through them and caused a large swelling afterwards. She squeezed slightly with her fingers above the elbow, washed the place and inserted the needle. The almost black blood welled out like a thundercloud in the salt-solution in the syringe.

"What are these tests for?" said Primus.

"Just the usual checks, I expect," she said. She seldom knew why a ward requested a certain series of tests, just as she seldom knew the patient's diagnosis.

"I heard on rounds there was one result that was too high."

At that moment, a highly conspicuous woman came into the ward, an overripe beauty of about forty-five, Greten guessed. The woman was wearing shoes with very high wedge heels made of cork, and a thin red-and-black flowery dress, with a long slit down the side. You could see a bruise on her thigh. She was wearing a black straw hat with a wide brim. Her mouth was thickly painted and full. Under one arm she had a shiny black handbag, and under the other a box of chocolates as large as an evening paper.

"Oh, gracious me!" she said in a deep, almost masculine voice. "Is this where Primus Svensson is?"

20 Primus had never seen the woman before. She introduced herself, kissed his cheek, handed over the box of chocolates and sat down on the visitor's chair by his bed.

"Well, well, so you're Kitty, are you?" said Primus. He was not quite sure whether he had heard the name right. Bernt had been extremely secretive about his private life since his divorce. But Primus knew that Bernt had had several quite lengthy relationships. Perhaps he had mentioned a Kitty the last time?

"Bernt's such a nice man," said Kitty. "A lot like his father."

Why had she come instead of Bernt? He didn't know whether to feel flattered or not. If they had both come, he would have been very pleased, as if Bernt at last respected his father sufficiently to introduce his new wife to him—or whatever she was? Kitty was not wearing a wedding ring.

"Has Bernt got a lot to do?" said Primus.

"He's terribly busy! He just rushes from one famous professor to another. He's absolutely marvelous with people!"

That was a strange statement. When Bernt was really small, he had been open and trustful. But not as an adult. Primus found it hard to think of anyone more sullen, negative, or uninterested in his fellowmen. But perhaps he was misjudging Bernt. You couldn't tell from the way he treated his father, and he couldn't very well work as a salesman if he was an old sourpuss, could he?

"Are Bernt's sales doing well?" Primus said.

"Sales?"

"Yes, his sales of pills and tablets and things."

"Oh, Bernt doesn't sell things. He stopped doing that ages ago. He goes around *informing* people now. He gives lectures to doctors on the latest lines. And advances. You could say he's working in education. That's nice for him. He's always wanted to be a teacher."

Had Bernt wanted to be a teacher? That was news. Bernt had trained as an engineer, hadn't he? As far as Primus knew, Bernt had talked to his mother about becoming an inventor. But a teacher? How would Bernt be patient enough for that? He looked down at the box of chocolates lying like a breakfast tray on his lap.

"Would you like one?" he said, not opening the box.

"Oh, Lord, no, thank you!" said Kitty. "I haven't eaten chocolates for years. You must see, Dad—may I call you Dad? Bernt always says Dad. You see, Dad, I run a little boutique together with another girl. Customers are so critical these days. I have to keep slim."

So Kitty had a shop of her own? She must be all right then, even if she did look like a whore. It was all part of the job, he supposed. At least she didn't go around in shabby clothes. Lots of young people did that nowadays.

"Well," said Kitty. "Unfortunately Bernt couldn't get away. He had to deal with some foreign business contacts, so I thought why don't you go yourself, my girl, and pop up and see old Dad Primus. We're practically related. He's sure to need some help with something. Is that right?"

"No, thank you. Nothing that you could do, Kitty."

"But you tried to get Bernt on the phone, Dad?"

"Yes, of course. He simply ought to know I'm here."

"Who's looking after your apartment, then? And the allotment?"

"They're all right."

"But what about all your papers and business? Income and bills. Debit and credit, as we in the trade say."

"They send on my mail," said Primus. "It works fine."

"But you asked Bernt for some help, didn't you, Dad? With this and that? Of course, you need a bit of a hand from your only son."

"Well, he isn't here, anyhow," said Primus, feeling slightly miserable. Bernt was clearly very busy, but after almost eight weeks, he might have found just one moment to spare . . ."

"Well, I'm here!" said Kitty. "Bernt has sent the best he's got!"

"I'm grateful to you for that," said Primus, putting his hand on Kitty's.

"I've wanted to get to know you for so long, Dad. Bernt has told me so much about you and about your bike rides when he was a little tyke."

Primus felt a slight thickening in his chest. Perhaps he had been unjust towards Bernt, and Kitty here must also have a lot to do? With her own business, as well.

"How is your shop going, then, Kitty?"

"Don't talk about it! Oh, times are really bad! The sales tax keeps going up and the krona goes down. You can't rely on anyone these days, either. People steal like jackdaws. You see, we dealt mostly with imported garments."

"Dealt? Have you given up the shop?"

"We had to! So that's that. I might as well tell you, Dad. We've thrown in the towel, so to speak."

"Did Bernt have money in the shop, too?"

"Bernt, no! We've always kept our finances separate. Bernt is all right with his fat salary and leased car."

"What are you going to do now, Kitty?"

"Well may you ask! I thought I'd devote myself to the family. There's a job called "caring." I don't think we take care of each other nearly enough in this country, do you, Dad?"

"Yes, that's probably true."

"I'm not sure if you really trust me," said Kitty, looking hurt.

"Of course I do, Kitty dear," said Primus, patting her hand again.

"But you've said you don't want any help."

She was right there. He had been lying when he had said he didn't need any help. He had phoned Bernt in order to go through the bankbooks and talk about his funeral. Now he was better and the infarction healed, but they couldn't very well simply push all these matters ahead into the future.

"Well, Kitty, if you wouldn't mind taking some papers to Bernt, I'd be very grateful."

"Of course, I'd love to, Dad."

He pulled out the drawer and fished out his wallet and the list of questions he had meant to ask Bernt. Kitty put on her glasses and then handed Primus his own spectacle case.

"Here's the key to the apartment," said Primus. "The key to my safe deposit box is in the bathroom under the rubber mat by the tub. If Bernt would read the papers in the safe deposit box, it'd be a good thing. Here are the numbers of the bankbooks and the balances. If he could just transfer three thousand to the funeral book from the other book."

"He has to have power of attorney to do that."

"Yes, of course, that's true. Then he'll have to come here—"

"Here," said Kitty, extracting a piece of paper out of the shiny black bag. "I took the liberty of coming via the post office to fetch the forms. If you just sign this here. Down there."

"But this gives *you* the power of attorney."

"Yes, but I'm the person here, aren't I? You can't sign for power of attorney to someone who isn't here!"

That was true, of course. If only she had been married to Bernt, he wouldn't have hesitated. But it seemed a little strange to be handing over power of attorney to an unknown person.

"If you don't trust me, Dad, we'll just tear this silly form up," said Kitty, holding it up and tearing a tiny rip in it.

At that moment one of the nurse's aids, Yvonne, came into the room.

"Please, would visitors mind leaving the room," said Yvonne. "We've got Grand Rounds coming."

"Oh, my goodness!" said Primus. "Kitty, you'd better come back another time—"

"Just sign this, Dad dear." said Kitty, pressing the pen into his hand.

Primus adjusted his glasses and with a hesitant and trembling hand, he scrawled his signature, using the box of chocolates as a desk.

"Will you arrange for someone to witness it, Kitty?" he said.

"I'll fix everything, don't worry, Dad."

Within seconds, she was out of the door. Primus lifted the box of chocolates up, wondering what to do with it. It was too large to put in his nightstand, and he couldn't leave it lying there during the doctors' rounds. There was nothing else to do but to put it underneath the covers.

21 *Grand Rounds* had special significance. The medicine floor at Enskede Hospital was divided into five sections. Four of the sections covered two medical teams each and were supervised by a senior lecturer acting as Senior Assistant Resident. In addition, each team had an attending physician and two residents. The fifth team covered only one ward and in that the Professor was the Senior Physician. But the Professor was usually relieved of his duties as senior physician and so in practice that team was looked after by the eldest of the attending physicians.

In each ward, there were rounds every morning and every afternoon. Twice a week, they had major rounds, which meant rounds with the Senior Assistant Resident present. The rounds system had long been criticized and several alternatives had been suggested, but the old system prevailed. From the doctors' point of view, it was most efficient to walk around and see the patients. Then the doctors themselves could decide how long the rounds would take, whether they would seriously discuss every single patient, answer questions and make decisions, or whether they would make it a quick one, darting around and throwing out an encouraging word here and there, waving aside all questions or with an expression indicating that there were far more important things to do than talking to patients.

Grand Rounds meant that the Professor also did the teaching rounds for which he had no personal responsibility. Everyone except the Professor hated Grand Rounds. It was really supposed to be kept secret, so that the students couldn't read up about patients they otherwise knew little about. Grand Rounds also involved the whole class. The Professor would suddenly pounce on a patient and ask the relevant student to report on the patient. Then more questions would follow in front of the whole class, the ward doctors, the nurses—and the patient. The Assistant Course Director then noted down in his little grade book how the whole thing had gone.

The nurses had an agreement with the Professor's secretary, so that they knew in advance when Grand Rounds was looming, otherwise they would probably not have had time to get the place cleaned up properly. The doctors also usually knew what was going to happen, so they did extra rounds the evening before for safety's sake, arranging for new batteries of examinations and tests. You never knew what ideas might fly into the Prof's head. The students were often kept in ignorance of what was going on, but if they had good contact with the ward doctor, they might be tipped off, although that was strictly forbidden.

Professor Ask considered Grand Rounds an excellent way of acquiring informally and without advanced preparation some insight into the daily work of his empire. As head of the unit and the whole department, it was his duty to keep himself informed about the situation. The students also needed bedside contact with their course director and to see an experienced doctor at work. Quite simply, they needed a role model. Finally, the patients had a right at least once during their treatment to speak to the Professor. That was a guarantee of security. Grand Rounds was also a good method of getting past the hospital bureaucracy, so that the person with the greatest responsibility would have direct contact with the work in the field without an intermediary.

The whole company surged into Room D, where Primus was sitting upright in bed, his fellow-patients standing more or less at attention at the ends of their beds. Ask stepped up to Primus, introduced himself and shook him heartily by the hand. The fact that they had met before, when Ask had been around with the two doctors from Ghana, Ask had forgotten.

"Who is in charge of this patient?" he said, turning around to his forty-odd tribe of followers in white.

Martina came forward and stood beside the bed. At first it looked as if Ask had not recognized her. He looked interested in a friendly way, but then an icy gleam appeared in his eyes. Martina began rattling off her homework.

"Primus Svensson here is seventy-six. He is a retired typographer. He's had a hypotonia for at least eight years, and also some trouble which we have interpreted as angina pectoris. On the twenty-seventh of August, he had an M.I. As far as the EKG . . ."

"What else could it have been if not angina pectoris?" said Ask, looking out of the window over the heads of the crowd.

"It could, for instance, have been due to nerve compression from cervical radiculopathy."

"Or?"

"Some other internal organ other than the heart. The lungs, esophagus, gallbladder, perhaps."

"Hiatus hernia," said Ask. "Describe that."

Martina accounted as best she could for how the diaphragm muscles weakened and how the upper part of the stomach could press up into the thorax, which could produce symptoms that were occasionally mistaken for heart trouble. When she had finished, Ask said nothing, burying his head in the chart instead. Martina's friends made faces at her.

"What are the results of the laboratory tests at this moment?" Ask said.

Martina rattled them off.

"That's not quite right," said Ask, looking nastily at her.

Martina was confused. Nyström had tipped off the students about the Grand Rounds, and they had sat up half the night cramming on their patients. Martina was quite sure she had remembered the series of figures correctly. She found it easy to learn by heart, after three years of almost daily training at rattling off Latin names, chemical formulae and all kinds of lab results.

"Well?" said Ask.

She flushed and shook her head.

"Don't you think you ought to tell your audience that you have begun an investigation into hyperparathyroidism?"

"We haven't had any results from that yet. The question was what was the *present* situation with lab results."

"Don't say lab results. It's called laboratory results. Unfortunately you young medical students do not understand the significance of language. Language cannot be allowed to deteriorate in this way."

Martina didn't know what to say, so she simply shrugged her shoulders slightly helplessly, trying to catch Nyström's eye, but he was staring down at the floor all the time, shifting his feet. Ask shook hands with Primus again.

"Things'll work out for the best," he said. "As soon as the parathyroid test is done, you'll be told. Thank you for your cooperation."

The company surged out of the room. Nyström whispered to Martina that she should stay. She sat down on the visitor's chair and started explaining to Primus why they had taken tests of the parathyroid gland's function, that it was probably nothing serious, and was almost certainly a test showing a false positive result.

22 Vera Grondahl was the longest-serving of the staff nurses in Ward 96. She was in charge of the coffee fund. For long spells, the coffee fund was self-supporting because patients who had been discharged donated sums to it. At other times, the fund was at low ebb because the ward had not produced a sufficient number of profitable discharges. At the moment, there were only a few lonely coins in the bottom of the round aluminum can that had once had English honey-toffees in it.

Nurse Vera looked in her little blue book. They would have to take a collection. The only chance of avoiding that was if there were an "eviction round." Eviction rounds happened when the Senior Assistant Resident had been on vacation and came back bright, refreshed, sunburnt, and with the light of battle in his eye. Then in one fell swoop, he might discharge half the ward to make way for new admissions—to hell with it if the old ones weren't yet completed. You had to start again some time.

But Dr. Lock, who was the present Ass, i.e. Senior Assistant Resident, was at that moment doing a spell of military service. Vera took the can under her arm and went into the nurses' office. Two of the nurses on duty were sitting in there, Nurse Lizzy and Nurse Samantha. Lizzy was one of the old guard, while Samantha was a substitute, a Canadian with Swedish credentials. She had come to Sweden with her then fiancé, who was the Second Military Attaché at the Canadian Embassy.

"When's Lock coming back?" Vera said.

"Tuesday," said Lizzy. "We're sitting here just gathering up our strength."

"Sitting" wasn't true, because both of them were standing, Lizzy going through the medicine cabinet and Samantha in front of the mirror over the basin, holding a half-finished sweater under her chin to see if it fitted across her bust.

"We must buy some more coffee," said Vera. "And filter papers."

"How much do you want?" said Lizzy.

Vera didn't know how much she would need. The ward consumed at least two kilos of coffee in about four days. There was about a quarter of a kilo left, so if she bought two kilos plus filters, that would be about a hundred and twenty kronor. If she managed to get ten out of everyone, that should be enough. But of course not everyone was on duty and some simply hadn't got ten kronor on them just like that. When it came to the doctors and the students—Dr. Nyström was an exception because he even came and asked about the state of the coffee fund. Otherwise, the further up the hierarchy and the salary scale, generally speaking the harder it was to get anything out of them. The girls in the ward always paid if they had any money. Many of the doctors never paid at all. They couldn't be bothered with such trivialities.

Carola, the secretary of the ward, came into the office with the tape recorder's earphones like a stethoscope around the collar of her white coat. Every ward had a part-timer for secretarial duties, plus access to the typing pool that served the whole hospital.

"I'm getting a cold," said Carola. "Have you anything in that cabinet?"

"Do you believe in Vitamin C?" said Lizzy, taking down a large bottle of tablets.

"I heard someone talking about chalk down on 95."

"Calcium tablets?"

"Yes, if chalk and calcium are the same thing?"

Nurse Lizzy took down another bottle from the medicine cupboard, put on her glasses and read the instructions.

"Yes, that seems to be right," she said. "They're usually used for allergies. Have you got hay fever?"

"No, just an honest-to-goodness cold."

"Then I can recommend vitamin C," said Lizzy, handing her the bottle.

"I know someone who takes iron," said Vera. "To strengthen the mucous membranes."

Vera realized it was not the right moment to bring out her coffee can. When the nurses started prescribing, it could take quite a while. There was always someone who had a tip from other departments or hospitals. The medicine cabinet was the most sacred place in the ward. In construction it resembled a shrine, a triptych, that could be closed or opened out. Opened, it revealed hundreds of bottles in neat rows on the narrow shelves, standing there looking toward the center of the triptych. In the center of the medicine cabinet was the refrigerator with its transparent plexiglass door. Inside that were the bottles of intravenous solutions with shiny glittering caps, a Holy Family a head taller than all the other worshipping little bottles.

"Nothing helps a cold," said Samantha. "The doctors always say that."

The other two pretended not to hear what they had already heard innumerable times, that colds could not be cured. You could relieve them, perhaps, but not cure them.

"Of course calcium is justified to some extent," said Lizzy. "There's sure to be an allergic factor in all colds. Yesterday in the cafeteria, Solveig in Emergency told me that someone there used diuretics to reduce swellings. Then you escape that thick feeling in your throat."

"I reckon you could start with three aspirin," said Vera, who herself had found aspirin good.

"Have you got pollen?" said Carola.

"We tried to get some last spring. But Nyström wouldn't sign for it. But doesn't pollen help with resistance? Before you have any symptoms?"

"No, it's like Vitamin C," said Carola. "It helps the first day, but you have to take quite a lot."

"Have we come to the end of the ten milligram Valium?" said Lizzy. "I promised to take some back home to my old man."

Without noticing it, they had acquired company in the office. Hardy had crept in with his cart.

"Are you handing out prizes?" he said, sitting in the middle of half-written prescriptions on the little table.

"Come off it!" said Carola. "Funny man, eh?"

"I know everything about colds," said Hardy, taking one of his reference books off the trolley. "*Common viral infections*. I like reading aloud. Is it a *URI*?"

URI was slang for upper respiratory infection, in other words, a cold.

"Yvonne's got comp-leave," said Lizzy. "If you were looking for her."

"I've brought a book," said Hardy. "*Gulliver's Travels* for, what was his name now, Primus Svensson?"

"He's down having a kidney x-ray," said Samantha.

"He's got a fantastic little allotment over on the other side of the freeway," said Hardy.

"Yes, I heard," said Vera.

"From Primus?"

"No, from Yvonne."

Hardy slid quickly off the table and put *Gulliver's Travels* down on the edge of the sink.

" 'Bye then, you girls," he said. "Give this book to Primus from me, will you?" And he pushed off with his cart.

"Are any of you any good at knitting?" said Samantha, again clamping her knitting beneath her chin and standing in front of the mirror.

No one replied. Samantha was not especially popular. She was considered a bit of a snob who liked to fraternize with the doctors and students. It was even whispered that she had had an affair with Dr. Lock the previous summer. Someone had seen them together on one of the island ferries.

Vera Grondahl picked up her can and went out into the kitchen. It was time to put on the afternoon coffee. She was cross. She couldn't stand the nurses' chatter. They went on as if they owned the medicine cabinet. But when any of the rest of the staff, except Carola, wanted anything, then it was quite another story. The orderlies used to come to Vera to ask for tablets for headaches, cough medicine or nose drops. But Vera did not have a key of her own to the medicine cabinet. The

HOUSE OF BABEL 109

medicine cabinet was the nurses' own treasure chest. You had to bow and scrape for one of the girls who had menstrual pain or a toothache. Nurse Lizzy and the Ward Supervisor weren't too bad, but the younger ones, Samantha or Sirkka, they were hell. The girls had to crawl through half the hospital right down to the staff doctor to get a couple of aspirin.

23 Time passed, and November came. Primus started being up and about more and more during the day. He was a little tired, but otherwise felt well . . . except for his constipation. That always happened when he wasn't able to carry out his usual morning routines, porridge and strong coffee, then half an hour in the john with the morning paper. There was often a line for the bathroom here. Or else he couldn't relax. You could hear every sound from the bathroom.

No one bothered about his heart attack any longer. Instead they were investigating his parathyroid gland; Primus didn't really understand why. Dr. Nyström and that girl Martina had both said it was nothing to worry about, just a blood test that had gone wrong. But they continued. He had been to the biochemistry laboratory twice, and been made to drink some mess that looked like ordinary water. Then they had taken various urine tests. As recently as the week before, they had started talking about kidney stones. Did it hurt when he passed water and had there been any blood? No, it hadn't hurt, but he had had pains in the small of his back sometimes, of course. Not so much now as when he had been working at the printer's. They had x-rayed his kidneys and urethra, but still with no result. Only a preliminary one—and that of course came with no comment.

He had become the oldest inhabitant of Room D now. The engineer with the bad stomach had been transferred to Surgical, the policeman with the thrombosis in his leg had gone home, and the tram worker with the liver problem was dead. No one had said that he had died, but he had grown yellower and yellower and had thrown up so terribly at night. The hospital social worker had been in and talked about moving him to a long-term care room, but he had refused. Either he was going home or he wanted an operation. It had been very unpleasant. One night he had been taken to Isolation. Two days later, he was no longer in the ward. His roommates had asked after him, but none of the staff had known much, which meant they didn't want to say anything. Then Primus had seen the announcement of his death.

A new patient was a twenty-year-old boy who had been in many times before. He didn't talk about what was wrong with him, but rumor had it that it was bone cancer. In the bed next to Primus was an ex-primary school teacher with high blood-pressure, which might possibly be due to kidney failure. Unfortunately, Hardy the librarian had grown invisible, so there was no expert to ask. But the porter who pushed them to x-ray had indicated that the teacher had kidney failure. The fourth person in the ward was a taxi driver not yet fifty. He was suffering from some kind of anemia. He was as pale as porcelain and slept most of the time. They had punctured his breastbone to extract the bone marrow.

Primus was fairly content. He had company and care. It was not exactly fun being in the hospital, but he had plenty to do. The days went by, every hour apparently filled. When he had to go to x-ray or to EKG, he was almost annoyed, as if they had come and disturbed him, as if he were carrying out his work in 96. He did not want to leave it.

It was too bad about Alf, the boy with bone cancer. He whined over not being allowed a room of his own. He had a very expensive stereo with him and he lay there all the time with headphones on. But he didn't want to use the headphones. He wanted a room of his own so that he could play it loud. Alf's mother came to see him every single evening, but she and Alf hardly ever spoke to one another. After they had said hello, Alf put the headphones on again and became absorbed in the music. His mother just sat beside him, looking at him.

Today was Monday and a new bunch of students had come. Primus missed Martina, but she had promised to come and see him. The new students all had surnames beginning with S. One was called Svensson, of course, but Primus hadn't caught the other names yet. Yes, the one who had taken over from Martina was called Svahn, wasn't he? Svahn was a shy little fellow who seemed no older than Alf. When Svahn—what was the little thing's first name?—spoke, he held his hand in front of his mouth so that you couldn't hear him. Two of the students were girls, one of them very pretty and striking. Her hair had just been done and she was wearing large pearl earrings, a pearl necklace and yellow leather boots with high heels. She was responsible for Alf. But Alf was not interested, although the taxi driver, who was otherwise nearly always asleep, had sat up in bed and whistled after her.

In the dayroom Primus could mix with the other ambulatory patients in the ward. They were men and women, but most of the women were very old. Like a blessed old folks home. There were two who were very young, under twenty perhaps. But they were fairly ill and seldom managed to get to the dayroom. Dr. Lock was a specialist in the different forms of leukemia.

Primus had tried phoning Kitty once or twice, and late one evening he had at last got hold of her. But she had seemed tired and confused, at first unable to remember who he was. Bernt was not there, but out having a meal with some foreign contacts. Primus had asked about the bank papers. Kitty had been to his apartment and got the key to the safe-deposit box, but she hadn't spoken to Bernt yet. Bernt was so exhausted. She was waiting for the right moment. Bernt had asked her to send his regards and say he was missing Primus terribly. The next day, Primus had phoned Bernt's office in Södertälje and they had said that Bernt was off sick. Was that true? Bernt's affairs always had been mysterious. Primus had learned over the years that he could never rely on anything Bernt said.

24 On Tuesday morning, Dr. Roland Lock conducted his first major rounds in Ward 96 since his return from military service. Lock was a Naval Medical Officer, which meant he was paid a salary by the Navy every month in exchange for doing a few weeks' military service a year. He had been in a stone shelter in the mouth of Stockholm archipelago, running an underground military hospital, which had been very boring. Owing to a shortage of funds, naval maneuvers were running at half-steam, and the hospital had lain outside the actual war game. Instead, he had sat there peering down servicemen's throats in the mornings, sleeping in the afternoons, then drinking with his assistants at Trosa Hotel in the evenings.

But now there was to be a major round in 96. The day before he had been in his other ward, 97, and had managed to get rid of almost a third of the patients. Had that been wise? Ordinarily, it would have been, as there was always a line of new leukemia cases after he had been away. But he had forgotten one thing. In almost two weeks' time, the annual conference of the General Medical Council would be starting at the conference hall in Älvsjö, and that lasted a whole week. Not much skilled medical care went on in Sweden's hospitals during that week. He had seen a figure that said that about thirty to forty percent of the country's doctors were at the conference then. He himself usually let his rooms remain empty at the time, which meant he took in no more than absolutely unavoidable cases. Old people were allowed to stay filling up beds until the conference was over.

What was he doing now? 97 would be filled with a great many new patients during the week. Should he leave 96 alone? No, for God's sake, he would get down to it now. With some luck he might get through another generation of cases before the conference. There were ten days until then, weren't there? The surgeons teased the internals for prolonging their investigations for ever and ever. But not Lock. He considered he had what was called a surgeon's mentality: vital, an action man, not given to unnecessary brooding. People with a little push were needed in internal medicine.

Everyone joining in on the major round gathered in the office. Nyström, the interns—Lock had forgotten their names, there was such a damned quick turnover of interns. They did two weeks in each ward for training purposes. Then there were the students; 96 had changed since the last round. But he didn't mind about that—he gave lectures. Nyström saw to the daily arrangements. Then there was the Ward Supervisor, Nurse Berit, and old Lizzy. Samantha was there, too. Three nurses, not bad. The hospital social worker was there, and the dietician. On the very edge, he could just see some anonymous student nurses.

"Here we go," said Lock, jerking open the first door, into Room A.

In Ward A was a young director with a suspected M.I. and a pharmacist with cystic kidneys. Not much to do. They had both just come in. Lock greeted them and eyed through their charts. Then out again.

In Room B was an old man of over eighty who had paralysis of the face. They were fairly sure it was a small embolism in the brain causing it.

"No need to keep this one in, is there?" said Lock aside to Nyström.

"A bed problem," said Nyström.

Lock beckoned to the hospital social worker.

"Our social specialist will fix that, won't you?" he said.

The social worker shook her head wearily. There were no long-term care beds available, as usual. Internal medicine was becoming long-term in itself anyhow. Was becoming? It had been so for ten years. The other bed in Room B was empty. Excellent. When they were outside, Lock turned to the social worker and said:

"Either you fix a bed for our friend in there, or else you'll have to take the patient home with you!"

The social worker looked offended—couldn't she take a joke? She should be able to. This was no kindergarten, but a hospital, and patients who couldn't be treated should be sent to another institution.

The first person they came to in Room C was all ready to go home. Lock's spirits rose. Excellent, so he could pop a patient with Hodgkin's disease into that bed.

"Nurse, phone my secretary so that she gets in a new patient today."

"From you own list, Doctor?" said Nurse Lizzy, holding her pad.

Lock was a stickler for formalities out in the ward, but otherwise he always used first names, as long as there was no patient present. He couldn't allow people to take liberties just because he was the youngest in the unit.

"Dr. Lock, we can't do that," said the Supervisor. "We've a patient lying in the examination room who must come in here."

Always some kind of hassle. He turned on his heel and went out. There must be some old idler in Room D they could weed out. But it was impossible there as well. Primus Svensson had become practically a permanent fixture, but they'd found some disturbance in the serum level in his blood calcium. He went on to Room E, a four-bedded room for women. Two cerebral hemorrhages and two leukemias, a chronic lymphatic and an acute myelogenous. He said they were to puncture the breastbone of the latter. That had been done before with no conclusive result. In Room F was a woman in her forties with a gastric ulcer. They took her x-rays out of the large envelope and held them up against the ceiling light. A very clear "crater" could be seen in the mucus membrane.

"Can you tolerate coffee?" said Lock.

"I don't drink coffee," said the patient. "I'm a vegetarian."

"What about tobacco or alcohol, then? Or are you stressed at work? Or is your husband nasty?"

"I'm not married," said the woman.

Her complexion was slightly yellow, but the liver tests were blank. Some outdoor fanatics ate carrots so that they looked as if they had jaundice.

"What else do you eat beside granola?"

"Fruit, for example."

"What kind of fruit?"

"Whatever contains vitamin C."

"Such as?"

"Oranges."

"How many?"

He was on the scent now. He was usually right. If you had clinical intuition, then you had it. He could feel his nostrils involuntarily widening.

"Twenty. Thirty perhaps . . ." she said.

"A week?"

"No, a day."

Roland Lock was very pleased. No stomach could in the long run tolerate such consumption of citrus fruit without developing ulcers. He turned to the students.

"Whose patient?"

A small diffident youth, his label stating he was Fredrik Svahn, stepped forward.

"I can see no mention in the chart of this colossal consumption of oranges," said Lock.

"I didn't write it."

Lock read the top of the chart. No, hell, it stated there that it had been written by Lars Borg. The B group had changed wards, and it was the S students they had here on 96. He turned to Nyström instead.

"Well, that's it," he said. "The puzzle solved." Then he turned to the patient. "You can go home this afternoon. Dr. Nyström will talk to you about your diet. You'll live happily until you're ninety as long as you stay away from oranges."

Out into the corridor again.

"Nurse, ask my secretary to phone the patient I mentioned before. I can't remember the name, but he's a Hodgkin's."

"Is it a male patient?"

"Yes."

"I can't put a man in a room with three women."

No joy for long, then. Lock rushed through the rest of the ward without being able to pry loose a single male bed. After the round, they had coffee and cheesecake sitting down around the table. Lock would have liked to have had a quiet word with Nurse Samantha, but that didn't look possible this time. Anyhow, he had no time for females now. He had her home number and could phone this evening and suggest a meeting at the Holiday Inn, the motel alongside the conference hall where the GMC congress was being held. Holiday Inn? Wasn't it called something else this year . . . Star Hotels, was it? That'd work out. But now, hell.

"Give me the charts," he said to Nurse Lizzy, who was holding them.

He tipped back his chair and leafed through them. Primus Svensson? Hadn't the old boy already used enough of the taxpayer's money? M.I.'s weren't dangerous. Hell, all those M.I.'s! Nearly all large hospitals had special coronary units, but not Enskede, oh, no. M.I.'s were to be spread all over. That had been Ask's idea. He didn't really keep up these days. He considered heart disease the most important domain in internal medicine and that all wards had to be specialists in hearts. And what was the result? Intensive Care stole all the acute M.I.'s. The anesthesiologists ruled in Intensive Care, those self-important asses with all their tubes and apparatus. They could keep people alive, that they could, but a janitor could do that with that equipment. As soon as anything began to go wrong, a bell rang or a warning lamp blinked. Couldn't be more difficult than driving a bus. But Intensive Care had no more profound medical knowledge than that. They didn't know what the art of healing meant even.

Was this parathyroid examination necessary on Svensson? No. Most of those endocrinological complaints were incurable. And even if you took out the parathyroid glands, the old man was seventy-six, wasn't he? His heart half gone, too.

"I think we'll let Primus Svensson go," he said to Nyström. "There was nothing tangible on his x-ray, either, was there?"

"No. The boss was here when you were away. We couldn't do anything else but go on."

Oh, so Ask had been on Grand Rounds and poked his nose into Primus Svensson, had he? But that would be forgotten now. Though you couldn't be absolutely sure, because Ask's assistant made special notes for him. On the other hand, the Medical Council congress would be on soon. What would Ask be doing then? Ask was usually more than occupied preparing his various intrigues before the meet-ing of the Swedish Internal Medicine Association that took place at the end of the national conference.

"Discharge Primus Svensson," said Lock. "And give me some of that cake, will you?"

25 That same afternoon Primus Svensson was sit-ting waiting in a wheelchair in the corridor outside the office. He had been waiting for an hour and a half. Fortunately, he had managed to get hold of Kitty, who was coming to fetch him, but she had still not appeared. There were no windows in the corridor, and to save energy only every other light in the lightramp in the ceiling was on. This made the corridor striped, brilliant zones alternating with muddy yellowish-gray.

Primus tried once again to read the prescription he had been given by Dr. Nyström after their discharge talk. But he couldn't. His glasses had been packed and anyhow it was too dark where they had put him.

Nurse Vera, the staff-nurse, came out of the office with a book in her hand.

"The librarian was here and left this book," she said, holding out *Gulliver's Travels*.

He recognized the cover, but couldn't read the title. The cover was one of the old illustrations he remembered from his youth. They had certainly taken their time getting the book.

"How much does it cost?" he said.

"Nothing. Loans are free."

"I mean if I wanted to buy a copy? It's probably on the back, if you don't mind taking a look, Nurse."

"No, I'm afraid it's not."

"Oh, well, thanks all the same."

"Don't you want the book, Primus?"

"It's too late now. I'm going home today."

"Hasn't your daughter-in-law come yet? Shall I try phoning her?"

"No," said Primus. "Please would you phone for a taxi instead. I'll manage on my own."

"Are you sure?"

"Please phone for a taxi for me. And Nurse Vera—the coffee fund. Take three ten kronor notes out of my wallet here, will you?"

She took the money, pressed his hand, and went off to phone for a taxi.

26 Gustaf Nyström had managed to escape having to perform at the 1979 congress of the General Medical Council. The previous autumn, he had given a fifteen-minute talk on myocardial infarctions and psychological stress. But this year, Ask had excused him so that he could devote his energies to his thesis instead. Ask usually really pushed. Every division chief wanted as many of his own people on the program as possible.

Nyström showed his Medical Association membership card at the conference hall entrance. He came to this place twice a year, once early in the spring for the Boat Show, and now for the medical conference. He wondered which event attracted the most doctors.

The conference included more than twelve hundred lectures, symposiums, discussions, and meetings. The program grew thicker every year. In the old days, Nyström had gone to these annual conferences with great enthusiasm and curiosity. In those days, they had been held in the Public Meeting Hall in the middle of Stockholm, and at that time he had still thought he had a lot to learn, that he would hear the latest news at the conference. But over the years his enthusiasm had waned. Certainly he learned a thing or two, but then most of that was quickly published in the more important medical journals. Except what was really revolutionary—that never appeared either at the conference or in journals.

Most doctors went to the conference to meet each other and do their Christmas shopping at the NK department store. Naturally it was important and quite legitimate that they met each other. Many doctors were isolated in health centers, firms, or smaller hospitals far away from the university towns. For them, the conference fulfilled an important social function, but not for Stockholmers. There were already several thousand doctors in Stockholm.

Apart from these scientific activities, there were also exhibitions in the great open space. The various firms that produced apparatus and drugs had colorful booths staffed by striking women and well-tailored salesmen. Nyström went to that section first. He had four children between two and fourteen years old, and all of them, even the two-year-old, had learned to appreciate the ballpoint pens, cloth bags, calendars, gadgets, and other plastic gifts firms showered on their visitors.

At one stand they were serving a fizzy drink containing Vitamin C from a fountain—it tasted like soda pop—and they were handing out small rain gauges in the shape of a schnapps glass. It was hard to push your way through, but he managed. He got five rain gauges after some prompting, four for the children and one for himself. He had been collecting the worst advertising lunacies for several years. When he was old, he was going to open a museum of curiosities, then he was going to sit at the entrance with a cat on his knee and take the entrance money.

Luna Pharmaceuticals had one of the largest stands, with great posters advertising Harmonyl. Luna was handing out golfing caps. They were a brilliant red and had HARMONYL LUNA in luminous acid green paint on the brim. Nyström asked one of the representatives for five caps. When he got closer, he realized the man smelt of drink. Nyström didn't know how these salesmen survived, for the firms not only worked them hard, but also ruined their livers.

The largest home-based drug firm, Astra, had a very sober stand manned by two doctors. This was equipped with its own computer terminal linked with Medline for visitors to conduct literature searches in Astra's special area of interest. Just like their sister firm Luna, Astra dealt mainly in licensed patents or general goods of their own manufacture; very few original preparations. Several decades earlier, Astra had acquired access to a local anesthetic that had been experimented on by researchers associated with the medical school. Since then Astra had developed this anesthetic and it had become a major export. Luna, on its part, had had the equivalent good fortune of coming in contact with a young biologist who had happened to discover a new material for sutures. This plus its discoverer had been swiftly bought up. Those were the traditional procedures. But what would happen in the future? The drug companies now invested larger sums in research than many universities did, hoping to make discoveries internally before they were freely available to the scientific community.

Gustaf Nyström was one of the few doctors against this. Nearly all the others supported the drug firms' methods of working. Every objection from the public was regarded as socialization and an attack on free research. But Nyström couldn't understand that. If medical advances were made in universities and hospitals, then findings were presented in the usual order in theses and articles. Findings were noised abroad so that researchers out in the world could share them or check investigations in their own labs. That was the fundamental basis of free and open research. But the drug companies used the opposite principle. For them it was a matter of applying for patents as soon as possible and shrouding new medical findings, so that they could then market them and retain all the rights.

It was easy to laugh at the amusement park tactics the smaller drug firms used to advertise and market their goods. But they were relatively harmless. The dangerous ones were the large "serious" companies, whose staff appeared distinguished in gray suits, who did not strew bright ballpoint pens around. The truly professional companies were instead striving to take over medical research, pharmacological first and foremost. The phrase "brain-drain" was often bandied about within Swedish research, and this meant that accomplished researchers went to America where they would find better resources. But in reality the brain-drain did not go from one country to another; it went from the public and open to the private and enclosed.

Gustaf Nyström continued his hunt for toys for his four children. The Boat Show and the conference melted together in his mind and he thought he sensed great hulls of boats behind him, but when he turned swiftly around all he saw was a smiling lady in a white coat between glittering autoclaves. It seemed to him that the firm's products had suddenly changed name, as if he were staring at the hull of an Astra 95, a Draco 1700 TL, a Johnson & Johnson 22, a Roche Sea Cat, a Leo Great Dane, Tika Tornado, Kifa Cabin, or a Ferrosan Daycruiser.

Every annual conference included a major debate on some popular subject. This autumn the subject was *The Human Approach to Health Care*. Nyström set off for the section where the debate was to be held. Although it had not yet started, between four and five hundred people had already crowded into the room. A row of rickety tables covered with a green felt cloth were ranged up on the platform, a speaker's rostrum with the association's emblem on it to the extreme right, and plastic plants in pots ranged all along the edge of the platform.

Gustaf Nyström leaned against the wall and watched the debaters climbing onto the platform and finding their places. They all greeted each other warmly and politely, even those who would be regarded as bitterest enemies. A well-known professor from Lund appeared, a bright old man with a sly look in his eyes. Then came the representative of the national patients' organization, the medical correspondent of Sweden's largest daily paper, a lawyer from the Medical Association, a city councilor, a departmental head from the social services, the ombudsman from the Consumer Council, an author in jeans who had written a play on the Swedish health services, and a man with white hair standing on end like a dandelion. Was it Gustav Jonsson? No, it was someone from Swedish Radio.

After greetings from the chairman of the panel, who ordinarily was the Head of the Army Medical Corps, the introductory speeches began. Each of the nine delegates had five minutes at his disposal. Eight out of the nine overran their time by ten or even fifteen minutes. The ninth, the author of the television play, refused to make a speech at all. In ten words he said sullenly that he disapproved of the whole enterprise and did not wish to sit there discussing patients *von oben*. Nyström wondered why the man hadn't stayed home instead.

After the hour and a half the speeches had taken, Nyström gave up. He didn't think he had learned anything new about "The Human Approach to Health Care." One of the speakers thought it was shot to hell, another that it was problematical, a third that it was as good as could be expected, and a fourth that it was conspicuously absent. How could any debate be carried out with those starting points? Nyström left the warm room and went to get himself a cup of coffee.

He waved to an old classmate at the other end of the café. She was a company doctor in Borås now and she triumphantly held up a straw hat with a black ribbon. On the ribbon was Librium-Librium-Librium-Librium. Nyström answered by waving his red Luna cap; Harmonyl-Harmonyl-Harmonyl. He saw several acquaintances at other tables, but he couldn't be bothered with them or the same old talk about duties, superiors, winter sports resorts, tax breaks, absent colleagues, children and perks. Instead he tried reading the thick program. The problem was not that lectures of interest were lacking; on the subject of myocardial infarctions alone there were thirty. But he didn't have the energy and gave up. The torrent of information was all too great, and he felt impotent.

27 The medical class at Enskede Hospital was to have a party to make up for the canceled trip to Helsinki. Martina had thought a lot of her friends would be very annoyed with her because of the canceled trip, as she was the one who had got them to boycott the test. But no one had said anything, not even Bertelskjöld and Borg, both members of the ultraconservative medical society called Carolus Dexter, which fought for the reintroduction of letter grades.

They had not had a party for a long time. They had often had them in their first terms, but seldom with the whole class all at once. That was almost impossible; the preclinical courses at the Karolinska Institute involved a hundred and eighty students. But during their general year, when they were preparing for clinical duties, they had been no more than thirty, and then they had often had parties. They hadn't had one since they started the clinical course. Clinical realities were exhausting and many of them had also had to travel further. And perhaps more important, those on the course who had come direct from school had started getting married and having children. The time of *Sturm und Drang* was over.

They had formed a committee of which Martina was a member. She was always elected to all committees. The first controversy was over who was to be included in the party; members of the class only, members plus lecturers, members plus partners, or members plus invited physiotherapy students. One of the men, Janne, who was said to have slept with over two hundred women, was strongly in favor of inviting extra girls. But Martina spoke against it and got the others to agree with her. Martina promised rather acidly that she herself would look after Janne, if his "need" became too great. So it was decided it would be members of the class plus certain lecturers. One person was automatically excluded, their course director, Professor Ask. He wouldn't have come anyhow. If he mixed with students, it was on St. Lucia's Day, or at the Commencement Hall. Then he was only too willing to fraternize, preferably with the choir in their student caps, or even more so with their fiancées.

Many of them wanted to include Gustaf Nyström, then unity came to an end. Group C—Carlberg, Carlheim, Carlsson, Cassi and Coltin—wanted to have the assistant director for safety's sake, and because as drunkenness increased, they would be able to pump him about coming exams. But a lot of them considered their Assistant Course Director a total shit and ass-kisser, and that evaluation won the day. One or two of the other physicians were suggested and approved, but on the other hand, not one of the Senior Assistant Residents. There were indeed a couple of them who were excellent and efficient lecturers, but no real contact with the students had come about.

Where should they hold it? Three suggestions were made: the van der Linde vault in the Old City, Tionde Barn at the Karolinska Institute, and the Gasque Cellar in the student building. The first alternative was too expensive, the second too small, the third really too dull, but no one had the energy to find another alternative.

Who would pay? If they had gone to Finland, after pressure from Ask the drug firms would have contributed about ten thousand kronor. Could they raise that sum? What a party it would be with up to three hundred kronor per person to spend! But the firms would demand some kind of return. They would probably want to have representatives present. Someone would make a speech, at best a medico-historical chat, at worst something about a preparation for lowering blood pressure. Martina was very much against accepting "dirty" money.

"What do you mean 'dirty?'" Janne had said. "We all know it's mostly insurance money anyhow. Contributions the people of Sweden have paid in all honesty. How can you call that dirty money?"

Janne won, but as a punishment, he was delegated to approach the sponsors and find out if it were possible to pry ten thousand out of them. It wasn't. One of the firms was willing to give a buffet contribution of five hundred. Otherwise they all politely refused. Student trips were one thing, parties quite another.

So there was going to be pea soup and hot punch, as it was going to be a Thursday. After that there would be dancing with Janne acting as disc-jockey. Drinks could be had at the bar at cost. The buffet was crossed off the program. Martina had considered suggesting they should have a serious item, like inviting someone to speak on the teaching situation, or some other question of concern to the students. But she didn't have the energy. She would never get a majority in favor. During the General Course, she had tried to give an introduction to a party that concerned matters of equality, the differences between opportunities for male and female physicians; why, for instance, fewer women went on into research. But she had been shouted down, even by some of the women in the class!

Martina took part in the preparations, heating up the soup, counting bottles of punch, and keeping an eye on them. It was considered a perfectly legitimate student lark to steal the whole arsenal. The partygoers arrived. It was hard going at first, despite the fact that Janne and some others took around a homemade mixture of 190 proof alcohol and coke.

The doctors from the clinic were shy when they couldn't fulfill their usual function of leaders and big brothers. Gustaf Nyström was wearing an enormous knitted sweater and jeans. Martina didn't like that. He was too old. Why couldn't he dress like the other forty-year-olds in a blazer, polyester slacks, tie and colored shirt? She decided not to sit at his table, although she had noticed his eyes seeking out hers. Why should she sit with someone she already knew?

The actual meal went quite well. There were a couple of student-singers in their class who sang some drinking songs, the punch taking the place of schnapps. The Medical Association had also published a special song book, but no one really wanted to concentrate. The conversation drifted back into the usual old channels that arose in lunch rooms or student rooms. They talked about stupid patients, sadistic professors, possible jobs, and the fabulous sums certain senior students were said to be earning as weekend locums in the districts around Stockholm. Or in Norrland. One was said to have earned twenty-eight thousand in twenty days in Skellefteå.

The dance had been hard to get going although Janne held forth in his sexually loaded language. "Sexuality and cynicism," thought Martina. The common assumption that medical students liked occupying themselves with such things was true. She could easily fall in with the jargon. Why? Was it a way of protecting yourself? A way of saying that you really suffered from anxiety and compassion you couldn't handle? Or was it purely an attitude of superiority?

Gustaf Nyström asked her to dance, but he couldn't dance. He stood there rather awkwardly wagging his arms about and looking at his feet as if he were playing hopscotch.

"Come on!" she said. "Let's sit down."

They sat down in a corner, but almost at once he wanted to go and buy drinks. Was he afraid of her? She thought about her relations with Gustaf while he was gone. How did she regard him? He was almost the only sensible doctor in the whole clinic. He was all right, quite simply, human, didn't harass the students. He wasn't all that much in the prof's good books. But neither was she. There were several ties that linked them. But this evening, the rules were different, if they were going to be drinking together. She decided to censor all erotic impulses and not give him the slightest encouragement. Perhaps he wasn't that interested in sex? But nearly all men were when it came to the crunch, even the most formal, even very old men. She had been disappointed when she had realized that in her late teens. Now she tried to regard it as an illness.

"I'm thinking quite seriously about quitting," said Gustaf, after the first sip.

"But what about your thesis?"

"To hell with it. I've had enough of that circus."

"What are you going to do then? Is it easy to get a job?"

"I don't know. Yes, if you get out of Stockholm, I'm sure."

"You have a family, do you?"

He looked slightly embarrassed, as if his family were an unsuitable subject here. But then he shrugged and said:

"I've been married since sixty-five. We have four children, between two and fourteen."

What had Martina been doing in 1965? She had been nine years old then, going to school and writing letters to herself as an adult: do you think I'll ever have a horse of my own?

"What does your wife do?"

"She teaches English and French."

"What will she say? If you quit?"

"I don't know."

"You don't know! But haven't you discussed it?"

"Not yet."

"But you must see that if you leave Stockholm, she'll have to change jobs, too!"

She was a little angry, but mostly disappointed. Gustaf was all right, really, but the damn man couldn't even see he had to talk to his wife.

"Are you such an idiot you think you can keep your wife out of it? What's her name, incidentally? It sounds damned silly, you sitting here talking about 'my wife'."

"Marianne."

"Why haven't you talked to Marianne about it?"

"Because I don't know what I want to do myself."

"Why do you have to know that? Surely you have to talk to Marianne *before* you decide whether to leave Enskede or not!"

"Perhaps so."

She tried to calm down. What did she know about Gustaf and Marianne's relationship? What had someone else's marriage got to do with her anyhow?

"I only meant you know best about that, of course," she said, smoothing things over.

The conversation came to an end. They sat there uncomfortably, Martina waving to Janne in the disc-jockey box. But she got no response. How serious had she been when she'd promised to "look after Janne" if his need got too great? Perhaps she had been serious, unconsciously? Janne was very sexy. Some men were. He was rowdy, conservative and rather unpleasant. But if she were honest, she would certainly consider sleeping with him. There was an attraction about men with bad reputations.

"Shall we go?" said Gustaf suddenly.

He didn't wait for her to reply, but emptied his glass. "Go?" thought Martina. What did he mean by go? He needed to talk, that was clear. He had supported her when there had been trouble and he hadn't told Ask who had been behind the boycott. O.K., now it was her turn. And this party was a failure, anyhow. Several people had already left although it wasn't even eleven yet. She felt it in her bones that she was already on her way out.

"Where to?" she said.

He didn't reply, but just looked rather sheepishly at her. So she would have to decide for herself—as usual. Where to? Home to his place? Idiotic. To some pub or other? To the Victoria? They wouldn't be allowed in there. No, she couldn't face sitting with Gustaf in some grubby drinking place. What would they do if they didn't hit if off, and simply exchanged polite nothings?

"O.K.," she said. "Back to my place then. But I have to get up early tomorrow morning."

Gustaf went to phone for a taxi. Martina went to the restroom and paid the waitress.

Martina lived in a student apartment on Körsbär Road. She had not had time to make her bed that morning, and the whole place looked like hell in every other respect, too. The ironing board was out, two newly-ironed blouses hanging from the ceiling light. Alongside the bed was a small table and two bat-wing armchairs of canvas.

"Wine or tea?"

She got the bottle of wine from the refrigerator. It was half full. She had to wash up two mustard glasses. She took a bag of potato chips in with her.

"What do you live on?" said Gustaf.

"Student loan. And I've worked as a nurse's aid in the summers."

"Everyone should have health care experience before starting to study medicine."

"Wouldn't work," she said. "The trade unions are against it. They're afraid there'd be fewer jobs."

"Silly, isn't it?"

"I don't know," she said. "Practical experience is important. But it wouldn't be fair in itself if a whole lot of privileged students came along and swiped the jobs from people who needed them more."

He looked lost in the tattered armchair, already on his second drink.

"Why do you drink so quickly?" she said amiably.

"Oh, sorry," he said in embarrassment. "I didn't mean to drink up all your booze."

"Are you worried about something?"

"Yes, I am actually. I'm not usually in the habit of going home with female students at night."

"What about male ones, then?"

"No, I don't have *those* inclinations."

"I wasn't talking about sex," said Martina. "Why can't one go home with someone if there's something special to talk about? Whether the person concerned happens to be male or female?"

"Well, of course one can."

He was so oddly defenseless. Gone was the security he radiated in the hospital, his quiet, rather dry humor. He just looked terrified. Totally confused!

"Why do you want to be a doctor?" he said.

"Why did you?"

"I studied the humanities until I was twenty-four. Then I didn't know what to do next. Nearly all my family were doctors. My grandfather was a professor and heart specialist. My father was a neurologist. Mother is a pediatrician. I had an elder sister who studied medicine. In some ways I was the prodigal son."

"And you returned to the house of your father?"

"Yes, I returned to the house of my father, started studying medicine, married a girl I'd known since I was at school, and had children. And now I'm here. Sometimes I think I made the wrong choice, that I'm bluffing my way through life."

"Everyone thinks that some time or other."

"I often think I'm simply inadequate, that patients have a right to demand much more of me than I can give. That I'm ignorant, lazy, slovenly . . . what you will. A phony in my private life, too. I'm a kind of phony daddy to my children. I often feel as if I were the same age or even younger than my own children. If only they knew! If they really knew how *small* their father is! He looks big because he clumps around on stilts that don't show under his trousers. I try to look happy most of all in my marriage. Sometimes I'm too tired to be happy. Then I blame the patients or that I've been on duty. Or our goddamned professor. But I don't tell them the truth, that I no longer know who I am in my own family. What does my wife, I mean Marianne, think about sleeping with me? I don't know. It seems to work. But does it? Or is she bluffing, too? Is my second youngest daughter bluffing when she says she loves me more than anyone else in the world and she wants to marry me when mommy is dead? I'm forty-one. I should feel free and strong. I know that most people envy me. Medicine is the finest profession of all. But I don't know. The only thing I know is that it isn't at all what I thought it would be. Sometimes I want to sit down and cry, for hours and hours. Other times I want to sit down and laugh because I was born into the best country in the world, have the finest profession, a high income, and a family that would look great in the weekly magazines. *Angst* about luxury? Yes, of course. But it happens to be the only *angst* I have access to. What will happen to me? What will I be in ten years time? Then I'll be over fifty. When you're forty, you realize life isn't endless. You can't change profession. There are perfectly clear time limits. You have twenty-five years left until retirement. What can you do in that time? You know the years are getting shorter and shorter. Sometimes they're as short as three months. If I'm good, I can become a senior lecturer by the time I'm forty-five. Then perhaps a Senior Physician in Småland or Norrland. How could I stand that? I've been a junior physician in a small town once. I know what that's like. You can't go out into town without half the hospital knowing. You're forced to mix with other doctors' families with whom you've nothing in common. Just look at the radical doctors, the ones who created the Socialist Medical Association, for instance. What has become of them? They're in backwaters in the countryside in small hospitals, trapped by bourgeois values. They're on call or on backup call perhaps once or twice or even three times a week. When do they have time to think? Or to live?"

This was too much. Martina got up and opened the window. People confessing too much was embarrassing. She wasn't shocked, but maybe slightly depressed. His life could easily be what hers was going to be. What was it like to be a single woman doctor in the countryside? It was good that Gustaf was straightforward about it, but what was he demanding in return? People who opened up always wanted something in return, love, pity, encouragement, to have their fears allayed, or else they were asking for the same openness in return. Now I've shown you *mine*, you must show me *yours*. She did not want to confide in Gustaf; she was not ready for that. If she once started and really got going, heaven knows where it would end! Perhaps she would rant and rave on for hours. Could he stand that? She couldn't just close her eyes and allow herself to fall helplessly into his arms. Gustaf probably wouldn't stay to catch her, but would run like a frightened rabbit instead. The few middle-aged men she had known well had been like that, radical and nice on the surface, worldly-wise and educated: a rather false safeness and big-brother stuff. But when it came down to it, they were scared stiff, just wanting to run away. Last year she had had an affair with a married man. Never again! Never, never, never! It had been degrading.

She rested her arms on the window sill and looked out over the city. The apartment was shabby, cramped and thin-walled, but the view was fantastic. She could see all the way over to Södermalm, squalls of wet snow swirling over the city. The red, green and blue neon lights looked smudged at a distance, the orange street lights with haloes around them. She tried to see as far south as possible. Could she see the red warning lights for planes on Enskede Hospital roof? She half-closed her eyes and leaned further out, the snow striking her forehead.

She heard Gustaf moving in the chair. Time to pee? Men were always going for a pee.

"The john's on the left in the hall. Don't go into the closet by mistake!"

But she heard no steps retreating. Instead, he came up behind her and she stiffened. Gustaf stood close to her and put his hands onto her bare arms. Very slowly, he pressed up against her.

"What do you do now, Tina, my girl," she thought. "Push him away? Fall weeping into his arms? Joke my way out of it? Start chatting about the view? Explain that I do indeed think you're a great person, the only one of the doctors I really like, but that I can't possibly get involved in a relationship with a man who's almost twice my age, who's married to someone called Marianne, and has four children by her? Stupid! What difference does age make? Or appearance? He's not good-looking. Kind of mousy, actually. Now he's going to kiss the back of my neck," she thought. "God how—" But he didn't.

"Here we are, standing like a couple of idiots!" said Gustaf, laughing.

She leaned back and laughed, too. The tension snapped. They were two friends laughing at the stupidity of life. They laughed and swayed back and forth, out into the wet snow, back into the warmth—then she swung around and turned her face away so that he couldn't kiss her.

"Let's go to bed," she said, walking swiftly away from him.

She undressed in the bathroom, hastily washing between her legs and putting in her diaphragm. She got cream on her fingers and had to wash again, all the time bubbling with laughter. Was he standing out there looking foolish in his underwear?

When she went back in, he had turned out the light, undressed and crawled into bed. She poured out the rest of the wine into two glasses and took them with her over to the bed. He sat up and took one and they both emptied the glasses before she, too, crawled in.

They kissed and hugged for a long time. She felt herself swelling and becoming wet. She tried to take his penis but he turned away, and they went on again. He heaved her over on her side and lay pressed against her behind and back. That felt good. That's what it should be like . . . not just charging ahead. She slid out of his grip, turned over onto her back, spread out her legs and pulled him down over her. Gustaf got to his knees. Was he doing something to himself? She closed her eyes. Then he came over her, pressing himself down. She raised her hips to meet him. But he was totally limp.

He tried several times, pushing and pushing, but nothing would go in. Pressing, wriggling. She tried to reach him and help him, but he held her away. In the end he let her grasp his testicles and she went on for a long time, but it was no use.

"Christ, what a man I am!" he whispered. "My whole being wants to except that tiny bit."

She heaved herself over him and lay flat like a fish on his chest. She was terribly sleepy now, but Gustaf's heart was thumping hard. After about three quarters of an hour, he eased his way out of bed and said he had to go home.

28 Lars Wastesson was the new Director of Luna Pharmaceuticals. He found it remarkably stimulating to change jobs, although he was over sixty. His career had been eventful. At twenty-seven, he had received his M.D., and become a senior lecturer in physiology. Then he had gone over to internal medicine and become a heart specialist, like so many of his generation. At thirty-nine, he had been the youngest professor of internal medicine in the whole of Sweden and had transformed his clinic into one of the most active in the country. But after a few years, he had realized that sound medical development demanded broader foundations. He had gone into politics and run for the People's Party, but the party had suffered one of its many major reverses, and Lars Wastesson had instead become Chairman of the Swedish Medical Society. He was nearly always on leave from the clinic. After a schism, he had resigned from the Society and devoted himself to educational matters. For the previous three years, he had been an investigator in university administration, but he had considered that a dead end; he was not the type of person to be creative in a bureaucratic set-up. So he had accepted the directorship of Luna.

Why Luna? The salary, just over half a million, was not the reason. He was not particularly interested in money. But he had long since had shares in Luna. The Medical Association also had shares in Luna, and it had turned out to be an excellent way of gaining insight. During his period as Chairman of the Medical Society, he had also been on the board of Luna. But Lars Wastesson's interest in Luna was on the ideological level, even his greatest enemies admitting that. To a man who had devoted forty-five years of his life to Swedish health care, it was obvious that the drug industry could not just be left to drift. There were many tendencies within the industry that could be criticized, short-term investment, faulty information, and far too loose a grasp of the future. During the seventies, the Swedish drug industry had lost more and more of the market to the large foreign firms such as Geigy, Roche, Boehringer, Ingelheim, Pfizer, ICI, and all the rest. A number of younger colleagues, with their limited experience, had attacked the drug industry in order to undermine its credibility. In the hopes of nationalization, of course. He could understand them, but did not agree with them. In a society such as ours, with a long tradition of mixed economy—why in God's name should the drug industry be any more efficient and more serious in the hands of the state? The drug industry had happened to become the special target of the Marxists. Whenever it came to throwing bricks, the drug firms were always the first targets. Why? It was immoral to profit from people's illness, they said. But a large number of Swedish people were nowadays connected with the health service, and consequently earned their salaries and wages from the lame and the sick, the ill and the tormented.

Lars Wastesson's ambition was to change things from within, to weed out what was neither serious nor efficient, to improve relations with the medical profession and researchers, to expand international cooperation and give Sweden a cogent pharmaceutical industry that could export and compete with the giant firms. Although he himself was reluctant to make the comparison, a parallel could be drawn with the manufacture of arms. By exporting, products could be tested. By arm wrestling with the best, you could assess your own strength. He knew he had nearly all the big guns among the politicians behind him. There had been some unrest and attempts at coups among the leaders of the Social Democrats, but Olof Palme was no revolutionary romantic. When it really came to the crunch, you could depend on him. The free market and free research had nothing to fear. On the contrary, in time, more capital would come to the drug industries with revenue sharing, whatever it might look like. That was excellent. That employees had some say in things was also excellent. In the debate on nationalization of the drug industry, employees had been almost united in their opposition; no paralyzing bureaucracy for us!

What would happen if all the forces for the good did not support the home industry? Either it would wither away, collapse and cause unemployment, or else the German, Swiss, and American giants would buy their way in and take over the firms.

Lars Wastesson did not usually call himself Director; he still referred to himself as Professor. His vision was of a serious Swedish pharmaceutical industry increasingly taking over medical research and development, both of which were atrophying at the universities owing to lack of money and erratic recruitment into research. With an increasingly rigid university bureaucracy, the industry would be a stimulating refuge for creative people who realized the extent to which the state of health of the nation depended on more effective drugs.

Luna's administration had been reorganized when Lars Wastesson had been appointed, making him a working chairman on the pattern of other Wallenberg concerns. And the Director's function had been doubled so that Wastesson had at his side an Administrative Director responsible for finance and marketing. Wastesson himself was to be concerned first and foremost with development.

Although it was not directly one of his tasks, a number of sensitive staff matters had landed in his lap. He had taken the initiative for this himself. With his long medical experience behind him, there was no reason to retreat from sensitive issues such as transfers, sick pay or pension matters at all levels. He had nothing to do with the unionized employees. Luna's company doctor and welfare officer took care of them.

What was he going to do with this Bernt Svensson? A tragic and unpleasant case, a man who had slaved away for nearly twenty years out in the field, constantly traveling, and who had proved to be excellent over a long period of time. But no longer. From the middle of the seventies onward, he had begun to slide. Too much drinking, not only at work, where unfortunately it did occur, but also during his free time. And now the authorities had taken away his driver's license. That did not look so good. In 1977 and 1978 and during the first half of 1979, Svensson had taken no fewer than 318 days off sick. Wastesson leafed through the medical records from the company doctor's office, noting that the diagnoses were back trouble, bronchitis, back trouble, gastritis, fracture of the wrist, psychological disturbance, and now an abdominal examination. But the true diagnosis was a drinking problem. How far gone an alcoholic was Svensson? No delirium, no epileptic fits as far as could be seen. But he might have gone to another doctor for that. Unfortunately, confidence between public health services and private was such that Luna could not automatically share health records or computerized diagnoses.

Lars Wastesson stretched out his hand to press the green "Come In" button, but then stopped, and instead went and opened the door himself, asking Bernt Svensson to step inside. Svensson put out his cigarette in the waiting room's overflowing ashtray and sullenly went in.

"Well," said Wastesson, after they had sat down, not at the desk, but in two of the group of armchairs. "As you know, we're a little troubled about your health. How are you, by the way?"

"Fine, thank you," said Bernt curtly.

Wastesson smiled broadly and gazed at Bernt for a long time. He had that slightly brown skin that a layman might mistake for suntan. His cheeks were also slightly too round. The man looked quite simply as if he had a hormone disturbance. The skin on the backs of his hands was shiny and taut, his gaze steady but rather hard, a little rigid. Presumably he had taken a drink . . . but like all alcoholics, he had that remarkable ability not to smell of it. How did they manage it, actually?

"The last time we met was in Älvsjö, wasn't it, at the annual conference? I came down to see you when you had those severe abdominal pains."

"I remember."

Bernt Svensson had become acutely ill with violent abdominal pains that had in fact soon passed. Wastesson had wanted to send him to the hospital, but Svensson had obstinately refused and taken a taxi home instead. It might have been an irritation of the pancreas or an ulcer. When Wastesson had felt his abdomen, the liver had been clearly palpable.

"I don't understand why I have been called in," said Bernt Svensson. "And why have you got my medical records here? Isn't it enough that I consult the firm's doctor?"

"You're free to go to whomever you wish. Naturally. It wasn't your health first and foremost I wished to discuss, but what you think about your work. And to be quite honest, there's a connection between the way you do your work and your health."

"It's my back," said Svensson. "I've wrecked my back with all that driving. I've driven over a hundred and ninety thousand kilometers for Luna."

"That's really impressive!"

"But now I've got Greater Stockholm. I can take a taxi when my back cracks up."

"I've seen your traveling expenses, yes. That driver's license business was unfortunate, by the way."

"What business?"

"That they happened to have taken it away."

Svensson did not reply, his gaze rigid. Was it from hatred, or because he had to concentrate his intoxicated brain to follow?

"As you must see, we're a little troubled," said Wastesson, feeling his own features adapting. He really *was* troubled. Both on Luna's and Svensson's behalf.

"I can't think why. I've been off sick a bit, I know. But when I'm at work, I manage as well as anyone else."

"Well, now, is that really in keeping with the facts?"

"What do you mean?"

"If you think carefully, I was thinking about that collapse of yours at the Opera Grill in August."

"In August?"

"Perhaps you don't remember? You had some kind of blackout when you were having dinner with the drugstore people."

"There's nothing whatsoever wrong with my memory! I got sick. I had eaten shellfish, and even in the best places . . . How did you know about that, anyhow? No one else from Luna was there."

"If anything unusual happens, we usually know about it."

"From whom?"

"That doesn't matter. I don't want to be brutal toward you, but naturally you must be as aware as I am that you've been having a bit of a problem with alcohol lately."

"I don't understand what you're talking about."

"Don't you?"

"If someone's been going behind my back saying I was drunk at the Opera Grill, then first of all, that's a lie! But of course I smelt of wine, if that was what it's all about. We had had a couple of bottles of Petit Chablis with the mussels."

"You know, Bernt," said Wastesson. "I've been a doctor for almost forty years. I know what's wrong with you. An experienced clinician as I am doesn't make mistakes of that kind. Why don't you tell the truth? Then we can go on and try to solve the problem."

"Doctor?" said Svensson. "I thought you were Director here now."

"Director *and* doctor."

"So you think you can just go down to the firm's doctor and fish out my records, do you? And then sit here throwing a whole lot of diagnoses in my face? That really is the damned limit. There's something called confidentiality! That applies to company health services too!"

"Naturally. But between doctors there's no confidentiality rule, as you surely know. If the information is available to the patient."

"You could have asked me first! Perhaps *I* don't think it's in the patient's interest if the Director of the company goes rummaging through my health records."

"My dear Bernt, I'm just trying to help you. We could have taken a hard line and more or less given you your walking papers. But I prefer to see this as a kind of rehabilitation task, as a problem of a sociomedical nature. Instead of using reprisals."

"What had you thought of doing then?"

"I want us to come to some mutual agreement on that point. But first and foremost, we must agree on a starting point, and tell the truth about what is wrong with you."

"My back!"

Wastesson sighed. This is what came of trying to help. He should have let the welfare officer deal with this. The welfare officer and the rehabilitation group. But it was too late now. As he had started trying to solve the problem on the basis of trust, he would have to go on.

"I'd thought of suggesting a new job for you, Bernt," he said. "We'd like to make use of you here in head office. We had thought of creating another post in the Literature Department. We need someone who knows his stuff. But there is one but . . . we must agree that you go for treatment for your alcohol problem. Either to our doctor here, or to someone else. And we retain the right to ensure you fulfill your part of the contract and really do go for treatment."

Bernt Svensson did not reply. He stared so intently at Wastesson that the latter had turned his eyes away, no longer sure whether Bernt Svensson could see either him or the room they were in. His gaze was turned inward.

"Think about my suggestion, Bernt. It's a chance. I hope you take it."

"I want to speak to my own personnel staff association. Things shouldn't happen like this."

"Of course, of course. I'd be the last person even to think of stopping you. Talk to your association. Then they can pass the matter on to the rehabilitation group."

"I've no intention of talking to any rehabilitation group! I'm going to ask my association to look into how you can sit here and be both employer and doctor at the same time. I haven't a chance."

"It really is unfortunate that you take it like that."

Bernt Svensson rose and pointed an accusing finger.

"Why do you go on calling yourself Professor? You're no longer a professor. You've resigned your professorship. Now you're a director! Aren't you ashamed about that?"

Lars Wastesson had to admit that in some ways Svensson was right, but the title he used made no difference now. He didn't need a title at all. Lars Wastesson would be enough, both inside and outside Sweden. But if you've been a professor for a long time, the title almost becomes part of your name, as if he had been baptized many years ago as Professor-Lars with Wastesson his surname. Why change it? He could well do without the title himself, but he had a feeling the board would rather he retained it. If he was going to change anything here at Luna, then relations with the board had to be as good as possible.

"Yes, well, Bernt Svensson," said Wastesson wearily. "I think we've rubbed each other the wrong way quite unnecessarily. And in that situation, I suggest you prolong your sick-leave, while I wait for the association and the personnel to act."

Bernt Svensson was on his way out, but then he stopped.

"I'll manage!" he said. "I've no intention of bowing and scraping. If I'm not appreciated here, then I can go somewhere else."

"Where to? Be realistic. For your own sake!"

"I'm thinking of starting up on my own!"

Svensson walked out and slammed the door behind him. Wastesson remained sitting in the low armchair, picking his nose. What a wretched business. The man's aggressiveness he could dismiss as rashness. Some patients couldn't control themselves. But it would be unfortunate for Bernt Svensson if he did not understand what was best for him, if he couldn't grasp that a transfer or a disability pension was a good offer considering the position he found himself in. Found himself? There was a concept called "self-induced illness." But Wastesson didn't like the expression, as it sounded so moralistic. One simply had to be realistic. Bernt Svensson was finished. If he understood that and wished to cooperate, then they could arrange for a soft landing for him. The alternative would be a crash.

Wastesson left his place by the low conference table and went back to the revolving chair behind his desk. He sank into it and kicked out with one foot so that the chair slowly revolved. What Bernt Svensson had blurted out about his title was interesting. According to academic tradition, a man who left his chair had a perfect right to continue calling himself professor. But how did the law stand on that point? He had never felt the need to find out before. What could happen if Svensson were right? Naturally he wasn't, but some pop-lawyer— there were some who were out for the drug industry—might start digging around in the matter. Naturally he and Luna would win such a battle, but the possibility of some bad publicity could not be excluded.

Well, that could easily be arranged. There was something called Adjunct Professor. A deserving researcher within the drug industry could offer to lecture for a few hours a month free of charge at the Karolinska for instance. In return, the Institute arranged for an Adjunct Professorship. As there was no cost to the state, the whole thing was simply a matter of form. There were already several people in other drug firms who had acquired titles as professors in this way. The initiated knew that you could buy academic titles in Sweden. What was so peculiar about that? Nothing at all—both the previous and the present government had expressed their approval of the procedure. In such a small country, research could not afford to appear naively pure at heart in relation to trade. All good forces must work together.

29 It was good to be home again. For the first time in many years, Primus could sleep in the mornings, not waking until half past five when the newspaper boy clattered on the stairs outside. Largely speaking, he followed his old routine, but it was odd how easy it was for some things to get left out. Suddenly he didn't know where he kept the sugar lumps, or what time the morning news started. But he soon had a new routine, which also included his medication. He had tablets for his blood pressure, diuretics, potassium to replace the potassium that vanished with increased urine output, tablets that counteracted bladder pressure at night, tablets to lower the cholesterol in his blood, and vitamin and iron tablets. In addition, he had been given instructions about a new cook book with low sugar and low fat recipes.

He had asked if he should return for a checkup, but that had not been necessary. Dr. Nyström had referred him to the district doctor. Primus had never been to the present district doctor, but under any circumstances, that was where he was to go for blood pressure checks and renewal of his prescriptions, as the outpatients' department of the hospital was unfortunately far too overloaded to cope with that. But Primus was slightly anxious about going to the district doctor, suddenly appearing there with empty medicine bottles. What if the doctor had different views on what treatment he should have?

On the fourth evening, Primus did something that filled him with great pride. He took all his bottles, except the vitamins, emptied them down the toilet and flushed them away. He had to flush several times, watching with fascination pills to the value of several hundred kronor simply disappearing. Why had he done it? It was a quick decision. The idea had arisen and five minutes later, it was done. He wanted nature to take its course. He had a slight twinge of conscience when he thought about Dr. Nyström, a very nice man, but otherwise—no! They were probably excellent tablets but they were intruders. He had seen a number of older people anxiously fidgeting with their dozens of pill bottles, as if the very bottles made the decisions, not themselves. What kind of life was that?

On Sunday, the sun had come out after a frosty night. Primus went down into the basement to see whether his bicycle was there, but it was gone. Had the police taken charge of it, or had they just left it lying? He would have to phone. But when he came up from the basement, he felt he would never even be able to get onto a bicycle, not to mention cycle the two kilometers to his allotment. He was totally exhausted. There was no elevator in the building and it was only with an effort that he managed to mount the three flights of stairs to his apartment.

He had grown thin and his clothes hung loosely on his body, but that was to the good; he'd always been rather on the large side, especially the year after his divorce when he had done all the housekeeping himself—then he'd been downright fat. Perhaps he would have to buy some new trousers? He was not attracted by the thought, as he was afraid they would laugh at him when he went into a clothing store. But perhaps there was some store for workers where they didn't mind if his suit didn't have the right cut. When he went out to the bathroom, his trousers hung like an empty barrel around his waist . . . lucky he had suspenders!

His face had shrunk. He could see that when he shaved. His nose was thinner and there were more brown patches at his temples, patches that had started melting together. He was pale, too, almost yellow, his forehead shining like marzipan that had been out in the sun.

A week after his discharge, his doorbell rang. He looked through the peephole. It was Bernt.

"Come in, Bernt," said Primus, trying to put his hand on Bernt's shoulder, but Bernt evaded him, went in and sat down on the sofa without taking off his coat. Primus remained standing.

"I'll put the coffee on. You've time for that, haven't you?"

"No coffee for me, thanks. My stomach. But if you've got a beer?"

Primus fetched a pilsner and poured it into a glass beer stein. Bernt took a gulp, then pulled a large envelope out of his inside pocket and flung it onto the table.

"You're crazy, Dad! Handing over your whole fortune just like that!"

Primus sat down on the sofa beside Bernt and opened the envelope. Inside it were his bankbooks and some papers from his safe deposit. It looked as if the whole contents of his bank account was in the envelope.

"That was nice of Kitty—"

"You're crazy! She's crazy! No one seems to be goddamned sane these days."

Bernt got up quickly and went over to the color television.

"What did you pay for this?"

"I got it from Mrs. Brundin who used to live downstairs."

Bernt sat down again.

"Do you know anything about Kitty? Do you know who she is at all, Dad?"

"I thought you lived together."

"I don't know about live together. Lived . . . I suppose so, now and again. But that's over now. Do you see? Kitty's nuts! So are you, for that matter."

What had Bernt been up to now then? Clearly he must have had a fight with Kitty.

"If it hadn't been for me, she'd have swiped the whole lot! How stupid can you get? She'd put all your assets into her own safe-deposit box. And hidden the key."

"Then no harm's been done, has there?"

Primus looked in the bankbooks. The money was untouched.

"Do you know how I got them back for you?"

"That's not my business."

"I had to beat her up. She was as drunk as a skunk. But I clouted her until she came around. She promised to fetch the things out of the safe-deposit box. Then she tried running away instead! But I found her. I know where she usually goes when she gets thirsty. Did she want to cough up? Not on your life she didn't! But then I said I'd get the fuzz on to her. Now, Kitty, I'm going to ring the police and tell them what you're up to. Did you know Kitty's done time, Dad?"

"I don't think you should talk like that. You yourself have . . ."

"Done time, yes! Of course. Once. Drag all that up again, go ahead, do. How I destroyed your life. What happened to *mine* you didn't give a damn about. A convicted son. My son has fallen foul of the law. Bloody hell, Dad. Hypocrite is a mild expression!"

"Have you read my note?"

"What damn note?"

"About the funeral."

"What damn funeral?"

Bernt had obviously not read the note. Just as well, as the conversation had now developed, just as well to keep off the matter of his funeral. He looked at Bernt. Anyone could see that he was a hunted man. But how could he get through to his son? How?

"But you've seen that I've left you a little bit," said Primus.

"Seen where?"

"In the bankbooks."

"Nothing would induce me to poke my nose into your affairs. You'll have to see to them yourself. That's best, eh? So that nothing crooked happens, eh?"

"Sometime, Bernt . . . I'd like you to know that I wish you well."

Bernt leapt up from the sofa again and strode out to the refrigerator to fetch another beer. But there was none. He came back again and stood staring down at Primus.

"Your face is all yellow! Look at yourself in the mirror. You're as yellow as a saffron bun."

"I've been in hospital for eleven weeks."

Bernt went out into the hall.

"Next time you'll have to get your old bankbooks back yourself. So hang on to them!"

"Thanks for your help."

"Don't mention it. The whole fortune. 'Bye then."

"Bye. When are you coming . . ."

But Bernt had already slammed the door behind him. Primus sank back onto the sofa. "I'll write to Bernt," he thought. "Then he can read it in peace and quiet. It was clearly too soon for us to be able to talk directly to each other." He ran his hand across his face . . . yellow? He went out to the bathroom. Yes, he *was* yellow, unless it was the light. When he looked really close, he could see that even the whites of his eyes were yellow.

30 Kerstin Löwenberg was an assistant physician at the Årsta western district medical office, which involved a few months practice before her required courses and her medical exams. The idea was that this should be supervised, but that was seldom the case. Assistants were used to fill vacancies. The permanent doctor at Årsta was on leave in order to be able to reduce the line of patients at his flourishing private practice at home in Essinge. So Kerstin Löwenberg was the only doctor in the office.

She had an unusual background. In the fifties, she had been a first-class swimmer and had then trained as a physical education teacher. Only a few weeks after her final exam, she had fallen victim to one of the last polio epidemics in Sweden and had ended up in a respirator. Gradually her paralysis had begun to give way, but now over twenty years later, her legs were still totally paralyzed. During the years of rehabilitation, she had begun to dream about becoming a doctor. In 1969, she had started at the Karolinska Institute and now almost ten years later, she had got as far as an assistant physician. She was forty-six years old. The disease that had afflicted her so badly was nowadays a totally unnecessary disease. With the Salk vaccine, modern medicine had achieved perhaps its greatest triumph. When preventive medicine's fiercest critics, Illich and others, were discharging at full blast, there was always an ace in the hole that could be slammed down on the table—inoculation against polio.

Kerstin Löwenberg used crutches. The examination room had been refurnished so that she always sat in a revolving chair beside the green examining table with a small high desk on her other side.

Primus Svensson was lying on the table with his upper body bare, his fly open and his long underwear around his hips. She put her hand under his knees and lifted them so that he was lying with his knees bent.

"Try to relax," she said, digging her hands into his flabby yellow abdomen.

There was nothing special to feel, no hardening, no protruding edge of the liver, no tenderness that made her patient start.

"Thank you," she said. "You can get dressed out there and then come back in."

He shuffled out. She took his chart and struck its edge against the table. Icterus, that is, jaundice, that much was clear. The liver's bile pigments escaped into the bloodstream and colored the skin and whites of the eyes saffron yellow. But a thousand different things could cause jaundice. A small gallstone could block the exit from the gallbladder, and the bile then made its way out into the blood. But there was nothing to indicate gallstones. It could be a tumor, of course, blocking it, but not one in a position where she could feel it. Then it might be an infection, hepatitis. There were two main types: one infectious in the usual way through water or feces, the other infectious through sores, injections or blood transfusions. As the patient had recently been in the hospital, there was a lot to indicate it was the latter, a very unpleasant form of hepatitis often spread by drug addicts. Many employees in the hospital had caught this type of jaundice, a few of them had died, and quite a number had been off work for as long as a year. She suddenly realized she should have used gloves when she had examined him. But it was too late now.

What else could it be? Alcohol, of course, or some other kind of poisoning. Mushrooms? No, not at the end of November. Some chemical? There were perhaps fifteen thousand artificial chemical combinations in a modern community. Only a few hundred of these had been adequately investigated, the rest being potential poisons and in principle able to cause almost anything; tumors, diseases or disintegration of the liver and nervous system.

She stretched out for a handbook on internal medicine lying under the table, but then stopped. It didn't make any difference. There were no resources for a correct diagnosis here in the district office. Primus Svensson was a case for the hospital.

When he came back and had sat down, she said:

"I don't want to worry you, but as you know, jaundice can be serious. The cause of it must be found. And I can't do that here. You'll have to go to the hospital."

Primus Svensson did not seem surprised.

"In that case, I'd prefer to go back to 96 again."

"Ninety-six? Oh, you mean Ward 96. In the medical ward at Enskede?"

But that couldn't be arranged. Analyses of jaundice were a sensitive field. As soon as there was the slightest suspicion of it being what was called transfusion hepatitis, which was jaundice transmitted via the blood, ordinary hospitals refused to admit the case. The patient was then remitted to a special ward in one of the isolation hospitals, where the staff were specially trained and had greater protection.

"Can I take a taxi to the hospital from here?"

"No, not today. It's not that urgent. I'll send a referral that they'll get tomorrow. Then they'll phone you from the hospital and tell you when you can come."

"To Enskede? But to another ward?"

Kerstin Löwenberg pressed her intercom.

"Nurse? Nurse . . . a jaundice analysis. Could be transfusion. Who takes that? Roslagstull?"

The nurse hesitated before answering. Stockholm was like a great crossword puzzle. Different hospitals and clinics had different areas of jurisdiction. If you lived in Årsta and had a coronary, then you went to Enskede; gallbladder operations belonged there also, but mild psychiatric problems belonged to St. George's, severe ones to Långbro, gynecology to Söder Hospital, pediatric diseases to Huddinge, tuberculosis to Uttran, long-term care to Högdalen and infections . . . ?"

"I think it's Roslagstull," said the nurse over the intercom. "But I'll phone and make sure."

The areas of jurisdiction could be altered at short notice, should a clinic close for vacations, for repairs, or because of staff shortages.

31 Bernt Svensson was sitting in a taxi in a line of vehicles on the Essinge road. They had phoned to say his father had just been admitted to Roslagstull Hospital. It was quarter past five in the afternoon, dark and sleet was falling. All three lanes into the city were jammed and there were several rotating blue lights a few kilometers ahead by the tunnel beneath Marieberg. Something had happened. Bernt had driven this stretch himself several times and there were often jams by the tunnel. Inattentive drivers coming at high speed from the south did not have time to brake.

Bernt did not feel especially irritated. He had realized he had to go to Roslagstull, as they had phoned, but he did not want to see his father. So it was all right sitting there in an immobile taxi. He'd done what he could, but until now he had avoided seeing Primus.

Why didn't they have continuous supervision of traffic on the most overloaded part of the Essinge road? One or two permanent towers on the side or across the road, where police could control and direct the traffic? Traffic along this road was always reckless, the speed limits constantly exceeded and lane switching common. Cars could be traveling at over ninety kilometers with only a short distance between them. But perhaps there was a secret agreement somewhere between the army and the police for instance? Let the Essinge road stay the battlefield it is, otherwise surgeons in the city hospitals would never get the war-surgery training they needed.

Bernt smiled and brushed the thought away. You couldn't make money out of that. But there was another idea that you really could make money out of, and that was trading in used medicines and drugs. That's what he was going to do when the Luna job fell through. The trade could not only be very profitable, but it would also be a good way of giving Luna a kick in the pants as a final thank you.

Every year, about two and half billion kronor worth of drugs were sold in Sweden. How much was really used? Difficult, very difficult to say. But there had begun to be a few investigations into the matter. One from Jämtland maintained that between five and ten percent of packs were never even opened. Many were opened, but the contents remained untouched. An even higher percentage remained half or three-quarters full. Several thousand old people who died each left behind them drugs worth hundreds of kronor. In the Malmö region, 1.2 tons of drugs were destroyed every year. In the whole country, the drugstores destroyed about twenty-six million worth per year. Anyone managing to get at some of those unused thousands of kilos of drugs in some cunning way would be able to make a small fortune.

Most medications lasted for several years, their durability printed on the labels. Bernt was thinking of starting in a small way at first, going around some of the larger old people's homes in Stockholm and getting to know the old people and asking to look in their bathroom cabinets, cupboards, nightstands, shoeboxes under beds or wherever they kept their bottles. There were bound to be many medicines prescribed for complaints that no longer existed. He would offer to take them away—at worst pay for them in—no, not in cash, but with books, perhaps, illustrated Bibles or medical books. When he had collected a decent store of unopened, fairly recently prescribed medications that were in demand, he would offer the lot to the Druggist Company at a cheap rate, half price, say.

There would be problems. There were drug regulations and restrictions, but at the same time there were economy campaigns on the go at the moment. "Recycling" could be referred to. If you got some journalists behind you and a couple of members of parliament—Center Party people?—the authorities would not be able to stop him easily. On the contrary. With cooperation from the Red Cross, Bernt could become the leader of a drug-saving campaign. Local authorities would save several hundred million and everyone would be pleased, except the drug industry. He laughed out loud.

After two ambulances with their sirens wailing had passed in the opposite direction, the line began to move. Thousands of cars started moving jerkily forward in toward town. After another fifty-five minutes, the taxi had managed to crawl past North Station Street, North Toll, Svea Square, Roslagstull, and drive up the hill to the hospital. He asked the taxi to wait and went in to find out in which of the brick pavilions Primus was.

He was in luck and ran straight into the doctor on call. But Primus Svensson had unfortunately not been admitted at all. Some complications had arisen since they had telephoned Bernt. This was how things were. Primus had been referred to Roslagstull for a jaundice analysis, and they had booked him in for the following week. But Primus had been taken ill during the night with stomach pains and vomiting, so had phoned the doctor on call. He had said that Primus should take a taxi straight to Roslagstull, as he was already due in there. At Roslagstull they had at first decided to admit him, but now his symptoms were no longer right. Everything pointed to an acute attack of gallstones instead. And that was a matter for the surgeon. But for surgery, Primus Svensson should go to Enskede Hospital. So they had sent him in an ambulance to the Enskede Emergency Room. That's what had happened.

Bernt went back to the taxi and asked to be taken to the Tennstop restaurant, where a couple of journalists he knew usually hung out. He considered he had done enough for his father that day. The old man wasn't exactly hovering between life and death. So he would start preparations for the recycling of used drugs as soon as possible.

SECOND TREATMENT

1 Sten Ossolovsky was the Director of Enskede Hospital. On some days, he had meetings from morning to evening, meetings with heads of departments, staff organizations, building committees, politicians, the Council for Artistic Decoration, the Finance Department, the patients' ombudsman, representatives from the Health Service Planning Department, the delegation from the Joint Commission for Coordination of Local Authorities, the Health-and-Safety-at-Work Committee, the Energy Conservation Group, or the Fuel-Usage Association.

He was an austere man who rarely lost his temper or showed any emotion. To be top administrator in the Health Service was one of the most exposed positions within the public sector. He was seldom thanked for anything, and more often was blamed, accused, harassed, criticized on radio and television, and clamped between central authorities, local authorities, and decision-making parties. Within the Health Service itself, as were other administrators, he was regarded as a bad joke. The professional staff, especially the doctors, daily made fun of him on their rounds, in lectures, at lunch, or in operating rooms, at clinical meetings, or conferences. He was accused of everything: incompetence, interference, power-seeking, cowardice, bureaucracy, laissez-faire policies, being overpaid, an opportunist, lazy, a workaholic, and totally lacking in understanding of the essential needs of the Health Service. Sten Ossolovsky was said to be a totally insensitive and medically ignorant top bureaucrat who had never seen a sick person in his life.

He took criticism fairly calmly, but he did not exactly turn the other cheek in humble self-criticism. According to him, the expanding health service was in the long run a gigantic fraud, in which billions were spent in the wrong places, while other screaming needs remained without funds. He disliked most doctors, especially the senior men and professors. The doctors had the strongest union in the country. The doctors used their magical power to mislead people and politicians. It was the medical profession that was steering and manipulating the health services toward a greater and greater technocracy with little chance of supervision. How were they able to do that? Because people, politicians included, were frightened of doctors. Rightly or wrongly, doctors were considered to hold life and death in their hands. When it came down to it, the most fearless critics paled at the thought that even they one day would, with certainty, end up in the hands of the doctors.

Before the first meeting of the day, Sten Ossolovsky was trying to answer a letter. The Palace wished to know whether Enskede Hospital's newly-opened maternity unit would undertake Queen Silvia's next delivery. The Karolinska Institute had previously been used and had had its maternity unit re-equipped as a result, but that did not fulfill the demands the police now made for the security of the royal family. From a security point of view, Enskede Hospital was the most suitable of all the hospitals in Stockholm. The surveillance system was advanced; nearly all doors between wards could be locked from a central point. The windows were of reinforced glass, so that confused patients could not try throwing themselves out of them. The hospital itself was situated in an enormous open area, so the traffic to and from it was easily controlled by helicopter.

What did one reply to such a request? Was there any hurry? According to the press, the Queen was more or less constantly expecting a child. But presumably the exact date of a possible birth was a state secret. He would not be told that. The only person in the hospital who would be told that in good time was the Professor of Obstetrics and Gynecology. Sten Ossolovsky scribbled "Speak to chief Ob-gyn man" onto a telephone message pad and fastened the note with a paper clip to the Palace's formal missive.

The first meeting of the day was about the hospital's Emergency Room. Overloading had now reached catastrophic proportions, the staff were threatening mass-resignation, and the mass media were threatening exposure. Several studies had already been made. At present, one was being carried out by Ants Kurck, a Professor of Education, on the orders of the hospital board. The Institute of Education was not behind the project, but Kurck's private consultancy firm, Pedinvest Ltd., was involved, which was quite usual when an investigation was required in educational, psychological or sociological areas. Academic consultancy firms were expanding as never before, ever since the introduction of the new work-environment laws.

The first man to arrive was Levi Jonsson, Head of the Work Safety Department. Then came Kurck and his assistant, Hannes Gordon. Rolls and thermoses of coffee were ready on the round table. They all sat down and Ossolovsky poured the coffee. By the time they were having second cups, the committee's fifth member, Frank Nylander, Professor of Surgery and responsible for the Emergency Room, arrived. Nylander was wearing white sailing plimsolls, white cotton trousers with knife-edged creases, a short white jacket and a white shirt, his gold doctor's ring and his wedding ring suspended on a gold chain around his neck. His face was tanned, his eyes very bright, and his hair gray and stubbly. On the collar of his white jacket was a coin-sized patch of dried blood. Sten Ossolovsky wondered whether it had been deliberately put there, a *Légion d'honneur* in blood.

"I repeat what I've said a hundred times before," said Nylander. "I want a special Senior Surgeon for Emergency. An independent Senior Surgeon responsible for the surgical cases."

"As you know, the board has to agree to such a maneuver," Ossolovsky replied benignly. "But today, I thought we'd find out a little of how Kurck's and Gordon's task is progressing."

Clearly Gordon was to speak, because he picked up some yellow papers. Sten Ossolovsky suspected that Kurck was perhaps not quite up on all the details. Gordon scratched his untidy black beard and started.

"We should perhaps emphasize that this is a pilot study to give us some idea how one carried out a real study along the lines we have suggested. In addition, we wish to emphasize that this study is scientific in the sense that we will not be proposing any direct concrete measures. We will try to respond to certain proposed hypotheses."

"I hope that's quite clear," said Kurck. "Measures are not our business."

"Naturally not," said Ossolovsky, glancing at Levi Jonsson. Ossolovsky was quite convinced that any possible results of this investigation would be used in quite a different way from whatever the educationalists had intended. The results would be the weapon used in negotiations. On the basis of the results, both the Head of Work Protection and the Professor of Surgery would produce demands for new appointments. Naturally. Otherwise they would be idiots, would they not? In the power game, those were the big guns. Appointments, Appropriations, and Premises, often known as AAP.

Hannes Gordon produced a number of preliminary results: slightly more than eight hundred patients had been interviewed and the dropout rate was small. Fifty-five percent had come directly to Emergency without first seeking help elsewhere. They had since reckoned in Emergency that two thirds of these could have been treated at a lower medical level. Forty-five percent had made from one to seven attempts to contact the district doctor, the district nurse, the doctor on call, or private practitioners, including company medical officers. Of those who had used the telephone for this, almost half had been told to go directly to Emergency. In retrospect, this information was judged exact in about fifteen percent of the cases.

"What does this cost per day?" said Nylander.

"Sorry?" said Kurck.

"I was just wondering what you charge per day to sit down in Emergency asking people questions?"

"I don't know whether the financial arrangements are public . . ." said Kurck, turning to Ossolovsky.

"Certainly," said Sten Ossolovsky. "The interviews cost twelve hundred kronor per person per six hour stint, including insurance benefits. On top of that come the costs of setting up, administering, and evaluating the project. All in all, the pilot study will cost sixty-three thousand."

"And if there is going to be a larger study, a 'real' one, as the gentlemen here call it?" said Nylander.

"We don't know yet," said Ossolovsky. "That will come up later."

Nylander was on the warpath now, as always when it came to money. Only a month earlier, he had made an attempt to get rid of the people who ran the computers in the surgical unit. He wanted the money for health care instead. Nylander was a very unbureaucratic person when it came to money. On one occasion, he had hired a surgical nurse at his own expense, and on another he had bought two horses for a course project. The horses were to be used for serum production.

Hannes Gordon continued with his figures. Professor Nylander cleaned his nails with a paper clip and Levi Jonsson industriously took notes without saying a word. The safety at work protection representative was the most powerful person in the room, the one who had the most influence, and was most motivated by the power game. He was the only person in the room Ossolovsky felt to be an equivalent opponent. Nylander could of course be troublesome locally but in the upper reaches, he was nothing. Hannes Gordon was a hibernating Marxist, and Ossolovsky had very little confidence in Kurck. Kurck was no true professor. He had worked his way up in the U.S.A. and then got a professorship in Åbo in Finland. In Sweden, he had somewhat tenuous ties with the academic world, his main interest being in Pedinvest Ltd., and the column on sex matters he ran in the country's most popular evening paper.

"Let's go down and look at the reality!" said Frank Nylander, slapping his hands down on the arms of his chair.

The two educationalists looked astounded, but neither Jonsson nor Ossolovsky reacted. They had seen all this before.

"Why not?" thought Ossolovsky. The meeting was nothing but mock fencing, a maneuver in face of the new agreements. They wouldn't learn anything they didn't already know perfectly well. It might be troublesome if the educationalists demanded information on the continuation of the study. Kurck had given an estimated budget of 830,000 kronor, plus a percentage for inflation. But there would never be any further study. That had been an unspoken agreement between board and staff organizations from the start. A small study, *yes*. A large and expensive one, *no*. No one wanted results that would eventually work against certain other aims. But the educationalists were still blissfully unaware of this.

"Why not?" said Ossolovsky, getting up. "I'd very much like to make a little educational visit under the direction of the Head of Emergency."

Levi Jonsson did not move a muscle, but glanced at his watch, and Nylander showed great enthusiasm, virtually shooing the others out into the elevator. Kurck hesitated most. He had never been to Emergency, only seen plans of it.

Although it was still early in the morning, there was a great deal of activity in Emergency. The first busload had just come in. A Finnish gypsy family of about twenty people, half of them children, had been sitting in the waiting room half the night. Two ambulances arrived with the victims of a collision between a commuter train and a switch engine. In the Observation Ward, the section of Emergency with a small number of beds for patients under Observation, sorting out was under way. All those admitted during the night either had to be discharged or placed in another ward. Nylander took the other men with him as if on an ordinary doctor's round. He didn't talk about organization or work conditions in Emergency, but instead asked patients and staff questions about symptoms and case histories.

In one of the smallest rooms in the Observation Ward was an old man with jaundice. Crowded into the room were two doctors, the surgeon as well as the physician on call, eight medical students, two nurses, an orderly and two janitors.

"What's this now?" said Nylander, stepping in with all his troupe except Levi Jonsson, who had escaped to another meeting.

"Well, there's a slight division of opinion here," said the surgeon on call. "This patient has been in Medical recently, in 96. I reckon you can have him back," he went on, turning to the physician on call.

"But he has quite different symptoms now. He was with us for an M.I. Now he seems to have a blockage in the bile duct, according to the doctor on call at Roslagstull."

"An obvious case for analysis," said the surgeon. "We don't know what kind of jaundice it is."

Professor Nylander thrust some of the others aside and began to feel the patient's abdomen. The patient started and groaned.

"He's tender in the epigastrium," said Nylander. "With subtle guarding."

Nylander pushed his way out of the room and started washing his hands in the anteroom basin.

"I'll have him in with me in my ward, although we're already doubly overcrowded. The welfare of the patient comes first in Surgical."

Sten Ossolovsky smiled inwardly. That was the tale today. On another day not a single damned soul, half dead or no, would be allowed in.

2 The teaching situation at Enskede Hospital was a trifle confused. In several university hospitals, they had started combining courses in internal medicine and surgery into a two term block, within which both subjects overlapped. They had intended to do the same at Enskede Hospital, or EH as it was called in everyday language. But the surgical unit at EH had been delayed, first because of a holdup in building caused by lack of funds, and then because of Nylander's special demands for operating rooms. A couple of extra scrub areas had had to be built to reduce the risk of what was called perioperative infections. So the Course Directors had not been able to integrate medical and surgical courses until the beginning of December.

Martina Bosson and her group had been in anesthesiology for two weeks before their real surgical duties had begun. Anesthesiology had of course been important and exciting in many ways, but it was real surgery they were all longing for. Now at last they were to be allowed to operate. The teaching consisted of the usual lectures and demonstrations and then ward duties. They had been allocated Ward 12. On Tuesdays and Thursdays, they admitted or discharged patients. Mondays, Wednesdays and Fridays were operation days. Then the students had to assist with those patients whose charts they had written up. The concept "assist" could be slightly misleading. Students often had to stand holding a forceps with no chance of seeing what was happening in the actual operation area. Sometimes they had to be content with the seats above, from where they viewed the operation through small windows, looking down into the room. There was also complex color television equipment for closeups, but that was never used.

Before Martina had come to Surgery, she had been somewhat suspicious. Surgery had a reputation of being a heroic specialist subject in which hard men in white and green constantly struggled against death with scalpels in their hands. Naturally, that was a cliché, like so much else in medicine, but it was a valid cliché in the sense that it was the only image the students had. She also knew that a great many students dreamed of becoming another Herbert Olivekrona or Clarence Crafoord, or rather, world famous brain or heart surgeons. But surgery was similar to other clinical subjects; in reality it was no cowboy activity. It involved complicated events which the staff dealt with to the best of their ability. But as so many of the factors involved were unknown or uncertain, the work was only partially under control. It was also difficult to evaluate contributions. Serious complications seldom arose, minor complications often did, and then a number of patients would be just as fit, or even better off if they were not operated on at all.

Despite her skepticism, Martina enjoyed it enormously. There was an atmosphere of activity and vitality in Surgery. In Medicine, it was often slow and slightly tedious with all those endless analyses. The patients in surgery were also on an average younger. Many of them were there because of injuries they had received in road accidents or at work. But injuries received in free time activities seemed to be more common than accidents at work. One man had had his car fall on him while he was changing a tire, another had fallen off the roof of his summer cabin, a third had run over his feet with a power mower. Among the women, there was one with deep burns from a camping stove exploding in a tent, another had had half her scalp torn off when her hair had caught in an electric mixer, and a third had slipped and stuck a steel knitting needle into her spleen.

Despite the many injuries, most of the patients were there for other reasons: gallstones, stomach ulcers, intestinal tumors, or obstruction of the blood vessels in the abdomen. Among the latter were many alcoholics with cirrhosis of the liver and consequent rupture of the veins in the esophagus. Every large surgical unit had its specialty. At Huddinge they transplanted kidneys and at the Karolinska they operated on the heart. Enskede's Professor Nylander was a specialist in major abdominal operations.

His assistant in Ward 12 was Magnus Mattson, who was really an ear man, but he was now doing his general training—to be an ear specialist you had to do a stint in Surgery. Before he had started on ears, he had been a histologist. Twenty-seven years old, he had gained his doctorate with a thesis on the structure of the inner ear in guinea pigs reared in a special noise case. He had continued his research at the ear clinic and invented a semipermeable earmuff. Tens of thousands of workers in industry needed protective muffs against excessive noise. One problem was that useful sounds like conversations, loudspeaker messages and warning signals were also excluded. Magnus Mattson's muffs could exclude certain sound frequencies and let through others. The invention was not yet quite complete. Magnus Mattson was in a hurry to finish his training. He wanted to be an ear specialist before he gave up his hospital career and became head of medical research for Sonab, a well paid free post, with generous expenses for international trips and royalties on every pair of muffs.

Martina liked Magnus Mattson, oddly enough, for they had very little in common. She was a socialist and critical of much in medicine. She wanted either to be a psychiatrist or to work in public health. Mattson was not interested in politics, which meant he was conservative, and had a naive but immovable faith in the blessings of technology; and he could see no conflict whatsoever in earning a fortune from a medical discovery. But in the everyday work of the ward, he was honest, open, optimistic and amusing. He was a "whole" person. Martina was pleased every time she met a "whole person." Most people were broken, destroyed, neurotic, closed, afraid, false or introverted, when you got really close to them—when they could no longer keep up a façade, a role, or a sheet of glass in front of their faces.

But she was not uncritical. She knew more or less how it happened. When students were faced with clinical realities after almost three years of theoretical studies, they started frenziedly looking for models on which to base themselves. They learned the medical profession by imitating the doctors. They imitated their way of speaking, way of holding a stethoscope, wearing white coats, speaking on the telephone, treating patients, and addressing the rest of the staff. That these models might have totally different views on life and politics than they themselves had did not matter much. It was the professional role itself they imitated. That had been the worst thing at first, during their general year, but on each new course, they started the imitating process all over again, endeavoring to learn the right behavior as quickly as possible, making the right sounds and the right gestures. They had mastered the art of frowning heavily like the internists, so now they had to learn to be like surgeons. Martina had once said to members of her group that studying medicine was like being in a drama school as much as a school of knowledge, but they had thought she was joking.

Martina tagged behind Magnus Mattson wherever he went and whatever he did, on rounds, eating cake, at x-ray, scrubbing up for the prescribed time before an operation, putting in stitches, on duty in Intensive Care, straightening fractures, prescribing, or having a smoke and bragging about his semipermeable muffs that were going to save the Swedish export industry. She even started smoking again although she had stuck it out for two years now. The fact that only a few weeks ago she had had another model, Gustaf Nyström in 96, she had now forgotten. Gustaf was no longer her model. He was her lover.

3 There was a line in the pre-op room outside the operating rooms. Nilla, the scrub nurse, was in charge of the corridor and pre-op that morning. Patients not yet anesthetized waited there. They were called down in turns from the different wards. It was a job that demanded organization. Nilla had to keep track of how the work was progressing in the different rooms, which doctors were operating and in which order. Sometimes there were sudden changes in the order or a patient was struck off the operation list. Emergency cases also sometimes came from the ER. If there were a complicated traffic accident, the whole program might collapse and already semi-anesthetized patients had to be revived and sent back to their rooms.

There was stagnation at the moment because Room B was "dirty" from an infectious patient having been there the previous night. So the whole room had to be cleaned. The night staff had not had time to do it, so the day staff had had to set about scrubbing. But no one had told Nilla in time, so now she had pre-op full of beds containing half-drugged patients.

Nilla hated "the corridor," for it was not only a stress area, but also involved a problem of authority. In the old days, they had had only qualified nurses assisting the surgeons. But a new training had been created owing to the shortage of nurses, and produced what were called scrub nurses. These assistants had a more restricted training than a nurse's and in the ORs carried out the work equally well, even better, some people maintained. But they were not registered nurses. In some hospitals, relations between OR nurses and assistants were poor, for it was never quite clear whether assistants had any authority over nurses. Although Nilla was one of the most senior there, she had not been allowed to take over the position of acting head during the head's maternity leave without a prolonged fuss.

Nilla thought neither the orderlies nor the cleaners obeyed her as willingly as they did the nurses, and that was strange. Nilla had always thought herself to be a secure person with natural authority. Now it seemed as if her security had drained out of her and she had become touchy and uncertain. Were they talking behind her back? Whispering that Nilla was incompetent and had only an assistant's training?

One of the patients would have to be sent back up, but which one? She went in to ask the advice of the anesthesiology staff, but they were busy or had vanished into Intensive Care. The operating surgeon was really the person who decided which patients should be postponed if necessary, but the surgeons hadn't come yet. Well, someone had seen the gynecologist—no, he'd rushed off down to the labor ward. Nilla went out again.

In pre-op, the orderlies were shaving the patients. A conscientious objector and an ambulance driver getting further training were standing on each side of a bed trying to hold an old woman down; the woman was panic-stricken and confused, and she wanted to go home. The outpatients were also coming in. There would be hardly any room between the beds soon.

Nilla looked in on all the patients who had already had some premedication. Thirty minutes before at the earliest, the patients were to be put onto the various operating tables and wheeled in to be taken over by the anesthesiologists. She had to keep track of how the patients were to be placed. If anyone were placed wrongly on the actual operating table, she might have to start all over again from the beginning. One particular thing she was scared stiff of was that the OR staff would mistake right for left. That had never happened yet at EH, but it had happened at other hospitals that patients had had their right foot amputated instead of the left. The risk was always greatest if the patient lay in an awkward position, sideways or face down. At first Nilla had written with a marker pen R or L on the calf of some patients, although that was really the surgeon's job.

She also had to check whether all the necessary tests had been done before the patients were wheeled in. That was really a ward job, but according to the regulations, whoever was in charge of the corridor should also double check. She started leafing through the papers of the already pre-medicated patients. A "yellow jaundice," Primus Svensson, was in the first rank. Everything seemed in order, no diabetes or anything else that might cause trouble?

"How are you feeling?" she said. "Things'll calm down a little once you're in the room."

"My mouth's so dry. Could I have a glass of water?"

"I'm sorry, no. You mustn't drink anything now," said Nilla, shivers running down her spine. From his chart, it appeared that this man had just had a coronary, but neither the surgeons nor the anesthesiologists seemed to have noticed. A medical consultation and another EKG should have been carried out.

"Haven't you been to EKG recently?" Nilla said.

"What?"

No, she shouldn't rely on information from patients. She'd better phone the ward. She went out to the office and phoned Ward 12, but both telephones were busy. Did she dare send the patient straight back? That would solve one problem and lessen the pressure on preop. Who was operating? Number 12 was the professor's ward, but he hadn't come. She went in to the preparation room for some help.

In the preparation room, one of the anesthesiologists was just administering a spinal anesthetic. Nilla approached cautiously and had to wait a few minutes until the critical moment was over. Then she held out the papers.

"Would you mind helping me with something," she said. "I've got an elderly man out there with yellow jaundice. But he had a coronary sometime in September. There hasn't been a new EKG."

The anesthesiologist yawned and took the papers.

"Is this one of old Nye's patients?"

Old Nye was Professor Frank Nylander.

"He's in 12. But they haven't put on the list whether it's the Professor or Mattson operating."

"But I'm the one administering the anesthetic. I'll come out and have a look in a moment. Old Nye doesn't like having his list messed up."

Nilla went out. Most of the anesthesiologists were nice if they weren't too harassed. It was crazy there wasn't a doctor, neither an anesthesiologist nor a surgeon, in charge of the corridor. Anything could happen there. Patients could pass out from shock—not to mention nursing students or other strays. Nilla had heard from people doing military service that when they were operating, the army worked on quite different principles. They placed their most experienced doctors at the entrance to sort out and judge which patients should go where.

She put Primus Svensson's chart back on his bed and said:

"The anesthesiologist's coming soon."

He propped himself up weakly on his elbows and gasped:

"First they said it was gallstones, but then they said it wasn't gallstones, and I could go home. But then yesterday they said they would have to open me up to look. What do you think, Nurse?"

It wasn't uncommon that patients in pre-op asked why they were being operated on. Hadn't they been properly informed? Yes, they had, she reckoned, most of them. But some patients seemed to find it hard to grasp what they'd been told, as if they screened themselves off. They couldn't "assimilate," as the doctors sometimes said, couldn't take it in.

If she had been able to, Nilla would have referred him to Nylander or Mattson. They were the people who had decided to operate, but neither of them would see the patient until he was already anesthetized. There was no one else to refer to. Ducking the issue, she said:

"The anesthesiologist will be here soon. Lie down, now."

At that moment the telephone in the office rang and she hurried in to answer it. On top of everything else, she was responsible for all incoming telephone calls.

4 Ralph Parret was the name of the anesthesiologist who anesthetized Primus Svensson. He was not especially worried about the absent EKG. A coronary could never be forecast. It was probably better for the patient if he had an M.I. with ventricle fibrillations or total arrest down here in the OR, where it would be spotted within seconds. Up in the ward, people could lie there dying of an infarction without anyone noticing.

"We're off now, Primus," said Parret, pressing the plunger of the hypodermic syringe of barbiturate.

It worked beautifully, Parret following its course by watching the pupils and flicking the patient's eyelashes with his forefinger. Swiftly and quietly, Primus went under. Parret intubated him, which entailed placing a rubber tube into his throat to ease his breathing; the tube was attached to the respirator. Primus was given curare and so was unable to breathe himself, the apparatus taking over. While Parret rigged up the cloth screen between himself and the lower half of the patient, a nurse and an orderly started washing his abdomen. During the actual operation there was a sharp line drawn between the surgeon and the anesthesiologist, the borderline marked with a cloth screen across the patient's throat. South of the border, the surgeons reigned.

He switched on the oxygen supply and checked the patient's blood pressure. He could follow the beat of his heart on a small oscilloscope. He yawned and waited. He had had a couple of extra calls that night and had not slept for more than two hours. Slept? He had lain there twisting and turning, dozing. On some nights, he took a Librium to enable him to relax, but that was a dangerous habit. One shouldn't start taking tranquilizers regularly when on duty. Not only was it difficult to wake up, but some pills also relaxed one's muscles. They had had two caesareans, one after another, that night. One could not stand fumbling around then. He knew that many of his colleagues were exhausted by continuous duties, but they seldom mentioned it. Least of all did they mention having cheated a bit with tranquilizers.

Ha, now the time had come! Frank "Nye" Nylander came in with his hands held out and raised as if in prayer, in his wake Mattson and two students, all with their hands raised in prayer. Old Nye leaned over into the domains of anesthesia and said:

"And is my patient resting safely in the arms of Morphia?"

Parret made a gesture of victory by forming a circle with his fore-finger and thumb.

"Contact," he said, in his homemade aviator language.

The nurse helped the doctors and students on with their coats. Nylander had his glasses put on his nose and asked for a mirror to check that they were all right. Everyone there had been glad that Nylander had at last got himself some bifocals. Earlier on in the autumn, he had obstinately gone on wearing two pairs of glasses during operations, but then one morning he had leaned over too quickly and the top pair had fallen straight into the patient's open abdomen.

The operating team gathered around, Nylander on one side, Mattson opposite him, a student on each side, then the surgical nurse with an orderly diagonally behind. They looked like beekeepers in their paper hats and white veils. Their costumes were often changed. A few years earlier, OR staff had all looked like priests and bishops. Then they had looked like executioners when close fitting caps with ear-flaps had been the rage. When hospital cross-infections were common, they had looked like astronauts heading for the moon. But this autumn the Central Purchasing Agency had launched the beekeeper fashion.

Nylander was given the scalpel and said without looking at the patient:

"He's tense!"

Parret got off his circular stainless steel chair and looking over into surgeon's country, said:

"No."

Nylander let the end of the scalpel bounce against the patient's abdomen.

"The patient's tense!"

"Everything under control here," said Parret, sitting down again.

There was constant bickering between surgeons and the anesthesiologist: the former constantly considered the patient's state too near to the surface, too badly anesthetized and their muscles tense, while the anesthetists considered the opposite, that the patient was perhaps too deeply anesthetized.

Nylander made no more fuss, but started the incision. Parret half-rose to his feet again. It was a pleasure to watch Nylander working. There was something sensual about his way of dealing with organs and instruments, as if he were sculpting or baking bread. Nylander was probably the most skillful surgeon Parret had ever seen in action. A great many of the others were also good, but some were always working against the clock to create new records. Others were crazy about making as small incisions as possible so they could hardly see what they were doing inside the body. Others made far too large openings to have a panoramic view of things. But if Parret himself were ever to find himself on the table, only one person would be allowed to operate and that would be Nylander.

Parret had taken a course in surgery under Nylander, at a time when Nylander had been only a senior lecturer. He had become a professor late in life because he had not been pushing enough within the scientific world. His thesis had been very poor, some people maintaining that he hadn't even written it himself. But Nylander had had powerful defenders. He was the last of the old Stockholm gang, a junior under Johnny Hellström, assistant to Jack Adams-Ray and in joint harness with the legendary "Torsan" Thorsen.

Nylander was a fantastic doctor. He seldom used patients when he was demonstrating indications for surgery, instead acting all the parts himself, limping around the lecture hall with an appendicitis, writhing and vomiting with gallstones or bellowing with a kidney stone. But of course he was slightly crazy. In his younger days he had been a great singer of student songs and a drinker. He had once been editor of the medical student rag, *Guts*, renowned for its low humor. He had also been Junior Épée Champion, but with increasing age and increased income he had become passionately fond of sailing. He owned two sea-going yachts. One was moored at Dalar Island, the second at Cap Formentor in Mallorca and used for winter sailing. It was part of all his residents' duties to take turns as crew, but most of them did that with pleasure. Nylander was a gregarious man and anyone who had crewed for him always had the most incredible stories to tell. Nylander sailed as he operated, by intuition. He had little use for nautical charts or x-rays.

"Now let's see, as the blind man said," said Nylander, putting his hand into the incision and feeling around inside the abdomen. "The liver is glossy and as good as a child's. Fancy having a liver like that at the age of seventy-six. He's refused a good many drinks, that he has. And here are the stones in their little bag. We'll soon relieve him of those. What's his name now?"

"Primus Svensson," said Parret, glancing down at the chart.

"Is he the eldest child?"

"Don't know," said Parret. Such details were seldom in surgical charts.

"He's got a younger brother," said one of the students.

"Then his brother's probably called Secundus, I imagine," Nylander went on. "What the hell have we here?"

Nylander had to extend the incision slightly to reach.

"Damned if there isn't a metastasis sitting here right under the gallbladder! Yes, indeed, just look at this now, here's the little blighter . . ."

Mattson and the students were also allowed to feel and look. Parret looked again at the chart. After all that, it had been a tumor blocking the gallbladder, but had perhaps temporarily tumefied again. A liver metastasis meant that the patient was inoperable, so he was very surprised when Nylander said,

"We'll scrape the blighter away when we take the gallbladder."

"Is there any point in that?" said Mattson.

"We'll have a try. I remember when we operated on Kalle's old mother. The old girl had a huge metastasis in the liver. But we took it out as it was Kalle's very own mom. And would you believe it, the old girl lived for five years!"

"Shouldn't we get the pathologists to take a quick look first?" said Mattson.

There was the possibility of taking a portion of the metastasis, freezing the portion and trying to find out what kind of cells were inside it. If you were lucky, you could localize the actual primary tumor, the one that had sent out the metastasis.

"No," said Nylander, who once again had his hand right inside the incision. "I've found it. It's in the corpus pancreatic. And it'll have to stay there."

So Primus Svensson had pancreatic cancer, a tumor in the pancreas. That was almost impossible to operate on. All you could do was a palliative resection, a temporary operation to relieve the symptoms.

"We'll take out the gallbladder and dig out the metastasis. Perhaps that's what's obstructing, but I can't feel any round duct. Blood, please."

Primus Svensson had already received half a unit of blood, but now there might be severe bleeding, if they cut into the soft, blood-filled liver. Parret fixed up another unit. The operation continued calmly and safely. Nylander was not one to be hurried or irritated because an operation had taken a different turn from what he had first thought. He liked that, just as he liked bad weather at sea. He didn't like fair-weather sailing in any area of life. On a younger patient, Nylander might have decided to make a larger clearing in the abdomen. But in contrast to a number of his senior lecturers, Nylander was discriminating. He did not wish to play the hero at the expense of an old man.

Half an hour later, the actual operation was over. The surgeons inserted a draining tube and began stitching the patient up. Nylander himself stitched all the way out, a job otherwise usually handed over to an assistant. But Nylander never handed anything over. From one point of view, that was a failing, because his subordinates received less practice in that way. Neither did other professors usually bother with such trivial things as possible gallstones. But for Nylander, no operation was too insignificant.

When for all practical purposes everything was finished, Nylander drew back, pulled off his gloves, and came around to Parret. Nylander solemnly shook his hand like a conductor thanking the leader of the orchestra.

Parret began to bring the patient around from the anesthetic, following the progress by watching his pupils. He shut off the respirator and went over to manual artificial respiration, pressing the black rubber football-shaped bladder, pumping a few times, then waiting and letting the bladder fill. Then the bladder began trembling with the patient's own first hesitant breathing. Spontaneous breathing had started. The rest went according to routine. Parret loosened the clamp below the trachea tube's little red rubber bladder and cautiously drew out the tube, replacing it with an ordinary tube of hard plastic so that the tongue would not block the windpipe. Primus Svensson could now be handed over to the Recovery Room.

Ralph Parret went off into Operating Room E to see how things were going for one of the nurse anesthetists administering anesthetics there. But it was unnaturally quiet in Operating Room E, as if suddenly muffs had been put over his ears. He saw the staff tiptoeing around as if they were on the other side of a glass wall. No respirator was sighing. The patient was naked, only the head covered. A team of doctors from the neighboring Huddinge Hospital was in the process of excising the kidneys from a corpse, a young man whose brain had been destroyed. They had to excise the kidneys as quickly as possible, rinse them clean and then freeze them. They specialized in transplantations at Huddinge and had a patrol that could turn out at any time of the day or night and take the kidneys of young people who succumbed in traffic accidents or died in some other sudden way.

They also had a special immunological department at Huddinge, which helped minimize the possibility of transplanted organs being rejected. There was nothing like that at EH. Although EH was a more recent hospital, there was a distinct risk it would fall behind. None of the fashionable items was invested in there, neither immunology nor tomography.

5 One moment the room was very light and it was possible to imagine that you were in a dairy with freshly whitewashed walls, the sun shining through the open door. The intense light was reflected in milk bottles of polished metal and in the panes of glass, reflections from the sun flickering on the ceiling and the smooth walls. The sounds were as brittle as tinfoil.

On other occasions the room was blacked out. Primus felt he was floating on his back just under the surface of the water in a vast pool. Here and there in the pool were gigantic milk bottles cooling, as large as silos. He tried holding his breath, his lungs almost bursting; then he could stand it no longer and he drew in a deep breath of the cold green water. It rushed down his throat and out into his body, which was as empty as a vaulted cave or the stomach of a huge whale. He himself was the prophet Jonah thrashing both arms and legs to reach the last remaining air bubble under the top of the vault. A kitten in a sack.

He was drifting farther and farther away from the edge of the pool and slowly sinking to the bottom. The pool hadn't been cleaned for a long time. The bottom was covered with rubbish, half-rotted paper, slashed rubber tubes, old fuses and bottle tops. Black grass was growing in tufts. He kept getting entangled, one blade after another swirling around his body, across his forehead, his eyelids, his nose, his windpipe and midriff. Then they began hauling him up. A thousand

Lilliputians were swimming around his body, fastening ropes and windlasses. He saw the rusty brown bottoms of small tugs hauling him toward the edge of the pool. They couldn't stop him in time and he hit the long side of the pool with a bang against the concrete. He was waterlogged now, the tip of his nose and his eyes on the water line, little dwarfs crowding around, trying to cling to his body and constantly diving off from the edge of the pool. He could feel he was being lifted, great portions of his body now above water level, his feet, his knees, his thighs, his stomach, his chest and mouth. His ears were still below the green surface.

The Lilliputians were building a drill tower on his stomach. Laboriously they hauled and pried logs from the quay, the largest the size of pencils. The tower was a framework, narrowing toward the top like an anti-aircraft tower. Inside the tower was a thick drill of steel, driven by a small toy steam engine that they also placed on his stomach. The Lilliputians started digging a hole right into the center of his stomach, then they sank the drill into it and started. The little steam engine jumped and vibrated, the drill very slowly spinning farther and farther down into his bowels, light-colored blood spurting out like gushing oil straight up through the tower. Deeper and deeper they drilled, through his stomach, into his intestines, and when they reached his spine, the drill burnt to a standstill in the slivers of bone. He screamed.

"There we are, Primus," said an endlessly soft voice. "Time for your shot now. Just try to relax."

He looked up. The end of the bed glittered, the window, the steel frame with the flask, the taps on the basin, all as sharp as knives. The nurse straightened up and put the empty plastic syringe into the bowl. She took his hand in hers.

"You'll soon be able to sleep again, Primus."

Soon be able to sleep again, Primus, soon be able to sleep again, Primus. It wasn't cold any more. It tingled and prickled in a million spots all over his skin, endlessly good. He sank into a dry friendly warmth, the Lilliputians gone. His stomach was whole again. He felt large and powerful, a fat zeppelin slowly drifting up into the sky.

6 Bernt got up out of the visitor's chair, after sitting there for almost twenty minutes, gazing at his sleeping father. It was horrible looking at someone who had once been strong and was now so small and helpless. Bernt left the room.

There was a smell of candles, coffee, ginger cookies, and mulled wine in the corridor. The office was empty. A small gnome made of red wool was fastened to the glass door with adhesive tape. Someone had put a crumpled angel's cap on top of the desk lamp. It was the morning of St. Lucia's Day. Bernt went on into the coffee room, where the table was cluttered with cups, cake dishes, paper mugs, and a whole lot of red wooden candlesticks in the shape of half eggshells, each one with small round wooden feet. All the candles had been blown out, and there was a stink of candle wax. At one end of the table sat a pimply youth, his feet in their enormous white clogs draped over the back of the next chair and a comic in his lap.

"I'm looking for Dr. Mattson," said Bernt. "We were to meet at half past ten."

"They're probably on rounds. Ask at the office."

They had been making candles in the washroom and the candles were hanging upside down, the wicks tied to a broom handle.

Bernt retreated and went on. *Doctors' Offices*, it said on another door. After the words Doctors' Offices was a small blue triangle and the words *Scalpel Street, Level 4, Room 1099*. There were similar signs on every door in the corridor. Bernt opened the door and went in. As he had expected, the room was empty. It was a small room, the window looking out onto an airshaft about seven by seven meters. Inside the shaft, the top of which was invisible although he put his nose right against the glass, hung several full size rag-doll figures clinging to thick ropes. It all looked like a gigantic model of a gymnasium. "Artwork" to enhance the dreary view.

There were three desks in the room, two back to back, the third crosswise against the other two, each one equipped with identical objects; a green desk pad, a small table lamp with an articulated stem, a pen tray in black bakelite filled with paperclips, and a flat recorder with a hand microphone. On the recorder lay a heap of dusty dark brown records. The other thing that differentiated the desks were the advertising objects. On one was a stand-up calendar in pink plastic, on the second a blue postal scale from Luna, and on the third a pair of plastic men attached to a long string. If you put the string with its weight over the edge of the desk, the two plastic men wobbled slowly toward the edge. That was medical information from Dumex about the medication called Somadril Comp.

Bernt rummaged around in the letter trays on the shelves: prescriptions, notes, EKG strips, electrolytes, results, dictated records with memos clipped to them. In one of the trays was an instruction book for an Audi 100. The rest of the shelves were stuffed with drug catalogues and a couple of handbooks. He sat down on one of the revolving chairs and looked at the only ornament on the free wall, a large color photograph with a bearded human face superimposed on an owl. The advertising text below was so unobtrusive he couldn't read it.

How many doctor's offices had he seen in his day? A hundred? No, seven hundred, or thereabouts. Doctor's offices in hospitals were seldom interesting, in fact boringly alike, the only thing varying being the density of inhabitants. Here the three doctors in Ward 12 shared the same office, but in the old hospitals in the city center, all the residents in one unit might have to share one small grubby common room. The senior physicians were better off, of course, some of their rooms with good furniture and oil paintings of their predecessors on the walls.

The most interesting were in the country, those of district practitioners and doctors in private practice. When Bernt had been traveling around Norrland, he had seen most of them over the years. Some doctors barricaded themselves into small cells lined from floor to ceiling with medical literature. One medical officer of a whole province was an amateur painter and hadn't a single book in the office, only dismal little watercolors of dwarf birches. Another was passionately fond of fishing. A third exhibited all the presents he had received over the years from patients. A fourth was a keenly zealous educator and had his room filled with anatomical charts and plaster models of the human body from which it was possible to extract all the organs and then put them back again with the aid of small pegs and hooks. A fifth collected strangely shaped tree roots. A sixth had his walls covered with marksmanship medals displayed in shallow showcases. A seventh had wallpaper photographs on all four walls, creating the illusion that you were in the middle of a wood.

Bernt had quite often functioned as a kind of social worker for lonely doctors. Many of them were trapped in their districts, bound by long hours and huge distances. Several had probably been loners from the start. Some of them had no contact whatsoever with the nearest clinic or general hospital, except when they sent patients there clutching their scrawled referrals. Some of them drank. One had twelve children and devoted his time to his own findings. The only regular intellectual contact many of them had was with their pharmaceutical salesmen. The rep was their courier, their continuing education tutor and closest confidant in medical and personal matters. Bernt had mediated in several marital conflicts. He had witnessed contracts and wills, given advice about sinking a well, and had pronounced his views on appointments of district nurses.

Some doctors could be ghastly, but they were usually in the larger towns. Some wouldn't even speak to him unless offered an expensive lunch first. Others would not deign to talk to him but would gracefully accept an envelope of offprints after the last drink, while others on the other hand drained him of information. Some wanted only female reps. Bernt had to telephone to Södertalje for someone, drive her to the doctor's house and wish her luck. Younger substitutes liked going out dancing. More than once, Bernt had dredged up two girls on the same evening, one for himself and one for his customer.

But most of that was more or less ancient history now. The old guard was beginning to die out or be pensioned off and everything was becoming more efficient and businesslike. You couldn't bribe anyone directly any longer. You had to make detours. It had to be golf strokes, research trips, conference fees or grants for somewhat slapdash clinical tests. Bernt preferred the old system. In the old days, a rep really had been able to maintain personal contact, be human, in fact.

The door jerked open and three people came into the room, Dr. Magnus Mattson and two students, a man and a woman. The girl flushed and snatched a whisp of tinsel out of her hair. They greeted him and sat down, Bernt remaining where he was at one of the desks, as if the room were his, not theirs.

"We've met before, I think," Bernt began. "When I was an area manager for Luna. Weren't you at Sabbatsberg before?"

"No, Karolinska, ears," said Mattson.

"Of course, yes. With Hamberger, eh? I see he's got his picture in the portrait gallery at Gripsholm these days. Among the other leading lights."

"Gripsholm?" said Mattson. "I thought they only had King Erik XIV on the walls there."

The students grinned. They were red-eyed, too. Had they been up all night? Or was it just home-brewed drinks? The hospital pharmacy was always very busy on St. Lucia Day mixing secret and individual recipes for the various wards.

"Well, perhaps we ought to talk about my father," Bernt went on. "He's not so good, is he?"

"He was admitted for what we interpreted as a biliary obstruction. The tests indicated a stone, that is, nothing malignant. But unfortunately that proved to be wrong."

"So he's got a 'neo'?" said Bernt, trying to keep up with hospital slang. Malignant and neo meant cancer.

"Your father has a pancreatic tumor. It's in a bad place. He also had a small metastasis in the liver. We took it out, but the primary tumor is still there. Unfortunately."

"What happens now?"

"Well, he'll stay here for the moment, of course. But if he heals as he should, it'll be a matter of moving him after a while. To some kind of convalescence."

"To a long-term care hospital?"

"More or less, yes. There's nothing much we can do for him from a surgical point of view, I'm afraid."

"What about radiation or chemotherapy?"

"This type of tumor is not especially responsive to that. But we'd thought of asking the radiologists if they think it's worth it. The question is really just how active we should be. Mr Svensson is seventy-six, isn't he?"

"You think he might as well die then? As soon as possible?"

Mattson shifted and the students looked horrified.

"It would be more merciful if it didn't take too long," said Mattson.

"I don't want him to die," said Bernt, feeling a wave of heat swamping over him.

"No, I understand," said Mattson. "It's difficult for us all to accept when someone close to us—"

Bernt wasn't listening any longer. He felt the tears welling up and pouring down his cheeks. The three people in white looked upset, none of them looking at him except the girl, who was peering cautiously at him from under her bangs. Naturally they wanted him to take out his handkerchief, blow his nose and leave. But he wasn't going to.

"I'm really sorry," said Mattson. "But none of us can—"

They were totally indifferent! Naturally, they couldn't imagine what he felt like. For doctors, both patients and relatives were another race, a lower species who might be ill, die, be tormented, or grieve. They themselves in their white coats were above such tribulations. They were untouchable.

"Get out!" said Bernt. "Go! Go on your rounds or what the hell you like."

They stared dumbly back at him, then Mattson and the male student got up.

"We're really very sorry—" said Mattson, heading for the door. "Do by all means stay here until you're a little calmer. The nurse is in the office if you want anything."

The girl who'd had tinsel in her hair stayed where she was.

"Go on, you go, too, so I can cry in peace!" said Bernt.

But the girl did not get up. Mattson put his hand on her shoulder, but she did not get up. The two men left the room and closed the door carefully behind them.

"Go on!" repeated Bernt. He was feeling panic-stricken now, for he realized he was sitting there making a fool of himself. What the hell did he care about Dad! How many times hadn't he wished Dad dead! Dad always seemed to him to appear at the most unsuitable moments. Whenever he pulled open a closet door, he was quite prepared to find Dad standing inside saying: "I saw through the keyhole what you were up to!"

Bernt got out his handkerchief, blew his nose and said:

"I'm sorry. I lost my head."

"You don't have to apologize," she said. "If you don't mind, I'd very much like to know more about your father. I admitted him when he first came into Medical, in 96."

What did this little girl know about life? How old was she—twenty? Twenty-five? There had been a time when he could guess exactly to the year how old a woman was, at least, if she were under thirty. But now, now he could mistake a seventeen-year-old for a twenty-seven-year-old, or vice-versa.

"I've always felt *watched* by my father," he started, but then he stopped. Would she write down everything he said? Would it be included in the chart? Would she report during the next lecture to thirty sniggering students what Bernt Svensson had poured out about his dying father?

He decided to go on because Martina Bosson, as it said on her badge, seemed to be approaching him with no ulterior motives or fingers crossed behind her back. He started telling her, not very coherently. He told her how his father had abandoned his mother during the difficult years of the change of life. How Dad had sold the house and thrown Mom out onto the street so that she had had to move in with her mother, whom she had never got along with. Dad had also maintained that Mom was mentally ill and tried to persuade Gran to commit her. But Gran hadn't agreed, although she was over eighty. Dad had tried to get Mom declared incapable of managing her own affairs so that he could keep all the money from the house.

All this had happened when he himself had been doing his military service. He had disliked it very much. That had been in 1948, hard times with double pressures. The army hadn't really realized the Second World War was over, but on the other hand, they had soon realized the huge threat of the Cold War. Military service in 1948 was preparedness against both the Second and Third World War simultaneously. Dad had never understood that. He was a superannuated old warrior who was now a corporal in the National Guard. He had done everything to get Bernt to sign on to become a reserve officer.

He told her about the matchstick pictures, how terribly pedantic Dad had been about them, supervising every single match Bernt stuck on. Once Bernt had taken an almost completed picture of a sea-eagle, gone down to the boiler room, broken the picture in two by stamping on it, then thrown the bits into the boiler. Dad had asked about it, of course, and Bernt had helped him look for it, in the attic, under the stairs, in the potato cellar, behind the trash cans. They had cycled out to the allotment together to look.

For Bernt, Dad personified the concept "guilty conscience." As soon as he saw Dad, he felt guilty and had to search his soul. What have I done now? There was always something: he'd lied about a test at school, stolen a coin out of Dad's desk drawer, made a fool of Dad in front of his friends. As soon as he saw Dad, he felt accused.

What had made things difficult was that Bernt was almost certain that a long time ago he had been very fond of his father. When he was really small, two, three or four years old. When they'd cycled around the Stockholm area, and Bernt had been given a white pilot's cap that could be buttoned under his chin. Even then, Dad had begun to be ingratiating. Mom had not had a bicycle. They couldn't afford that. Dad had laid claim to Bernt for himself. Dad was like that, false, demanding and dishonest about money.

He'd also been violent on certain occasions. If you weren't careful, he'd beat your bare behind. Dad used to make Mom tell him how Bernt had behaved during the war. If he'd done anything bad, there would be a smack. The last time that had happened, Bernt was as old as eleven. He had borrowed an airgun from a friend and shot holes in Mom's raincoat hanging out for an airing. Dad had beaten his bare behind then. It had felt like being raped.

Dad had liked swimming very much, too. On warm summer evenings, he had cycled out to Drottningholm with Bernt on the bar on a child's saddle. There he had hired a rowing boat and rowed out to one of the smooth round rocks of Kar Island. Then both of them were to go into the water although Bernt didn't want to. Dad took him by the shoulders and jumped in, although he was screaming his head off. When they came up, Dad called him a coward. It was infamous. He had deceived Bernt, too. Bernt had been learning to swim, but it had not been going too well because he was afraid of getting water up his nose. So Dad had said to Bernt: "You're good now. You can swim as well as a 'gray stone'" and Bernt had gone around telling people he could swim like a gray stone, not understanding why they laughed at him. It hadn't been until a few years later that he found out that gray stone and gray seal weren't the same thing.

"If I'd had any brothers and sisters," Bernt said to Martina. "I probably wouldn't be sitting here today. They would have looked after Dad. What do I owe him? You tell me that—what do I owe him?"

7 She was no more than forty-three, but she looked ten years older in her black suit, black stockings, old-fashioned shoes, and small, round hat with a full veil. She was carrying a large gray bag in her hand. She had many names. Her real name was Margarete Hansen. She was Danish and was a Danish certified nurse, but her certificate had long since been taken from her. She had worked with a gynecologist in Aarhus who had made large sums of money from illegal abortions. After that, she had tried to keep away from Denmark. She still had her diploma from nursing school and had done several locums in Gotland and northern Norway, where they hadn't checked up on her registration. One job had lasted over two years. But all that had come to an end. In Sweden, it had taken only a few days for the payroll office to check with the national computerized register. You couldn't sail under false colors in Sweden.

Sometimes she nursed old people. Private nurses did not have to be registered, but there was often trouble with the family if someone died. She had been accused of all sorts of things, from stealing the silverware to fiddling with wills. Naturally, they were all mistakes. Her prison sentence was also a mistake, and was only because the relatives had been totally uncooperative and not realized how much pressure there is at the end, how the nursing had demanded all her attention, and she simply hadn't had time to keep accounts of all the money the patient had asked her to take out.

She had worked as an "aide" at Enskede Hospital a couple of times and learned her way around. She would have preferred to get money from the Department of Medicine, but she dared not go there, as that was where she'd worked as an aide. But they didn't know her in Surgery, so the risk there was minimal. She drew the veil down over her face and went into Ward 12. The doctors' office was on the right in the corner. She knew you couldn't see the door of it from the nurses' glass box. She opened the door and went in. The room was empty. Two white coats were hanging by the basin behind the door, together with a thin yellow leather jacket. She felt the jacket, but it contained only a bunch of keys. One white coat was completely empty, presumably having just come from the laundry. In the other, she found a book of luncheon-vouchers in the top pocket. She popped them into her gray bag. Her cheeks grew hot when she found a wallet in one of the big pockets. She listened before opening the wallet, then looked through it. It was unnecessary to take whole wallets, as they could be traced. But the fat wallet did not contain what it had promised. There was only sixty kronor cash in it, plus four different credit cards. The credit cards were in the name of a man, so were no use to her.

Her head bowed and a crumpled handkerchief in her hand, she left the doctors' office and made her way along to one of the small rooms at the opposite end of the ward. In the corridor she met an orderly, who respectfully stepped aside for the lady in mourning. There was nothing at all in Room A: no beds, no chairs, nothing. The floor shone, the surface in one corner still dull from the wet floorcloth. What were they doing? Trying to scrub away the hospital-acquired infections!

She went on to Room B. A lone patient on an i.v. was in there. The patient, an emaciated old woman, was asleep or in a coma. Just as Margarete Hansen reached the nightstand to pull out the drawer, someone came to the door, a youngish man dressed in white from top to toe, a stethoscope carelessly draped over one shoulder. She identified him immediately as a medical student. Instead of pulling out the drawer, she leaned over the unconscious or sleeping woman and kissed her on the cheek. Without a word the student immediately retreated.

There was a prayer book in the nightstand drawer and she took it on an impulse. It might be useful to walk around with in her hand. She left behind an unopened bag of raspberry candies. An insurance premium, too. There was a bunch of keys in the drawer, too, and for a moment she thought of taking them. The patient's address was on the insurance premium, but she had never broken into an apartment. It would be much more difficult to explain her presence if she were found in a strange apartment. So it was safer to walk around the hospital in mourning clothes.

She backed out of Room B. Since the student had seen her, perhaps it would be wiser if she went to another ward. But she hadn't taken anything except the prayer book. That was harmless. Everything seemed so quiet for the moment here in 12. There might be lots of activity in another ward. She was very curious, too—walking into an unknown isolation room was very exciting, like getting a large, well-wrapped parcel that might contain the most wonderful presents. She had thought about this many a time. Why did she steal? The money she took, after all, tended to be frittered away like toy money. She bought all kinds of unnecessary things with it, only respecting the money she herself earned. It must be her curiosity that drove her to steal: curiosity, excitement and the feeling of power. To be able to do anything, to be able to do what all the other little gray people didn't dare do, the ones who were quite happy to sit at home in front of the television and experience crimes vicariously.

There were two beds in the next room. The one by the window was empty, but there were fresh flowers and a razor on the nightstand. An elderly man was in a bed with a railing on it, by the door. The top part of his body had slipped down and he was asleep with his mouth open and one of the pillows half over his face. He was harmless. Quickly, she went over to the empty bed and sat down near the nightstand with her back to the sleeping man. She spread out her veil to make a screen. There was a plastic roll of fifty coins in the drawer, presumably for the telephone. She put the coins into her bag. There was no wallet. But there were five color photographs in a plastic folder. The photos must have been taken on some festive occasion and were of a dozen or so dressed up people in various groups. One of the photos was of a table loaded with presents, a sundial, a toaster, books, flowers, an enormous round box of chocolates, and two happy birthday cards, made of elaborately folded banknotes. She glanced back at the bed. There we are! The wallet was under the pillow. She swiftly fished it out and let it vanish into her bag.

"Mr. Jansson is having a dressing changed," said the old man, whom she'd thought was out like a light.

HOUSE OF BABEL 185

At first she didn't want to open her mouth. She was afraid that her slight Danish accent would be noticed, but the man went on:

"They've just been to fetch him. It usually takes quite a time. You'd better go and ask the nurse."

The old man had propped himself up on his elbow and was smiling at her. He was very pale.

"Can I tell him you were here?" the old man said.

She screwed up her nose and said in a slightly forced tearful voice: "Thank you, so kind of you."

She wanted to run past him, but didn't dare to. Instead she walked slowly with heavy dragging steps toward the door, enjoying it all in the middle of her terror. Acting like this, acting someone you weren't, getting people to believe it, taking them in, it was—yes, it was amazing! But there was no legal place for such activity in society, if you weren't a professional actor, if you weren't sufficiently independent, of course, and managed to overcome it. If you weren't supreme at it, if you weren't someone who dared take the risk and act outside the well-enclosed stages. Stealing was like having wings.

8 Gustaf found it difficult to get away in the evenings. It was Sunday midday and he was lying in Martina's bed having a late breakfast, after having come in and awakened her at ten o'clock. This was the third time they had been together. After the first inglorious occasion, he had been prepared for her to reject him, but she hadn't; she had shown quite clearly that she wanted to be with him.

Their second meeting had been marvelous. Gustaf had lied at home and said he had to do an extra duty. Instead he had had dinner with Martina at the Metropol and afterwards they had gone back to her place and made love together four times. Then with his loins aching, he had driven her to the hospital the next morning. He had felt flayed for several days afterwards.

Was he in love with Martina? He didn't know. Neither did he really dare try to find out, because if it turned out that he was truly bound to

Martina, everything would be extremely complicated. A divorce now, with four children, would be impossible for both him and his family. Anyhow, he would not be able to take the initiative himself. If Marianne did, that would be a different matter. But would Marianne take the initiative? Wouldn't she prefer to put her head in the sand to avoid seeing anything? He had been unfaithful twice before, once when he had been in the U.S.A. But that didn't count, as Marianne couldn't possibly have noticed it on him when he had returned. The other affair had been a relationship of a few months' duration with a woman who was a resident at Enskede. It had lasted for one whole spring. Marianne must have noticed, but neither of them had said anything. Marianne had seemed tired and miserable, but nothing more. When the relationship had come to an end, Gustaf had returned with renewed energy to his marriage. Both he and Marianne had lived as if they had just fallen in love and they had decided to have another child, their fourth.

"They miss you in 96," he said to Martina, who was brushing crumbs off her breasts. "The gang we have at the moment is unusually boring. You should see the kinds of admissions they write up. God Almighty!"

"It's more fun in Surgery," she replied. "Though I hadn't expected that. I thought it'd be awful and they'd just try to make us into knife-happy robots. But it isn't like that. It's fun. Things happen. You feel you're being useful. When I did my first radial fracture down in Emergency, I was blissful for several days."

"It'll pass," he said. "When you've done your tenth, you just find it tedious. It's the same when you deliver your first kid on the maternity rotation. You feel like buying the whole crowd champagne. But when you've delivered twenty, your jaw nearly cracks with boredom."

"Well, it's fun as long as it lasts," she said. "You know, in Medical it's sort of grandiose in some way. Intellectual, or whatever you call it. No, not intellectual. Pseudo-intellectual. Like some damned protracted rituals. And you never know if anyone is any the better for it."

"Ever heard of diabetes? Or pernicious anemia?" he said, trying to find more examples of diseases from which internal medicine had saved people's lives. There were lots of them.

"I don't mean that. But in Surgery you see results more immediately. Someone is admitted and has a real pain in his abdomen, is really ill and has a temperature. You take out his appendix and at once you've changed everything, perhaps even saved a young person from peritonitis."

"And if you can't operate?"

"What do you mean, can't?"

"Are you so sure it's impossible to cure appendicitis in any other way apart from surgery?"

"How do you mean? With penicillin?"

"Perhaps. But no one dares try seriously. Operating has long been the accepted way of treating appendicitis. Perhaps conservative treatment with antibiotics and fluids, for instance, would be just as good. Or even better. But how can you find that out? To prove that, you'd have to stop operating, shall we say, on every other appendicitis. You'd operate on half and not operate on the other half. Then you'd compare the results. If it then turns out that it's just as good not to operate, then you'd have made a great find, you'd be praised and become a professor. But if the results were worse in the non-operated group, you'd have had it. You could be sued for malpractice. Then you would have been carrying out unethical research, robbing patients of the treatment they had a right to. Do you see? In fact, you're trapped. You're flogged on to continue with all those thousands of more or less necessary appendectomies."

Martina slid down under the covers, grasped his knees and shook him.

"You're so terribly sensible, Gustaf. So tremendously sensible. Come on!"

"No, I have to pee."

He got out of bed and went off to have a pee. He found it hard to start. Perhaps he hadn't really needed to? After sex, the various nerve ganglia in his loins were entangled and didn't know which direction to go in. He had an erection as he stood leaning over the toilet bowl with his hands against the wall. He closed his eyes and tried to think about something neutral. The car? The car was not neutral. He was afraid Martina would leave traces in it, hairs, a lipstick, place the seat belt in a way no one else in the family did. Should he change cars? How much was a SAAB 95 that had done fifty-four thousand miles worth? He felt it coming. He'd deceived his loins.

They made love for a second time that morning and Gustaf felt like Valentino or Marlon Brando in bed. Nothing was impossible. He could steer things at will. He held back until Martina's orgasm was almost over, then let go with a bellow and collapsed like a sack on top of her.

"Shall I come out?" he said a few minutes later.

"No, no."

"But I weigh almost eighty kilos. How much do you weigh?"

"Fifty-seven. And a half."

"That's twenty-three kilos difference. I'll squash you."

"Squash me!"

But a moment later he had to get up and go for a pee again. He felt foolish, almost as if he were an old prostate patient. But there were natural explanations. First he had eaten an ordinary breakfast at home, yogurt, juice and three cups of tea, then barely an hour later he was eating another breakfast, fruit yogurt and lots of black coffee.

"How long are you staying?" said Martina, when he came back.

He was disturbed by the question. There was no accusing tone in Martina's voice, but it sounded like that all the same. You don't support me. You just want a couple of lays now and again and then you trot off home! He looked at his watch that had landed under the bed. It was twenty to twelve.

"I must be home by half-past one. We've got relations coming for brunch."

"Where are you at the moment? Officially, so to speak."

"At the hospital, going through some papers. Things that have got piled up. It's happened before."

"What was her name that time?"

"Don't be silly," he said, slightly offended. "I quite often have to go in and write out charts or sick-notes. Then there's my research, too—funny, now you mention it. I'd forgotten to ask you something. You filled in a Social Readjustment score on an M.I. sometime in August or September. But you put a question mark I wondered about. I was going to ask you about it. And now it's popped up again."

"I remember," she said. "That patient's in Surgery at this moment. He's got pancreatic cancer."

"Pancreatic cancer? Well, I'll be damned. Thought we were looking for something endocranial. Typical. The chemists gave us a clue, but it was a false one. They missed the pancreatic tumor completely. Pancreatic tumors are deceptive. They often start with a thrombosis somewhere. In this case an M.I. What are you going to do with him?"

"Nye opened him up himself and looked. We were looking for a stone that was obstructing somewhere. Primus, his name is, do you remember? He got icterus and turned yellow after you'd discharged him. But we were just doing an explorative laparotomy."

"We were just doing an explorative laparotomy? Oh, my dear little surgeon."

He could feel an erection coming again and he tried to part her legs to get at her clitoris.

"Don't! It's my turn to go to the john now," she said, pushing him aside none too gently.

He lay down with his hands behind his head, staring up at the ceiling. Was he happy? Yes, this is what it should be like. But it couldn't go on like this. Hell, he thought, grasping his limp member and pulling back the foreskin. On Sundays, between ten and one, I'm happy.

9 Primus was sitting in his wheelchair in the day-room of Ward 12, waiting for Bernt. The dayroom was partitioned down the middle with a glass wall. On one side was Smoking, the other side No Smoking. In the smoking section were about a dozen people, men as well as women. Surgical Ward 12, like practically all wards at Enskede, was mixed. From the side where Primus was sitting, the smoking section looked like a large aquarium in which various currents were swirling, almost as if the potted plants and greenery swayed as someone walked past. People were moving behind the glass in slow motion, playing cards or board games, or just sitting staring at the columns of cigarette smoke floating up toward the ceiling. There were two beds in the smoking section. In one was a patient with both his arms and legs in casts, weights fastened to his legs with thin steel wire. An orderly was sitting on the edge of the bed "feeding" the patient with a pipe.

In the No Smoking section, apart from Primus, there was a patient in a bed behind a screen of crinkly light green plastic. He was an "overflow." Primus could see out of the window by craning his neck. Snow had fallen during the night and now in the late morning the sun was shining low over Enskede, the freeways black and shining, as if painted in with black ink. The yellow light-ramps across the freeways were switched on despite the bright sunlight. There was a straw advent star hanging in the dayroom window that was also switched on. It would soon be Christmas.

Primus was feeling fairly well now. Yesterday they had taken the drainage tube out, so he was not in any real pain, mostly pressure and pulls. But when he coughed or strained at all, it felt like knives cutting inside him. And then he itched, too, an urgent creeping itch underneath the dressing itself, but also on other parts of his body, his chest, between his shoulder blades, on his neck, knees and the tops of his feet. This was because of the jaundice. When it got better, it itched, as if the saffron were oozing out of all the pores of his skin to evaporate and disappear. He had been given tablets for the itching, but they made him terribly sleepy. He hadn't taken any that day, because Bernt was coming and they were to talk to the doctor, so Primus wanted to be clear-headed.

What would happen? They had taken out those gallstones that had been obstructing the bile duct. The operation had been a great strain but had otherwise gone well. He was still very weak. Simply raising his arms to comb his hair was like a day's work. But he didn't comb his hair every day, for raising his arms was one of the movements that gave him pain inside. He didn't have much of an appetite, either, not even for coffee. He felt slightly nauseated at the sight of food, but that was an advantage. Then he didn't eat so much, and so didn't have to ask for the bedpan and sit there straining. Straining was the worst, worse than coughing. He didn't remember much of the twenty-four hours after the operation. They had presumably injected him full of morphine. But what he would never forget was when the physiotherapist came and forced him to cough, and then walk once around the bed. After that he'd felt as if he had boxed for twelve rounds against the world heavyweight champion; he was hanging over the ropes, in other words, more dead than alive.

What would happen next? He had been much too weak to go straight home, and he couldn't stay there in 12. The beds there were only for people who were to be operated on or just had been. As soon as things began to heal, you had to go somewhere else. One of his fellow patients had had a piece of his intestine removed and a new opening put in his belly. Ten days afterwards he had had to move, although he had had a much more severe operation than Primus. It'd be all right if it was possible to get a place in some kind of convalescent home, but did you have to manage everything on your own there? If so, it would be impossible. He could still only walk a few steps on his own and sit up for no more than a few hours. Would it have to be a long-term care ward instead? He felt distaste at the very thought of "long-term," imagining huge, old-fashioned rooms full of emaciated senile wretches lying moaning in their own mess. No! It couldn't be like that today. It was probably something like life in 12, though slightly more indifferent, perhaps, a slightly slower tempo. He liked it very much in Ward 12. There was so many more younger people there and cheerful things happened, too. When someone had his cast off, for instance, the whole room could cheer.

Miss Laijla came into the dayroom.

"Hasn't your son come yet? Doctor's nearly finished the discharges."

No, Bernt had not appeared and it was twenty-five minutes past the agreed time. But it had snowed in the night, so perhaps he hadn't been able to start the car.

"We'd better be off anyhow," said Miss Laijla, starting to push the wheelchair toward the corridor.

The corridor seemed almost dark after the bright sunlight of the dayroom. Two orderlies were polishing the floor and there was a strong smell of disinfectant. Laijla pushed him over to the doctors' office and parked him outside.

"My son hasn't phoned, has he?" he asked, to make sure.

"Not as far as I know," said Miss Laijla. "But I'll ask Nurse Cecilia."

His eyes followed her as she walked toward the office, her wooden sandals pattering on the newly polished floor. Just as she was about to swing around the corner by the open door, she fell, crash, bang! Primus was just about to start up from his chair when the pain caught him in the solar plexus, leaving him speechless. Carefully he let himself back again, holding his breath. Miss Laijla was already on her feet again, rubbing her hip. She seemed to be scolding someone inside the office. Then she vanished, but almost immediately thrust her head out again and waved dismissively to Primus. So Bernt hadn't telephoned.

It was a new doctor today, a woman of about thirty. She opened the door herself and pulled the wheelchair into the room. There was no one else there. Primus had hoped that Martina or one of the other students would be there, but they must be at a lecture or whatever it was they did. The new doctor shook his hand.

"I'm Lena Willard. I've taken over from Dr. Mattson."

"Has Dr. Mattson left?" said Primus. He had arranged this meeting with Dr. Mattson.

"He's gone back to the ear clinic. Now let's see . . . wasn't your son going to be here, too, Mr. Svensson?"

The new doctor seemed very formal. Practically no one in the whole ward had called him Mr. Svensson before. She wasn't looking at him, but leafing through his chart.

"I don't know where my son is. He must have got held up somewhere."

"I suppose he has spoken to the doctors here before. About the outcome of your operation?"

"I don't know anything about that."

"What have they told you, then, about the operation?"

"That they found the stones. And took out my gallbladder."

"Was that all?"

What did she mean? All? What else had they said? They had said that the jaundice was due to an obstructing stone—or that it might be due to that. Wasn't that true?

"I suppose I'll be discharged soon, won't I?" he said, hesitantly. "I won't raise any objections this time. If the social worker can arrange for a place in a convalescent home, if that's possible, or if I have to go to a long-term place. I suppose I'll have to accept whatever it is."

Dr. Willard looked questioningly at him, then gazed out of the window for a long time before impatiently leafing through the file of papers again.

"There's no hurry about a discharge," she said. "But it would have been a good thing if your son had come. Then we could have talked about all this together."

"Thank you," said Primus with great warmth. He hadn't dared hope for that. He would be able to stay in 12. If they didn't discharge him this week, then he'd be able to stay over Christmas. That was a great relief, not having to spend Christmas in a strange hospital. He knew several people who would be here over Christmas. The coming Christmas would be the first for Surgery Ward 12. They hadn't yet moved in the previous Christmas. Miss Laijla had been one of the first to come and she had said that the whole ward had looked as if it had been bombed, with loose wires in the ceiling, heaps of plastic bits and chunks of concrete. They were going to celebrate their first Christmas properly, he realized.

"Can we get your son on the telephone?" said Dr. Willard.

"Yes, the nurse has got the number out there."

"Have you any objection to my phoning him, Mr. Svensson?"

"No, of course not."

It was a good thing they wanted to keep contact with Bernt. He was ashamed that Bernt hadn't come today. He didn't want to telephone himself and ask. Bernt got so irritable. It would be better if the doctor, who was a neutral person, telephoned and arranged an appointment.

"I suppose you can't tell me how long it'll take?" he said.

"You know what you're suffering from, don't you?" said the doctor. She wasn't looking directly at him but at his right shoulder. "As far as I can make out, Dr. Mattson's told you your diagnosis, hasn't he?"

"Yes, indeed."

"I'll be quite honest with you. We might have to operate again. You realize that, don't you? Should there be another obstruction."

He didn't think what she had said had anything to do with him at all. Operate again? "I'll be quite honest—" who was she talking about? Bernt? About one of the other patients, someone who was really *bad*?

"Is there anything special you want to ask about, Mr. Svensson? I realize it must be very difficult for you. That it's hard for you to assimilate all this, as we say."

He was struck dumb. He couldn't say a single word, not even open his mouth, even if they'd tried prying it open. Neither did he move, nor even blink. If he sat absolutely still, without moving a single muscle—quiet as a mouse, if he held his breath, perhaps the doctor wouldn't notice him sitting there in the wheelchair. There was just a chance she hadn't seen him. Still, sit still. Let her sit there talking away to herself. Soon Miss Laijla will come and pull him into the dayroom, and then the danger would be over for this time.

10 Sture Ohrn was the chairman of the municipal union organization at Enskede Hospital. In a large labor-intensive hospital, that was almost a full-time job, rather than a voluntary duty. The employers understood that completely. He cooperated closely with the administration and in many matters, they took the same line. There was no need to go looking for trouble unnecessarily.

He was in the Bed Center. The hospital had two large bed centers responsible for used beds. The one he was in at the moment was on the top floor of the hospital and was called in everyday speech the Blue Bed Center, where ordinary beds were dealt with. The beds were still cleaned off with a spray cleaner between uses, but they did not receive any more thorough cleansing. For that there was the Clean Bed Center down in the basement culvert system. There was an automatic bed-washer there, and a sterilizing room for sterilizing the whole frame. That was where beds from the red zone were dealt with, from Intensive Care, the Kidney Ward, and other places where people had to be sterile. There was a red elevator from the Clean Bed Center that took clean beds straight to the relevant wards.

"Blue" wasn't nearly so automated as "Clean." Here in "Blue" there was a wide belt, a conveyor belt of rubber matting on which the newly-arrived beds were placed. At walking pace, the bed-belt then passed through Dismantling, where four men tore off the old bedclothes and threw them down a shaft into open wagons that took the bedclothes on to the central laundry. The empty beds then slid on to Washing where they were sprayed with cleanser and dried with cloths. Then they went on to Making where they were made up with clean bedclothes. Finally they went into the largest room, Delivery, from which the various wards could fetch them.

Sture Ohrn and the Municipality had been very much against the building of the Blue Bed Center. Neither did they approve of the Clean Bed Center, but it was one of the means of combating hospital-acquired infections, so they were neither able to, nor dared do anything about it. But "Blue" was unnecessary. It was stupid to build this kind of conveyor belt in a modern hospital. Industry was just getting rid of such things. Why then should the health service get involved in old systems that were known to create a poor work environment for whoever was forced to work there? Monotonous, repetitive work that strained people's backs and joints, a type of work in which employees could not decide the pace of work, but were simply forced to keep up with the speed of the belt. Demands for job-rotation that had come from the union side during the seventies could not be fulfilled in a conveyor belt system. Every operation was divided up and categorized. The atmosphere was also wretched, far too hot, and dusty from the bedclothes, while in Washing it was damp from the steaming soap. There was also the risk of staff getting their fingers or clothing caught in the switchpoints between the different conveyor belts.

In both Bed Centers the staff consisted almost exclusively of immigrants, most of them Turks with a poor grasp of the language. They didn't need to know much to make beds. Sture Ohrn was also aware that most of the Turks had two jobs, and when they weren't there making beds, they were washing dishes in some restaurant or cleaning offices at night. Here in the hospital they were called "coolies." It was an apt expression. Without hundreds of coolies in the basement, in the culverts, in the attics, in the kitchens and laundries, this great Stockholm hospital would simply cease functioning.

The Bed Centers were not a subject of conflict between the administration and the union, for both had been against them. But the plans had already gone so far when the union and the newly-appointed hospital director started objecting to them, that it was too late. They simply couldn't redraw the plans of half the hospital just to alter the bed-cleaning system. That would have cost millions and delayed the whole building of the hospital, and although it might have resulted in a system that would provide a better work environment, in the short run it would have been less "efficient." As the centers were manned by immigrants who never stayed long at the hospital, someone else had to deal with the back troubles, strained joints and the spiritual monotony the bed centers produced.

How could this have happened? At some time, during the early stages of planning, someone, whoever it was, had taken a decision that had resulted in this workplace which no one wanted. No one?

Naturally someone had wanted it like that, someone who hadn't understood what it meant and someone whose living came from installing conveyor belt systems. Was that a fair accusation? If Sture Ohrn were truly honest, he would have replied: We're the guilty ones. We taxpayers who take every opportunity of avoiding having to pay higher taxes, and to hell with whether some anonymous Turk is better or worse off.

He nodded to two of them making beds. He didn't know most of them, or rather he couldn't remember whether he had spoken to them. The turnover here was among the highest in the whole hospital, and that said a good deal. Ordinary wards could replace their whole staff of orderlies within three or four months. So much for continuity of health care. But what was going to happen when so many employees stayed no longer than students doing a stint of practical work?

Sture Ohrn went into the Pathology Department that was alongside the Blue Bed Center. He passed the Large Autopsy Room with its ten polished, stainless steel autopsy tables. Sometimes all ten of them could be occupied at this time of the morning, but today there was only one single cadaver there. It was an elderly woman. She was very fat and both legs had been amputated at the hips. The pale flabby hands did not even reach beyond the actual body.

Beyond the Large Autopsy Room was the Small Autopsy Room, where they did post-mortems entailing special risks of infection. The two draining-board-like tables were empty, as usual. The next room was Microscopy and beyond that, the Preparation Room. Alongside Preparation, Sture Ohrn had his own office. He did very little work for the Pathology Department these days. For many years he had worked for the National Forensic Station in Solna, as a post-mortem porter, then later mostly as a technician in the animal experimental department. But Pathology at Enskede had no experimental animals of its own. All research was concentrated in a special building, Research House. So Sture Ohrn lacked any real work, and the authorities let him keep this bogus job to enable him to do the union work.

His office was piled high with files and papers and above the shuttered cabinets were rows of stuffed birds of prey. Preserving and stuffing birds was his hobby, and he had also been an enthusiastic hunter. Nowadays, he had very little time to spare for such activities, but when he retired he was going to take up his hobby again. Unfortunately the destruction of wildlife had gone so far now that it would be difficult to complete his collection of Swedish birds of prey. He had a peregrine falcon as well as a number of others, a hobby-falcon, a merlin, and a kestrel. He also had an ordinary goshawk and a sparrow hawk. Of the smaller marsh harriers, he had both a grayish-white female and a lead-gray male. When he had stuffed the male marsh harrier, he had mounted it with outspread wings so that the long black band on the underside of the wings should show clearly. Some taxidermists tried deception and hid this mark of recognition, so that the bird would be taken for a blue marsh harrier. He would never have a chance of stuffing a blue marsh harrier, alas. Not even when he had undertaken professional taxidermy had he ever had a blue harrier through his hands.

There was a newspaper clipping lying on his desk. *In certain circumstances it has appeared that in some cases employees do not conform with the present agreements and regulations in relation to, for instance, working hours, sick leave and notification of absence. Unfortunately staff problems relating to abuses of various kinds are also found in institutions. Similarly, events occur in which criminal offenses are established or suspected . . .*

He broke a match in two and wedged it between two teeth that were irritating him . . . *Such cases, if established or suspected, should immediately be reported to the police.*

He laughed slightly wearily. Now they really had gone over the top up there in the office, sending things like that out just before Christmas and doing it so clumsily that you read about the wretched business in the newspaper before it reached you through their own internal mail. He remember a similar memo in 1977. There had been one hell of a row, and those responsible had more or less had to apologize.

And now exactly the same thing again, only two years later. Did they never learn up there in the office? No doubt there was some truth behind it all, he had to admit that, now that he was sitting there in his private office. Of course many of them cheated over working hours. In Intensive Care, for instance, they were prepared for thirty-three patients, but sometimes there might be no more than ten in there. Naturally, people went home a few hours earlier in such situations. Similar problems had arisen in Surgery, where it was said that nurses and aides went to the hairdresser's in working hours. But what large concern existed where that didn't happen? When it became too flagrant, it could be dealt with internally. The union wasn't interested in slovenliness and disorder, either. When such things came out, they were always waved about during negotiations.

Abuses of various kinds . . . that was laying it on a bit thick. On the union side, both working hours and free time had been spent helping a number of their people with drinking problems, making sure they stayed in some kind of work instead of being forced into a disability pension or being disciplined. So now people with drinking problems were to be reported to the police, were they? True, it was written into the management's agreement that as far as *first* offenses were concerned, they could be dealt with within the union, or by the staff medical officer. But it was part of the times that some employees with drinking problems relapsed not just a second or third time, but also a tenth or a fifteenth time. In those cases, the agreement between union and hospital management was that the person with the closest contact with the sick man, so to speak, should arrange for his treatment. That was the system within almost the whole of the public sector. And those idiots in the central management . . .

Idiots? No, it wasn't that simple. They probably knew perfectly well what they were doing. They knew that memo, in fact an exact copy of the infamous circular of 1977, would arouse bad blood with the various directors of the hospital as well. Sten Ossolovsky was no doubt sitting up there in his office grinding his teeth over the same document as Sture Ohrn now had in front of him. Ossolovsky was a shrewd man. What was the management up to? Hadn't they jumped the gun a bit? This year's agreement had been ratified only a few months ago . . . was it already time to put out the nets for the next one? Must be so. This was an attack. The document was just a trial balloon. During the 1980 negotiations, these questions would be brought up and weighed on the scales. Greater efficiency, stiffer controls, clocking-in in individual wards, greater demands on able-bodied workers, more compulsory early retirements. By making a document of this kind public, the management hoped to sow discord between the hospitals' employees who kept their noses clean and those who found it hard to comply. The young and healthy and efficient would be set against the old, the weak and the hopeless. That was how they honed the knife when they wanted greater efficiency. Employees would be deceived into hostility toward "less desirable elements" within their own ranks.

What would the elected representatives say about it? Not easy to know. Politicians avoided such issues like the plague, and outwardly nonpolitical officials from the management appeared instead. But you never knew whether politicians were behind them. Some of the economically-minded moderates? Some well-meaning but confused member of the People's Party? Or some amateur politician from the Center Party? But unfortunately it might also be someone from his own party. The Swedish labor movement was not untouched by the winds from the Right and the shortsighted discussions on efficiency of recent years. It was not only employers who wanted more severe measures taken against absenteeism due to illness.

11 Edit Wahlgren was eighty-one. Seven years earlier, the sight in her right eye had begun to deteriorate, requiring more and more light for her to be able to read. Stronger glasses had not helped. Her left eye was still sound, but when she looked in the mirror, she noticed there was a kind of weak gray light like a pearl behind the pupil. She had cataracts.

Some time later, she stopped using the bad eye completely, managing well with one eye as long as she was doing things she was used to doing. But of course, sometimes she poured the coffee outside the cup as her depth perception became impaired. It was much worse out of doors, as she found it difficult to judge where to put her feet. She had fallen a couple of times because she hadn't noticed curbstones. She disliked going out after dark; the maze of lights and shadows confused her. She had stopped going on escalators altogether. She carefully noted which subway stations had elevators or ordinary stairs. So in this way, her life became more and more restricted, but she could still read and watch television. She loved color television: a whole world entered her tiny apartment in the evenings. She liked the wildlife programs and documentaries on exotic countries most. News and current events made her turn it off. She thought she'd been through quite enough wars and catastrophes, and the young could worry about them now.

When she was seventy-eight, her good eye began to blue slightly, too. The ophthalmologist had said there was nothing to do but wait. He had also suggested an operation to remove the milky lens on the bad eye. The absence of that lens could be compensated for with powerful glasses. Edit Wahlgren had taken her time deciding. She knew perfectly well what was happening and that she would be almost totally blind if they didn't operate, but she had always been very careful of her eyes. Naturally, people were always careful of their sight, she had thought, but for her, her eyes were of special significance. When she had been a young girl, many people had told her she had "soulful" deep blue eyes. Her life and memories were also strongly concerned with sight. She could easily remember and imagine things visually. As a girl she had painted watercolors and her dream of becoming an artist was still with her, although she laughed at herself . . . silly old thing!

Now she was lying on a table in the physiology unit in Enskede Hospital. They were going to do an EKG to check her heart before operating. The table was hard and cold and it embarrassed her that a man was in charge of the examination. At first she had thought it was a girl when she had seen his long blond hair, and she had been shocked when the person had suddenly addressed her in a deep bass voice.

"Now, Mrs. Wahlgren, dear, would you mind just unbuttoning your jacket."

She had turned away from him as she did so, then kept her eyes closed as he squeezed her breasts and fastened the contacts and wires. She had had EKGs before, so she knew what happened. He had set the apparatus in motion for a few moments, rustled the strips of paper and then said everything was done. As he took away the electrodes, he wiped away the ointment with a paper towel and buttoned up her jacket for her. She opened her eyes:

"Look at this," he said, holding up something that must have been a long strip of paper. "This is called the P-wave and is a registration of how the atria contract. This tall spiky one we call the QRS-complex. That's for the ventricles. And this is the T-wave."

"Thank you very much," she said, without having seen or understood any of the demonstration.

They were so friendly in the hospitals these days, telling you lots of things you hadn't asked about. It had been quite different in the old days, quite different when she had had her Hasse. Then the whole room had lain at attention when the doctor came on his rounds. She plucked up her courage and said:

"How does it seem? My heart?"

"Great, Mrs. Wahlgren, just great," said the young man. "I really envy you your heart."

She laughed, almost as if he had been flirting with her. But she realized that you weren't declared in the clear quite so light-heartedly. A doctor had to look at the EKG. It couldn't be left to just anyone whether her heart was all right or not. This whole business of health was so complicated. She was grateful to be allowed to live in a country with such good doctors. The day after tomorrow, she would have an operation. An associate professor would be operating. She had been disappointed when she had discovered the surgeon would be a woman. Stupidly enough, she had assumed all eye surgeons were men. Now it was to be a woman. But it would be all right, anyhow.

She thanked the young man. He wanted to help her to the door, but she waved him aside. She wasn't blind yet! They had given her a white stick, or rather, a cane, and she had rejected it at first, as it had seemed shameful, but then she had given in. You couldn't really be so choosy when you were almost eighty-two. She walked with small dragging steps out to the waiting room, just able to discern a few people there, but she didn't try to look any closer. Instead she concentrated on finding the right door. They had brought in a bed-patient, which meant she didn't really recognize the waiting room because of the bed. Suddenly, her shin struck something hard and smarted with the pain.

"Edit? Edit Wahlgren, is that you?" said a man's voice she recognized.

She turned to the right and saw that she had collided with a man sitting in a wheelchair. She did not recognize him.

"Hello, Edit. It's Primus Svensson here."

"Primus?" she said.

"Yes! Get yourself a chair and sit down."

Another patient helped her pull up a chair. It *was* Primus Svensson. She had seen him, seen his face quite clearly, but she would never have recognized him. She remembered Primus Svensson as a rather large man, a man with a definite paunch. Axel, her now dead husband, and Primus had done their military service together and their families had started getting together. At first she had been rather scared of Primus, because he looked so stern. Silent and stern. But he hadn't been like that at all. He was a very nice man, though slightly formal at the same time. Axel had said it was because of his funny first name. If you were baptized "the first one," then you had to keep yourself to yourself out of shame.

"This is a fine hospital, isn't it?" she said. "I feel I'm living in a hotel."

"And the food's just as good as in a restaurant," said Primus.

"You can't see that on you," she said. "You've been dieting."

She was appalled when she had said it. Primus was nothing but a shadow of his former self, his face tiny and wrinkled, his body as thin as a youth's. But his color was good, his face really tanned!

"Your color's good," she added. "Have you been down south?"

"No, I've had jaundice."

"I'm sorry to hear that. But you must be better now, as you're sitting up."

"I was just going to say I'm fine. But actually I'm exhausted after the operation. They took out a gallstone that was blocking somewhere so the bile was going into my bloodstream instead."

"So you've had a gallbladder operation, then?"

"Yes. But the worst's over now. They forgot to check my heart before the operation. So they're going to do it now. Better late than never. And what about you? It's your sight, is it?"

She told him about the coming cataract operation. Then they went on to other things, families and children. Primus knew that Axel had died in 1969. He had seen it in the papers, but it had said that the funeral had already taken place. He had meant to do something about it . . . but, well. . . They talked about Ellen, their divorce and how Primus and Ellen had started seeing each other again toward the end of Ellen's life.

"And your Bernt?" said Edit. "He's done really well, hasn't he? A director, or something, isn't he?"

"Pharmaceutical salesman. He works around the clock, so I hardly ever see him."

An orderly came up to them and said it would soon be Primus's turn.

"Would you like a hand back to your ward?" she said to Edit.

"No, thank you," said Edit. "I had some help getting here. All I've got to do is to go back the same way. Well, Primus, it was really nice to see you again. I'm still living in Högdalen. You'll find the number in the telephone directory. Couldn't you come and visit me?"

"I live in Vreten," said Primus. "And I'm in the directory, too. But I'll phone you. When do you think you'll be back home?"

"They've got to try out my new glasses, too. But perhaps we could try in a month's time or so, when Christmas is over?"

"Fine. I hope to be home by then, too. It takes time to get back on your feet after an operation."

"Yes, so they say. Goodbye, Primus. Regards to Bernt when you next see him!"

She got up and walked toward the door, which was quite visible to her now. Go straight down the corridor to the elevators, then take the elevator up to Level V, that was all she had to do. It took time to get an elevator. Twice one stopped about ten meters away and rang "Free," but before she had time to reach it, the doors slammed shut again. Once she got her stick between the doors, but it was easy to get it out again; the door edges were covered with soft rubber.

At last she managed to get an elevator. At first, it went down in the wrong direction, but then it went up again. A whole lot of people in white pushed their way in. She asked one of them to press the Level V button, but they must have done that already. The elevator stopped and a nice man in a short white jacket held his arm against the door so that it would not close again. Now all she had to do was to go straight ahead to the next elevator, and then turn first right to where the eye clinic was.

There had been a great crush when she had gone to the EKG department, but that had been three hours earlier. Now there was not a soul to be seen. That was what it was like in a hospital, sometimes like you were in a railway station in the Christmas rush, and a moment later it was as desolate as when you were cleaning an office building in the small hours. She took things calmly and had no difficulty finding her way to the next elevators, then recognized the automatic doors on her right at once and stepped onto the rubber mat. The doors hissed open and she went on into the corridor. After about thirty or forty steps, she came to the next bank of automatic doors, and beyond them was her ward. There was a funny smell. Was it glue? Or some kind of latex paint?

Almost immediately beyond the second bank of automatic doors, she tripped over a bucket she had not seen in time. She fell and felt a sharp pain in her left hip. She passed out for a moment, then came to again and couldn't remember where she was. If she lay quite still, her hip didn't hurt too much, but as soon as she tried moving her leg, it felt as if her whole skeleton were falling to pieces. It was hard to see. For the first hour or two, a powerful searchlight from the building site outside was shining in through the window. But when the searchlight was switched off, the only light came from a temporary naked bulb hanging above. But she could see that she was in a half-completed corridor, lying on bare concrete. There were loose wall panels standing about, and thick cables and wires curling along the floor. There was a smell of cement and a musty odor she recognized as laminating paint. She did not cry out once. What use would that be? All her attention was concentrated on trying to lie so that the bone splinters in her hip did not rub against each other. She was sure someone would find her, if no one else but the construction workers arriving early the next morning. If it wasn't Saturday, that is!

12 It was the day before Christmas Eve, late at night. Martina felt caught out as she carried her heavy suitcase up to the room for doctors on call. There were several such rooms in a row, and she did not want to be seen. But the short corridor was quite empty and Gustaf had left his door unlocked as agreed. She went in and switched on the light. The room was cramped but well-equipped, bewilderingly like a motel room, with its wide, fixed bed and colorful blanket as a bedspread. By the bed was a telephone table, and there was a flat clock-radio on a shelf behind the pillow end of the bed. The radio was on and she could hear faint, nondescript music coming from it, rather like on a plane before it takes off. There was a birchwood desk, a chair, a small armchair beyond it, a standard lamp and a small round table with a large ashtray on it, all the furniture in light-colored wood. There was nothing whatsoever personal in the room, no clothes, no briefcase, no books, only a faint smell of cigars. As Gustaf did not smoke, that must have been from some previous occupant.

She looked into the shower room. On the edge of the basin was a yellow leather shaving kit she presumed was Gustaf's. She went back into the room and sat down in the armchair. It was ten to twelve. They had agreed to meet between half-past eleven and midnight. Any earlier would have been pointless. He had to have a cup of tea with the Emergency staff at half-past eleven, and then there was always a patient to be discussed. But with a little luck, they might have five or six hours to themselves. If their luck was out, they would not see each other at all.

Should she go to bed? It was silly just sitting there. If he came, they would go to bed anyhow, and if he didn't, she'd have to try to get some sleep as best she could. She started unpacking her case, taking out her toothbrush, a textbook on general surgery, the plastic case with her diaphragm—no, she put it back again. Her period had stopped only yesterday. It'd be good not to have to mess about.

She undressed, brushed her teeth, took the textbook, and crept into bed. She felt good. It was better meeting here than at home, where there was always such a hassle when he had to go. She never knew how long he would stay. It was usually three hours, but she usually spent the last half hour thinking: he's going to say he must be off now. But here conditions were more equal, someone else deciding when Gustaf should come or go. She could stay until about eight, when the cleaner came. Gustaf had told her it had been the custom before that someone from the department, perhaps a student nurse, brought coffee for the doctor on call. But that had been abolished now. Thank goodness.

She opened the heavy textbook and tried to read about ruptures and inguinal hernias, then started humming a tune: "Gallstones, hernias,

and varices—almost all our patients have one of these. la, la, la, la, la."
She couldn't understand the illustrations in the book, and yet they
had plodded through the anatomy of the groin for almost a week
during their second term of theory. Everything she had learned
seemed to have vanished, the imprinted details having had no meaning whatsoever two years earlier. It was like learning a map of a city by
heart, a city you had never visited nor were ever likely to. Now she was
right in the center of it and didn't even know where the four points of
the compass were. In other hospitals they had instituted review lectures in anatomy in the surgical rotation. But that hadn't been possible at EH. The teachers had no formal obligation to go out into the
clinics, and many of them preferred to stay in their nice safe laboratories.

That same morning, Martina had seen her first hernia repair, per-
formed by Lena Willard. It had started out almost completely wrong.
Dr. Willard had got lost and the surgical nurse had pointed this out,
making a suggestion as to how the problem could be solved. But Lena
had taken no notice, not even bothering to listen. Martina had been
upset and had said she could at least listen to the nurse. But no.
Instead the operation had been held up and the patient had had to lie
quite unnecessarily under the anesthetic for three quarters of an hour
until one of the older surgeons came to have a look. And then it turned
out that the nurse had been right.

Martina's relations with Lena were already poor. They did not
think in the same way at all, and they spoke wholly different languages. Lena was ambitious, theoretically knowledgeable, and always
went to the core of problems, and yet things still went wrong. She
could not take advice from any subordinate, only from a superior. She
was pedantic to a point of lunacy when it came to fulfilling the Senior
Surgeon's intentions. She could talk for hours to a patient and understand nothing, thinking she was being friendly, when in fact she was
oppressing people. Martina thought Lena was a tragedy, both to herself and to the patients. Why was this? Not from lack of willpower, but

some people simply were not suited to the profession they had chosen, and Lena would presumably never change. She would work and strive even harder, going deeper and deeper into a cul-de-sac.

It was depressing to think that of a woman doctor. There were already far too many prejudices against working women and women doctors, so this was all grist to the reactionaries' mill. The other doctors tried not to give the show away, but there was a noticeable change as soon as Lena came into the room or sat down at the same table for lunch. They were all exaggeratedly friendly toward her, or they ignored her, pretending to be busy peeling the skin off their potatoes. They stopped talking about anything important. When she left, they sighed with relief. But very seldom was anything ever said openly against her. Loyalty between doctors was almost unbelievable. It was as strong as a blood bond. Naturally internal criticism arose, but outwardly a united front was maintained. Sometimes she thought of the medical profession as a powerful close little group of colonials battened in behind spiky palisades. Their attitude to the savages outside was friendly, caring and in many ways self-sacrificing. But the boundaries had to be drawn quite firmly, otherwise medical language and with that the whole of western culture would be engulfed.

Martina fell asleep after a vision of white men in cloth helmets with neck-protectors in retreat from an attacking front of old people in wheelchairs thundering across the savannah, great rolling clouds of dust behind them.

She woke again to find someone lying on top of her. She cried out and tried to heave the person off, and then realized it was Gustaf making love to her. How long had that been going on? He was hurting her; she was too dry. She put her hand down and ran her fingers swiftly once or twice over her clitoris to moisten her vagina. Gustaf was still wearing his undershirt. Had he just rushed in and hurled himself onto her? She tried to make eye contact with him, but he had his forehead buried in the pillow, his teeth against her shoulder. She sensed he could no longer control himself. He worked faster until he came, leaving her behind. Then he rolled off her, turned off the light and almost immediately started snoring. She was now more awake than ever and lay there open and empty. She put her hand on her pudendum but did nothing. She was too embarrassed.

If it had been any of the men she had previously been with, she would have been angry. But it felt right with Gustaf, even better than if he had come up, kissed her awake, and talked for a while, then started on the slow exciting foreplay. She put her hand on his stomach, which was soft and slightly flabby like a child's cheek. When he had an erection, his penis swelled hugely. She used to kiss it and burrow her nose in his pubic hair. Sometimes there was something animal about an orgasm, the world outside ceasing to exist, her head turning white inside, and it could be incredibly wonderful. But it could be just as wonderful with all senses intact, noticing how things were for Gustaf, too, instead of striving on in total self-absorption.

During the weeks they had been together, their relationship had changed. The early curiosity and openness had gone. They had acquired habits together, not only meeting on Sunday mornings, but also in their way of making love. There were fewer improvisions. She knew what Gustaf would do next, how she could caress him, and how she couldn't without risking him losing his rhythm. It was a little dull, but also safe. There was a great feeling of home in their intercourse.

Their conversation had changed too. The almost complete openness that had existed after their fumbling start had gone. There were certain areas they rarely or never touched on. Marianne was taboo. She could ask about his children, but not about intimate relations. They did not even mention Marianne's name. It had become magical and it had been Martina who had decided that was how it should be, that Gustaf must protect what was sensitive, so that he did not need to feel he was betraying anyone. What were her own taboos? The future, first and foremost. They never talked about how they regarded their relationship or its continuation. At first, he had asked her how she wanted him to caress her, but he didn't do that now. She was slightly disappointed, not so much about the sexual side, but that they couldn't speak openly. Not speaking openly was against her way of functioning. But Gustaf couldn't cope with it. He was a man, and almost twenty years older than she was. Would it have been easier with a younger man? No. Her experience of her contemporaries was that men of her own age could be even more vulnerable and scared about not being regarded as men.

She slept for a couple of hours and was awakened by Gustaf speaking on the telephone to Emergency.

"A status asthmaticus has come in," he said.

"I'd like to come and watch."

He didn't say no, but she saw by his look that she couldn't go. They couldn't go trotting down to Emergency hand in hand at five o'clock in the morning. She could. But he couldn't.

As he was already pulling on his underpants, she pulled him down again and took his penis in her mouth. Then they made love. She came almost at once. He hurried off and she fell sound asleep, almost missing the clock radio as it buzzed half-past seven.

Gustaf had left two large paper shopping bags full of Christmas presents in the room. He must have been out shopping in the afternoon immediately before going on call. She took out an oblong parcel and shook it. The parcel contained a fairly light firm object. As she was putting it back in the carrier and slowly tipping the parcel over, it said "Mama."

13 It was ten past five in the morning of Christmas Eve. He had used his last remaining coins to take a taxi to Enskede Emergency just before two o'clock in the morning. They had seen who he was immediately and shown him into the special waiting room for psychiatric patients. He had not been able to stand it in there for long and had rapidly begun to deteriorate. He was quite alone in the waiting room, a row of four upright steel and plastic chairs starting to threaten him. They did not change shape or even move, and they looked just as they had a few minutes before, but now the chairs were *inside* him, the whole waiting room a picture inside his head. If anyone suddenly came in through the door, that person would be trampling around inside his own brain and he would be unable to protect himself, able only to sit there watching his own anguish and helplessness.

He had rushed out into the main waiting room and cried out that he had to see the psychiatrist on call at once before his paranoia really took off. An orderly and a nurse—her name was Mona and he had come across her before—had told him to go back into the small waiting room and not disturb the other patients. Disturb? There were a few straight guys there with pains in their feet or heart—who in the hell was disturbing whom? He had sat down on the floor and refused to go back to the solitude of the psychiatric waiting room. The orderly had stood holding onto his arm for a while, but had not dared pull him; then they had given up and fetched him a chair. He had sat down with his head in his hands to protect his eyes against the far too sharp impressions. Patiently, he had sat there for over an hour without uttering a sound, but his pulse had risen to two hundred, so he had gone out and found all the staff in the coffee room. He had asked for an injection, whether a psychiatrist was there to fix it or not. He could fix it himself. He had suggested ten different means, strengths, doses and quantities. Nurse Mona had said that there were some people who had nothing better to do than just read up on medical details in books and learn them by heart. Then he had accidentally knocked over a candlestick and gone back out to his chair again. They would not provoke him! He had managed to keep away from the whole medical scene for four whole months. They would not be allowed to sabotage anything now. Everything would go calmly and peacefully. He sat holding himself rigidly still on the chair to stop it flying up into the ceiling with a crash like an ejector seat.

It was now ten past five. Where the hell was the psych on call? He got up and went over to the glass window of Reception and tapped discreetly on the pane with his signet ring. Nurse Mona appeared, waddling out like a penguin with her large stomach.

"Excuse me," he said. "I'm sorry to disturb you, Nurse. But I must have somehow lost my place in line. I'm not asking for any favors. I'm just asking to have my rightful place in line back again."

"Sit down," said Nurse Mona. "Your turn will come soon. The doctor is trying to get a post partum psychotic transferred to another hospital."

"That's when the milk goes to their heads, isn't it?" he said.

Nurse Mona summoned the orderly over the intercom. Why? He realized he might just as well go back to his chair. He rolled up his sleeves and massaged the crooks of his arms. They were a bluish-greenish-reddish color, the needle marks like tick bites with a small black spot in the middle. He scratched and scratched, but they itched more and more. Suddenly the orderly was standing in front of him.

"Calm down, will you?" the orderly said.

Calm down? He had already clenched his right fist and shifted his weight to his right foot to get in an uppercut, but trembling all over, he managed to control himself. No overstepping the mark! They would not win!

"Sorry," he said. "I only asked a simple question."

The orderly clumsily put his hand on his shoulder for a moment, then went back to the office. Now it was the light that tormented him most. The ceiling light was as strong as a camera flash. The sharp rays were not only trying to penetrate through his eyes, but also through the flesh itself, down through his hair, through his skin, drilling through his skull like a laser beam into his brain! He got up and banged his forehead against the wall. He must put the light out. With his hands over his eyes, he tried to look at the room through a narrow slit between his fingers. There was no switch. But if he could lie face down in a dark examination room . . . he walked swiftly across to the door leading to the examination section. The corridor beyond it was empty. He caught sight of an open door to one of the examination rooms and stumbled over to it. Inside the room were several white-clad people around a bed for heart cases with the head propped up. A woman was sitting up in the bed breathing so that it whistled and hissed all over the room, her face bluish-red and her eyes protruding like black grapes.

"Let me lie in a dark room!" he said, curling up, waiting to be beaten.

"Could you perhaps help me with this man until the psychiatrist comes, Doctor?" said Nurse Mona to a doctor he had never seen before.

"Let me just lie in a dark room before I coagulate," he begged.

"Put him in Number Six," said the doctor, and one of the girls took him away. He threw himself down on the bunk and pressed his face into the plastic pillow. The orderly turned out the light, but left the door open. They were probably afraid he might do something to himself. He lay there for a long while with every muscle tense, then felt his body starting to relax, almost as if he had had a shot already. The image of a hypodermic got stuck in his brain's slide projector and whatever he did to remove it, it stayed there like a rock, an image of a rather thin disposable hypodermic of transparent plastic, with a blue protective cap over the needle. All his imagination concentrated on the blue cap. He had to get that off and see the sharp, beveled point. Then the cap was moving downward. It apparently caught on the needle and stretched, but then it loosened. He got up on his knees on the bunk and pressed his clenched fists to his temples to be able to concentrate. Only a centimeter at the most was left before the heavenly vision of the needle-point would be exposed, shiny and naked . . .

Someone came into the examination room and switched on the ceiling light. He collapsed into a fetal position on the bunk, as if lightning had struck the back of his neck.

"So . . . sorry," said a young girl in a foreign accent. She was holding a red three-branched candlestick in her hand and was wearing thick yellow cleaning gloves.

Slowly he sat up and watched the cleaner going over to the little steel table along the short inner wall of the room, spread out a paper table napkin with small spruce sprigs in the corners, then place the candlestick in the center of it. When she turned to leave, he grabbed her with one hand over her mouth and the other in her crotch. She doubled up with a groan. He put one knee into the small of her back and pushed as hard as he could. With a dull thump, she crashed into the wall, turning without a word and seeking the doorway with her eyes, and with the edge of his hand he struck her just where her neck rose from her right shoulder. She collapsed and remained lying on her side. Swiftly, he closed the door and tried to wedge the back of a chair under the handle, but it was a rigid handle and could not be jammed.

He didn't bother to examine her face further. That was unnecessary. Deep down inside him, he was quite convinced this little slut had been persecuting him for over a week. When he had gone into the supermarket, she had been at the register. In the wine merchant's, she had been disguised in a green overall. When he had bought cigarettes, she had been in the kiosk, and he had kept catching glimpses of her in the Christmas crowds in the street, each time in different clothes. But he wasn't deceived. Now at last he had caught her in a trap. Now he would have to render her harmless for good. Otherwise he would have her at his heels for the rest of his life.

He considered his shoes for a while, a soft pair of Playboys. He would destroy her, trample her to pieces. He went over to the body and tried jumping onto her feet, but he slipped off and almost fell. So instead he jumped on her knees. It felt like jumping on a doorstep, numb, soundless. He would trample her hips to pieces, then further up, jumping on her chest, her neck, then finally on the head that lay to one side.

He was just about to continue, when he realized what was going to happen. Instead, he leaped up onto the examination table and stood there with his back to a corner. Wasn't anyone going to come soon? Why did no one come and save him! He daren't go over to the door, take away the chair and call for help. He beat against the walls with the palms of his hands to attract attention, kicking with his heels at the corner behind him. He felt like a rabbit with a boa constrictor in the room, a great fat white snake lying stretched out on the floor, feigning death. The snake would slowly start moving, then stretch out its head onto the surface of the steel table, then start wriggling further up.

He had killed a girl. Was she dead? He got down on his knees and peered down from the bunk as if he was trying to see something on the ocean floor from a jetty. Was she breathing? A great wave of joy swept over him. Now they would take him in. Now they would look after him forever. He would no longer have any will left at all. Other people would take over responsibility for him for the rest of his life. But if the police came, if the cops got here before the hospital staff . . . then he'd be beaten up as never before in the whole of his violent life.

With one leap, he was out in the corridor. He slipped out into the waiting room and sat with his head in his hands, breathing deeply. After he had sat there for about a quarter of an hour, he saw the psychiatrist . . . whom he had met before . . . coming down in the elevator and walking across to the counter with glass windows.

"Hello, nurse. Didn't you have a patient for me?"

14

Bernt drove the green Volvo up toward the multi-story car park's closed grids. Some distance before the grid was a red and white striped bar and a thick orange metal column beside it with a slit in it for passes. He stuck his Luna card in. The bar jerked up very quickly, almost as if weightless, and the first red light changed to white. He crawled toward the grid as it slowly but surely started to rise. Not until it had vanished completely did the other red light change to white and he could drive into the hospital car park.

He had not drunk a drop for over twenty-four hours. If he happened to get caught by an unexpected police patrol, he was sure he would be able to talk his way out of it without having to show his license, the license he no longer had, the license he had been forced to return to the authorities. But it was hardly likely the traffic police would have extra roadblocks up on Christmas Eve. They were probably all out on the main roads checking on the jams, or they would be on leave after all the overtime put in on Lucia Day. The ordinary police would be at home having an early Christmas meal, in preparation for the tide of domestic troubles that would start in the evening.

Dad had asked him if he could go around via the apartment in Vreten on the way. Dad had a couple of hours leave for Christmas and he had not been back to his apartment since before his operation. Bernt drove the car into one of Luna's reserved places and locked it carefully. Despite prolific security measures, thefts from cars and of cars themselves were common.

He was almost half an hour too early when he walked into Ward 12 and Dad was still eating a meal. No, not eating, but pretending to eat. In a couple of weeks, he had thinned down enormously and become a wrinkled thin old man. His skin hung on him like borrowed clothes.

"Hi, Dad. I'm a bit early."

Dad immediately pushed aside his almost untouched plate and took his wallet, glasses, handkerchief and keys and put them in his pockets. Bernt had to help him with his shoes and jacket.

"I don't think you'll need an overcoat," he said. "We'll either be in the car or indoors."

"I feel so cold since the operation. Can you understand that?"

Yes, Bernt could understand that very well. He was told where he would find the overcoat. Then Dad asked for a wheelchair to go down to the exit. Bernt was surprised, quite simply unable to imagine Dad asking for anything like a wheelchair as long as he was even conscious. Now the old man slowly got into the chair with great suspicion and care, then sat slumped in it, his head hanging. As they walked along the corridors, he didn't look around once, but just stared down at the floor in front of him, like a child on a switchback unable to take its eyes off the rail to avoid being sick.

Bernt didn't know what to say when they were alone in the elevator. He couldn't ask about his health, could he? He had been just about to say: "Is the food good?" But that was stupid. Dad seemed tormented by food.

"Can you drink coffee?"

"Tea, weak tea," Dad replied.

Inside the garage, Bernt first backed the Volvo a little, then helped Dad into the passenger seat and left the wheelchair in the car park beneath the *Reserved for Luna Ltd.* notice. His eyes strayed from the wheelchair to the notice several times. Life had its little joys. Pity he wasn't a photographer.

"Can we drive by the allotment?" said Dad, who was slumped in his seat without his safety belt on. Bernt did not try to persuade him. It would be almost impudent to force him to wear a belt when he was . . .

"We're not allowed to stop on the freeway above it. But we could curb-crawl past it if you like."

Bernt was not in the slightest amused by the idea of stopping on the freeway that ran about ten meters almost directly above the allotment. The police would pick you up on that kind of traffic offense, but didn't give a damn about things like ninety percent of all drivers exceeding the speed limit. They could stop him crawling past the allotment, but he couldn't bring himself to refuse Dad that. It would probably be the last time Dad would have a chance to see his beloved allotment.

They had to make an eight kilometer detour to get into the right lane in the right direction. Bernt drove well out to the right on the soft shoulder of the freeway. The traffic was fairly light. On weekdays there were mostly heavy trucks on this part of the freeway, vehicles going to and from the Årsta warehouses or one of the other great transport terminals.

"Can you see the allotment, Dad?"

"I can see Jonsson's hut."

Bernt could see nothing himself as he was on the left of the car, and he also had to keep an eye on the rearview mirror to avoid a truck running into him.

"Couldn't you see ours?"

"Don't know. I've never seen it from up here."

"We'll drive around again."

Dad protested lamely, but Bernt drove off the freeway and took the road past Enskede Hospital and around south again before setting back into the right lane. Eleven kilometers according to the speedometer. When they approached the allotment for the second time, Bernt switched to the police band on the radio Luna provided all its cars with. He hadn't thought of that before, it was so long since he had driven. Although he was on sick-leave, Luna hadn't made a fuss about the car. No doubt they thought it was like tearing the clothes off people's backs to take away a man's car. He listened to the police messages but everything seemed quite dead in their area, though there was tremendous chatter going on about a Saab on fire on the Essinge road. He stopped, got out and helped Dad walk over to the railing. If the police came, Bernt would say his father had had to get out to vomit.

They stood there looking down for a couple of minutes. Bernt had never seen the area from above before, either. A short distance to their left was a netting-covered spiral staircase leading down to a newly cleared site. It was some kind of emergency exit off the freeway, but he would never get Dad down those narrow stairs. They would probably both get stuck. The area looked almost grotesquely small from ten meters above, almost like Legoland, the toy-town in Denmark, where Bernt had once been on an outing from a pharmaceutical conference.

The snow had gone for the moment, the soil damp and inhospitable, almost all the plants brown, gray or blackened. The allotment area looked like a rusty junkyard of discarded metal sheeting, old barbed wire and reinforcement bars from some factory backyard.

"The windows are still whole," said Dad, pointing down at their cabin.

"Their cabin" thought Bernt. He no longer recognized it. His memory of everything was so much larger, more beautiful and colorful. It couldn't be only because of the December weather. Dad's cabin had been a fine pale green with white gables. Now it was gray and patchy like a shed of oxidized metal.

"Well, that's that then," said Dad, walking on his own back to the car and getting in, as if he had gained some strength.

When they had got up speed again, Bernt said:

"Listen, Dad. What about taking a trip into town before going back to the apartment? Then you can have a look at the Christmas decorations."

"If you keep to the South."

Typical of him. His parents had always regarded all parts of the city north of the great sluice gates with the greatest suspicion. No one went there willingly. Bernt wondered whether they could even have found their way around there. Yes, Tegelbacken, and the Central Station, they knew them, but the rest? Did Dad know how to get to Sture Place, or Östermalm Square? Had he the slightest idea where the Wennergren Center was?

They drove along Ring Road for a while, then turned off down toward Medborgare Place. Very suddenly, the traffic grew heavier and they almost came to a full stop. Bernt swore . . . now they would be stuck there for hours. Not that he was in any particular hurry, but he felt uneasy with Dad there. What would they talk about? They couldn't start bickering as usual, could they, not on Christmas Eve and with Dad soon going to die?

He turned in on one of the narrow, one-way streets that lay just south of Medborgare Place.

"We could take a little walk around if you like."

"Not for me, thanks. My knees aren't up to much after the op—"

"How are things *really*, Dad?" said Bernt, at once regretting it and his inability to avoid controversial subjects.

"All right, you know. I met Edit Wahlgren the other day. Do you remember her? She was married to Uncle Axel. We agreed to get together after Twelfth Night. She's got cataracts, poor thing."

"Could you manage that, Dad?"

"I'll have to take a taxi—"

"Taxi? But will you be well enough? Don't you see that I want to know how you are?"

"I'm not complaining."

"No, you don't complain. But you're bloody not well, Dad! Anyone can see you're in a bad way. I'm sorry, but I really want to know how you're feeling. Don't you see? I want us to be honest with each other at last. For the time we have left together—"

Hell! Why had he said that? Dad didn't understand what it was all about. He thought he'd had an ordinary gallstone operation.

Why don't you tell him, Bernt had said to the new doctor. But she had been evasive and tried to get away with saying: "When he wants to know, he'll ask." Not Dad! He wasn't that kind.

Suddenly Dad placed his wrinkled little hand on the wheel just beside Bernt's own right hand. No, he couldn't cope with this. It was too much . . . too . . . sloppy.

"You've got cancer, Dad!" he shouted. "Haven't you figured that out?"

Dad looked at him, neither in anger nor sorrow, just looking as if Bernt had asked whether he had a fly in his eye or a pimple on his cheek.

"It's all right, Bernt," he said. "I know you mean well. I'm not the one having a difficult time. It's you."

Suddenly it was like talking to a contemporary, not his formidable Dad any longer, but another person, a man who simply happened to be his father. But otherwise it could have been anyone, someone he'd known for a while and begun to regard as a confidant.

"Do you know you're dying?" said Bernt.

"I don't think about it much. It's unpleasant. I try to forget. It works pretty well, actually . . ."

Bernt didn't believe him. If Dad knew that he was going to die soon, then he was probably going through hell, at night at least, or in the early mornings when he couldn't sleep. He must feel fear, fear of the pain, fear of the black hole of the grave.

"Tell me about yourself and how things are going for you, Bernt."

A few weeks before, such a question would have made Bernt get out of the car and slam the door. Now the question sounded true. He began to tell him, about that Kitty bitch, about him having nowhere to live, the trouble at Luna, about how he was on sick-leave at the request of the company doctor but he reckoned they didn't want him back. About how they would probably force him to apply for a disability pension on the grounds of his back and nerves. He told Dad everything, except about his drinking and his license. That was not necessary. Dad had always warned him about drinking. So he didn't tell him that. Booze wasn't really the most important thing now, anyway.

He had thought he would start crying or collapse when he'd poured out all his misery, that there would be an awful sloppy reconciliation scene between him and Dad. But it wasn't like that at all. They sat there discussing things quietly and calmly like two people who trusted each other without fuss or declarations of friendship.

It was quite late by the time they got to the apartment in Vreten. Dad was too tired to go up, so he handed over the keys and asked Bernt to fetch one or two things, saying:

"Take the opportunity of having a good look around. You can live there if you like."

15 Professor Frank Nylander had started lecturing again after the Christmas holidays. Today's subject was the diseases of the pancreas. Old Nye was a lecturer of the old school, using neither slides, overhead projectors, nor flip-pads. On rare occasions, he scribbled a word on the blackboard in his great loopy utterly illegible handwriting. Otherwise he relied on his verbal and dramatic talents. He never used notes, instead roaming freely around the subject, chatting informally, pouring out his own very personal experiences, getting sidetracked with pleasure and staying there until the end. The students were taught as much surgery as they were gossip about the complaints of famous people and the private lives of great pioneer surgeons such as Sauerbruch, Billroth and Dupuytren. Travel reminiscences were also a common occurrence. These were often his memories from the Finnish Winter War, though even more often adventures at sea. Old Nye had an incredible facility for becoming involved in emergency medical situations wherever he happened to be. He had done an amputation on board a lightship he had happened to be passing, with the aid of nothing but kitchen implements and a box of tools. He had done a tracheotomy on a Belgian restaurateur seeking refuge in Corsica, and he had also intervened in several traffic accidents. How much was true and how much fantasy was impossible to make out. The students came in numbers, as there was no better entertainment to be had in the whole medical world of the capital. But Old Nye's lectures had one basic failing. You couldn't pass exams from them, as they were far too erratically prepared, leaving great areas quite untouched, and containing so many oddities that genuine facts were drowned or pulverized by theatrical monologues.

After the actual lecture, if Old Nye's performances could be called that, came regular demonstrations with patients. In principle, the responsible student was supposed to speak about the case and Nylander comment. Then the students were allowed to step forward and look at an interesting deformity, or feel a stomach, throat, loins, testicles, or whatever was being demonstrated at the time. Then the patient was either wheeled or walked out, and treatment and prognoses were discussed.

As an interviewer of patients, Old Nye was always friendly and genial. But soon after the interview had started, he himself took over both questions and answers, describing pains the patient hadn't even mentioned and imputing to the patient experiences and reactions as if he was not the Professor of Surgery, but some superannuated old producer at the Royal Theater.

The first demonstration case of the day was a middle-aged man with a pancreatitis, an acute inflammation of the pancreas. The man was well enough to be able to walk on his own and sit down on the demonstration chair by the lectern.

"Mr. Sandelin, would you be kind enough to tell us a little about your illness," said Nye. "Our young friends here need to know a little about the realities of life."

"Well, it started with me feeling pretty rotten generally . . ." the patient began.

"And then you were afflicted with something like a punch in the upper part of your stomach!" interrupted Old Nye. "You got a high temperature and felt really ill. You'd never experienced anything like it. You realized your life was at stake. Blood appeared in your stools. You turned pale and sweaty. The pain was unendurable, like a knife, a sword thrust through your stomach and diagonally up and out through your shoulder-blade. Violent vomiting occurred—spouting like a volcano!"

"Well, something like that, if you like—"

"And you'd done quite a bit of drinking before that, hadn't you?"

"I don't know what you're implying," said the patient sullenly.

"You'd done quite a bit more drinking than usual before that," said Old Nye. "No point in bickering over that. You've never been one to turn down a drink, have you, Mr. Sandelin? You've always liked to have one with the boys, haven't you? Well, we won't go into the reasons for that here . . . perhaps trouble with the old woman, or your male parts refusing all amorous signals. Work was hell, or let's say your ship caught fire. Enough. You tried drinking Bacchus himself under the table. You quickly slid down the familiar track and couldn't stop, and a drink became your breakfast egg; then you drank until you felt your whole brain turn red. And like a bolt of lightning, or perhaps the God of Thunder, Thor himself, dropped his hammer into your stomach, and you were afflicted by an absolutely unendurable pain in your solar plexus!"

The patient ceased even trying to get a word in edgewise. Old Nye went on for a while longer, and it was time for the students to have their turn. Then something happened that Nylander had never experienced before. Mr. Sandelin refused.

"I want a fee," he said with hostility.

"What?"

All movement in the lecture room ceased, students on their way down from the benches suddenly quite still. Those who had started getting up remained crouched with their hands on the desks in front of them, and Old Nye himself forgot to lower the upraised arms that had just welcomed Thor's contribution to medical history.

"I wish to be paid," said the patient. "Because I am partaking in the teaching."

"Who promised you payment? Has my assistant raised your hopes that if you came down here and held forth on your alcoholic background, then you would be paid for it? You've never been made such a promise, Mr. Sandelin. No such pledge would ever have passed the lips of anyone in this unit. It is even less likely that anyone would have ventured to have drawn up a contract entailing payment for a patient who has had the great advantage of treatment in a great teaching hospital."

The patient got up to leave. In the doorway, he turned around and said:

"I just think that anyone who partakes in the teaching should be paid for his contribution. Thank you."

Members of the audience expecting any comment or an outburst from Old Nye did not have their hopes fulfilled. The intermezzo was far too insignificant for that. The Professor immediately went on to enact the torments suffered by Charles XI in the icy cold apartments of Three Crown Castle before dying in 1697 of cancer of the pancreas that spread to the peritoneum. After a couple of forays into other famous people who had suffered from this incurable form of tumor and been treated in the old Eira Hospital, it was time for the second patient demonstration. An orderly from Ward 12 wheeled in a bed on which Primus Svensson was lying. Old Nye stepped forward, pressed both Primus' hands and started off.

"Mr. Svensson, would you be kind enough to tell us a little about your illness and how it brought you here to the Surgical Unit? Well, on second thought, perhaps it's not necessary to trouble you. But it would be nice of you if the young doctors-to-be here could feel your stomach."

The Professor gestured to the frightened orderly to take off the covers and pull Primus's nightshirt up over his chest. Then he felt for himself. As he squeezed, he did not look at Primus's abdomen but at his face to be able to register whether it hurt or not.

"Well, here we feel a widespread hardening below the right arcus. It has quite a different consistency than what you would expect from an ordinary enlargement of the liver. Come forward and feel."

The students hesitantly started coming down. Several of them knew Primus Svensson and others realized what was in question, so were either embarrassed or reluctant. The patient was lying there exhausted and emaciated, a bowl alongside him. It was hard to know how much he was aware of what was going on, or whether he even knew that he had been wheeled in for a demonstration in the lecture room. Nearly all of them hastily squeezed his abdomen lightly, as if afraid of being infected, not by the disease, but by death itself.

When the demonstration was over and the bed was about to be wheeled out, Primus started becoming agitated, fumbling with his hands for the bowl and turning his head restlessly.

"He's going to vomit. Help here, please!" said Old Nye, lifting Primus up into a sitting position. "The bowl for his majesty, the Pharaoh!"

But the orderly was much too terrified and remained clinging onto the bedhead. Primus vomited thinly and with great effort, yellow mucus running over Nylander's hands. The vomiting ceased and the bed was wheeled out. Old Nye struggled out of his white coat, stuffed it into the waste-paper basket and washed his hands in the basin by the door.

"A surgeon must not be afraid of getting messed up," he said cheerfully, wiping his hands on a towel that he did not hang back, but flung away so that it caught on the overhead projector. "And now to the treatment. Inoperable tumor in corpus pancreatic? What do we do? Anyone? Nothing! If there's a total biliary or intestinal obstruction we can intervene to relieve it. But otherwise the patient is beyond medical treatment. He is no longer a case for the Surgical Unit. It is not our job to deal with terminal treatment. The patient has been here waiting for my lectures to get to pancreatic surgery. Now our friends in the long term care wards will take over."

16 Martina's group was on duty in the Outpatient clinic. After the lecture, they went off to the surgical unit outpatient department to practice examinations and writing up charts on the patients. They stitched up wounds, set minor fractures, lanced boils, talked to patients who were to come in for further examination; and they were present when the surgeons did checkups on patients later on. Then they removed casts, took out stitches and tested the mobility of fingers, wrists and anything else that had been treated. They also had to accompany the surgeon on call that day.

The most remarkable aspect of Surgical outpatients was the fast pace of work. On some days, more than a hundred patients would be seen. The surgeon on call had an average of two minutes for each patient, so a great deal hung on the surgeon's knowledge and ability to make quick decisions, as well as perhaps primarily on his personality. Certain doctors were so anxious to keep up, they flew around like frightened hens with coats flapping, pecking at everything and everyone. Others took no notice of time, pedantically and fussily approaching their tasks, altogether too conscientiously, with the result that perhaps half the patients had to go home again after waiting for four or five hours. Not all of them went home, of course, as some took the elevator down to Emergency, where they knew no one could turn them away.

On this day, Dr. Folke Johansson was on call. He had worked for many years as a mission doctor in Ethiopia, but had been forced to leave the country in 1977. On their first day, Martina and the rest of the group, Hasse, Carl, Lars and Signe, who had joined them after Juan Bosco had left, had all been both suspicious and curious about Folke Johansson. For one thing, he was old, fifty-three according to the register. They had never come across such an elderly resident before.

Secondly, he was a Christian. How did a Christian surgeon work? Did he start praying when things went wrong, trying to save the souls of patients, or what? And a doctor who had worked for over twenty years in Ethiopia, wouldn't he be rather behind the times?

After a few days, they were all enthusiastic, even Carl Bertelskjöld, who had a very rigid concept of success in life and did not willingly bow to anyone lacking a doctorate. Folke Johansson had a medical divining rod built in between his ears. He didn't bother with numbers and other artificial methods of arrangement, but with fantastic precision, went straight to the patients who were most ill. The others had to wait, but no longer than necessary. Folke always succeeded in clearing off the line before the office closed.

He allowed students to do as much as possible on their own, but never left them entirely to their own devices. They never needed to feel abandoned to situations they could not cope with, a common occurrence with the other doctors. When the students had been in Anesthesiology, for instance, they had not done anything, only watched, right up until coffee time, and then the anesthesiologist had just left the respirator, the i.v.s, and all the rest of the space apparatus with a laconic: "I'll be in the coffee room if anything happens."

The nurses hadn't been totally satisfied with Folke Johansson at first. In an outpatient clinic, the Nurse, Nurse Stina, the Senior Nurse especially had much more say in things than in ordinary departments. No disturbance of routine was tolerated. But then Folke had come along with his gentle but determined ways. Even Nurse Stina, the only person in the whole of EH Old Nye was afraid of, adapted herself to Folke's milder routines. How had this come about? Martina thought about it a great deal. Why were some people born doctors, apparently always doing practically everything right without stirring up heaven and earth or appearing the slightest under pressure?

During their course in clinical psychology, the students had occasionally talked about what made a "good" doctor. Not all the students had discussed it, perhaps sixty percent of them, the rest absenting themselves. Clinical psychology had such low status among the students that it was quite natural for a majority simply to absent themselves, especially from seminars and group exercises. Psychology was generally not considered to be a science, but just talk, and people involved in it either communists or members of the Small Birds Society. This attitude was reinforced later during their long medical training because the majority of the medical profession at the Karolinska Institute agreed with it.

What is a good doctor? This could be expressed in many various ways, one way being that a good doctor should master three arts or skills: he or she should be *knowledgeable* in an all around way in the purely medical field, and he or she should possess the quality of *empathy*, the ability to put oneself into the thoughts and feelings of other people. Thirdly, every doctor should have a minimum of *self-knowledge*, know his or her own reactions, preferences, inhibitions and blind spots. If it hadn't been so controversial, Martina would have liked to add a fourth quality: political consciousness.

Folke Johansson fulfilled all these demands, although his training had been old fashioned, and he had scarcely had any opportunity to keep up with recent discussions on medical training. Martina thought it was unfair. Why should a person be a born doctor? The very thought was reactionary, that inborn qualities could make themselves so evident. Did that mean that you couldn't learn to be a good doctor? Or learn empathy and self-knowledge? That must be at least partly true, otherwise her whole concept of the world was shaken. But as her training progressed, the more students and doctors she met, the greater her doubts grew. There were always hopeless cases, but she had never thought there were so many. The majority of students and doctors were "semi-hopeless." They mostly meant well, but they never really got going. There was a sluggishness about them that sometimes seemed like an occupational disease. Gustaf Nyström was one of the better ones, of course, but he was sluggish, too. What really happened to people training to be doctors? Was their environment socially destructive, or did nearly all of them suffer from some kind of mysterious poisoning, a softening of the brain? Was it the formaldehyde? Or the fumes from anesthetics? Was it the actual printing ink on these thousand-paged textbooks? Anyhow, they seemed to have been poisoned, as if their very imaginations had more or less coagulated. "One day I'll be like that, too," she thought. "Why should I escape when so many other people haven't?"

That day, something happened to make Martina deeply ashamed. A week before she had been on night call and had stitched up a cut on a woman's middle finger. She had not been under Folke Johansson's supervision, as Palle Österholm had been on call that night and he regarded students as a labor force. He taught very little and instead simply distributed tasks. So Martina had stitched up the cut in the woman's middle finger. Now the woman had come back to have the stitches removed, but when she tried to bend her finger, it would not do so normally. The middle joint bent as it should, but the outer joint protruded *upward*.

"What shall we say about this, Martina?" said Folke Johansson.

She did not know what to say, as the tip of the finger was pointing in the wrong direction. Suddenly, all her painfully acquired anatomical knowledge was useless.

"The tendon has been severed," said Folke. "When the finger is flexed, the two parts of the tendon divide on each side of the joint, with the result that the distal phalanx is extended instead of flexed."

It was as simple as that, and yet had gone wrong. Would the woman have to go around with a protruding fingertip for the rest of her life?

"The tendon was severed when you cut yourself," Folke said to the patient. "And unfortunately we didn't notice it. But no great harm has been done. I'll speak to the hand surgeons. They can put a little matter like this right in next to no time."

The woman thanked him, and despite their mistake, seemed satisfied and grateful. What would have happened if she'd made a fuss and had wanted to make Martina responsible? Would Martina have been liable? You weren't taught that. She had no idea what her legal position in relation to the patients was.

They continued after Folke had asked Martina to write a referral to the hand surgeon. The next patient was a man who worked in the hospital kitchen. He had tennis elbow, an inflammation of the epicondyle around the elbow. It was not the first time. He had been treated several times with steroid injections in the Outpatient Clinic.

"Hmm," said Folke. "I've seen three of four like these from the kitchen. What do you do up there?"

The patient didn't answer his question, but instead smiled gently and said: "Yes, yes. Thank you. Thank you very much."

Was he a Turk, a Greek, an Assyrian, a Kurd, an Algerian, or what? She felt quite helpless when she came across some immigrants. The distance was *too* great. How with the best will in the world could she understand or imagine how these people lived? They got the heaviest, the dullest, the most dangerous and the worst-paid jobs. It was too much for her. As if there weren't enough misery among native Swedes. Why should she as a Swede worry about foreigners *as well*? She was ashamed at the thought, realizing that the step from there to pure racism was frighteningly close.

Folke Johansson always found time for coffee without rushing, and while they were drinking theirs, he said:

"If I were you, I'd pay a call on the kitchen and see how they work up there. I've already seen three or four tendinitis cases. More are sure to come."

"When could we have time for that?" said Carl Bertelskjöld. "We haven't finished here. And x-ray lectures start this afternoon."

"You can go now, if you like. I'll manage. Get up there and take a look at the kitchens, all of you."

Martina and Hasse wanted to go, but not Lars, Carl or Signe.

"I'm here to learn clinical surgery," said Carl. "Not to go diving around kitchens."

"Do as you please. You're adult people," said Folke Johansson. "Judge for yourselves what is relevant and useful."

"You have to do that sort of thing on social medicine courses," said Signe. "Then you go around looking at things. On the hygiene course, you also have to visit places of work."

"Sometimes it's a good thing to see things in their right context," said Folke.

That's it, thought Martina. When you're on the surgical rotation, you're only interested in surgery. You immediately forget, for instance, all your internal medicine, becoming almost hostile to what you'd learned the month before. What would happen after Surgical? When you were doing psychology, you'd despise all surgeons, all those adventurous knife-happy heroes. In obstetrics, you'd only be interested in deliveries. In Pediatrics, everything to do with adults would seem foolish, almost unnecessary. Why should you expend energy on a whole lot of old-age pensioners when there were ill *children*? A common mode of thought through the whole field of medicine was lacking, an overall approach. There was no language common to all. The numerous medical dialects could at best only complement each other, but were just as often contradictory.

17 Willie Kindlund was responsible for Dishwashing. All dirty dishes, both from wards and cafeterias, were loaded onto a conveyor belt that took the trays down to Dishwashing. There they simply had to keep up with taking the trays off the conveyor. There was room for some piling up, but three minutes was enough without anyone unloading during the rush hour and Dishwashing was transformed into an enormous rubbish heap of overturned trays.

The china on the trays was scraped clean of leftover food, then sorted into large wire baskets, different ones for glasses, silverware and china. At every dish return station and in every ward, instructions were displayed on how things were to be placed on the trays, but the staff ignored them. When pressure was great after lunch and dinner, Dishwashing was as sweltering as a boiler room, the huge machines rattling like the chains of an ice-breaker.

Willie Kindlund had a colorful background. During his military service he had been in the merchant marine. Then he had been a caretaker in apartment buildings, a slaughterhouse worker, a motorbike messenger, and in time a kitchen hand on the ferry boats to Finland. When EH had opened, he and two friends had escaped to Dishwashing from a Finnish ship that was to be unexpectedly docked. Willie Kindlund was fifty-nine, and since he had started at EH, he had managed to keep his alcohol consumption down to eight cans of beer a day. He had not had it so good for many years, his income reasonable and his working hours fixed. Compared with the galley on board ship, Dishwashing at Enskede Hospital was almost teetotal and he could keep a hold on himself.

It was half-past three and they were having a break. The conveyor belt had stopped, and the dishwashers were cooling off with their doors open. It was growing cold in Dishwashing, condensation dripping from the ceiling. One of Willie's subordinates was swilling down the floor with a hosepipe, another behind him mopping with a broom. They had to get the grease off before it set hard. At certain times of the day, the floor tiles in Dishwashing were as slippery as lard.

Willie Kindlund had nine people under him and he ruled them with an iron hand. Most of them had been seamen and Kindlund knew them personally. Many of them had at various times also done dishwashing jobs in restaurants. All of them had one aim in common, to get on to the established staff of cafeterias or hospitals. Of the nine of them, five were Swedes, three Finns and one a Dane. Kindlund's intention was gradually to acquire an entirely Swedish crew. The worst thing he could imagine was some blackie trying to get in.

So he was concerned with caring for his staff as actively as possible. All of them drank to some extent. Kindlund permitted this, but he was the one to decide on individual rations. Absence due to sickness there was among the lowest in the hospital, and whoever was away could reckon with personal reprisals. Some of them also handed over their wages to Kindlund and then drew them out piecemeal. Apart from his banking activities, he also dealt in houses and apartments. If anyone was going on holiday, Willie arranged for extra jobs during the time. No one was allowed to fall into penury. Willie saw Dishwashing as the last bastion of Honor and Manhood before the foreigners and housewives definitely threw men overboard. He was no romantic. He was quite convinced that that day was coming.

He was sitting in the coffee room with his two closest friends whom he had himself named Bill and Bull. Willie was very dissatisfied with Bill. Kindlund's rehabilitation program included everyone in Dishwashing, if possible getting rid of any too evident tattooing. Kindlund himself had had the plastic surgeons remove tattooing from both his forearms, where nowadays two patches of hairless transparent skin now glistened. Bill had a large splodge, a clumsy double-eagle, on the back of his left hand, but he did not dare go to the plastic surgeon, as he was insanely frightened of all doctors.

"You're a little rabbit turd," said Kindlund. "They peel it off in half an hour, with a kind of plane."

"I don't see why I have to."

"Because it's a badge of class."

"Yes, but anyone can see I come from the bottom, anyhow."

"As soon as anyone sees you, they think, 'That guy's been a sailor.' Or done time. That's the first thing they see when you apply for a job, if you're tattooed."

"But I've got a job, for Christ's sake."

"For the moment, for the moment."

"He'll have to go off sick, too," said Bull. "If he's to have an operation. He might make things worse for himself."

"Aren't I like a father to you?"

"Yes, yes," they both said together.

"In your time off, too?"

"Yes."

Someone came from outside Dishwashing, a small delegation with a girl in the lead, two boys behind her, not one of them a day older than twenty-five. Willie rose and stood in the doorway to the coffee room. What sort of bunch was this? Spies from the personnel department? Some damn fool from the union?

"Can I help you?"

"We're students from the surgical rotation," said the girl. "We're on duty in the outpatient clinic and we've had quite a number of patients coming from the kitchens. We were just wondering what it was like to work here?"

"No one from here's been to the clinic," said Willie.

"Yes, they have, several people. With what they call tennis elbow."

Willie glanced swiftly over his shoulder at Bill and Bull sitting at the coffee table. They both shook their heads.

"As I said, Miss. No one from here."

"But I mean from the kitchen department in general."

"This is Dishwashing. I'm not in any way responsible for the kitchen department in general."

"Oh, I see."

"We didn't know the kitchen had different departments," said one of the boys.

"Well, it has. Anything else?"

He looked at them without curiosity. They were students and were going to become doctors. Snotty kids. But they'd soon learn to give orders, becoming stiff-necked noncommissioned officers or good judges of horseflesh. As long as they had the sense to keep away from Dishwashing and didn't come disturbing honest folk.

"Could we possibly have a look around?" said the girl. "We're trying to get to know the different work environments in the hospital, you see."

"What for?"

"Well, a lot of people's work makes them ill. Bad backs, or, well, like in here for instance, with all the noise from those dishwashers when they're working."

"No noise here," said Kindlund. "Ask the gentlemen here. They'll tell you."

"It's as quiet as an office here," said Bill.

"Silent as the grave," said Bull.

"Yes, I suppose this is a newly built hospital, of course," said the girl, looking pleased. "Haven't you any problems at all, then? Lifting things and so on. Those great dish baskets?—"

"We have our routine," said Kindlund.

"We've also heard—" began one of the boys.

"—that there are sometimes drinking problems in this kind of workplace," the other one filled in. "Have you a special scheme to deal with the people who have problems with . . . er . . . well?"

"Does this look like a pub?"

He gestured invitingly toward the coffee room, where Bill and Bull were sitting staring over their spiked coffee, Bill slowly withdrawing his tattooed hand and thrusting it under the towel he'd tucked into his trouser belt.

"Do you get visits from inspectors? Or the safety engineers?"

"If we need them, we telephone for them."

"Oh, I see," said the girl, looking disappointed. "We wondered if we came back again in an hour or two, would you be working then? Could we see how you work when the machines are going?"

"Don't think that can be managed."

"Only for quarter of an hour or twenty minutes?"

"I can't be responsible for that. I should ask the hospital director, in that case. I've no power to promise such things myself, see?"

Supposing the damn bitch went to the director? And came back with a piece of paper in her hand? What would he do then? Send them straight to the safety representative to get the paper approved.

Someone else came into the corridor between Dishwashing and the coffee room, a tall thin man of about fifty. His name was Edwin Björk and he was an old naval hand. Every three months, he went to the barber, put on his best clothes and came to Enskede Chest Clinic to have his sicknote filled in in expectation of his pension application. Björk was an idiot, thinking Kindlund was prepared to let anyone with rotten old lungs into Dishwashing! Especially someone in line for a pension! And yet Björk faithfully left his tribute every three months, a whole bottle of schnapps.

"You'll have to excuse me, Doctors," said Willie. "I've got a visitor here."

"Sorry to have bothered you," said one of the boys.

"And thanks very much indeed," said the girl. "For spending so much of your time answering our questions."

"Not at all," he replied breezily, making a stiff little bow he had learnt when doing his military service as a steward on board the destroyer *Puke*.

18

Bernt had installed himself in Primus's apartment. He was not feeling well. The previous evening he had been to Kitty's to get his things. They had talked and drunk a good deal and the visit had ended in a "reconciliation," which had meant exhausting mechanical sex in the small hours when he was too drunk to feel anything. He had gone home in a taxi and on the way had taken a powerful sleeping pill. Now it was eleven o'clock in the morning. The alcohol was retreating from his body and his heart was beating violently. He had a portable medicine chest in his demonstration case consisting largely of sleeping pills or tranquilizers. He took something to reduce his blood-pressure, a so-called beta-blocker, that had recently become popular against various forms of heart fibrillation, stage fright, psychosomatic heart troubles and hangovers.

Then he had lain down again on the sofa bed with several pillows under his head. His stomach wasn't feeling too good, either. If he lay flat, his stomach threatened to push up into his chest and then up into his throat. He tried to sleep, but that made him so giddy, he had to lie with his eyes open and try to focus them onto something. The nearest object was the excessively large color television set on its steel stand. There was a small cloth on the television set, and on that a Stone Age man sawn out of plywood he had made in woodwork at school when he was ten.

On the right of the television was the window. He didn't want to look at that because it was too bright. On the wall to the right of it were five matchstick pictures all crowded together, one of two elks, another of a Viking ship, one of a waterfall with snow-capped mountains in the background, and one of a windmill and—then the telephone rang. He let it ring, but after rather a lot of signals, he lifted the receiver, unable to bear the sharp metallic sounds any longer.

"Hello, Bernt Svensson? Is that Bernt Svensson?"

"Yes, it's me."

"Runo Adler here. I've been searching for you all over the place. Like a maniac. How are things with you, so to speak. I should ask?"

Runo Adler was employed as a salesman at Luna and had recently been elected secretary of their local staff organization. Drug salesmen had had poor union support for a long time, but for the last two or three years, almost everyone had joined, oddly enough at the suggestion of their employers.

"My blood pressure's not too good."

"I'd no idea you were a high blood pressure man. You see? But as we're now on that subject, they want to take your case up in the adjustment group. I picked it up on the way and thought I'd just give you a call and find out a bit more. You've been off sick for quite a while now, seven weeks, isn't it?"

"Six."

"That's it, six. Anyhow, we were beginning to wonder out here just what you wanted. Wastesson is said to have had a talk with you about another job. Head office job, or whatever. But listen—well, what do you think about it? The management's actually been leaning over backwards, you know."

"What's all the damned hurry? Six weeks off sick. You can have at least three months on the insurance before they even start looking at your papers."

"Reorganization."

"Again?"

"No, it's probably the same thing that just keeps going. Ongoing reorganization."

"Let them ongo as much as they damn well please."

"Can I be straight with you?"

"Oh, hell."

"Straight from the shoulder, frank, so to speak?"

"Of course."

"You're in a bit of a spot."

"I know I'm in a bloody awful spot."

"Good. Well, Section Grouping's being abolished."

"That's old news."

"Yes, but listen, it's being abolished *inside* Greater Stockholm."

"What?"

"That means the hook you're hanging on suddenly isn't there. The whole business's coming directly under Marketing. There's no line organization left. What do they call your job? GS something. Wait, I'll look it up."

"GS twenty-six."

"Greater Stockholm twenty-six doesn't exist from the new year onwards. The girls in Pay are in despair. They don't know how to account for your salary any longer. It ended up with their doing your card manually. Do you see? You're off the computer."

"I'm quite within my rights to be off sick. There's no reason to make a fuss now. Not until I become a ninety-day case."

"I'm only trying to stall a bit. We'd hoped for some cooperation. I realize you're feeling slightly better. But when the train's gone, it's gone. We can fix a corner for you where you can hang out. In the Literature Search Department. We can't do more than that."

"What about the new laws about not sacking people after six months' employment?"

"Yes, I know about them. They can put you in some closet down in the basement and have you copying out the telephone directory in reverse alphabetical order, until you break down and accept a disability pension. But from the union point of view that seems to us a poor solution."

"Things are in a bit of a mess at the moment, you know . . . my pop, my dad . . . my father's dying."

"I'm sorry to hear that."

"Yes."

"So you want a further respite, do you?"

"Yes."

"We're already working retroactively, you know. Your appointment ceased formally at the new year. But O.K. Let us know, will you?"

"Sure."

"When?"

"How the hell would I know?"

"There's no reason to . . . oh, sorry, I wasn't thinking. Phone me when . . . well, phone when you can. Shall we leave it at that?"

Bernt put down the receiver, and, his body rigid, he went out to the kitchen and took two cans of beer out of the refrigerator. He fell into the brown armchair with stained legs and pulled off the ring of the first can. The beer felt cold in the hollows of his head. The future? He had given a lot of thought to trading in surplus drugs, undoubtedly a good idea. Why should several tons of perfectly usable drugs to the value of millions of taxpayers' money every year be quite unnecessarily flushed away or burnt? If nothing else, they should be used up by the vets. But it would never be possible to carry out the plans in reality. Bureaucracy coiled like layers of barbed wire around the whole matter. Bernt Svensson—he knew himself well enough for that—was not the man to have the patience to crawl, cut and squeeze his way through the entanglements of bureaucracy.

His other idea was a better one. It wasn't a new one, true, but he knew from reliable sources that it could be very lucrative, and also there was a touch of idealism about it. He had thought of opening a health farm. He wouldn't need an enormous amount of capital. You rented or bought a large old house in the country—no, hell, you got hold of some old army huts out on some abandoned shooting range! Then you equipped the place sparsely, because in this context spartan surroundings were an advantage. A number of small cabins with narrow beds, in principle like a sleeping car, a ribstool on the inside of the door. The room temperature would be kept low, about fourteen degrees centigrade, even somewhat lower at night. One of the huts would be turned into a combined gymnasium and dining room. The cost of food could be kept low, mostly concentrates; you could probably make an advantageous contract with one of the larger frozen food firms, Findus or Felix, and buy up their stock for vegetable concentrates. In other words material problems were minor—except one—there would have to be a toilet in every room, as laxatives were the foundation stones of most health cures.

He was now quite enthusiastic and opened the second beer can. The great problem was ideological, or however you put it. There must be some kind of philosophy behind it all. Waerlandist, vegetarian, anthroposophy . . . best to avoid touching on the established homeopaths. That market was already fairly tied up: in principle a cartel just like the one the drug industry had formed. He would have to find something of his own, but it wasn't all that simple. But he could "rediscover" something old, something to do with the Incas, perhaps? They were sure to have had plenty of secret scripts on longevity and good health. He'd soon fix it.

Then he would also need access to personal authority. A physiotherapist was obvious, and a psychologist or a yoga teacher perhaps, and most important of all would be a qualified doctor to supervise everything. The doctor didn't have to be there more than about twice a week, to examine new arrivals, for medical advisory work and discharge interviews. Damned shame he wasn't a doctor himself. But there were various possible candidates. He would go to Luna as soon as possible and get his personal card index, in which he had listed all the doctors he had dealt with over the years, their qualifications, interests, special features and other things a clever salesman might find useful. He had noted down those who had trouble with the tax authorities, too. The more he thought about it, the simpler it seemed to become. You got a manpower grant and a local development subsidy, then contacted some anthropological researcher who could dig out some suitable old scripts . . . then you fixed up some doctor. He knew from experience that a great many Swedish doctors thought the increasingly bureaucratic health services were a threat to good patient-doctor relations. The private practitioner section was shrinking.

Company doctors were bullied by the union. The solution was a health farm.

19 Gustaf Nyström was sitting in his research office in Research House. After the turn of the year, he had been granted sabbatical leave for research, or rather it had been forced upon him. Ask's secretary had brought him an already signed application, the period of time was also filled in; three months.

His work seemed even more meaningless than ever, nor had he any kind of inspiration whatsoever. Indeed, inspiration was hardly demanded for research these days. Discipline, persistence, and the ability not to think too much once decisions had been made were required instead. Creativity had its place at the start during the "designing" stage, but then it was like running along a familiar track, plodding on, not giving up because one or two landmarks happened to be covered with undergrowth. In short, research was boring. Some people could cope with boredom and some couldn't. "Why can't I function like the others?" thought Gustaf. "Why can't I adapt. It'd be for my own good." He no longer believed the research he was doing would be for the good of patients. But he himself would benefit from it. That was the twig he was perched on.

"Am I depressed?" he thought. Some things pointed in that direction. He woke early in the mornings and lay thinking about his research, about Martina, about his age. Fourth, and not before, came his family. They weren't truly real to him. He was a husband and father of four children. "Or am I?" he often thought.

He moved sluggishly. Colors, if colors existed in January, had dulled. His surroundings were an endless, detailed porridge of black and white. He looked at his desk lamp. It was a perfectly ordinary lamp with the usual yellow metal shade and mobile stem. It was the most nauseating lamp he had ever seen. He shifted his gaze to the telephone. It was pale gray, and there were certainly several million like it. And yet the telephone threatened him, not in the usual old way all doctors knew when the telephone suddenly rings and you have to rush off. No, it was threatening him as an object, as if it would slowly start sliding forward on the desk and press him against the bookcase behind. The bookcase—he didn't want to look at it! It screamed out his failure: Pilot Study I, Pilot Study II, References, Correspondence, Social Readjustment, Scores, Theoretical Background, Patients 1970–75. And below the bookshelves were all those files full of forms. Nothing would be simpler than taking them out and altering a few checks here and there, moving checks upward in the experimental group and downward in the control group, producing in the results a nice couple of "clusters" separating the material. The chances of anyone discovering the fraud were minimal. Why should he be the one to be so damned honest that he refused to do that? What was the moral? No one would suffer! Who would suffer from Gustaf Nyström showing in his thesis that "transfer at work" was a heavily loaded factor for solving myocardial infarctions?

The honor of a research worker, they called it. What was that? What kind of honor did Erik Ask have? What kind of responsibility? Or compassion for patients? Or political insight? The answer was so banal that he could hardly bear to think about it. There were different kinds of honor: one for the weak and one for the strong.

"Hello, Gustaf!"

He started as if he had been caught out with his fly open. Stefania was standing in the doorway. She was a lab technician and often worked late in the evenings for one of the researchers in the physiology lab.

"I've put the water on. Do you want some coffee?"

He hesitated. Martina was coming by this evening. He didn't want Stefania to see Martina. There was quite enough gossip already.

"I thought you were on your way home."

"Home? I've got to stay until six tomorrow morning. Then he's taking over himself."

"He" was one of the clinical physiologists, Herman Lahren by name. The physiologists were among the most powerful in the hospital. Research House had been built to their specifications and had been equipped to look like a branch of the Karolinska Institute.

"It'd be nice with a cup," he said, stretching his arms above his head and yawning.

"Come and get it then."

"Have you made it already?"

He put on his white coat and followed her. He left his own door open, as if leaving a trap for Martina to fall into, hoping she would slip in quietly without making any fuss or sound.

Stefania had put out two plastic cups on the counter top, a cloth under them. Two rather stale-looking pastries lay on the cloth. The water for the coffee was boiling in a glass flask over a bunsen burner, the flask rattling about as great bubbles swirled up toward its narrow neck.

"What are you doing that's so important?"

"Bleeding mice."

She put a large heap of instant coffee into the cups and poured the hot water over it. A timer rang.

"Something is calling you," he said.

"It can wait."

He raised his cup, then put it down again as it was far too hot, and looked around with distaste. It was a small laboratory: a sink unit, a work bench covered with a black, painted wooden board, a couple of steel stools, a set of drawers, a few stands of test tubes. In the middle of the room were several small glass aquariums on a stand. Each aquarium was like a square, transparent plastic tub with netting over the top. Small glass tubes for food and water were thrust down through the holes in the netting. There were several white mice huddled up in the corners of each tub, their pointed pink tails sticking out.

They had nothing to say to each other. Every evening when he was working in his room and Stefania was on duty, she came in and asked him if he wanted some coffee. Then they sat there waiting impatiently for the hot coffee to cool. Once or twice he had felt obliged to attempt to say something about his own research, but she hadn't listened. He couldn't make out whether that was because she didn't understand, whether he expressed himself too academically, or whether she simply wasn't interested. He had decided on the latter. She didn't care what the hell he was doing. But some time during the course of the evening she clearly needed another human being's company for a few minutes. That happened to be him.

He gulped down the coffee to wash down the stale pastry, then got up to hurry back to see if Martina had arrived unnoticed. But then he sat down again, feeling no particular desire to see Martina. He closed his eyes for a moment, trying to imagine Martina naked, sitting on him, or lying with her legs apart, or on her side with her backside up and waist down. But he felt nothing. He put his hand in his coat pocket and felt in his crotch, but his penis did not react.

"Do you want to see?" said Stefania.

He nodded. She had laid things out for an extraction. Before starting, she pointed silently at the various bits of paraphernalia, as if counting them. Then she pulled a glove onto her left hand, lifted the netting of a plastic tub marked with blue tape, and took a white mouse out by its tail, its eyes shining pinkly, its white whiskers twitching. Its nose, ears and tail looked as if they were made of pink marzipan. She held the mouse's head and picked up a small pointed glass pipette and jabbed it just underneath one of the mouse's eyes. When she released the rubber bulb on the pipette, a narrow stream of dark blood was sucked up into the glass tube.

"Can't that be done any other way?" Gustaf said. He had seen far too many animal experiments to feel any sense of disgust, but it seemed impracticable to have to stab out the eye of a mouse just to get a little blood.

"This is the established method," said Stefania, putting the mouse back.

She picked out the small white bundles one by one, calmly and methodically, and jabbed an eye out of each one. They offered no resistance.

"Thanks for the coffee," he said, putting a few coins down on the bench. "See you."

"Same to you. Goodnight."

When he got back to his own room, Martina was lying smoking on the sofa. Her cheeks were flushed, her wooden-soled shoes kicked off, her white cotton slacks rumpled up around her calves. She had rolled her white coat up and put it behind her head. She was wearing a white T-shirt on which was printed *Thorax*, a souvenir from a visit to Thorax, the Finnish Medical Society.

He bent down and kissed her on the forehead after carefully closing and locking the door. She smelt of drink and tobacco as she blew the smoke up out of her mouth, smiling at him.

"Put that out," he said.

"Are you cross?" she said, stubbing the cigarette out in a matchbox.

"I thought you didn't smoke, except at parties."

"We've been having a party, you see. In Emergency. That damned Christer Bahlin, you know, the one I'm in Emergency with. He was going to do down the women good and proper. We'd been grumbling about always having to find the evening snacks, getting nice tasty sandwiches for the staff and so on. And we're supposed to be learning something, aren't we?"

"It was like that in my day, too. That's nothing to moan about," he said, sitting down at the desk. He put his hand in his coat pocket and felt his penis. It was still as limp as a dead slug.

"Anyhow, Christer Bahlin thought he'd made a contribution, and he went to town and bought masses of open sandwiches with cheese, olives, beef, grated horseradish and crab. Then they bought six bottles of Val de Loire instead of making tea. You should have seen Nurse Stina. She nearly threw Christer out. It ended with us drinking on our own. Then the others went off to a pub."

"Do you think it's wise to drink wine when you're working?"

"Just for once. It was only a lark."

"What about the patients?"

"Just for once."

Martina got up from the sofa and walked barefoot across the floor toward him, her T-shirt up above her waistline and the outsize surgeon's trousers flopping. Half of her stomach was bare, her navel hidden in its hollow, a narrow line of fair hairs running from the waistband of her pants to her navel.

"Why didn't you go off to the pub with the others?"

"I wanted to make love with you."

She smiled warmly and he was forced to cough to cover turning his gaze away. He couldn't cope with this. He couldn't in all honesty respond to her trust. She knelt in front of him and put her head down with her cheek against his thigh. He bent down and sniffed her hair. A solution to the situation would be to get horny with her. Now, this moment. Really horny, so that he didn't have to think too much. "Horny." What a foul word, sticky and mucky like sperm. She flung her arms around his knees and hugged as hard as she could, lifting his feet off the floor.

"The chair," he said. "Careful it's got casters . . ."

She began sliding forward on her knees, the chair gliding slowly backwards until it was stopped by the cabinet full of green files. Her head slid up at the bump, her forehead resting against his stomach.

"You look sleepy."

"Mmmmm."

"Go and lie down then."

She turned her face up to him, a small red impression near one eye from a button.

"A kiss?"

He bent quickly down, closed his eyes and kissed her. He was not thinking about Martina, but about Stefania a few doors away. How did she stay awake all night? Did she try to get some sleep between the ringing of the timer? In that case, where did she sleep? With her head on that black bench?

Martina's wet mouth slipped aside so that she could breathe.

"Let's go to bed . . ." she whispered, her head sinking again.

He looked at the sofa, a narrow government sofa with loose cushions covered in rusty red.

"Go and lie down. I'm just going for a pee."

When he came back, Martina had fallen asleep, lying with her half-naked back to him, her face buried in the crack between the back of the sofa and the seat. She looked as if she would suffocate. He took his own white coat and spread it over her. Then he wrote a note *Didn't want to wake you*, rolled up the paper and thrust it into one of her shoes. He switched the light out and drove home.

20 Hardy had been put in the security men's rest room. It was a narrow room with no windows, and had a green couch along one long wall. Hardy was sitting on a chair against the inner short wall. On the second chair, his back to the closed door, sat the hospital's head of security, Lennart Lilja.

"What now?" said Hardy. "Am I a sort of prisoner here?"

"If you answer my questions, maybe we won't have to call the police," said Lennart Lilja.

"But what have I done?"

"Let's start with identification. You admit that you're Hardy Ragnar Hedwall? Is that right?"

"Yes."

"You were previously employed as a substitute in the hospital library here at EH. When?"

"First of July up to the thirtieth of November."

"And you're now unemployed?"

"Yes."

"But you're a qualified librarian?"

"Yes."

"How come?"

"There happens to be a shortage of librarian's jobs at the moment."

"Good. Now to today. For what reason did you try to gain entry to the hospital Emergency Room this afternoon?"

"I was ill."

"In what way?"

"I just felt rotten. Temperature and a pain in my neck."

"How high was your temperature?"

"I didn't take it. I just sensed it."

"How high?"

"Well, over a hundred anyhow."

"But according to Emergency, on your arrival it was normal. How do you account for that?"

"On arrival? Three hours after my arrival. You have to wait, you know. It had gone down by then, I suppose."

"Your temperature?"

"My temperature had gone down that much, yes."

"You mean you presume that. It hadn't been taken before. There's only one certain measurement and that's what Emergency gave us."

"Yes."

"Then you tried to make out you were ill, among other things that you had severe pains in the neck?"

"I felt damned awful, you know."

"But you weren't."

"What?"

"You weren't ill at all. You were just pretending."

"Hell, no. I felt really lousy."

"But when it was suggested that you should have a careful examination, including a lumbar puncture, you weren't so keen any longer. How do you explain that?"

"I suppose I felt better."

"But you categorically refused to agree to an examination?"

"There's no law that says you must undergo a whole lot of examinations. It is the patient who finally decides."

"You've read up on it all, I see."

"Yes, I've had plenty of opportunities."

"In that case, you will probably have read about something called insurance fraud."

"When you set fire to the house, you mean? To get the fire insurance money?"

"I'm talking about health insurance fraud. If you try to draw on health insurance without being able to prove illness, then you're guilty of an offense against the national insurance laws. And that's precisely what you've done."

"Like hell I have!"

"How then do you explain that after you had refused a lumbar puncture, you then got off the stretcher and told the staff down in Emergency the whole thing had just been a joke."

"I just wanted to have a little fun with the staff to cheer them up."

"The head nurse, Nurse Stina, was not especially amused."

"No, not her."

"Wouldn't it be better if you told the truth, so that we can clear this matter up? You decided from the start, for reasons not yet established, that you'd deliberately go to Emergency, maintaining that you were suffering from certain medical symptoms which were not in keeping with the truth. Didn't you?"

"I don't know about that."

"Didn't you?"

"O.K. O.K."

"So the answer is yes?"

"Yes."

"Why?"

"Why?"

"Yes, why?"

"Because, well, because I . . . because I wanted to go back to my old job. You get attached to . . . you know."

"Have you heard of Wallraff?"

"Yes. That German who got into a hospital, yes."

"You wanted to use the same method as Wallraff had. You wanted to try to worm your way into Enskede Hospital by making out you were a sick patient in need of treatment. Is that right?"

"Yes."

"Why?"

"I wanted to see what it was like."

"What was?"

"It was like this . . . I trained as a librarian, but couldn't get a permanent job. Then I worked here and sort of got into the hospital world, so to speak. I thought about it quite a bit. Why not get more qualifications in a field where there was a shortage of people? But I thought it wasn't enough, just having worked in a hospital when it came to practical experience. Everyone's always talking about practical experience. The experience you need is as a patient. If you haven't been to the hospital, then you haven't. What the hell does a healthy person do? How could I get experience of what it was like being a patient? Well, there's your answer."

"So you're thinking of becoming a doctor?"

"A nurse first. Then go on, you know, and study medicine on one of those new courses for nurses."

"Are there a lot of you?"

"What do you mean, a lot?"

"Who're doing this? Getting 'experience' as patients."

"I really don't know what you're talking about now."

"Have you ever heard of the 'Health Front'?"

"Yes."

"You don't happen to be a member, do you?"

"Not as far as I know."

"Not as far as you know?"

"No."

"To get all this straightened out, I want you to tell me who else is involved in all this."

"No one."

"Think now. This could be very much more serious than you think."

"Could it? How?"

"Just think."

"I've no idea, you know."

"Then I will inform you that on the night of Christmas Eve there was an unusually brutal assault here in Emergency. Someone tried to trample a cleaning woman to death. The person in question later managed to get himself admitted to the psychiatric clinic here, from where he then absconded before the police found out who he was. Do you understand now why we look very seriously at all incidents concerning Emergency?"

"What do you mean by incidents? I'm not violent."

"I didn't say you were. But don't think I'm going to stand for all that patient-experience talk. What kind of lunacy is that? Or childishness? You weren't here for that, but . . . ?"

"I really don't think I'm obliged to sit here being questioned by you. You're not a policeman, only the security guy here."

"You may leave when you like. Let me just ask you about one thing. What actually happened with the Commissioner's car?"

"Whose damned car?"

"The Police Commissioner's. As you see, I know quite a bit about you . . ."

"Carl . . . ?"

"Shut up, Hardy. No names. We don't know if we're alone."

"Well, it was like this. Me and a friend were out in town in his Volkswagen beetle. Then we happened to see . . . the guy who hasn't got a name getting out of his car just in front of us and going into a house in the Old City. We did something else for a few hours, but then we happened to be cruising around past the same place, you know, and the Director-General's car was still there. Mostly just for fun, we got out and went over to the driver and said: 'Why do you sit here waiting half the night? Go home to bed and let hum-hum take a taxi.' Well, he just said something like 'I'm on duty,' and that was that. We pushed off. But what do you think happened next? They had taken the number of the Volkswagen and checked whose it was with the car register, and then they telephoned my friend's *employer*. He works at the City Hall. They asked what kind of people they employed! What do you think of that?! And they demanded an apology!"

"It's not a crime to talk to a driver."

"Exactly!"

"But it was a pretty stupid thing to do, all the same."

"Yes. Though he's resigned now. There's a new boss now."

"You got a bad mark, so to speak."

"Yes."

"Do you know how to get rid of bad marks?"

"That depends, you know, on things."

"You show a willingness to cooperate. It's a good way of getting rid of bad marks. What do you think about trying that method?"

"One does one's best."

"Good. Then we can overlook this 'practical experience' business. You in fact were . . . ?"

"I thought I might write something about the health service."

"Write?"

"Write a book, so to speak."

"Or a series of newspaper articles?"

"A book."

"That's not a one-man job, is it?"

"I don't know. I haven't started yet."

"To change the subject . . . have you been to Germany recently?"

"I went with a girl on a theater trip to Berlin for three days in December."

"Exactly. Over a Friday, Saturday and Sunday. Who did you meet in Berlin?"

"No one special."

"No one special?"

"No."

"Is that absolutely true?"

"Yes, unless I met someone in my sleep."

"Did you meet someone in your sleep?"

"No, lay off now. You keep trying to threaten me with this and that, one hell of a lot of implications. I faked a bit in Emergency, O.K. I've admitted that. I also admit I perhaps took a place from someone who needed it more. And in that way, I cost the health service something. I think that's enough."

"How far have you got with your book?"

"I haven't started yet."

"But before you start, you usually make notes, don't you? Things you have to remember? People who might be interesting to talk to?"

"Yes, of course I've a few notes."

"Could I just take a look at them?"

"Why should you?"

"We could make a deal. We'll overlook that little matter of attempted insurance fraud. In return, you bring your notes here and we'll go through them together, eh?"

"What would you get out of that?"

"I'm the best judge of that."

"But I don't get it."

"Then I'll tell you. This happens to be Stockholm's largest, most expensive, and technically most complex hospital. In itself *it* is a security problem. A whole lot of crimes occur here every day. Money and jewelry disappear, people get knocked down, things are stolen from the clothing store-room, from the alcohol store-room, cars are broken into, patients molested, drugs peddled, and recently you and maybe your friends trying to pose like Wallraff here, as phony patients. I am responsible for both material and personal security here. One day, when we least expect it, we could be the target of terrorist action. Where, when, and how, we don't know, of course. But just look around. The possibilities are frightening. A number of our patients are important people we have to protect. We happen—well, should it be that we had a *really* important person here in Maternity, a person with certain—um—royal connections, who in the past might have had something to do with Germany, I'm not saying who, of course, and I just say suppose, suppose some ill-disposed person—well, you can think out the rest for yourself. I'm employed here to be in charge of security, and I try to do that to the best of my ability. That entails keeping myself informed. About *everything*. About what may seem quite meaningless, but what one day might turn out to be the difference between life and death. For someone, some people, just who we do not know. We have several hundred foreigners employed in this hospital. That doesn't make security any easier. And then you come along with your silly, childish games. Infantile, of course, but even a blind chicken can pick up one thing and another. And it's my duty to keep track of the little bits of grain a blind chicken picks up."

"Yes, I suppose so."

"What about Thursday, two o'clock up in my office in Admin?"

"Thursday, two o'clock? Yes, that's all right—"

"And you'll bring all your notes along?"

"You'll be disappointed."

"We meet again on Thursday, Hardy."

Lennart Lilja put away his little gray diary with the council insignia on it, got up and shook Hardy by the hand. Then he lifted away the chair, put it on the couch, opened the door and held it open.

21 Primus could no longer eat or drink. He was receiving fluid and nourishment through an i.v. into his arm and a tube in his nose. Most of the day, he was more or less drugged. He thought he was an old log in stagnant water, slowly floating downriver. Sometimes he struck a stone, a sandbank or another log. He lay staring up at the sky.

But to see the sky, he had to close his eyes. The sky was a warm rosy pink, such as when you closed your eyes and looked straight at the sun through your eyelids. Sometimes he was disturbed by dark shadows. Those were the giants. Gulliver had become a dwarf now. From being chased by a thousand Lilliputians trying to catch, drill into, and live inside his body, Gulliver had recently been transformed and had shrunk. The day before yesterday he had been only twice as large as an ordinary person, yesterday the same size . . . and today the proportions had been totally reversed. A crow could have carried him in its beak.

He didn't want to look. If he opened his eyes, he saw the giants were wearing white coats, that they were nothing but the staff turning him over, changing the i.v. drip or washing him with washcloths. It felt safer floating on his back in a lukewarm river, while the giants strode mightily along the banks, now and again picking at him with a stick so that he should keep on course.

Sometimes he would float apart. That was horrible. When the morphine injection began to wear off, he could no longer keep himself together. The contours of his body were doubled and trebled, much as when one deliberately crossed one's eyes. He had to make an effort not to give in, not let the doubly-exposed bodies take shape and separate like drops of water. Then he might cease to exist.

And yet everything was fairly calm now. He had had terrible days when he had done nothing but vomit and be seasick. His skin had started turning yellow again and the itching had been indescribable. He had been made worse by the pain-killing injections, but now they had changed them to something else that he tolerated better. If he lay absolutely still and straight, with nothing but his nose and mouth above the surface of the water, he would be able to go on floating for a long time. He had to lie quite still and try to look like a log.

He could hear well. He seldom slept so soundly that he didn't hear everything that was said around his bed. They were doing the rounds now. He heard the professor's voice.

"Now here's Primus Svensson. How is he doing?"

"He sleeps most of the time," said Dr. Willard.

"And what about long-term care?"

Far away . . . it was hard to catch, there were so many people there; far, far away he heard the social worker:

"We're trying."

"He'll probably take off soon, anyhow," said Dr. Willard.

They left. The giants all turned their fat bulging backs and strode up the river bank. The danger was over for this time. "But what if I drift toward a waterfall?" he thought. "I'd prefer to fall feet first. Or on my side. I want to hear the sound in good time, too. I want an extra injection before . . ."

"Dad?"

Was that Bernt? Who else would say "Dad"? There was someone . . . or there might be someone . . . during the war when he had been called up, he had met a woman called Gun. Gun had worked as a cook at the Marine Research Station, where there were several hundred men to every woman. Gun was heartily sick of men, but she liked picking mushrooms. That was how they had got to know each other. After a while, they had started sleeping together. There had been talk of love and marriage. Gun knew he was married and had a son. They had had a fine warm relationship. Thanks to Gun, he had survived. Ellen had known nothing.

Then that autumn, Gun's period had stopped. They had been surprised, although they were both middle-aged people. Primus had lain awake for several nights wondering what he should do, whether he should divorce Ellen . . . but then Gun had said she would get rid of it. Primus had given her what cash savings he had, a hundred and sixty kronor. Gun went to Trosa and from there on to Nyköping. What had happened then? They had agreed to break it off. They were never going to see each other again. But what had happened?

"Bernt?" he said.

"I'm here."

Bernt put his hand on Primus's shin as if to assure him. Primus looked at Bernt. He could look at Bernt. He was no giant.

"How're things, Dad?"

Primus nodded that he was fine. It was difficult to speak, as his mouth and tongue were swollen and dry. Now he was on an i.v. he didn't need his mouth any longer. He wasn't used to talking, his jaw stiff like after going to the dentist.

"I'm living in your apartment now."

"Good."

Bernt had changed. He had come back, but it was too late. They would never have time to be friends. He had hoped for that, to have a son who would grow up as a friend. How many people had thought equally wrongly? Was it possible? Yes, it must be possible.

"Bernt. I want to tell you something."

"Yes. Can I help you with anything?"

"No."

"What is it?"

"In the war, when I was called up, I met a woman there. Her name was Gun."

"Gun?"

"Yes. You've never heard of her."

"You were together. You and Gun?"

He nodded. It was good that Bernt understood at once. He had often thought he must tell him about Gun. But it seemed as if Bernt had sensed it all along, as if that was why he had avoided his father. He had never thought of telling Ellen, not even when she had been ill at the end. It would have been betraying Gun to have told Ellen. But it was different with Bernt. He wouldn't hurt Bernt if he told him.

"She got pregnant."

"So I've got a brother or sister? That I don't know about?"

"I don't know."

Bernt laughed and patted his leg again. He looked really pleased and it was not a scornful laugh.

"It'd have been a good thing if you and Mom had had more children. It's probably not a good thing to grow up alone," said Bernt. "That's not an accusation. Just a statement."

"Ellen didn't have the energy."

"Did you have sex together, you and Mom, after I was born?"

Why did Bernt want to know that? That was nothing to do with him. That was between him and Ellen.

"I want to talk about Gun . . ."

"Of course."

"Gun went to Nyköping . . ."

"To get an abortion?"

The pain was beginning to come back, the last injection wearing off. He could tell that, because he was so awake. The more awake he was, the worse the pain. He tried to breathe with his chest only, as the physiotherapist had taught him.

"Are you in pain?"

"A little."

"I'll go and get the nurse. You shouldn't be in pain. They've damned well got to see to it you're not in pain."

"She'll come. I want to say that I don't know, I don't know what happened afterwards, whether she did what she said she was going to, or, well . . ."

"Why didn't you try to find her?"

"Not after all that."

"Did you agree never to see each other again?"

"Yes."

"People were crazy in those days. You had to punish yourselves, I suppose? Never see each other again just because of that. It's inhuman."

"Yes."

"You'd think it was the nineteenth century. But nineteen forty-three!"

"My generation . . ."

What could he say about his generation? Bernt wouldn't understand.

"But did no one ask for child support? If she'd had the child, she would have tried to get child support, wouldn't she?" said Bernt.

"No, she . . . she was so tactful."

Bernt laughed. Primus himself could hear it sounded silly. But it was true. You just didn't do such things. Gun didn't do such things. You didn't take money for abortions and then change your mind and come asking for money.

"My generation . . ."

"Your generation were so tactful you had to go out in the garden if you wanted to hiccough."

Primus closed his eyes. Now he didn't have to look at Bernt any longer. Now it was done. But had Bernt understood? Had he really heard? You never knew with Bernt. Sometimes it went in one ear and out the other. He changed the subject.

"How's the job going?"

"What do you mean?"

"You were on sick leave, weren't you?"

"Yes, until the end of February."

"Do you have to?"

"What do you mean?"

"You have to be careful about being away too long. You get behind. And . . ."

"And what?"

"They might give the job to someone else."

"That's what your generation thinks, Dad. That sort of thing doesn't happen nowadays, you know. They're all tied up now. Nowadays we have a right to be ill."

"But . . ."

"We've every right!"

"I only meant you should be careful. It's easier than you think to get people against you. Foremen and bosses. You've got bosses, too, Bernt, although you're not an ordinary workman."

Bernt didn't reply, but sat playing with his watch. Primus closed his eyes again. Bernt had withdrawn. He recognized it so well. When Bernt was small and he had asked about school, then Bernt had withdrawn. You had to be so dreadfully careful with the boy. The sharp pain in his belly came back again and he started breathing with his ribs, short panting gasps.

"Where the hell's the nurse?" said Bernt.

"Sit down."

"They can't let you lie there in pain!"

"They'll come."

"They're sitting gossiping in the coffee room, or knitting some-where. Ring the bell."

"They'll come."

Bernt moved over to ring the bell hanging on the trapeze above the top of the bed. Primus took his hand and held it. They looked angrily at each other. Then Bernt freed his hand and patted him swiftly on the cheek.

"I'm going now, Dad. Look after yourself."

"Don't go into the . . ."

"Yes, I will. I'll tell the nurse that you must have an injection. That's your right. Don't you see that tact business is all part of it. You'd rather lie there and . . ."

Bernt wasn't just angry now, he was wretched, his voice thicken-ing. Primus closed his eyes. Bernt would have to speak to the giants now. It was strange having an adult son, someone who could talk to the giants.

22 After having lain in a semi-torpor for several days, Primus Svensson was markedly better on the twentieth of Janu-ary and could sit up for short spells. The pain receded. Bernt was with him every day. They didn't say much but there was no tense silence between them, either.

Bernt had to leave for a couple of days to reconnoiter a bit for the health farm he was planning. As Primus's condition was not consid-ered critical, Bernt decided to undertake his journey. He left in the afternoon of the twenty-fourth of January. At nine the same evening, the patient in the same ward as Primus rang for the nurse. Primus was having severe breathing difficulties. The doctor on call was summoned, an EKG done, and they tried to contact Bernt. But no one answered the Gotland number Bernt had left.

Torben Gillberg, acting resident, was on duty in the Surgical Unit. He was going to be an anesthesiologist but was now doing his stint in Surgical. He did not like accepting help from other people. Primus Svensson had a pulmonary edema, which meant fluid had collected in the lung tissue and was making breathing difficult. The pulmonary edema had been caused by heart failure. If Primus had had another M.I. not visible on the EKG, that didn't matter, as the edema had to be treated first.

Torben Gillberg had to make certain decisions. The first one was whether he should treat Primus at all, or let him die. They could give him oxygen, calm him down with drugs and let him die, peacefully, it was to be hoped. Another question was whether the medical resident on call should be summoned. Pulmonary edema was an internal medical complaint, and in many hospitals they were very particular about keeping mine separate from thine, according to the specialty, about who should diagnose, treat and take the responsibility for the part of the patient that in this case was afflicted with pulmonary edema. Torben Gillberg dismissed the idea. As an anesthesiologist, he had worked in the Intensive Care Unit. There they treated pulmonary lung edema very much more effectively than Internal Medicine could; the patient was put on a respirator there.

Should he have Primus Svensson put on a respirator? In a smaller hospital, he would hardly even have considered the idea, but this was no small hospital. Enskede Hospital was one of the great flagships with excellent technical resources. Should they not be used? That depended on whose interests were involved. Primus Svensson in himself was nothing, a seventy-six-year-old ex-typographer of no special worth to anyone. His next-of-kin were not available at the moment, but there was nothing to indicate that relatives would demand intensive treatment. But there was another reason. Primus Svensson was in Professor Nylander's own unit. Nylander himself had operated on him. Why was Svensson there and not in a long-term care ward, where he belonged? Had Old Nye something special up his sleeve for this patient? As Old Nye was one of the country's leading specialists in abdominal surgery, was it not possible that something special had been planned? There must be some other reason why Primus Svensson, according to ordinary standards already beyond treatment, was still occupying one of the professor's beds.

Could he telephone Frank Nylander at half-past ten at night and ask? He certainly could not, nor even consider such an idea. The staff knew nothing, either. The night staff were on duty at this time, and they were rarely well-informed about the patients. They had not taken part in the rounds or conferences. What remained was to telephone the backup doctor on call, in this case, the Senior Resident, who should be consulted in difficult circumstances. The backup doctor tonight was Dr. Emmerich Wachsmuth. But the backup doctor in a large surgical unit was called in almost solely for major emergency operations. No one phoned him unnecessarily if they wished to remain in favor. Neither was Wachsmuth one of the unit's sunniest boys.

The simplest solution was always to treat the patient. The risk of criticism for being too active was considerably less than the risk of disapproval for standing around doing nothing. Swedish surgery was active, and also forced to maintain its activity in order not to fall behind internationally.

After a few minutes' thought, Torben Gillberg decided to transfer Primus Svensson to Intensive Care. The doctor on call there was a young girl he had recently had as a student. She would not make a fuss. He gave his orders and then phoned Intensive Care to warn them. They would have to keep the old boy alive until they found out who it was who was interested in him.

The night nurse in Ward 12, Nurse Irene, was angry.

"Do you mean we have to go down with him, Doctor?" she said. "Can't they come up from Intensive Care and fetch him? He may take a real turn for the worse, Doctor. I've got several really sick patients here, and can't just go off and leave them."

Torben Gillberg shrugged his shoulders and left. It was no business of his who supervised the transport. They would have to settle that for themselves. Anyhow, he had a long line waiting for him down in Emergency, and an appendix that they were already anesthetizing up in the O.R.

A short while later, Primus Svensson was ensconced in Intensive Care, drugged so that he would not resist the respirator, the respirator pumping oxygen into his lungs to press back the water. By about one in the morning, all the tubes, wires and i.v.s had been connected and checked. An emergency lung x-ray had been taken at his bedside and according to the oscilloscope on the ledge at the head of his bed, his heart was beating fairly evenly. His blood pressure was steady and the blue color began to fade from the tips of his fingers and lobes of his ears. The respirator was watched over by an aide, a young man studying Egyptology and supporting himself by working as a night aide. He had to keep an eye on the connections and the red warning lights. If anything happened, bells rang and lamps winked, inside the ward as well as out in the office. The nurse came around approximately every thirty minutes, suctioned the tubes clean and gave injections so that the patient would be sufficiently drugged.

At six the following morning, the aide was changed. The new one was also a student, a young man in nursing school who took on this work in his spare time to augment his income. The situation was otherwise unchanged, the same regular respirator rhythm, pschyyyi-click, pschyyi-click, grinding on and on.

The morning round was headed by the Senior Assistant Resident, Victor Peipus, who went through the night's charts and reports.

"So Torben put Primus Svensson in here, did he?" he said. "I can quite believe that. What use is that supposed to be?"

He looked at Primus for thirty seconds as he lay there in the bed, his bare feet on view to all. Then he looked at the blood-pressure chart, the fluids and laboratory tests, the EKGs and the chest x-ray plate. Victor Peipus, originally from Estonia and wise to most of the miseries of the world, did not want Primus in Intensive Care. There was no sensible reason, only because a creep of a doctor hadn't dared make an unpleasant decision a few hours earlier, and now he was in a difficult position. It was one thing ending up on a respirator, but quite another coming off it. It was hardly likely that a seventy-six-year-old with advanced cancer and pulmonary edema would ever be able to breathe again on his own, even if the acute situation was relieved. He would be lying here a long time, if worse came to worst. The alternative was to switch off the respirator.

If Primus Svensson did not come off the respirator that day, Peipus would also be forced to do a tracheotomy. Hitherto Primus had had a tube down through his mouth into the windpipe, but if that were allowed to stay for any length of time, there would be pressure injuries to the trachea and vocal chords.

"Put him on the tracheotomy list and telephone Ear," said Peipus to the nurse. The Ear-Nose-and-Throat surgeons did tracheotomies.

When Peipus came back on the afternoon rounds five hours later, the situation was unchanged. He could wait no longer. Primus Svensson could lie there for weeks and a tracheotomy had to be done. Peipus was very annoyed. He had treated a great many seriously ill patients in this unit, who would not have survived without the advanced techniques Intensive Care had available, traffic accident victims, children who had drowned and had been resuscitated, poisoning from overdoses of sleeping tablets, heart attacks . . . but there had to be definite limits. Hitherto those limits had been left to individual doctors, left, it was hoped, to the good judgment of those concerned. But that was no guarantee.

Alongside Intensive Care was a special tracheotorium, and on that afternoon there were two patients on the list, Primus Svensson and Sylvia Bjurström, a young woman with an incurable disease of the nervous system that had paralyzed her respiratory muscles.

At half-past five, one of the patients' names was crossed off the list.

Minutes beforehand, Primus Svensson had had a sudden heart failure. The alarm went off, bells rang, red lamps winked into the eyes of the terrified aide, a girl who had taken the Royal Theater's course for producers, but who was now unemployed in her own profession. Two male nurses came rushing in from the office, tipped up the bed, threw themselves over Primus's chest and pulled up the machine they used to shock a stopped heart into action again with electricity.

By chance, Victor Peipus happened to be there at the time. He slipped in behind them, looked on for thirty seconds at the excitement all around Primus, then said calmly:

"No more now."

23

Bernt Svensson was standing on Grötlingbo Point in southern Gotland. He had been given a lift there by an old business acquaintance, Dr. Johan Melin. They had first met when Melin had been acting as locum for the local Medical Officer in Örnsköldvik. At the time, Melin had been medical head of research at one of the minor drug companies, and they had met several times. Then they had drifted apart when Melin had become an army doctor in Fårösund. Nowadays he had a private practice in Visby, but spent most of his time dealing in houses.

Grötlingbo Point in January was not a pleasant spot. During the previous few days, snow had fallen to the depth of two meters in places, then thawed. A fresh strong breeze had dried up some of the water, but then it had started freezing again. The sand had been driven up into irregular frozen waves, at the bottom of which were black frozen pools.

The two huts were about fifty meters from the shore, a dilapidated concrete bunker on one side of them, a rusty navigation mark on the other. The shore itself was edged with broken driftwood, smashed fish boxes, bunches of seaweed frozen into barbed wire formations, light bulbs, bottles and blackened old shoes.

There was nothing much wrong with the huts themselves. The

army had maintained the barest necessities, the roofs were whole, the façades covered with tiles, even the window frames replaced. They had water and electricity. But there were no approved drains; the existing drain ran out into a shallow ditch. Johan Melin had recently purchased the huts at a government auction, and now he wanted 430,000 kronor for them. There was no mortgage on them, but a local bank had promised to look with favor on any applications from a solvent speculator.

Bernt said nothing about the price, as it would not be a good thing to argue about that now. Instead he wrote down in a notebook everything that would need doing. Drainage 30,000, 18 separate toilets, 25,000?

"How much do you think it'd cost to make a new road?"

"Road? I thought the patients would be coming on bicycles, or on foot? Didn't you say just now that private cars were to be forbidden?"

"Yes, but you need a road for transporting things. We can't carry everything."

"A road? That'll mean negotiations with the council. And they're great ones for wanting their pound of flesh these days."

The place had many advantages. It was isolated, just as Bernt had imagined, and not even in summer would there be very many tourists there. It was a long way to the shops and eating places. The countryside was suitable for various kinds of physical exercise. There were market-gardeners with year-round produce near at hand. But that would be too expensive, of course. Much too expensive! For the time being. With a bit of skill, he might be able to reduce the price. Who would want a couple of old army huts? Though you never knew—it looked as if anything sold nowadays.

The real problem was staff. Not ordinary staff. Gotland was screaming for that kind of less well-paid job, but qualified staff, doctors, physiotherapists and psychologists. The psychologist could wait. Melin could be appointed medical officer for lack of anyone better—true, he was crazy, but people were tolerant. The hardest nut to crack would be the physiotherapist. He would have to hunt one out.

Otherwise a nurse would have to do. He knew there were a number of nurses in the area who had married and got stuck on farms. A nurse with a further qualification in osteopathy, perhaps?

"You don't want to buy a mill for your private use, do you?" said Melin, when they had got back in the car.

"A mill?"

"A large fully-equipped mill with electricity, water and drainage? You must have somewhere to retreat to, surely."

"I was thinking of living here if it comes off."

"To be on the spot always? Perhaps that'd be necessary to keep an eye on things. No, I was just thinking you might be interested in a mill. I've got one over in Hablingbo. I'm showing a Stockholmer it this afternoon. The other day I had a Stockholm restaurateur who wanted to buy a church."

"A real church?"

"Yes, Sundre Church. A fantastic place down on the south point. Painted medieval vaulted roof and all. Electricity and water. He was thinking of opening a steak house."

"He can't do that, can he?"

"No. Not allowed by the government. I have better contacts with the local council. But in a few years' time . . . if the Church separates from the State, if the Swedish economy goes on sliding downhill, and Gotland churches continue to fall to pieces. Because that's what they're doing. There are no funds to repair them, not until they become ruins. I'm convinced when the time comes, they'll be prepared to let in private capital."

Melin had a few calls to make on his car telephone, so Bernt had time to think.

They drove back toward Hemse. He was not sure he wanted to involve Melin in his health project. Melin was crazy. He couldn't do much harm as a doctor. Eccentric doctors had a special capacity for winning the confidence of patients. But Melin would interfere in the finances. He wouldn't be satisfied with an hourly fee, but would want a partnership or some kind of share in the profits.

When Bernt got to the reception desk at Hemse Hotel, there was a telephone message for him. *Phone Enskede Hospital Intensive Care Unit.*

He phoned immediately and was told that Primus had been transferred from Surgical and the situation was as could be expected. He tried to talk to a doctor in charge, but that couldn't be arranged at that moment. He hung up, phoned again, introduced himself as Dr. Svensson and asked to speak to the doctor in charge of his father. A young woman answered.

"Monica Dahlberg."

"Dr. Bernt Svensson here. Hello. I don't think we've met. I'm a doctor at Luna. I understand you're in charge of my father. What's the situation?"

He was given a long account of the pulmonary edema, the transfer to Intensive Care and the present state of affairs. He asked a few more questions, trying to avoid using professional terms. He knew a lot of medical terms, but not all of them. It was better to speak ordinary language than get caught with a wrong term. One would be enough to expose him.

"We're considering doing a tracheotomy," said Dr. Dahlberg. "Perhaps you have an opinion on that?"

She sounded scared. It was no joke treating doctors or their relatives. The hierarchical system did not work in such cases. You couldn't be categorical, or avoid sensitive matters, or be evasive. Bernt had experienced it before and heard doctors talk about it. In a case like this, it was natural that the doctor in charge was trying to shift responsibility on to the relative, on to "Dr." Svensson.

"Do what you think best," said Bernt.

"Wait—no, I thought I saw Dr. Peipus, who's the Senior Resident here. Perhaps you'd better talk to him. I think he's in Surgery. I can ask the exchange to put you through."

"No, thanks. It's good of you, but I'll ring again later. Thanks very much."

He put down the receiver, not daring to carry on with the bluff. He might be able to deceive a little girl like that, but hardly the Senior Assistant Resident. What should he do now? It was just past four o'clock. He had thought of spending the evening and night at the hotel. Melin was to pick him up the next morning in the car and take him to Visby airport.

A ferry went from Visby to Nynäsham in an hour's time. There was sure to be plenty of room on it. On the other hand, he had a plane ticket. But could he get a seat this evening with that? He clenched his fists and thought. Take a taxi first, get the driver to check over his radio if there's a seat on the plane, if not, take the ferry. There wasn't a minute to spare.

He was in luck. At twenty past four he was in a taxi on his way to Visby. He would just about make it. The distance to Visby was about fifty kilometers. It was dark, the snow swirling horizontally across the road. The taxi driver was very helpful and contacted the airport. There was a seat on the plane. But they were expecting fog and could promise nothing. He decided on the ferry and arrived at the harbor with five minutes to spare.

He sat down in the television lounge. Both sets were switched on, a children's program on one and an educational repeat on the other. The salon was almost empty, a couple of long-distance truck drivers were sitting sound asleep, and a family with small children had spread out hard-boiled eggs, grilled chicken, bread, butter, apples, milk, and Pepsi-cola in cans. Five scruffy servicemen had spread out playing cards and about twenty beers. A few minutes later, Bernt had had enough and went to telephone Enskede. It was twenty past five. A nurse told him the situation was unchanged. He bought two light beers, drank them, then sat in a corner and dozed off for a while. He telephoned again just before seven. When he gave his name, there was a silence on the other end. He heard the nurse asking the doctor on call in the background.

"Hello!" he said.

"Just a moment . . ."

Whoever was speaking had put a hand over the receiver. Then the voice came back again. It was the same person speaking, but her voice was quite changed, distant, solemn and formal:

"I'm afraid I have to tell you—"

He didn't hear the rest, or rather, he heard perfectly well what was being said, but he couldn't get the words into the right order. They seemed to come spasmodically, in the wrong order. "Unfortunately," at half-past seven," "tried to contact you", "heart massage", "unexpected fall in blood pressure", "sorry".

"Would you mind saying that all over again," he said.

Even before the nurse had had time to get through it, he had taken it in. He established quite calmly that Dad was dead. What was that to do with him? It was as if someone had read out any old newspaper notice to him. An old man was dead. That was both natural and merciful. It wouldn't change anything very much, either. They had seen so little of each other.

He sat for a moment feeling arid and distant. He was bored. He pulled out the timetable and looked at his watch, then synchronized his watch with the clock in reception. Then he took a short walk, looking into the almost empty dining room and going on up to the salon with airplane seats. He sat for a few minutes in a seat facing straight ahead to the fore. Snow was piling up into the angles of the windows.

His eyes grew hot and the tears began to fall. Then came the abandoned desperate weeping, his jaws trembling, his nose running. He threw his head from side to side and felt like smashing the windows to get some air. Then he was furiously angry. He went into the lavatory and banged his fists on the metal wall, at first angry with himself for being such an idiot as to go to Gotland when Dad was dying. Then his anger was transferred to the dead man. What the hell did Dad mean by going and dying just today, when it couldn't have been more inconvenient? Just as if the old man had lain there waiting just for this day, just as the weather was changing, in the middle of a collision between snow and driving banks of mist, just this afternoon—

After a while, he could weep no more and his head felt empty and dry. He tried to imagine his father in front of him. Primus was not at all his usual self. One moment he was huge, more than two meters in height, large, dark and archaic, a sullen heroic figure from Antiquity now, a statue in the Kingdom of Death, dismissive, incorruptible. The next moment he was the happy dad of the thirties, cycling with Bernt on the bicycle bar, lying on the floor tickling him, or striding in early one morning, his arms full of birthday parcels that he tipped onto the bed.

Dad was dead. Couldn't he have his father back just for an hour? The last time they had spoken, the conversation had ended with Bernt being angry because Dad had asked about the job and being off sick. If only he could see Dad just for a little while, so that he could settle that little skirmish. Naturally Dad had a right to know the position, to know Bernt needed help, that he felt he was sinking, that he was trying to keep afloat with a lot of airy-fairy plans about surplus drugs and health farms. If Dad returned from the dead for an hour, Dad—he had supernatural powers now—would be able to tell him what he should do with his life. There was no one else to do so.

Before he left the lavatory, he took another swing at the metal wall with his fists and the tension lifted slightly. For the rest of the journey, he sat slumped in one of the airplane seats, missing his father, not just the seventy-six-year-old father, but Dad at all ages. It was a little foolish. The cycling thirty-five-year-old Dad had "died" long ago, as had the Dad who had come home on leave in gray uniform with the Coastal Artillery's dark red cloth markings on his collar. Dad at the allotment. Dad on his way to the print shop with his lunch box. Dad and Mom standing hand in hand below the merry-go-round at Skansen.

Why couldn't he "grieve away" the young forty-year-old Dad and get rid of the sixty-year-old middle-aged Dad? Then there would be nothing left to grieve over except the old man, finished with life, whom he liked but realized would be better off if he died? Now the entire family album had burnt away all at once, remote idylls from the thirties and forties crackling in the flames.

24 Martina and Gustaf were in bed in the Esso Motel, on the corner opposite the enormous IKEA furniture warehouse. They lay side by side like two stacked chairs, the upper threaded over the lower. Gustaf was asleep. Martina felt his snuffling mouth slipping further and further down her right shoulder-blade. His penis had also become limp and was slipping out.

They had stolen a day off. Gustaf was officially at a cardiology meeting in Malmö for the day. She had not needed an alibi. They had come to the hotel at one o'clock in the afternoon, Gustaf nervous when they had registered. He had paid in advance, as they had to be away "early to catch a plane from Arlanda." Martina had also had to register—according to the law, the porter had assured them, looking up at the ceiling.

Up in the room, they had spread a picnic out on the bed, wine, cold roast beef, *pain-riche*, potato salad, Boursin cheese, and pears. By three o'clock they had cleared it away, undressed, got into bed and fucked. Then they had slept, woken, fucked again and switched on the color television. Like two children in a great sled they had sat back in the bed, the covers up to their chins, watching the Muppets. They had decided to go down and eat, but Gustaf had become horny again and they had started intercourse in a way that gradually became rather determined and boring, because it came to nothing, ebbing away when Gustaf had lain behind her. And fallen asleep.

Martina was wide awake. She couldn't see the television. The sound was switched off, but colored shadows were flickering across the white ceiling like clouds. She was also hungry, and it would soon be nine o'clock. Several emotions were crossing her mind. She was feeling dependent. She huddled into Gustaf's arms and felt small. Sometimes she had to feel small, a little girl, a weak woman. In reality, of course, it was exactly the other way around, she strong and independent, and Gustaf weak and dependent. But not at this moment; tonight he was the strongest person in the world.

She had changed a great deal during the last six months. Nearly four years ago, when she had left school, she had also changed, but her personal development had stood still until the autumn of 1979. What had changed? She was growing up into a doctor. That sounded silly, but it was true. Earlier on during her studies, she had felt outside it all. All those theorists she had met, had been forced to meet, at the Karolinska Institute, all those anatomists, histologists, physiologists, chemists, bacteriologists, immunologists and statisticians, they had been quite a different breed. People from Mars. Skilled, efficient, successful, intelligent. But what use was that when they were dressed in green spacesuits with one large eye in front, a round cyclops like a goldfish bowl?

During her early days at the hospital, she had felt more like a patient than a doctor. The whole apparatus of medical care had been frightening, incomprehensible, indescribable in any of the languages she had hitherto learned to speak. She had often been upset. She had taken the patient's side against the staff. She had been critical of most things, of the teaching, the treatment, even of the whole concept of health care. She had read Illich, Gorz, and Navarro, and agreed with them in turn. Medicine was almost a hundred percent bluff and humbug, industrialized society's sophisticated mechanism to rob people of the experience of themselves and mastery of their own bodies.

But now that all sounded crazy, especially Illich. She was still critical, but she realized now that she had obviously crossed a border into another kingdom. She was now a citizen of the white-coated. Had she stayed in research at the Karolinska Institute, she would have felt just like one of those green people, she was sure, a perfectly satisfactory person from Mars.

She had been initiated. She understood so much more than most people. Doctors weren't just a conspiring priesthood; they *knew*. They could do things no one else could do. Saving life was a remarkable thing to know how to do. Generations of clear-thinking people all over the world had thought out and created modern medicine. Could they all be wrong? It would be very arrogant of a young girl to think that.

But perhaps she would be thinking the opposite tomorrow! Where had her critical sense gone? From indignation it had gone over into joking. She laughed at mistakes and stupidities, a superior collegial laugh. Take Old Nye, for instance. Wonderful Old Nye, who should be given a place of honor when Skansen opened a special department for stuffed surgeons. She couldn't be indignant with Old Nye. Like Old Nye's latest bit of bravado. A patient whose chart Martina had written up, had asked for a copy of it after his discharge. The patient had telephoned Martina, who had promised to speak to the surgeon. In law, the patient in this case had a right to see his chart. But the attending physician had gone to Old Nye, because Old Nye himself had done the operation. And Frank Nylander had refused—he had never yet shown any patient a chart. She had been astounded. How could he be so arrogant? The patient had gone to the hospital director, but Old Nye had still refused. That was the position six weeks later. Doctors in the unit had told her that patients, lawyers, administrators, patients' ombudsmen and the Medical Association had all had several confrontations with Nylander, but none of them, despite sometimes years of battle, had succeeded in getting him to hand over a single chart.

She was not angry. Even if it was absurd, she still thought it strong of Old Nye to stand out like a figure of fire and a champion of freedom in an increasing bureaucracy, as he would have described it himself. She giggled; she felt completely ambivalent. Supposing she worked hard enough on her own as a doctor? Nearly all doctors worked in a kind of vacuum. Supposing she did that, she would soon be transformed into a real doctor, one who was no longer ambivalent. That would be as good as being here forever in Gustaf's arms and feeling dependent.

"Wake up!" she said, jabbing her elbow into his chest. "I'm starving."

He whimpered, rather like a dog dreaming in its sleep, his arms and legs jerking, his teeth nibbling at her shoulder blade.

"Up Amaryllis!" she said, twisting out of his arms. They had agreed to leave the hotel at half-past eleven at the latest, so Gustaf's arrival home would coincide with the evening plane from Malmö.

He stayed in the same position, then opened his eyes wide and said: "Where's my tie?"

"You didn't have a tie."

He looked as if he were falling asleep again. She bit him behind the knee. Suddenly, he rushed up and stood beside the bed, his arms above his head, scratching in his hair, the beginnings of a paunch evident, his member hanging small and wrinkled, the foreskin back.

"Where's my tie?"

She jumped up opposite him, leaned over and gave him a smacking kiss right on the spot where the knot of his tie would have been.

"There!"

Then she gave him a good shove, and he fell flat on his back onto the bouncing bed. She lay down on top of him.

"Where's my tie . . ."

But he was awake now, only teasing her now, joining in on the game.

25 Yvonne Meyer had been on sick leave for two months owing to a skin complaint on her hands. When she was at work, she was the despair of the personnel office. She had been originally employed as an orderly, but could hardly continue as that because her hands couldn't stand chemicals. Without anyone really noticing, her period of employment had slid past the six-month limit and they could not dismiss her now, because of the new laws. There was no other job for her. To gain time, they sent her on a KYH course. KYH stood for Know Your Hospital. This morning she was to make the acquaintance of the Pathology Department.

Sture Ohrn, union representative and employed in Pathology, was showing them around. The group consisted of sixteen people, five future nursing orderlies, a laboratory assistant, three student nurses, four conscientious objectors, a security guard, a journalist from the regional authority staff paper, and Yvonne. Ohrn started with a run-down of the work of the department. In Pathology, they dealt with tissues and cells. Surgical slides, samples from gynecological exam-inations and cells from coughed-up mucus were fixed, colored and put under various kinds of microscopes. In that way, pathological changes in individual cells and tissues could be directly observed. Their as-signment was to help put the surgeons on the right track as quickly as possible, for when operating, surgeons sometimes did not know what type of lumps or tumors they came across, whether they were malig-nant or benign. In other words whether it would demand considerably more intervention than had been planned.

Yvonne was not especially interested. She found it hard to stand upright for any length of time. The blood ran out of her head and her arches ached. She looked at the birds of prey in Ohrn's room with nausea. Supposing all those hawks, falcons, owls or whatever they were suddenly came alive and dived down from the shelves and started hacking out your eyes before you even had time to blink?

The group moved sluggishly through the various rooms, watching technicians freezing small bits of flesh with carbon dioxide snow and then cutting the bits into cellophane-thin slices. There was a strong smell of different chemicals and Yvonne felt sick.

"Well," said Sture Ohrn. "That's that. Any questions? Otherwise it's time for a visit to the autopsy room, where an important part of our work is carried out. This is voluntary, of course. But it's interest-ing, I can assure you. But if any of you men or women, feel, well, yes—"

Ohrn sniggered in a way that made Yvonne angry, like a challenge, so she had to stay. The only person to drop out was the man from the government security force. The rest moved toward the wide double doors, above which was an illustrated notice stating: Autopsy in prog-ress. No admittance.

They went into the Large Autopsy Room with its ten elongated tables of stainless steel, a strip-light hanging from the ceiling above each of them. At the end of each table was a small high sink with taps, a hand spray and sponges. There were bodies on four of the tables, three men and one woman, their heads propped up on wooden blocks. One body was waxy yellow and goosefleshed, the others grayish-white. Yvonne held her breath and glanced up at the two great round ventilators in the ceiling. Very carefully, she drew in her breath. The only smell was of detergents.

A tall man in white came in from the inner room, wearing a short-sleeved coat and thin rubber gloves with long cuffs on his hands.

"This is the Senior Pathologist himself," said Sture Ohrn. "Dr. Nordal Nansen-Vold. Hello, Nordal, here's today's lot."

"Welcome to my department," said the Pathologist, with a slight Norwegian accent. "We have three cases today. The first I will be opening up myself so that you can follow a complete autopsy. We will work on the other three as usual."

He took a bundle of charts off the window seat and leafed through them.

"To summarize, this patient, whose name is Sievert Gard, was born in 1924. A civil servant by profession, he had earlier been quite fit in most essentials. His wife says here that last Sunday night he woke up with a chest pain. She called an ambulance that took him to Emergency. In the ambulance, he was given heart massage and artificial respiration. In Emergency, d.c.-conversion was immediately introduced. They also injected adrenalin directly into the heart. However, the patient did not revive and was certified dead half an hour later."

The pathologist put down the bundle of papers, grasped a knife with a short blade and swiftly made a long incision from the throat to groin.

"It is a matter of taste whether you go to the right or the left of the navel," he said, cutting a little arc to the left of the navel. "For my part, I always go to the left."

Sture Ohrn had been out and changed and was now also wearing a short-sleeved white coat and gloves made of condom rubber. He stood opposite the doctor, holding a large sponge. Practically no blood appeared, only a few almost black trickles. The pathologist dissected the flesh and skin away from the front of the chest so that the ribs were exposed, then cut through the ribs on both sides of the breastbone with the aid of a large pair of articulated scissors. When they lifted away the platter of bone, the rest of the organs in the body were exposed: the pink spongy lungs, the heart sac like a boiled white cabbage leaf, the glistening reddish-brown liver, a green twist of intestine protruding between the yellow fatty lining of the abdomen.

An attendant behind them started working on the other three bodies. Yvonne changed places so that she had her back to the window-seat and could see everything. She did not want to be taken by surprise. The pathologist was now working inside the first body, cutting and pulling. After a while, he cried out: "Look!" then hauled out the entire contents of the thorax, lungs, heart and various tubes she couldn't identify, and lifted the whole mess onto the little sink unit at the end of the table.

"Come over here, now," he said, carefully rinsing the organs with the hand spray. "I start here and cut up the actual heart-sac . . . and here we find a quantity of serous fluid. That's more or less normal. Now we free the actual heart . . . there we are! Don't be afraid. Come closer so you can see properly. According to the EKG we should now find an occlusion in the right branch of the coronary artery . . . and there it is! See!"

He held up the loose heart with his knife, cut right through a white string, and then scraped white sediment out of the blood vessel.

"And here's the criminal! A thrombotic embolism in the coronary artery that had obstructed the flow of blood to this part of the heart. With fatal results."

He took the heart in his left hand and with a few neat slices, cut it open to demonstrate the heart valves. Then he sliced the heart tissue and showed the extent of the infarction, stating that the heart tissue was another color there, but Yvonne couldn't see that.

Then they went on to the abdominal organs. They put a large clamp above the stomach and another at the end of the intestine and when they started working, there was a smell of shit. Yvonne retreated and pressed her back against the window-seat. The attendant working on the other bodies had now come to the fourth. He had turned back the skin from the neck and dragged the neck and scalp skin down over the body's face. The body looked like a bank robber with a grayish-blue face-mask. Then the attendant took an electric circular saw and ran it around the skull, the saw squeaking and squealing.

The pathologist and Ohrn had started lifting the abdominal organs over to the sink. Yvonne closed her eyes and swallowed. She was not going to stay much longer. She turned around and looked out. The autopsy room was at the very top of the hospital so the view was stunning, a pale sun shining over the Enskede field and blue ski tracks criss-crossing it. It had been eighteen degrees below zero centigrade when she had left home that morning.

"Now, let us sum up," said the pathologist, "We have here a fifty-six-year-old official who according to his wife was under pressure at work. Mostly quite healthy and well. One night he suddenly has violent chest pains and he dies within the course of a half an hour or so. During the autopsy we find a fresh obstruction of Arteria coronaria dextra. The diagnosis is clear: acute myocardial infarction. We also find signs of hardening, of general arterial sclerosis in the abdominal aorta and the valves."

When they went over to the next body, Yvonne wanted to leave, but she didn't know the way out from Pathology to the parts of the hospital she was familiar with. She'd better stay; better than making a fool of herself.

The second patient was a woman born in 1899. Her name was Olga Tannendorff and she had originally come from Lithuania. She had died of cancer of the uterus. They were asked to step closer and look down into the woman's lower abdomen through the incision in the abdominal wall. But Yvonne declined. She didn't like the smell and at the same time, she was embarrassed on behalf of the dead woman, feeling like a Peeping Tom. Not even people's most intimate parts were left in peace here.

The pathologist was interested not only in Olga Tannendorff's lower abdomen, but he also devoted great energy to searching through her liver, extracting small pieces and putting them into glass jars for microscopy.

"According to her chart, this woman ran a studio where they did textile printing. It can be presumed that she inhaled or in some other way absorbed the solvent that at least theoretically can cause cancer, most of all of the liver."

Yvonne felt faint when they came to the third body. She had not recognized him, but when the pathologist read out the chart and mentioned the name Primus Svensson, she remembered. He had been in 96 last autumn. She would probably never have remembered him except for his funny name.

She didn't want to look, so withdrew past the last body. She could cope with looking at dead people she'd never seen alive, could distance herself from them. In fact, perhaps they'd never been real live people? But she couldn't do that with Primus. She had spoken to him, washed him, fed him and even shaved him.

The attendant, now clearly finished with the preparation of the fourth body, came up to her.

"Don't you feel well?"

"I'm all right, but I'd like to sit down."

He pulled out a steel stool for her and sat himself down on the window-seat. Yvonne looked carefully at the stool to see if there was blood on it before sitting down on the extreme edge of it.

"He's right famous, this one here," said the attendant, pointing to the body with a sawn-off skull. "Author and newspaper man, he was. I was reading him only yesterday. Had a cerebral hemorrhage playing golf. Just dropped dead like that. It was all over the front page yesterday. Perhaps you saw it?"

Was he joking? Who played golf in January in eighteen degrees of frost? But perhaps it hadn't been so cold the day before yesterday.

"Can you play golf in the winter?" she said.

"If you're eager enough," said the attendant.

The faint feeling had gone, but her ears had started to ring now. The attendant went on chatting about the "right famous" man, but she heard nothing, as if he were a great distance away. Neither could she hear a sound from the others, who had now turned their attention from Primus Svensson to the last body. There must be something wrong with her ears. The whole world was like a silent film!

Ohrn had begun to stitch up the first body with a large shoemaker's needle. Yvonne got up and went out. She stopped in the corridor and massaged her ears with her finger tips. The high note inside her head, a monotonous piping sound, disappeared, and ordinary noises came back. She took an elevator at random and went downward, not caring where she came to as long as it was a long way away from the autopsy room.

26 Rabbe Chymander was from a Swedish-Finnish family. The C in his surname was silent, so the name was pronounced Hymander. Rabbe was twenty-seven and a qualified dentist. At first he had thought of studying medicine, but had not had the qualifications, so he did the next best thing, odontology. He had never practiced his profession, with the exception of the compulsory practical work he had done during his studies. He had instead recently taken over his father's undertaking business, a relatively easy choice. He had compared being a dentist for eight hours a day until he was sixty-five and doing more or less the same thing every day, with launching into a dynamic trade where he would have a much freer hand. As a dentist, he would earn a reasonable salary, but not a good one, and presumably his real earnings would be reduced in the future. In the undertaking trade, prices were, if not exactly free, anyhow not yet regulated by the health service. National insurance would almost certainly come to include burial grants in time, but even when that day arrived, undertaking would have so much more to offer in comparison with dentistry. There was a larger choice of services to sell. The number of customers would also grow as the population of Sweden became increasingly aged.

The key to success was called chain service. You didn't sell a service, you sold several services interlinked with each other. The idea of chain service had long since had a firm foothold in the undertaking trade. Most entrepreneurs dealt with everything that had to be done from the moment the body was allowed to leave the hospital until the thank you cards were sent off after the funeral and the tombstone was in its place. But Rabbe Chymander wanted to go further and create longer chains. He stepped into the elevator, took off his black hat, pulled off his white right-hand glove and pressed the button to the. Chapel.

The Chapel lay alongside the autopsy room and the mortuary. In the autopsy room, the health authorities still reigned supreme, people met in the no-man's-land of the mortuary, and in the Chapel other forces ruled. Insurance funds, councils and health services took a back seat in there. Could the health services be pressed even further back? Perhaps. Rabbe Chymander was going to meet Sture Ohrn and Dr. Nordal Nansen-Vold. They worked together admirably. Undertaking firms had always cherished the health service. Before, when hospitals were smaller, they had kept track of who recommended what. If a nurse discreetly referred to a particular undertaker, she could reckon with a floral tribute for Christmas. That was how Father Chymander had worked before he had handed over to his son and moved to the Costa del Sol. But that was no longer valid. In the big hospitals, it was almost impossible to keep personal contact with the nursing staff, and neither were younger nurses so impressed by floral tributes; in fact perhaps even suspected that parts of them had already done recent service as coffin decoration in some undertaker's chapel, and then had been rapidly enhanced with moss, little gnomes or robins— recycling on individual initiative. As head of the firm he couldn't go into all the details. No, younger nurses would prefer foreign travel; the nurse who produced the most customers would win a vacation, perhaps. A nice idea, he thought, but clearly quite impossible for a serious firm.

The elevator stopped on the top floor and he got out, gathering up his coat tails quickly so that they didn't get caught in the elevator doors that had a habit of slamming shut too quickly. He went into the mortuary, a row of small stalls without doors, separated from the wide corridor by black draperies. But these draperies were never drawn and had no purpose. Relatives had no entry there. This was a working place where light and space were necessary, as well as the opportunity to chat together while working.

Work was over for the day. There were completed open coffins in two of the stalls and at the end of the corridor was a brown oak coffin, standing on a low wagon, the lid screwed down. The wagon and coffin were holding open the heavy door leading into the viewing-room of the chapel. The place was being aired. He glanced quickly into the two open coffins. The covers were drawn up to the bodies' chins, white cloths of an open-work material covering the faces, the features just visible, as if the dead person had been snowed on. One coffin was Chymander's, the other Fonus'. He noted with satisfaction that his own firm had done the best job.

The coffee room was empty. He went into Pathology, through Microscopy, and on into Ohrn's office. But Ohrn hadn't come. Rabbe sat down and looked at the birds of prey, wondering whether they had moth in them. He had prepared this meeting with great care. Like all departments in Enskede Hospital, Pathology complained that their resources were inadequate. If someone, Chymander's for instance, could reinforce these resources in an acceptable way, then Pathology would naturally look upon cooperation with especially favorable eyes. Actual autopsies could hardly be brought into the chain service, though Rabbe had touched on the idea, thinking fleetingly of having moonlighting pathologists running a kind of mobile autopsy service. He had decided that would be unworkable, but he could come in immediately after the autopsy. Chymander's staff could do the stitching and tidying-up on the actual autopsy tables as soon as the pathologist had finished. That would release resources for Pathology. The cost would not affect the health service, but would be transferred to "the other side."

Where were Ohrn and Nansen-Vold? He decided he would wait another quarter of an hour. Impatience could not be apparent in the undertaking trade. Where could he find staff for this new task that demanded both knowledge as well as experience? The answer was ingenious: he would need no more than the existing staff. Pathology's attendants could do exactly the same work as before, putting back the organs, stitching and tidying up, but under different management, as a well paid extra job for Chymander's. If these payments happened to be earned during ordinary working hours, that had nothing to do with Chymander's. In the old days, attendants had done a number of services for a consideration. Embalming paid the best. Some of them had also had a "practice" in town, making arrangements for people at home. But people rarely died at home nowadays—though perhaps things would improve if this new "thinking" within the health service continued, with its emphasis on decentralization. Famous people had said on television that they wanted to die at home. When that day came, Chymander's would not be found wanting.

Where were they? Rabbe pulled Ohrn's desk calendar toward him. There were several meetings written in. Today, it said KYH Course, then nothing else. He went out into the corridor and knocked on the door of the large corner room labelled "Senior Pathologist Dr. Nordal Nansen-Vold." No one there. In the Small Autopsy Room, he found a secretary taking a pair of skiis out of a cabinet.

"Has he gone?" he said.

"He's at Småland Street at this time of day. He's got his own firm there. Cyto-Service. Do you want the number?"

He thanked her and left. So they had forgotten the meeting. Things like that happened and you just had to put up with it. He went into the secretary's room and borrowed the telephone, first phoning his wife at her dental practice, asking her if she could play squash in an hour—he needed to relax. She could. Then he rang Sten Ossolovsky's secretary to check an appointment for the next morning. He had no wish to come all this way in vain a second time. But it was all right, the time was down in both the secretary's and the hospital director's calendars.

He was going to talk to Ossolovsky about the new crematorium. Enskede was the first hospital ever to have one of its own, and Rabbe Chymander had a number of suggestions to make. The local council had hitherto run the crematorium, the rest of the hospital being the responsibility of the regional council. The solution was naturally that the crematorium should be leased to Chymander's or perhaps a consortium of several entrepreneurs. Why not? Many public authorities rented out staff cafeterias to various companies. Everyone would gain if Chymander's took on yet another link in the long chain.

A game of squash would be good. He had to allow himself some relaxation. He was to go to the Therapy Center in Stockholm that evening to discuss group activities for the bereaved. If only people with the same kind of problems could get together, they would be able to help each other. Life had to be seen as a series of links hooked onto each other.

27 Martina had had a preliminary oral in orthopedics. Before they started working in Orthopedics, they had to be examined to show they knew what it was all about. She was sitting in the hospital cafeteria. Inside the main entrance was a long irregularly shaped hall, the outer part containing the information desk, cloakrooms, and a security post. The inner part contained a kiosk, convenience store, bank, post office, library, pharmacy, and the cafeteria. In the middle of the cafeteria was a pool shaped like an oak leaf. There were plastic fig trees, large-leafed plants, and palm trees here and there. The actual café furniture looked as if it had been intended for the garden: white enameled metal chairs of wrought iron.

It was nearly three o'clock, and most of the people there were patients and their visitors. Some of the visitors had parcels of food with them for the patients. That seemed crazy, pure nineteenth century. Some patients were in wheelchairs and others had walking-frames. A young girl was sitting with her plastered leg stuck straight out, swinging rhythmically in her wheelchair, two friends having rigged up a little tape recorder on the table. All three had their eyes closed, apparently unaware of each other's presence. A patient, a middle-aged man, came slithering into the cafeteria with his i.v. dangling from a tall steel frame on wheels.

Martina had a moment to spare before her next lecture, an extra one that had been pushed in at four o'clock despite their protests. She took out her pad and a pink felt pen, a silly color, but she had no other. She was going to write to Gustaf. What should she say? *Thanks for everything, Love M.* Ugh! Or rather: God! Her head was whirling. She and Gustaf couldn't go on like this; it would have to end sometime. She had long been aware that she did not mean much to Gustaf. He liked talking to her and sleeping with her, sometimes. In between, he seemed uninterested. What did she *really* mean to him? A little extra fun, a chance to relax, someone who appeared on all occasions without making demands, on all occasions that happened to suit him? He was always the one to decide when they should meet. She couldn't telephone him at home. Neither did he like her visiting him in the hospital. Generally speaking, he was often *embarrassed*. But then suddenly a day like that day in the Esso Motel would come along, and everything worked! She'd better put an end to it now, after a good session. Then perhaps she would gradually forget the failures and would remember him as something significant and positive in her life.

But it was damned difficult! How tied to Gustaf was she? She tried to take a negative attitude to him. Gustaf Nyström, forty-one, Senior Assistant Resident, on leave to write a thesis he didn't believe in, married to Marianne with whom he had four children, not especially good-looking, pale, a rather flabby paunch, sometimes impotent, sometimes as horny as a rabbit, holding mostly fair opinions, but ineffective, defeated, introverted, rigid . . . no, that would do; she just couldn't love a man like that. Love? Did she love him? No, but she was *tied.* She couldn't stop thinking about him, often critical thoughts, sometimes totally unreal dreams about Gustaf and herself going off to some distant underdeveloped country, or far up north, loving each other and making their contribution. But that sort of thing only happened in True Life magazines.

Damn you Gustaf, she started the letter, in her usual large handwriting, halfway between printing and writing. *Damn you Gustaf, you must see I can't cope with this any longer . . . you've become an obsession.* She scratched her head with the end of the pen. Writing this kind of thing was cowardly. She should say it straight out. How many times in the autumn hadn't she picked up the mail with trembling hand expecting . . . a friendly and considerate farewell letter from Gustaf. Thanks for everything. How she had hated him at those moments. The bastard, so cowardly that he—

Why didn't she get on well with her own contemporaries? She had had several brief affairs and also a couple of longer ones with younger men. They were constrained in a different way from Gustaf, more sensitive, more afraid, more childish. They didn't know much about life, either. What did Gustaf know about life? He could be amazing in the hospital: wise, calm, tolerant, reliable, open. What was he like at home? Probably a typical doctor, working too hard, unwilling to talk about illness at home, least of all about the family's. When things were difficult, he no doubt behaved at the table like a Senior Physician on his rounds. Now she was being unfair. She knew nothing whatsoever about Gustaf as pater familias.

If I try to contact you again, you should know it will be against my will. She couldn't write that, could she? That was putting the responsibility onto him. What would she do if she had a letter like that from Gustaf? She would have rushed straight over. Romeo and Juliet, like hell. She wrote on, trying to explain that she had decided quite definitely that there should be nothing between them any longer. Nothing more would come of their relationship. She had realized that for a long time. But she wanted to thank him for the Esso day. She hoped it had been as good for him. She signed the letter with a large M, with a flower growing out of the M. She might just as well tear it up? She looked out over the cafeteria to see if God, Fate or any other mysterious power happened to be sitting at a table holding up a Yes or No sign. There was never any help to be had from superior powers!

A man in a rather smart wolfskin coat was sitting at one of the tables. He took a small bottle of vodka out of his coat and poured a generous helping into his coffee. Her mouth watered a little. She would like to get very drunk just like that, quite unplanned. The man looked at her. He wants me, she thought. He's read about how girls sit around hoping for the zipless fuck and now he's got his hopes up.

But then she recognized him and was deeply ashamed. It was Bernt Svensson, the man who had wept up in 12 when he had heard that Primus had an inoperable pancreatic tumor. She wanted to hide or leave. She didn't want to meet him now that his father had just died. People grieving were terrible; it was as if they were trying to drag other people down into their swamp of tears. But Bernt Svensson had got up and was coming over toward her table.

"May I sit here?" he said, in a totally misplaced chivalrous tone of voice.

"Hello," she said, shaking his hand. "I'm sorry."

"What do you mean, sorry?"

"How're things?" she said, rummaging round for a possible forgotten cigarette in her coat. If she ever needed a smoke she needed one now, but there wasn't one.

"I won't offer you a vodka," said Bernt, patting his coat. "The little I've got, I damned well need myself."

She realized she was smiling, a wide friendly smile. Her face turned quite rigid. You don't smile practically into the face of someone just bereaved.

"I'm to go and see him at three o'clock," said Bernt, slurping his spiked coffee.

"It's twenty past already—"

"But I daren't."

"Are you going to see—going to say goodbye to your father?"

"I'm going up to view the corpse, yes."

How drunk was he? Or was he talking like this because he couldn't control his emotions?

"Can you imagine, although I'm fifty-one, I've never seen a dead person."

"There are probably lots who haven't."

"Not even my mother when she died."

"Do you have to?"

"Yes. When my mom died, I didn't go and look at her. I thought it'd be horrible. But then I never really believed she was dead, that they were perhaps just keeping her hidden somewhere or something. If I don't go and look at Dad, perhaps I'll never believe he's dead, either. Do you see?"

It was strange, almost as if he were afraid of ghosts. But perhaps that was what it was. She couldn't tell. None of her relatives had died. If Gustaf died, would she go and look at him, to be free of him?

"What did you say the time was?"

"Twenty-past, twenty-five."

"I can't. I'll collapse in a heap. I'll throw myself over him, or he'll open one eye and glare at me . . ."

"I'll go with you," she said.

He didn't react, but turned his head and bit into the long hairs of the wolfskin.

"Listen, Bernt. I can go up with you. But in that case we must go now. I've got a lecture afterwards."

He didn't reply, but sat up and stared at the posters over by the kiosk, as if something very important had happened, a colossal catastrophe that completely overshadowed the problem of Primus. She felt no desire to help him any longer. Why did she always offer? Why should she start playing at Florence Nightingale?

"If we sit here for a while, then I won't have to go," he said.

"All right, if you don't want to."

"When they've cremated him, there won't be anything left of him, nothing whatsoever. Just a little powder. I find it incomprehensible."

"Perhaps it'd be best if you went up, in that case."

"I daren't."

She got up and tugged at the collar of the coat.

"Come on, let's go."

As they passed the mail box by the kiosk, she felt a sudden impulse to send the letter to Gustaf, putting the piece of paper with no envelope or address right into the box. It'd probably end up in the "addressee unknown" department. The Post Office would have to contact every man in Sweden called Gustaf and ask whether he had a relationship with M.

28 A trial lecture was being held. Karin Sundin, Ph.D. in industrial psychology, had applied for an extra lectureship at the Karolinska Institute. There was no special faculty of industrial medicine, only a couple of lectureships the Institute had been forced to set up after getting pressure from outside. For the moment, the hygiene and social medicine faculties had some kind of vague responsibility for industrial medicine, which had not been made any easier by earlier lack of cooperation. So Karin Sundin had no sponsor of her "own" to back and support her. She had been told by the university authorities to undertake a trial lecture and speak for forty-five minutes on an industrial medical subject. She had chosen *The Hospital as a Work Environment*. The lecture required an audience and this task had fallen to Frank Nylander, who had ordered the whole of the surgical rotation to attend this not particularly popular additional chore at four o'clock on Friday afternoon.

The lecture was to be judged by a jury consisting of Frank Nylander himself, and another member of the university board, the Assistant Professor of Experimental Immunology, John Möller. Neither of these gentlemen had any special knowledge of industrial medicine. There were also two assessors with no vote, one Martina Bosson representing the students, and the other, Kurt Lundqvist, a sixty year-old in a wheelchair because of rheumatism, who had been appointed as ombudsman for the patients. About half the surgical course had put in an appearance, as well as some members of Karin Sundin's family.

Martina wondered what it felt like to stand up there lecturing in front of a more or less unwilling audience, who knew nothing about her subject. But presumably it wasn't nearly so unpleasant as presenting a thesis. Things did not start well. Old Nye arrived ten minutes late, bade Karin Sundin welcome and said:

"On the way here I was delayed by an unexpected environmental problem—we've got ants in one of the rooms for the central ORs, although it's four floors up. No one can explain how they got there. The other day I sent a couple of ants down to the bacteriologists to hear what they had to say. But they're more used to lesser bugs down there, bacteria and viruses. Anyhow, welcome, Dr. Sundin, and perhaps this problem of the ants could be your introduction to your lecture on—*Environmental factors in*—what was the title again?"

"*The Hospital as a Work Environment.*"

"Yes, exactly. Well, perhaps you'd begin then."

Martina saw Möller pressing a button on his watch. The first demand was that the whole lecture should take exactly the stipulated forty-five minutes. Karin Sundin, a plump, graying-blonde woman of about thirty-five, started by handing out about ten pages of stenciled papers. Martina leafed through hers quickly; no text, only drawings of various people in a hospital, a nurse, a cleaning woman, a custodian, an administrator, and so on.

"I thought we could do as follows," said Karin Sundin. "I will show you an exact copy of the pictures you have on the overhead projector. If you wish to make notes, you can do so on the blank space below the drawings, then you needn't waste time trying to write on the pictures."

"Good idea," thought Martina. So many lecturers showed such a large number of pictures and tables on the various projectors, there was often no hope of keeping up. Then the lecturer said something that made Martina sit up.

"Well, I thought I would ask you members of the audience to make you own views known. You all have some experience of the hospital environment, which means you already know a great deal about what it is like in a hospital. Please go ahead and give your opinions."

There was dead silence. Was Karin Sundin quite mad? You didn't ask medical personnel questions. They weren't used to two-way communication. They were trained to listen and take notes, not to discuss. There might be a few questions after a lecture, and if you were brave you could hold up your hand and ask to have some definition explained, even during the actual lecture, but that very seldom happened. So now there was a deadly silence. Möller sighed and looked up at the ceiling. Karen Sundin looked curiously at her audience. After a couple of minutes, she said:

"Is it a characteristic of a hospital environment that you hesitate to say out loud what you think?"

After another few minutes' silence, Frank Nylander raised his hand. It looked very foolish, as if he were a little schoolboy.

"I will not allow Professor Nylander to speak," said Karin Sundin. "This lecture is directed to the students."

Old Nye looked disconcerted and put down his hand with a slight laugh. Martina realized she would have to intervene, otherwise it would be a catastrophe. But before she had time to think out a question and hold up her hand, several of her companions had also started waving hesitantly.

"Transfusion hepatitis," said one.

"You mean infectious jaundice," said Karen Sundin, writing it down on the blackboard.

"Accidents from slipping on floors," said another student.

"Lifting heavy objects," said a third.

"Hours!"

"Shortage of staff?"

"Dry air."

"Unreasonable responsibility."

"Bad pay."

"Do you mean the doctors?" said Sundin, causing smothered laughter.

"Drugs and fatal injuries."

"Hospital democracy."

"Violent patients!"

Suggestions began to pour out and Karen Sundin did not have time to write them all down on the board.

"Well, perhaps we should stop now? Otherwise this will go on until tomorrow morning. What I am getting at, as I'm sure you realize, is partly to try to show how multi-faceted a hospital is as a working environment, and partly how much we already *know*. It is not really possible to maintain that lack of knowledge makes it difficult to find a satisfactory working environment. But first perhaps we should systematize a little—any suggestions?"

"Some of the factors are due to the physical environment," said Martina. "And others are—well, what could you call them—psychosocial?"

"We'll call them that for the time being."

"Political!" a voice was heard from the back.

"Sorry?"

"Po-lit-i-cal."

"Why do you look so skeptical?" said Karin Sundin. "Naturally a number of these factors could be called political. Someone brought up 'bad pay' just now."

With the help of the students, Karin Sundin went on writing various words on the board. After a few minutes, she had arrived at a system of headings that ran:

TRAINING

SALARIES

WORKING HOURS

STATUS

INFLUENCES

PHYSICAL ENVIRONMENT

"This is only an example of systematization," said Karin Sundin. "Other terms can be used and new terms can be added. But on the whole, I think these headings cover most things. Shall we try testing them out?"

She put a picture of a nurse in the overhead projector and asked them to look at the same picture on their copies.

"Well, let's start from the beginning. What training does a nurse have?"

There were a few scattered replies, nursing school, the secondary school nursing course, practical work in the hospital and so on.

"Then I'll ask the next question. Is the training adequate?"

"How could we know that?" said one of the students. "We aren't nurses."

"Think. You've been here over six months now. You've seen a great many nurses at work. What do they do? First and foremost, what might they find difficult if their training is poor?"

"Leadership and authority."

"Exactly. A nurse in a department may be responsible for fifteen or twenty fellow workers. But is she trained for that? Very little. Instead she is trained to nurse. Conclusion: many nurses do not have an adequate training. What conclusions do you draw from that?"

"That she makes mistakes," said a student.

"We don't have to express ourselves so moralistically," said Karin Sundin. "Let's say instead that the system can drive her into situations she cannot manage. What is the result?"

Profound silence again, Möller looking demonstratively at his watch, making Karin Sundin seem harassed for the first time.

"To gain time, I'll tell you. The result may be, for instance, stress symptoms, controversies, poor nursing—maybe she is finally forced to apply for sick leave."

They went on with other examples.

"What is the status of a hospital cleaner?" asked Karin Sundin. There was an embarrassed silence, and finally someone muttered: "Nix."

"Perhaps so. We know cleaning is extremely important work, among other things to prevent what are called hospital acquired infections. But how do we really regard the care of the premises? No comment necessary. What do you think a person thinks about her work when she knows everyone around her looks down on her?"

They went through all the other headings, at quite a fast pace now, Karin Sundin clearly determined to get to the end before Möller's watch began to buzz.

"What kind of future has an O.R. assistant? Retirement age is sixty-five. What do the last ten years of an O.R. assistant's life look like? When her back starts to make its presence felt, when her sight isn't so good, when she can no longer manage such long hours?"

The last subject they took up was a medical student.

"Talking about influences," said Karin Sundin. "We are agreed that influence is important when working environment is being discussed. Now I'm asking you what kind of influence you as students have?"

"On what?"

"On your work here."

"We don't work here."

"Don't you?"

"We're studying."

"Exactly. What influence do you have on your studies, then?"

Nylander was looking extremely uninterested now, Möller only interested in timekeeping. Martina glanced over at her "colleague" in the wheelchair. He looked terrified.

Three minutes before the end, Karin Sundin made a quick summary over what they had arrived at and Möller had to press the button on his watch before it started buzzing. As soon as it was over, the students poured out; it was Friday. Nylander went up and shook Karin Sundin by the hand.

"Thank you for a very interesting lecture, Miss Sundin," he said.

Then the jury withdrew for deliberations into the preparation room behind the lecture room. Nylander started.

"Well, that's fairly clear, isn't it? Quite original, really, but these trial lectures are actually only a formality."

"I don't think so at all," said Möller, looking angry. He was a handsome man of about forty with wavy fair hair. At the moment there were bright red spots on his cheeks.

"Oh, well, yes, then—" said Nylander. "What's your opinion, then?"

"That wasn't a lecture. It was a discussion group. The flow of facts was rudimentary, the level unacademic, the presentation unscientific. As a talk, it might get by, or as a senior high school lesson, perhaps even lower down the school. Nothing was said on "recent findings" for instance, or on the present problem of transfusion hepatitis. That would have been interesting for the audience. What evidence is there that pay influences working environment? No such points were put forward or even touched upon. I calculated almost four minutes wasted on silence. To sum up, a long-winded, unscientific and muddled performance. I shall not approve it. The lecturer was also far too ingratiating, sometimes almost painfully so."

"That may be so," said Nylander. "But then it wasn't meant to be anything else but an outline. You can't do much in forty-five minutes."

"All the more reason for concentration. A stringent and taut performance in forty-five minutes could easily cover the essence of Industrial Medicine. No names were mentioned, for instance. Not a word on Selye's theory of stress. No biological parallels were drawn at all. Nothing on such important areas as immunological problems in the environment, like allergies. I will account for what I have just said to the university. And I shall unhesitatingly recommend a fail."

"It wouldn't look too good if we aren't in agreement, of course," said Nylander.

"Everyone is free to change his position."

"The girl's not a doctor, you know," said Nylander. "We must take that into consideration. This is new, this business of the Institute accepting nonphysicians for lectureships. On second thought, it does disturb me a little. If it had been a large established institution—"

"We must make exactly the same demands on nonphysicians as we do on our own students," said Möller. "I find it hard to imagine a doctor delivering such mish-mash."

"I thought it was good," said Martina, who had been getting angrier and angrier. "What do you think, as representative of the patients?"

Kurt Lundqvist wriggled in his wheelchair.

"Of course, from the patient's point of view—but these are in actual fact staff problems. We usually try to differentiate between—"

"What the working environment in the hospital is like is extremely important to the patients," said Martina. "Poor environment must lead to poor care."

Möller turned to Nylander.

"Only you and I have a vote. I suggest we continue the discussion in private."

"Maybe, yes—"

"I protest!" said Martina. "We really must protest. We have no vote, but we do have the right to be present during the whole discussion. Read the statues for—"

"She's probably right," said Nylander grumpily. "You're good at that sort of thing, you students, knowing your rights."

Martina was slightly surprised that for once Old Nye was bowing to regulations.

"I have already called for a fail," said Möller. "I'll stand by that."

"The worst of it is that we probably have to try and come to some agreement," said Nylander. "We can't go to the university *in pleno* and speak against each other. The girl can repeat the trial. We've never refused anyone that before. Give her a tip about what we think. I'm sure she wouldn't find it at all difficult to present another trial rather more adequately. The woman's done a thesis, after all."

"I have my doubts about the way the psychologists handle their theses," said Möller. "But naturally, I would not oppose a repeat trial. No one need be judged on a single error."

"Then we can come to some conclusion, can't we? We'll let the girl repeat it. And regard today's session as an experiment."

"So you're in agreement with me over the fail?"

"Let's call it an adjournment instead. We'll take up a definite position after the next trial. Well, my friends, we won't keep you any longer. Thank you for coming."

Old Nye shook everyone by the hand and they all went out into the corridor, Martina pushing Lundqvist's wheelchair. It was just as well she had her hands occupied, as she was genuinely furious now. But what could she do? Should she have it out with Nylander? But she had already drawn attention to herself in the medicine rotation under Erik Ask. She wouldn't survive long if she crossed all the professors. It would be better if she made sure the question of trial lectures was brought up in the students' union. They at least had a vote there.

Karin Sundin was waiting in the corridor with a man of her own age holding a bouquet of flowers with the paper still around it. Two young children were clinging onto her, and the whole family was sitting in the window seat. They got up as soon as Nylander and Möller appeared. Möller ignored them, lit a cigarette, and quickly vanished into an elevator, no doubt in a hurry to get back to his cancer laboratory. At first it looked as if Nylander was going to sneak off. "God," thought Martina, "then I'll be forced to tell her she's flunked." But then Nylander changed his mind and put a hand on Karin Sundin's shoulder.

"Well, the university has the last word, as you know. You'll have to be patient for another week or two. I can tell you nothing more now, unfortunately."

But Karin Sundin understood. Tears came into her eyes and no one said anything else. Obviously, no one had expected this.

"If you push me to the elevator, I can manage after that," said Kurt Lundqvist. His hands were so deformed he found it hard to grasp the wheels.

Martina went over to the elevator with him. The whole day had seemed like a long nasty taste in the mouth, her farewell letter to Gustaf, the viewing of the body, and now this unusually clear demonstration of medical power.

29 Gert Jansson came out of Enskede Hospital Emergency with a prescription for Tryptizol in his wallet. He had left his taxi up on the island alongside the row of ambulances. He got into his cab, switched off the winking emergency light and switched on the light on the roof. He took the prescription out of his wallet and read it again. *Tabl. Tryptizol 25 mg No C, 1 tabl, 3 times daily*. The drug would not take effect for two or three weeks. What would he do about his depression until then? It was the fourth time he'd been through a Tryptizol cure to get rid of his depression, the fourth time in less than two years.

It was not particularly strange that he had become depressed and felt his life running out on him. He was twenty-nine. Until three years ago, he had been studying film at Lund. He had written a thesis on Swedish film-architecture between 1950 and 1960, but he had not been able to find employment with those qualifications. He had been forced to move to the southern suburbs of Stockholm with his wife and infant twins. As a student, he had occasionally driven a taxi. Now it was his occupation.

Two men came reeling out of Emergency with a plastic carrier-bag between them, the bag rising and falling as they slid apart and tumbled toward each other again. Gert Jansson switched the light of his Taxi notice off and drove away. He didn't like picking up passengers coming out of Emergency. He didn't want the taxi covered with vomit or to get involved in quarrels with desperate people who had been turned away from the hospital.

Instead he drove up the ramp to the main entrance of the hospital. It was usually slightly calmer there, though he could never be quite sure. But he couldn't afford to drive empty any longer. He had had to wait almost an hour for the promised prescription. There were two taxis outside the taxi station. He switched off the engine and pretended to be deep in the evening paper so that he wouldn't have to talk to his colleague in the taxi in front. He might be one of those talkative devils who came across and just got into the front seat. But he couldn't concentrate on the newspaper. He glanced through a long article on Queen Silvia's delivery problems, and the great question, which hospital had the best security?

The taxis shifted forward and the next time it would be his turn. He started sweating. He often got stage fright when he was in a taxi rank. Who would he get? His imagination was much too lively. When he drove someone to a distant place at night, he always sat with his shoulders hunched up around his ears, waiting for a gun or a knife to be pressed into his side.

An old woman was helped into the taxi in front. She probably had special ride coupons. Passengers with coupons were good, as they always paid and they never made a fuss.

He drove up. Several people came out of the main entrance at the same time, a young woman with a child in a folding stroller, a gang of young men in colorful American jackets, presumably medical students, a man leaning almost backwards with a white plaster collar around his neck, and a man wearing a black hat and an imitation wolfskin coat. It would be the latter. The man was holding a box in his hand, rather like a hat box. For the uninitiated, it might look as if the man were carrying money, a portable safe chained to his arm. Or a terrorist who had changed his mind at the last moment? But Gert Jansson was quite calm now. He knew the box contained an urn.

The man put the urn onto the back seat and got into the front seat. Gert glanced at him. Was he drunk? No trace of the smell of drink. Perhaps it was mothballs from the black hat. As an expert in film props, Gert Jansson could date the hat to 1962–63.

"Where to?" he said to his passenger.

"Where? Oh, yes, go toward Årsta and take the first exit road to the left."

"And then?"

"I'll show you."

A great many passengers did not give exact addresses, which wasn't surprising, as no driver could keep track of all the streets and alleys, especially out in the suburbs. He drove off. They took a wide loop south to get up onto the freeway to Årsta, and when they turned north again they could see the whole of Enskede Hospital in the afternoon sun, a grayish-blue airport terminal surrounded by approach ramps instead of runways.

"Drive slowly. It's here somewhere—"

"Are we stopping here? That's against the law. I can't stop here."

"Just for two minutes. Over there by that spiral staircase."

Gert Jansson slowed down. Were they really going to stop? He would for fifty kronor, but how could he get his passenger to understand that without actually asking straight out for the money? He slowed to crawling pace, switched on his winking light and turned to the passenger in the black hat.

"Stop," the passenger said.

He stopped. There was something uncompromising about the passenger's voice, which made it impossible not to obey. They both got out. The man carefully took the urn out and started climbing down the wire-encased spiral stairway. Gert went across to the railing and watched him. He wasn't going to sneak off without paying, was he?

Directly below was a snow-covered allotment area. The man in the black hat trudged in between the little cabins and snow-laden bushes, then climbed over the low gate to one of the cabins. Suddenly Gert realized what he was going to do—he was going to scatter the ashes in the snow outside the allotment! But what had that got to do with him? What did it matter to a part of the city that had tons of car fumes, sulphur fumes, radioactive fallout and sooty snow poured onto it every day? The ashes of a human being would probably be the cleanest and least harmful of all. It was nothing but superstition that they couldn't be scattered anywhere.

The man in the silly black hat and youthful too-short fur coat put the urn down in the snow. Gert carried a view-finder on a cord around his neck, a relic from his film days. He pulled it out and peered through it. That's what film directors did when they wanted some idea of the camera angle required. It was a perfect picture of the man in black and gray in the snow. It should be taken in color so that the almost indiscernible yellow in the fur would be hinted at rather than actually shown. Then he would lift the camera and slowly zoom back to the blue hospital in the background.

But the man didn't open the box. Instead he broke off two sprigs from a tough old yew tree. It looked almost impossible to get them off, the man twisting them around several times before they came away. He thrust the sprigs under one arm, picked up the box with the urn and slowly started retracing his steps. He seemed to be creeping away so as not to wake anyone in the little doll's house. A semi-truck and trailer went by, blowing its horn as the man climbed up the spiral staircase, and a wave of gray melted snow mixed with salt sprayed over the taxi. Gert jumped into the vehicle and held the door open for the man. But his customer did as before, first put the urn in the middle of the back seat before getting in the front.

"Where to now?" said Gert Jansson.

"Sandsborg churchyard."

They could see nothing through the left-hand window. Gert Jansson rolled down the window, thrust out his head, put out his left indicator and swung out into the lane. Once again they made a long detour around the hospital to get to the Årsta link-road and on toward Sandsborg.

AFTERWORD

A Conversation with P.C. Jersild

LEIF SJÖBERG

P. C. Jersild (b. 1935) is a Swedish physician who became a highly successful novelist. As medical adviser to the National Government Administration Board for some years, Dr. Jersild was able to view high official decision making regarding work environments. These experiences exerted a strong influence on his subsequent writing, in which he characteristically defined and discussed social maladies in the Swedish welfare state.

Jersild has nearly thirty novels and plays to his credit, as well as a sociopsychiatric study, *Recovery in Schizophrenia* (1970) which he wrote with J. G. and M.-B. Inghe. Jersild's novels have become best sellers and have been translated into major European languages; of them *The Pig Hunt* (*Grisjakten*, 1968) and *Children's Island* (*Barnens Ö.*, 1976) have been made into films. Besides Joan Tate's translations of *Children's Island* (1986) and the present *House of Babel* (*Babels hus*, 1978) in the Modern Scandinavian Literature in Translation Series, three more of Jersild's novels have appeared in English: *The Animal Doctor* (*Djurdoktorn*, 1975; trans. David Mel and Margareta Paul [New York: Pantheon, 1975]), *After the Flood* (*Efter floden*, 1982; trans. Löne Thygesen Blecher and George Blecher [New York: William Morrow, 1986]), and *A Lavender Shell* (*En levande själ*, 1981; trans. Rika Lesser [East Anglia: Norvik Press, in press]).

The following conversation with Jersild (pcj) was initiated in New York over a three-hour luncheon and complemented by an exchange of letters over the ensuing months. Excerpts from that correspondence are interspersed throughout the interview.

LS: Flaubert, the son of a physician, was presumably one of the first to introduce a clinical case in literature, in his novel *Madame Bovary*. Ibsen longed to be a physician, but he never made it, unless we could call him a precursor of Dr. Freud. At any rate, I believe I counted twenty-two physicians in his plays. So he may have fulfilled his wish vicariously through literature. Balzac went even further: there are said to be close to forty doctors in his novels. Chekhov also comes to mind; and in Maugham's *Of Human Bondage* Philip scattered his interest in art and in religion for a long time until he finally straightened out with his medical studies. How very different from any of these are the recent books involving physicians! What are some of the new directions in fiction about doctors, as you see them, with special reference to your own writings and those of Dr. Lars Gyllensten?[1] He had a promising career as a histologist at the Karolinska Institute, Stockholm, before he gave it up to devote himself to fiction.

PCJ: I don't quite know what significance there is, for instance, in the fact that both Gyllensten and I were physicians before we took up writing full time. I guess we can agree that there is something special about the medical profession. It always seems to have fascinated its practitioners as well as others. Much of this I consider romanticizing, as a vestige of the past, when medicine went hand in hand with magic and witchcraft.

As far as Flaubert and Ibsen are concerned, they are highly interested in clinical points of view. In their descriptions of pathological disease (such as the theme of syphilis in Ibsen), I think by and large these authors exhibit a form of realism; the case report is, after all, nothing but a shorthand life history in which the feelings of the narrator or physician are excluded in a kind of objective technique. Flau-

---

1. Lars Gyllensten (b. 1921), a member of the Swedish Academy and the Nobel Committee for Literature, is a distinguished novelist whose works treat complex philosophical issues. One of his most important works, *Cain's Memoirs* (*Kains memoarer*, 1963) is scheduled to be published by Ontario Review Press, Princeton, New Jersey, in their translation series.

bert's *Madame Bovary* was, incidentally, one of the models when I wrote my first novel, *To Warmer Lands (Till varmare länder*, 1961): one of the main protagonists is a young housewife in a suburb of Stockholm. The book had many tentative working titles, including "Madame Bovary in Blackeberg."

LS: I am now reading Chekhov's diaries and plays. Has any physician's work (beyond that of Gyllensten's) been a catalyst for your authorship?

PCJ: I have hardly been on the lookout for fiction written by physicians, but I can't fail to notice how fascinated I can be, for instance, by Rabelais and Chekhov. Chekhov in particular has given me much, but I did not read him thoroughly until about 1970 when I made a TV program about him. Sometimes I get it into my head that I know him personally, not the least when I study his letters. Or I imagine that I visit his house in Moscow and look at the comic strip he made as a young man in collaboration with his brother. Chekhov holds me spellbound for many reasons, perhaps first and foremost on account of his wide range: from the comic burlesque in the one-actor "The Bear," through the short stories, the great "comedies," so filled with clarity and sorrow, to the scientist Chekhov as he appears in his correspondence, and in *The Island: A Journey to Sakhalin*. He has both a clinical and a close relationship to the world surrounding him; he wants both to participate and to stand on the sidelines. He can say truths that hit home.

But I can also be irritated by him. I think that he sometimes tends to romanticize science; he seems to believe that if only the scientists were allowed to have their way, the world would become better. At the bottom of this I sense Chekhov's disdain for politicians and political realities, which I don't like. But much of this, no doubt, is due to the times in which he lived—medicine, after all, did not become truly scientific until 1880.

I think the profession of physician can stimulate a critical way of looking at the world; that one seeks truth *behind* what is said. In the medical profession it is often necessary to pare down to the truth; the first things that a patient relates are often merely superficial; it's important to penetrate beneath them.

LS: In the prefatory summary to your novel, *House of Babel*, you list the most frequent causes of death in Sweden and go on to ask whether, in spite of all the billions spent on medical care, there is any proof of an absolute and unequivocal connection between increased spending and an improved state of health in general or an increase in longevity. You state the Swedes have the medical care they deserve: but "that we cannot afford it is another matter." A Swedish newspaper critic objected that the novel had nothing to do with that Summary, since it didn't elucidate any of the major criticisms leveled therein. Do you think that was in any way a justifiable criticism?

PCJ: On the contrary, I think it was foolish and unwarranted. The Summary discusses the major, common questions in terms of care for the sick. In the entire Western world people by and large die from two complaints: hardening of the arteries and then cancer. In my novel the central character, Primus Svensson, first has a myocardial infarction (arteriosclerosis), then cancer. Alcoholism is mentioned as a great problem and is later exemplified through Primus's son, Bernt, who is an alcoholic. I would venture to say that in almost all essential points my novel gives substance to the ideas brought up for discussion in the Summary.

LS: How does *House of Babel* compare with other modern "hospital novels," for example, Samuel Shem's *House of God* and Dea Trier Mørch's *Winter's Child*?

PCJ: So far I have not myself read any novel which, like *House of Babel*, places the hospital itself at its center and then attempts to examine this complex microcosm in nearly all its nooks and crannies. I have not read Samuel Shem. Dea Mørch's excellent novel per se, tells of personal—but limited—experiences. Often *House of Babel* is compared to Solzhenitsyn's *Cancer Ward*, but the difference is quite considerable. While Solzhenitsyn takes aim at the Soviet system, I criticize a welfare policy that does not work.

LS: It is easy to imagine that you did not exactly endear yourself to your fellow physicians when you put nearly every medical position and point of view in the hospital under a magnifying glass. The first few chapters especially end up quite negatively—but the patients seem to like the care they get. What reactions did the medical establishment in Sweden have to your novel?

PCJ: They were rather interesting. First came a wave of anonymous hate letters, nightly telephone calls, and angry comments in the press. When the novel proved to be one of the greatest successes within living memory in the Swedish book market, that criticism was changed into a frequently devout fussing about me and my book. I think the initial reaction was more honest and that it better reflects how Swedish physicians do think.

LS: Did your novel and subsequent TV series based on it affect public health policy in Sweden as far as you can judge?

PCJ: This is hard to really know—but it is my private opinion that such was the case, that it became legitimate to call in and question the autocratic control of public health by the medical profession.

LS: Do you think that the solution to the problem of impersonal and costly health care would lie in a reorganization either of society or of the medical school curriculum?

PCJ: Well, certainly not through a general commercialization such as the Swedish New Liberal wants. It might be possible to pick out certain bits and move them into the area of private medical practice, but if society is to be in a position to offer all its citizens adequate care, then I think society must also be responsible for health care. But it will be pretty difficult to make alcoholics, the mentally retarded, those will senile psychosis, chronic diseases, and so forth profitable. We need a better distribution between inpatient care and outpatient care in Sweden; that process has, in fact, already begun. We must also have more efficient health care; the cost is now slightly more than 10 percent of the GNP (in the United States closer to 12 percent). The situation cannot continue like that!

LS: Many have suggested, Robert Bjork among them, that an infusion of humanities courses (focusing on serious literature discussing ethics, philosophy, and so forth) as is happening now in many medical schools in the United States, might help correct some of the problems that you have identified and described in the health care system. Do you think this might be so?

PCJ: Yes, I agree: education is clearly one way to achieve more humane health care. In Sweden a medical school recently opened in the city of Linköping, where they practice modern pedagogical, gentle methods, derived, above all, from the well-known progressive medical school of McMaster University in Hamilton, Ontario, Canada.

LS: Do you think that literature in general can affect the future?

PCJ: Why not—at least to some extent? *House of Babel* stimulated a public debate in Sweden, and so did my novel, *After the Flood*, which contributed to the debate on nuclear weapons. A widely read novel is genuinely a mass medium. And unlike TV programs and newspaper articles, it will remain available for a long time.

LS: Where would you place *House of Babel* in your own ouevre?

PCJ: In my ouevre *House of Babel* is the example of an attempt to create a *realistic*, community-oriented novel dealing with a controversial issue. It falls into one of my main trends, in which *The Pig-hunt, The Animal Doctor* and a couple of other works are to be found. On the other hand, it does not have much to do with the fantastic elements and the discursive passages that characterize my other books.

LS: As has been pointed out by several people, medical knowledge gives a great deal of power to the protagonist and his mentor in your novel *After the Flood*. How does that fit in with the social criticism implicit in that book and in *House of Babel*?

PCJ: It is true that medical knowledge constitutes a valuable and productive aspect of *After the Flood*. The same holds true for *House of Babel*. Health care is, first of all, governed by the physicians, the medical specialists, because they have a monopoly on knowledge. Only in the second place do we find the economists and the politicians. I think that these three categories of specialists must be able to talk to each other and, not least of all, to the common people, the consumers.

In this connection, I would like to point out that since *House of Babel* was written, almost ten years ago, the economic crisis in the health care system has become much worse, perhaps even acute. In the mid-1970s attempts could still be made to do away with problems through expansion. Now we have instead to rearrange our priorities, because society can no longer afford to let health care have a greater share of the GNP. As I see it, health care should be offered above all to anyone in need of it, regardless of ability to pay. Should we let those groups who are financially able buy their way past the health care lines and receive luxury care? My conclusion is that we cannot scrap the welfare state in spite of its bureaucracy, heavy taxation, and other side effects. I know no alternative system which can convince me that it is superior. Most physicians do not share this socialist idea of mine. They want to keep the privilege of power and their independent status. They think politicians should have nothing to do with health care and that physician and patient should work together directly. But you can't whip society's largest service sector into shape by only such means. Another reason for the physician's claims to exclusive privileges is that they make it simpler for physicians to do research on anything they want. Obviously they can also earn more money in a market-oriented system.

ls: In terms of *House of Babel* you stated that you endeavored not to portray living people, but, like other novelists, "snatched a trait, a detail here and there" and sewed together "bits from several persons into one character, adding a large portion of imagination." That certainly does not sound like a recipe for a disguised autobiography, yet it cannot be denied that your experiences as a medical student and later, as a physician played a most decisive role in your novel. As a major underlying factor you mention above all the relationship between you and your father. If there are, then, important similarities between the main protagonist, Primus Svensson, and your father, you also intimate that three other central characters are built on a division of your own self.

PCJ: As I have stated in *Professional Confessions* (*Professionella bekännelser*, 1981), they are "myself as a young, critical intern personified by Martina Bosson—an idealized portrait; myself as a no longer young and less than successful physician on the way to giving it all up, personified by Gustaf Nyström; and finally the one who is the closest to me in the entire novel, the alcoholic pharmaceutical consultant, Bernt Svensson, the son of Primus. The human-psychological kernel is actually how a son and his father find each other."

LS: Those are certainly partial "keys" to what appears to be at least partially autobiographical. Now, when you wrote the book it was a novel for laymen, and it was to serve as the foundation for debate. The book also contains romantic and erotic elements. What is your rationale for including sex in a book designed as the basis for cultural debate?

PCJ: I had long intended to avoid romance and eroticism; such things are overexploited in the hospital novels to be found on newsstands. I changed my mind while working on the novel. I am not sure this was a wise decision. But I did it, partly because it seemed like a distortion of reality not to include any erotic complications in the enormous working site of the Enskede Hospital, and partly because I had to give Martina and Gustaf, close to being protagonists, an opportunity to be utterly candid with each other, and such candor is found in bed.

LS: I live only a block away from a large hospital and find both advantages and disadvantages, but clearly you find the large-scale hospital an inappropriate idea. You feel the loss of unity in treatment and understanding of people in these hospitals. What do you see as the solution? Would the ideal hospitals be small "doctors' hospitals" or what? Have you changed your views since you wrote *House of Babel* in 1978?

PCJ: I have not changed my views, except in terms of unimportant details since that time. I still regard as abominations the large, iso-lated structures, such as were built in Sweden in the 1960s and 1970s. A hospital must be *part* of a total health services organization, and not some isolated, arrogant, exalted island. I think hospitals should be as small as possible. With good private practice taking on the everyday care of the sick, this would be possible. In Sweden the organization has been far too rigid. For instance, it has generally been considered that a perfectly adequate hospital would require twenty, thirty, or forty different specialties, preferably with their own departments. That is not necessary. Specialists can actually travel between various hospitals without having to be bound to a specific ward with so many beds, and the like. Physicians can also work both within a hospital and in private practice—that concept has been alien in Sweden but now is beginning to gain a foothold.

LS: The chapters in your novel about the large hospital generally begin with a name and a description of a person. This technique reminds me quite a bit of the old Icelandic saga; even in terms of working with several strands in the narrative. Characters fall in and out of the saga, as is fit; the light falls on them for a while and then fades. Only one person, Primus, is there practically all the time. I find it very appealing that a "little" man is allowed to unify the entire story, while still alive, and even after he is dead. In fact, I think it is quite an artistic achievement to manage to make Primus approach the centrality of the action although he has a seemingly inconspicu-ous, passive role as a patient. Even if your work in this respect occa-sionally appears contrived and the device is obvious, it is not disturb-ing. As a reader I can give Primus my sympathy and identify with this helpless pawn in the great game of life and death.

PCJ: I am glad you approve of the novel's basic structure—with Primus as the innocent center. I reasoned exactly as you do when I chose that technique.

LS: In *House of Babel* you blast the Swedish pharmaceutical com-panies. What kind of reform would you like to see them undergo?

PCJ: They commercialize pharmaceutical preparations more than necessary. But I don't believe in a nationalized drug industry, either. That would be too unwieldy. For my part I think the representatives of pharmaceutical manufacturers should not be allowed to sell directly to individual doctors. Each hospital or health care service should have a purchasing committee with sufficient expertise to offset the industry's advertisements. We have some of that now in Sweden. But there is still a lot of horse-trading done by the industry. It is very unfortunate that too large a share of research ends up in industry. Then the results are patented and are classified as a trade secret. As far as possible research should be carried out within free universities. I am sorry to say that the lack of public funding has caused developments to move in the wrong direction: the industry can afford to do research, so the state must restrict itself to predictably less profitable research.

LS: Apropos of the title of your novel. Babel and the Tower of Babel traditionally relate to linguistic confusion. In *House of Babel* it is striking how many non-Swedish names there are among the physicians and others who serve in "Enskede Hospital," as you call your imaginary institution just outside Stockholm. I have deduced the nationalities of the doctors from their names. Does this arrangement reflect the reality in today's Sweden—with about 10 percent of immigrants?

PCJ: The influx of foreign doctors has been considerable, and far greater than the 10 percent of immigrants generally. This was due not least of all to the fact that Sweden imported physicians to meet a shortage of doctors—which is now well on the way to disappearing.

IRONY AND SATIRE

LS: Assuming that satire is based on a certain view one has of oneself and of the world, how would you then characterize your view?

PCJ: I would like to mention, first, curiosity and a sense of wonder. Over and over again I find myself looking with wonder at the most commonplace things: often I realize that they are the same phenomena that filled me with wonder yesterday or the day before. I have the feeling I never succeeded in fixing or catching reality. It is a kind of naive, newly-awakened attitude containing a good deal of euphoria: "the world is new every morning." I can experience the same sense of wonder from my own ego—but with time I think my sense of identity has become stronger.

In other words, I would like to describe my relationship to the world around me as skeptical, antidogmatic. In political terms I could define myself as a humanistic socialist:—not the socialism of state ownership or something similar, but the socialism standing for justice and solidarity. Each person would be entitled to a dignified life and each person would have an equal value. That's why I stress the word *humanism*; I assume that everyone has basically the same need for security, love, work, and so on, as I myself have. I have also tried to expand this discussion to include other forms of conscious life—that of the more developed animals.

LS: How can it be determined that something written or spoken is intended as irony or satire? Does it happen that what you say or write is misunderstood?

PCJ: That is a difficult question. Very often I realize that what I write has an ironic tone without my striving to attain it. I don't know whether other authors choose when they wish to appear as ironic, but I do know that as for myself I experience it as something innate, formed very early in life. Perhaps it is, psychologically, a question of fear of the final, the definitive. Of course, to the ironic person there are always emergency exits.

It does happen that I am misunderstood, but perhaps not very often. Irony, satire, and humor did not rank very high during the leftist trend in Sweden at the beginning of the 1970s. This was natural when politics became dogmatic and infused with slogans. The dramatist hates irony, since it creates uncertainty. On rare occasions the right has given me its nod of approval when I have criticized Swedish bureaucracy; this I find unpleasant. I am not against the public sector in Sweden—on the contrary. But I believe it can be improved, it can be made more humane.

LS: As a satirist, do you feel that you are often forced to strike harder than you had intended—for certain effects?

PCJ: I believe the satirist only seldom is *forced* to go at it hammer and tongs; instead I think he falls for the *temptation* to strike hard. Restrained satire is almost always more effective than the overexplicit, the noisy. But it is very easy to raise one's voice. Perhaps distrust of one's readers or resentment for the wrongs of the past causes one to be taken in and then to exaggerate.

LS: Is there a good solution to this problem?

PCJ: To me the solution is in the insight that it seldom pays to go whole hog. There is also an inherent risk in certain media, such as the political revue. It goes without saying that in a written text it is easier to overdo it.

LS: Why do you think society, generally, is so suspicious of satire? This is true of the past as well as the present. Some satires border on caricature, which can be caustic by simple distortion, elongation, fragmentation, or burlesque.

PCJ: The answer is largely contained in your question. Satire and irony are not only critical; they can also be elusive, invulnerable. How can the offended politician defend himself against a cutting caricature that represents him and no one else, but doesn't spell it out? Satire, after all, says in principle one thing but means something else; and it is up to the reader to draw out that meaning. Satire therefore—more than any other style—makes a participant of the reader. The meaning is found through the reader, not in the language.

Those in power have always been vulnerable to laughter and ridicule. Who can oppose laughter? How do you kill an insinuation?

Burlesque in Rabelais, for instance, encroaches on tabooed subjects such as sexuality; burlesque impudently comes out with the dirty word.

When you mention the concept of fragmentation, I associate it primarily and generally to new forms of language. But then we get into a discussion that goes far beyond satire. But each new form, like modernism at one time, challenges and provokes precisely because there are no ready-made models—no interpretations given in advance.

OLD AND NEW MYTHS

LS: Many people assume, as does Lars Gyllensten, that we live in myths for which new ones will in time have to be substituted. Which myths would you prefer to have replaced? And with which new ones?

PCJ: I will bypass the definition of myth and just say that I conceive of myths as a collection of notions about reality; as a view of reality the myth must always be simplified in order to be comprehensible.

I would want to dispose of those myths that do not fill a positive role, that is, that present us with a false picture of reality. *False* to me means relatively speaking—that is, what was a useful myth yesterday might no longer be relevant today. These myths should then be replaced with better ones. In order to comprehend reality we constantly have to revise it, provide ourselves with better images of it, and remain conscious that these new images have a limited survival time.

To me, one of the ways to create new myths is to instill new life in old ones. Reality always surpasses art. But art is able, in a positive sense, to simplify and compress a multitude of chaotic elements so that we get manageable images of reality.

LS: Which examples in your own books would you mention as your contribution in this respect?

PCJ: In my novel *Children's Island*, I wish to smash the old concept that children are insensitive and unthoughtful; in contrast I write about an eleven-year-old who has "grown-up" thought and imaginative power but who lacks "grown-up" language to describe his thoughts and ideas. Psychologists have confirmed my view. *A Lavender Shell* takes up a long series of central issues; for instance, is the scientific, biochemical model sufficient to describe man's spiritual life? As far as I am concerned, the answer is negative—not even a religious concept can catch the "soul." In the final analysis there is no total concept of the world within which everything can be explained. Instead, it is a matter of constantly substituting a whole set of images or a whole system with another in order to approach reality; this connects with the discussion—often initiated by physicists—of the new concept of the world, the new paradigm.

LS: In *Professional Confessions*, which we have already referred to, you bring up the author's role—

PCJ: Yes, I reject both the old "genius role" and the currently quite common "amateur role" for authors—at least in Sweden. I disagree with the assumption that the result is not what is interesting but rather the intention and the social relations within (for example) a theater group. In opposition to that idea I wish to place the "professional role": writing (composing works of literature) in time becomes a profession rather like that of a scientist. One has to test and retest one's goals and one's methods again and again, learn from mistakes, learn from others whether one's work holds, develop, study new books, widen one's register, and so on. In the preface to *Professional Confessions* I have written that I wanted to produce a nonromanticized image of how it is to be an author.

LS: What is your view of inspiration? Is it at the conceptual stage, the preliminary stage, or during the actual work on a book that you feel euphoric?

PCJ: I experience at least two kinds of inspiration or euphoria: One is quieter and appears when daily work flows and feels good; it could also be described as the satisfaction of achievement. Thus it is an inspiration that one can work toward. The other type of inspiration is a keyed-up, ecstatic feeling. That generally requires finding a suitable idea, which usually manifests itself unexpectedly. An example of this occurred when I got the idea for *The Pig Hunt*. In a few short moments one morning in a half wakened state I saw the entire novel roll out before my very eyes. I had an enormous feeling of happiness. Later when I sat down to write the novel I had many a fine day of serene euphoria. So there is, then, a low-frequency "work inspiration" and a lightning-quick ecstatic "idea inspiration." It is also much more fun to complete a short piece, like a number for a revue than to contend with a novel for months on end.